FROM A CHIL... ...A
WHIRLI...
DRE...
I...

★   ★   ★   ★

"Only a gifted writer—and Maynard Thomson surely is that—could render so movingly the pain and triumph of the quest for Olympic gold."
—**Richard North Patterson**

"Entertaining."
—*Woman's Own*

"Fascinating. . . . a rich look into skating politics and a different culture."
—*Rainbo Electronic Reviews*

"Thomson writes action sequences well."
—*Kirkus Reviews*

"Well researched and knowledgeable. . . . Thomson uniquely blends the competitive world of figure skating with the traditions of Japan."
—*Professional Skaters* magazine

MAYNARD F. THOMSON

DREAMS of GOLD

WARNER BOOKS

A Time Warner Company

WARNER BOOKS EDITION

Cover design by Diane Luger
Cover photo by Herman Estevez

Warner Books, Inc.
1271 Avenue of the Americas
New York, NY 10020

Visit our Web site at
www.twbookmark.com

 A Time Warner Company

Printed in the United States of America

Originally published as a hardcover by Warner Books.
First Paperback Printing: January 2000

10 9 8 7 6 5 4 3 2 1

To Laura

When the dictates of our kami
Start to tingle within our mortal frame
There's no telling what folly it will
cause us to do.

Shinran-Shonin (1173–1262)

DREAMS
of GOLD

Prologue

February 2002: Salt Lake City

*M*aggie Campbell faced the judges. She stood comfortably, fingers loosely intertwined below her waist. She wore a small smile.

Her red dress was almost austere in its lack of beading and tulle. The only decorative touch was a six-inch cloth strip hanging from shoulder to wrist, suggesting wings. As she'd skated to her place at center ice, the skirt and top, fitting loosely, revealed, then concealed, the hills and hollows of her body.

She radiated youth, although at twenty-three she was the oldest of the potential medalists. She was willowy, though at five four and 112 pounds she had six inches and thirty pounds on one competitor. She appeared poised, eager, and unafraid, yet no more so than the young women who had gone before or would come after, for they were all great athletes who had spent their brief lives preparing for this moment.

She was in the final group to skate, the six leaders after the short program. In less than an hour three women would *ascend a pedestal. One would win the gold medal and stand above the other two.*

The world shrank around her, becoming no larger than the half acre on which she stood. The crowd disappeared, time stopped. She looked inside herself. Finding only joy, she reminded herself to manage it, remain in charge.

A chord sounded. The crowd stilled. Arms rising, thought surrendered to instinct. Her note arrived; she struck off.

Chapter 1

September 2000: Boston

*R*eaching for her nightgown, Maggie winced at the pain lancing up her side, praying it was only a pulled muscle. She'd have to get it looked at in the morning; the possibility that the rib had opened up again, with the Nationals barely four months away, was too grim to consider. She took two aspirin, eased into bed, opened Foucault's *History of Sexuality*. Harvard was full of students who did things better than anyone else; when she sat for her psychology exam, she'd be just another junior.

She turned on her cassette player. She never tired of the slow music for their long program, thinking of it as lovemaking set to music.

The Rachmaninoff had been Hunter Rill's idea. She'd opposed it at first, declaring it a pairs cliché, but he'd persisted, and he'd been right. Probably no other coach exploited the sensual undercurrent of skating as well as Rill; *Rhapsody on a Theme of Paganini* wouldn't do for a brother-sister team, but for Clay and Maggie, radiating a palpable sexual attraction, it was perfect.

She flipped through the textbook with mounting boredom before letting it slip to the floor; Rachmaninoff had more to say about sexuality, and in a language she understood. She turned off the light. The twinge in her side as she slipped her hands behind her head assuaged her guilt at not letting Clay talk her into Lofton Weeks's annual bacchanal.

When she was seventeen, and still skating as a junior, she'd been thrilled to be invited; it told the skating world that the man who'd been synonymous with American figure skating for almost fifty years had anointed Clay Bartlett and Maggie Campbell *prospects,* which was worth points every time they competed. When she was eighteen it was exhilarating to sip champagne and grow giddy at the thought of their first season campaigning as seniors. By nineteen it was starting to pall. At twenty, one half of the United States pairs silver medal team had gone home early. Now Maggie, at twenty-one, was pleased she hadn't even pretended.

The drunks and the skaters with eating disorders would be throwing up in the bathrooms. Association officials and judges would buttonhole her about their program, or their costumes, or the color of her lipstick. Red-faced, middle-aged skating fanatics would try to fondle her, while their wives showed off their cleavages and ogled Clay. Thirty seconds after some coach had deposited the four hundredth unwelcome kiss, she'd hear him telling someone she used drugs or slept with girls. Lofton Weeks would flatter and cajole until she'd want to scream. She'd made the right decision: she needed a quiet night at home.

The concerto was coming to the movement she loved best, *their* music, almost unbearably lush. She shut her eyes, letting the strings pulse through her, hearing the melody as the sound track to their triumph in Denver six weeks before.

That night had confirmed Maggie Campbell and Clayton

Bartlett as the heirs presumptive to the National title. It had been even more satisfying than the evening the previous January, when they'd won the silver at the Nationals. They'd skated well enough to take the gold, but understood that the association, and hence the judges, thought it was still Schuyler and Drummond's. That was the way of skating, so they'd kept quiet, waited, and worked. The win in Denver said their time had arrived.

Stepping onto the ice, they'd known what they had to do, and they'd done it. They'd owned the crowd from their opening lift, a Hunter Rill invention culminating with Maggie standing on Clay's chest-high left palm, his right hand bracing her calf. The roar, as she thrust out her arms and revolved, her head ten feet above the ice, was deafening.

Elements that had seemed a gamble when Rill put the program together, like the throw triple Salchow with less than a minute to go, hadn't seemed chancey at all when the time came—just a bit of work that had to be done. They'd have won even if they'd doubled it; that had been the safe choice, but they were skating to *win*, not to avoid losing. At Clay's whispered, "Triple?" she'd nodded; two seconds later he'd thrown her twelve feet through the air, spinning. When she'd landed, she'd known they'd won.

Their unison had been perfect. They had entered their jumps and spins together, revolved as one, exited with legs and arms at identical angles, identical points on the compass, moving as synchronously as parts of a watch. Going in, some had said the Lantsberg twins might be their match, but they'd lacked the unison. Not by much, but enough.

They were the only pair in the world with a triple flip. They landed side-by-side triple flips and triple toe loops seconds apart, and once again the crowd noise swamped the music, but they knew it so well that they never lost a beat.

When Clay fixed his pivot and lowered her into the death spiral, it was as though eyes, not arms, connected them. He winked at her as she swept around him, her curls sweeping the ice. They finished with Clay kneeling, she leaning back across his leg, his right hand cradling her neck. Their kiss was the only unscripted element in the four minutes and twenty-eight seconds, and it sent the crowd into a frenzy.

She heard Lofton Weeks, immaculate in his black dinner jacket, working the officials afterward: "The most elegant American pairs team in forty years. The best in the world, getting better every time out." Weeks always talked that way about skaters he hoped to sign to his professional tour, but she'd heard others echo the claim, so she dared to think it might be true.

She drifted off, as she often did, to music; her life moved to music.

Somewhere, dimly, an alarm sounded. Too soon, she thought, much too soon, and she reached to shut it off before remembering she hadn't set it. One eye opened on the glowing clock face.

One-thirty. Before she'd fully digested it she realized it had been the phone she'd heard. Distantly she heard her mother's muffled voice. Mumbling, then louder: "What? No! Is he . . ."

When she heard footsteps approach the door she knew, even before the door opened and her mother whispered, "Maggie? Maggie, it's Mother. There's been an accident."

Her heart raced, her stomach knotted. She bolted upright and switched on the lamp. "What happened?"

"It's Clay . . . he's been hurt."

Something squeezed her throat. "Hurt?" she whispered. "How badly? What's wrong?"

"That was Alex Bartlett. They're at the hospital. Apparently Clay was in a car accident."

"Is he all right?"

"He's banged up, but he's not in any danger."

"Thank God." Maggie sprang from the bed. "I've got to go. Which hospital?"

"Boston City."

Maggie pulled on clothes. "How did it happen?" she called from her closet.

"They're not sure. Apparently the driver lost control of the car coming off Storrow Drive. It went into a light pole."

Maggie stepped out of the closet. Her mother had settled on the bed. Her brother, owlish in his thick glasses, blinked nervously in the doorway.

"I don't understand—what do you mean, the driver lost control? Wasn't Clay driving? Was another car involved?"

"Clay wasn't driving. It was his car, but he wasn't driving."

"Then who . . . ?"

"Doe Rawlings."

Maggie ran out the door.

Clay's right eye fluttered open as she approached. "Hi, kiddo," he whispered. "Pretty, aren't I?"

His left eye, puffy and blue black, was swollen almost shut. A bandage covered one ear, another curved under his chin.

She went to him, fighting the impulse to shudder. "How do you feel?" His left hand was lying on top of the blanket; she picked it up and squeezed.

He squeezed back, his smile fading as stitches pulled. "Like I had an argument with a windshield, and lost."

"But why weren't you driving?" Seeing his downcast eyes, she cocked her head skeptically. "Too much to drink?"

He nodded sheepishly. "After being in training so long, it went right to my head."

"I told you to watch it."

"I know, I know. But Lofton was all worked up over our win in Denver, and I had a couple of glasses of champagne with him while he told me how much money he's going to make us when we turn pro. Some of the groupies kept bringing me beer, and of course Hunter was throwing back the vodka and wouldn't take 'no' for an answer."

She ran her finger down the line of his jaw. "Why do I suspect he didn't hear 'no' for an answer?"

When Clay Bartlett grinned he looked like a naughty twelve-year-old. "Once a year, Mag."

He could always disarm the schoolmarm in her. She rolled her eyes, sighing. "I know; I'm not blaming you." The smile faded as she remembered. "But why Doe Rawlings? How did *she* come to be driving?"

"By midnight I was ready to go, only I knew I shouldn't drive. I was in the lobby, calling a cab, when Doe came out. She also wanted to leave, but she'd come with Hunter, and he wouldn't be ready for hours, so she suggested driving me home, dropping me off, and I could come by for the car in the morning. It made sense at the time."

He frowned. "I must have fallen asleep, because the next thing I knew, I was trying to figure out how we came to be wrapped around a pole."

"Your parents say the police estimate she was doing at least seventy when she went into the turn, that's how."

The open eye fluttered. He seemed to shrink, his pale face lost against the whiteness of the pillow. "Christ, I had no idea. Why? I mean . . ." He swallowed. "Why?" he whispered.

"Because she was drunk, that's why."

His lips thinned. Shaking his head, almost angrily, he snapped, "No, she wasn't. She hadn't had a drink all night."

"Do you *know* that?"

He looked away, at the wall. "No, but she said she hadn't, and she seemed fine in the lobby."

"Well, the flunked the Breathalyzer."

He tried to sit up. "Oh, Lord." Grimacing, he flopped back against the pillow. "I can't believe it."

"She lied, Clay."

Maggie watched him trying to puzzle it out. "But why? We could have waited for a cab."

"Because she's a selfish bitch!" The rage broke over her. "Because she's Doe Rawlings, that's why." Maggie wished the brittle, hard words back as soon as she heard them bouncing off the antiseptic walls.

He blanched. Contrite, Maggie took a deep breath, willing her voice to remain calm. She began fussing with the sheet, tucking in a loose edge. "Don't you see? She'd decided she wanted to drive your car, and so what if she was drunk? She wanted to speed, and the hell with the consequences." Her mouth formed a tight crease. "What Doe wants, Doe gets. Hasn't it always been that way?"

"I suppose." His face was pale against the white pillow.

She pushed the hair off his forehead. It fell back; it always did. "Well, when I see her . . ."

His hand grabbed hers. "Don't, Maggie. Don't say anything."

She looked at him in amazement. "Don't say anything? She could have killed you."

"But she didn't." His head sank into the pillow. "Look—

think how she must feel: My car's wrecked, I'm beat up, and she's probably going to be cited for drunk driving. She's had a tough life; let's not add to her troubles. It won't help anything for you to get into it with her, and think how it would make practices."

"I've never found her presence one of the brighter parts of practice."

"Please, Mag—don't make me argue, not with my head feeling like this. Let's just forget it, okay?"

Her lips tightened, but she nodded, sighing. "Okay, it's up to you. But she's a selfish, thoughtless prima donna, and somebody ought to tell her."

He put his arm across his forehead. "Let it be somebody else, all right? We have to skate on the same ice."

"I said I won't say anything." She touched the bandage on his wrist. "What happened here?"

He held it overhead, studying it uncertainly. "I don't know; there was a lot of glass around—I suppose I cut it getting out. They put stitches in."

She shivered again. "Does it hurt?"

He waggled his fingers cautiously, shaking his head. "No, not really. More numb than anything else, like the rest of me." His eyelids drooped.

Maggie patted him. "Sleep now. I'll come back later." She kissed his forehead. He was out before she had her coat on.

As soon as she walked into the room the next morning she knew something was wrong. Clay, paler than before, wore an expression poised between fear and wonder. Two men, one in a lab coat, were standing by the bed. The man in a suit was rubbing his chin and nodding at something the other man was saying. Lettie Bartlett, smiling unconvincingly, was straightening her son's sheet, while Alex Bartlett was saying to the two men, "Are you sure? You can't be sure. Who else should we call in?"

"What is it?" Maggie looked from Clay, to his parents, to the strangers, back to Clay. "What's wrong?"

It was Clay who answered. "It's my right hand, Mag; it seems there's been some nerve damage. That's why it was numb."

"I don't understand." Maggie pushed between the two men, coming to stand by the bed. "What does that mean, 'nerve damage'? What's it mean, Clay?"

"It may mean looking for a tin cup, my girl." He forced a grin. "Maybe I'll qualify for handicapped parking. Think what that's worth in Boston."

"What?" Maggie thought he must be joking, then saw the tears tracking his mother's cheeks. She looked at the two strangers, willing agreement. "That's ridiculous. You're going to be fine. You just have a cut. You'll be fine in a few days. He will be, won't he? Won't he?"

Lettie Bartlett put her arm around Maggie, snuffling. "Shh, shh. They don't know anything for sure. It's just a . . . tentative finding, isn't that right, Doctor?"

The man in the lab coat nodded. "Of course. We've got to do a lot more tests, and then there's physical therapy once the injury heals. We don't know how much function he might recover. Why, I've seen—"

"But our skating . . . we've got to train . . . how soon . . . ?" Maggie clutched at Mrs. Bartlett; dimly, from down the corridor, she heard children chanting a nursery rhyme. She thought she might be losing her mind. "Tell them, Aunt Lettie—tell them they've got to get him well right away. We've got to skate!"

"Skate, miss?" The second man, the one in a suit, looked

at her reassuringly. "He'll be skating in a couple of days, if that's your worry."

Maggie sighed, suddenly weightless. Mrs. Bartlett's arm slid from her hands. "Thank God." She reached for Clay. "I was so—"

"There's nothing wrong with his legs," the man continued, "he just won't be picking anything up for a while."

Chapter 2

*H*unter Rill stood by the side of the Charles River Skating Club rink, a frown disturbing the sharp planes of his face. In skates he was almost six feet tall, and since he was a slender man—barely ten pounds heavier than when he'd been competing—he cut a handsome figure in the red sweater with the yellowing "U.S. Figure Skating Championships" patch on it. This morning he wasn't feeling handsome, though, or dashing, or even "well preserved," which he'd recently overheard a matronly woman saying of him, to his disgust. He was feeling all of his forty-four years, the vodka he'd drunk the night before, and acute annoyance that he had to attempt to instruct the uninstructible.

He ran his hand back through his thinning light brown hair as his eyes followed the pudgy boy working his way around the ice. The arm movements, that was one problem. They were absurdly tentative: little, halting jerks rather than the florid gestures demanded by the bombastic flourishes of the *William Tell Overture*. The boy, his face frozen into a rictus, might have been having some sort of fit on the ice, so graceless were his arms.

And the pliés—the boy was supposed to be bending his

knees and ankles, raising and lowering his hips while thrusting his shins against the tongue of his boots. Without a proper plié he would never be able to control his edges, much less jump decently, yet the boy's knees and ankles might as well have been fused for all the movement they showed. Instead, every few seconds he bent forward at the waist, so that he resembled a toy bird, bobbing its head over a glass of water. It would have been funny, if Hunter Rill could find hopelessly clumsy skating amusing.

Unable to stand it any longer, he reached over and stabbed the tape recorder resting on the rail beside him. The boy was so oblivious that he skated another fifty feet before realizing the music had stopped. He looked at his instructor, the pale, doughy face reflecting his confusion as Rill waved him over.

Rill glared down at the hangdog adolescent. "Do you *think*, Steven, you might try doing it as though God had given you joints? Would that be possible, do you think?"

The boy shifted his skate blades back and forth. "I guess so, Hunter," he mumbled.

"*Look* at me, Steven. I can't hear you when you don't look at me."

The boy made unsteady eye contact. "Yes, Hunter."

"Good. Now, Steven, let's try it again, only this time *try* connecting your movements to the music, all right? Like this."

Rill pushed the button and strode onto the ice. Half a dozen strokes had him speeding down the length of the rink. As the orchestra's "barump-pa-pa, barump-pa-pa" reverberated through the arena, he flung his arms, first one and then the other, as though trying to grab the pennants hanging overhead. At the same time he did deep pliés, compressing his weight against the ice, rising, sinking, repeating the motion.

He skated back. "Now, do you think you can do that, Steven? Because if you can't, we're going to have to go back to the exercise bar for the plié drill. And that's not as much fun, is it?"

The sudden change in the boy's expression told Rill he remembered all too well how his Achilles' tendons had felt after Rill had plopped him in front of the exercise mirror and drilled him through fifteen minutes' worth of pliés, all the while barking, "Up, down, up, down," occasionally showing him what "down" meant with a heavy hand on his shoulder.

The boy didn't know Rill was bluffing—his mother had made it all too clear that the next time her precious came out crying, she was going to find another skating instructor. That wouldn't do; there were already too many holes in his day, and now he'd lost Bartlett and Campbell—$36,000 a year, gone. He had to temper the wind to the Stevens in his stable; they couldn't skate, but they paid the rent.

He softened his tone. "Remember, Steven—you have to be able to do a nice plié before you can jump or spin. You want to start spins soon, don't you?"

"Yes, Hunter." The boy sounded uncertain.

"Of course you do—and you will. You've got real talent, Steven. Don't think you're not making progress—I'm always hardest on my best students."

Something like hope came into the boy's eyes. He mumbled his gratitude.

"Sure—you'll be doing Axels in no time." When pigs fly, Rill thought. "Now why don't you go out and try it again."

The boy made his awkward way back to center ice, and Rill punched the tape recorder button. He glanced at his watch. Thank God there were only five more minutes of this. Then he had a down hour, since the Purdue girl had quit on him.

Good riddance, except for the money. Kelly Purdue was a rich, lazy brat who'd be overtaxed skating third dwarf in the ice show chorus line. She'd run out bawling when he'd finally had enough of her shirking and chased her from one end of the rink to the other, swatting her with a skate bag, until she'd dropped.

Out of the corner of his eye he spotted Darcy Hazel—fourteen years old and one of the top juniors in America—about to step on the ice. His hand shot out, grabbing her by her braid.

"Ouch! That hurts!"

Rill kept a firm grip on the pigtail. "I *told* you, Darcy, that you were not to set foot on the ice until you lost three pounds. Don't you remember?"

"But Hunter, I did! This morning at home . . ." The girl's eyes filled.

"I don't care about your scale at home, dear." He dropped the fat braid and bent over to look the girl in the eyes. "We weigh in on the scale in the locker room, and Linda told me *that* scale said you'd lost only two and one-half pounds."

"But Hunter, I . . ." She started to snivel.

"Two and one-half isn't three. Is it, dear?"

"But . . ."

"Is it?"

"No," she quavered. Other skaters, scurrying out of range, cast nervous looks over their shoulders.

"You go down to the exercise room, and you *lose that half pound*. You will *not* go on the ice until you have lost it. Do you hear me?"

"Y-yes, Hunter."

"Good—we can't have you going into SkateAmerica one *ounce* overweight. Now, get going."

Rill watched the girl slink off, not the least concerned that *she'd* run out on him. If she broke a leg, he'd have to tie her down to keep her off the ice, and her parents worked two jobs apiece to support her skating. Those were the kind who complained only if they thought you were being too easy on their little investment.

Parents like that wouldn't admit they viewed the coach as their pension fund manager, of course; they didn't want to be quoted saying, "Yeah, I worked my kid like a plow horse, took away her youth, gave her an eating disorder, transported her a thousand miles from her father, and saw to it that the only book she'd ever read was the USFSA rules, all so I could cash in when she hit." Not the kind of copy that contributes to a wholesome, marketable image. So they talked about "building character" and "just wanting what's best for Susie." That's why he knew he could grab Darcy Hazel by her braid and haul her off the ice; her mother would rip the thing out by the roots, if that's what it took to make weight.

The thought cheered him so much, he actually meant the smile he wore when Mrs. Hotchkiss arrived to pick up her son.

"Oh, we had a fine lesson today. Didn't we, Steven?" His hand kneaded the boy's shoulder. "Yes, ma'am—this boy is going to be a *skater.* I'm delighted I made room for him, just delighted." He rubbed the boy's head and didn't look at the check she handed him until mother and son were out the door.

He watched Doe Rawlings at the far end of the rink. Her skin had a luminescence, and even thirty yards away he could feel the warmth she radiated. At eighteen she was the most beautiful woman he'd ever seen. It wasn't supposed to enter into scoring, but of course it did; her face and figure were worth a few tenths of a point almost every time.

She was practicing her triple lutz/triple toe combination. He shook his head in wonder; the lutz took so much momentum that it was astounding the girl had enough left for the triple toe, but Doe was stringing them together as though playing hopscotch. It would dazzle the judges at the Nationals.

Rill's pulse raced, as it always did when he thought about Doe's future. His future, really. He strolled back to his office, whistling noiselessly.

He decided a restorative was in order and was just reaching for the desk drawer when the door flew open. His hand jerked back at Maggie Campbell's bark: "I want to talk to you!"

She stood in the doorway, hands on hips, eyes boring in on him.

"Maggie—this is a pleasant surprise. I—"

"Don't give me that." She advanced on him, forefinger stabbing the air. "You fixed it. I know you did. Well, it's not over!"

She stood, glaring, arms crossed over her chest, chin outthrust. "Don't think you can get away with this."

He looked up at her calmly, though he thought her quite formidable for her size. "Maggie, what *are* you talking about?"

"I talked to the police. They told me there aren't going to be any drunk driving charges filed against your little protégée."

He gave her his boyish smile. "Well, I won't lie to you— I'm relieved to hear that. Now—"

"Liar!" The finger shot forward. "You already knew. They said you told them she had a reaction to a new *antihistamine*."

"That's true. Her doctor backed it up." Leaning back in the swivel chair, he locked his hands behind his head. "Doe has allergies."

"That's such a lie! She was *drunk*. Friends of mine saw her throwing back drinks all night. *That's* why she flunked the Breathalyzer."

Rill arched his eyebrows. "Odd Clay didn't notice."

"There were three hundred people there, and Clay wasn't with her until they left."

"Ah, I see." He shrugged. "Well, Lofton Weeks told the police he didn't see her take a drop. I believe several others spoke to the same effect." He turned up his hands helplessly.

"Sure—protect the crown princess. You haven't heard the last of this, you know. I've written the association."

Rill sighed. "That was silly, Maggie; the association isn't going to do a damn thing. You're talking about the United States ladies' champion. In a few months they're expecting Doe to repeat at the Nationals, a month after that to take the World title, and less than a year after that to win the Olympics. Do you really think they're going to sanction her because you wrote a letter? This case is closed. It's exactly as though Clay blew a knee skating. Sad, but it happens all the time."

Maggie clenched her jaw to keep from screaming. "We'll see. We'll see how the association feels about a skater destroying another skater's career like that—whether it thinks that 'happens all the time.' "

"I think you're going to find that the association is far more concerned with the future than the past. But I want you to know how sorry I am this happened. You deserved better. If you'll let me, I'll bend heaven and earth to get you another partner."

Maggie looked at him disdainfully. "Sure—so you can

collect your fees. No, thank you. I don't want anything from you."

He shook his head. "I'll do it even if you go to another coach. I've seen very few skaters with your sense of the relationship between movement and music. A lot of skaters go into pairs because they don't have the tools to be competitive in singles, but you were a terrific singles skater when you came to me, and I don't doubt you'd have gotten even better. Maybe good enough to have pushed Doe—who knows? And you made Clay; I wouldn't have given a nickel for his chances until you came along."

Maggie's nostrils flared. "That's ridiculous; Clay's a magnificent skater."

"Thanks to you he became a great pairs skater. But five years ago he couldn't keep a partner—he had a lousy work ethic, and was getting by on raw talent. He was just about at the end of that game when you arrived and showed him what it took. Now you should go on with someone else."

"Who's going to help Clay go on?" Maggie heard her voice catch and knew she had to get out. She whirled, bolting for the door.

"*He* will," Rill called after her. "And if I know Clay, he'll manage just fine."

He watched the small, straight figure stalking down the hall, feeling he'd lost something. He was tempted to call her back and tell her not to throw herself away on Clay Bartlett, but she wouldn't listen.

He pulled the pint of vodka out of the desk drawer and took a sip; yes, that helped. Soon he was feeling quite content.

Later, when Darcy Hazel appeared in his doorway, her face white, Rill was in a congenial mood. "Got it off, have you, Darcy?"

"Yes, Hunter."

"No tricks now?" The question was academic—he could see the string of drool on her sweater.

"No, Hunter."

"That's my girl. You won't be sorry. Now, get out there and work on that sit spin—you've been wandering off center recently. I'll be out in a little while for your lesson."

The girl nodded eagerly, distress forgotten. Rill, thinking she really was a nifty little skater, watched her scurrying toward the rink. He was quite fond of her.

Chapter 3

*M*aggie sat with Clay in his parents' sun room. A warm Indian summer sun brought out the colors in the maples. She'd always loved New England fall days, but now she saw death and despair in every fluttering leaf. She sprang to her feet, circling the room angrily, dropping the blinds.

The latest test results were back, and there wasn't much to say, beyond the doctors' bromides: "There's always hope. Great strides are being made. Perhaps . . . maybe . . . in a few months . . . in a few years . . ."

Clay half groaned, half laughed. "I've got a flipper. You might as well have a trained seal as a partner, Maggie." He clapped his hands together. "Arf, arf!"

"Don't! It's not funny, Clay." She hated the shrillness she heard in her voice, which she'd been hearing more and more.

He grabbed her, pulled her to him, stroked her cheek with his good hand. "I've got to joke, Mag—I'm too old to cry, and that's the only other choice I see." He looked at the magazine lying in his lap, shaking his head. "The Lantsbergs set to win the Nationals. My God."

"We'll get our turn next year, that's all. We've just been pushed back a year." She covered his hand with hers. "You've got to think positively—your parents say—"

"My parents have the same attitude they had when my father's business failed: 'Oh, everything will work out.' What they really mean is, 'Nothing's too important.' My father never took anything seriously, so he can't imagine that I do."

He lifted his right hand, examining it curiously. "It looks all right, doesn't it? But it might as well be made of wood, for all the use it is. I'll never skate with you again. Not competitively."

Maggie blinked back tears, words tumbling out: "That's not true! Your fingers can move. That means there isn't permanent damage. Once the cut's completely healed you'll recover your strength, I know you will."

"It *is* completely healed, Mag. What you see is the best I'm going to get."

Their eyes moved to the hand resting in his lap, cradling a sponge rubber ball. She saw the tendons in his forearm flex. The fingers squeezed, barely compressing the ball. "That's it. I can hold a newspaper, drive a car. But I'll never have anything like full strength again. We have to face it—my pairs days are over."

"It's too soon to say that; in a few months you might—"

"No, Maggie!" He cut her off almost angrily. "It's time to see things realistically." He lifted the hand two feet above the arm of the chair and brought the back of it down with a thud. "See that?" Specks of dust hung in the still air.

"That didn't hurt?" she asked, afraid of the answer.

"Hurt? I can hardly feel it. It's as though I was wearing a boxing glove; there's sensation, but it's distant. And when I try to work the fingers, it feels like something's holding them, keeping them from moving right." He raised his arm again.

Maggie grabbed his wrist. "Stop it! Stop it, please!" She pressed her hands against his wrist, just above the fresh, vivid scar that ran like a lightning bolt from the base of his thumb to the outside of his forearm.

In July, at Denver, that hand, cradling her hip, had thrust her high over his head, lifted her as it might a baby. He'd held her in a star lift while they'd revolved to Rachmaninoff, and fifteen thousand people had applauded. That hand had once torqued her so hard in a split triple twist that her rib broke. Now it was powerless to resist her pressure. She brought his wrist to her lips.

His free hand cradled the back of her head. "You've got to get a new partner, Maggie."

She recoiled. "I won't!"

"You have to. I'm going to have to get a job and finish school." He squeezed her neck. *"That's* positive thinking." His breath stirred the fine hairs curling around her ears.

She lost her fight with tears and turned away. "Damn it!" She drew her forearm across her eyes, flinging a crumpled letter across the room. "It's unbelievable! Rill was so smug, so sure of himself! She destroys your career, almost kills you, and nothing happens to Miss Rawlings, the USFSA poster girl. 'That's a police matter; if they didn't think there was any reason to charge her, we have no reason to do anything.' So association officials pressure the police to drop it, and then use the fact they dropped it to justify having the association not do anything."

Clay leaned back, shutting his eyes. "Maggie, would wrecking her career get mine back? Please—just leave it alone." He massaged the numb fingers. "Sometimes bad things just happen. Stupid things."

"Well, it didn't just 'happen' to you, you know. She killed my chances, too!" A spasm twisted her insides, and she clutched her stomach. "I've dreamed of going to the Olympics since I was six. I've worked my whole life for that. And when my father died, I swore that one day I'd stand by his grave with my medal on, because he, he . . ."

She clapped a hand over her mouth. "Oh, my God—what's happening to me? You're the one who's hurt."

"Don't, Maggie—please don't." He looked away, ashen. "Do you think I haven't thought about that every day since this happened? What it does to you? That matters so much more than what it costs me. But don't you see—dwelling on it won't change anything." His eyes pleaded with her. "It's just . . . over."

Maggie sank to her knees. "I hate her," she whispered.

"Don't, Maggie. It was an accident. Even if—"

"She's *always* been trouble. Since my first day she's been horrible."

"It's not her, Maggie. I—"

"I *know* she's the one who ripped my dress last year."

"You *don't* know that, you're just—"

"I know she nicked my blade before we went on that time in Providence." Maggie clenched her fists. "The way she looked at me when I had to come off, she *wanted* me to know."

"Maggie, you're imagining things. She's just . . . awkward."

She went on, talking to herself: "I blame myself; if I'd been there, this wouldn't have happened."

"Maggie!" He gripped her arm. "What's done is done."

She jumped to her feet, throwing off his hand. "Damn it, what's it take to get you angry?"

His head snapped back as though she'd slapped him.

"Something to be gained by it," he said softly. His arm circled her waist, pulling her onto his lap. "One of us has to think realistically. So let's get you a partner. Now, I've heard that Ham Barnes and Judy Hebert aren't getting along. Ham's a damn good skater, and—"

"Ham Barnes?" She looked at him in horror. "He doesn't belong on the same ice with you. Oh, God." She felt the tears starting again.

"Maggie, I know it's rough. But you've got to start someplace, and time is running out."

"There's no time! Even if I found someone tomorrow, there's no time! We'd never be ready."

"You wouldn't make Salt Lake City, probably, but—"

"I'll be too old for the next Olympics."

"There's still the Nationals, Maggie, and the Worlds. Not this year, but a year from now, two at the most, why—"

"No! I'll never skate with anyone else. I'll quit first."

"Don't say that, Mag." He enveloped her in his arms. "You can't give up your dream."

His hand might have lost its strength, but his arms were still powerful. They clung to her as if he needed to reassure himself of her reality.

"You were part of the dream," she whispered.

"Maggie, listen to me. You were born to compete. And not just to compete—to *win*. To be the best." His thumb stroked her cheek. "I remember when you were little—ten, maybe. I would have been thirteen. We raced around the pond, and I won. You made me go again, and I won. You made me keep racing until I decided to let you win, so I could quit. You got ahead, then stopped. When I caught up to you, you hit me as hard as you could, right on my ear. 'Don't cheat me,' you said. Like an angry little ferret. 'Don't ever cheat me again!' And you took off, remember? My ear hurt like hell."

Sniffling, she nodded. "I'm sorry."

He chuckled. "I doubt it. Anyway, you got what you wanted. I lit out after you, as fast as I could. I was going to *kill* you when I caught you. Only I couldn't. We'd *still* be running around that pond. You were yelling, and throwing sticks at me, and any time I got close you put on a burst and pulled away. I finally gave up. I never beat you again, either."

He patted her hip. She began coiling his hair around her forefinger, marveling that hair could be so fine and soft; she thought hers was like rusty steel wool. "You weren't training as hard as you should have been."

He nodded. "I sure wasn't. Not until we started skating together, and you shamed me into it. Oh, God, Mag—you got me so much further than I had any right to expect."

She bit her lip, rejoicing in the smell of him, the familiar, warm comfort of arms that had carried her safely across miles of ice. "We brought each other."

"We did, but you wanted to win more than I did; if you hadn't shown me how, I never would have known what it felt like to be a winner. I never knew what it took, Mag, until you showed me. You're so much better a skater, it made me reach in a way I never had before."

"I'm not."

"Of course you are." He took her chin between thumb and forefinger. "Maggie, you *have* to compete. I don't—I can live without it. But I don't think you can. Not until you've won it all. Now, let's get you a partner."

"No!" She shot to her feet. "I'll skate, but not with anyone else!"

"What do you mean? How can you—"

"I'll go back to singles."

He looked at her incredulously. "But you haven't skated singles in over five years."

"I can get back into singles a lot faster than I could be competitive with a new partner. I'll only have to worry about me, not about someone else as well."

"Who will you get to coach you? Rill won't, not with Doe."

She made a spitting sound. "Rill—if he hadn't always treated her like a little blond goddess who can do no wrong, this wouldn't have happened. I wouldn't train on the same ice with her. As far as I'm concerned, I need to see her on the ice only once."

"Once? When?"

"The Olympics. She took our medal; well, I'm going to do everything I can to take hers. And I know who can help me get it, if anyone can."

Once she made the decision she was obsessed with the shortness of time. Less than seventeen months; not a day to waste.

Their last night together they made love, the first time since the accident. They had eaten at a little Italian place on Charles Street, Maggie picking, for once not needing willpower to resist. Then they'd walked up Beacon Street to his apartment. There was a harvest moon, its buttery light masking the litter and graffiti, restoring dignity to the rows of nineteenth-century brownstones. She thought of the first time she'd noticed how stately a city Boston could be; she'd miss that.

In the apartment he built a fire. The night didn't need it, but he knew she loved fires. He struggled awkwardly with the logs, flashing such defiance when she reached to help that she turned away, not looking until she heard the kindling crackling. She settled beside him, and they sat, staring into the flames.

He put his arm around her waist. "I'm giving up the apartment, Mag. The lease is up this month, and I'll move in with my parents until I can find something cheap enough. Without the skating money it's impossible."

"Must you? I feel like this place is ours." She looked around the living room. She liked the fact that he kept it neat; she seemed to foster clutter wherever she was, but Clay had a sense of order. "I . . . I have some savings, and—"

He cut her off. "Thanks, but you'll need that for training."

He rested a finger on her lips before she could press him. "I'll be fine. When I get a job I can find a new place."

"What about college?"

"Maybe next summer; I need to earn some money first."

"Oh." She thrust the poker into the fire, muttering, "Money." They sat, watching the fire, saying nothing for several minutes.

He touched her arm. "Does this disgust you, Mag? You can tell me the truth." He turned the hand slowly, looking at it as though wondering whose it was. "Does it make you sick, to think of it? I haven't wanted to . . . you know. Not without knowing. I couldn't stand to think of you . . . putting up with something that disgusted you, just to please me."

She kissed the fingertips—slowly, one by one. They were cool and dry. He was the most beautiful man she'd ever seen, and she still found it a miracle that he wanted her, loved her. Her mouth moved to his palm, then to his lips as she tugged at his shirt.

He took her swiftly, with few preliminaries. Afterward she clung to him hungrily, pressing her slender athlete's body against him, willing herself to believe she could hold on forever.

The act itself was more a chance to give him pleasure than a source of great physical release for her. When they made love she never felt the dizzying volcano of passion and sensation people spoke of, the thing that convulsed his body and left him panting and spent soon after he entered her. Yet afterward she always felt a glow, a soft, languid sense that the woman in her was realized, that all was well. She would hold him as long as he would let her, imagining that she was in some way attached to every woman who had ever held a man, back to the beginning of time. Now she fought the thought that this would be the last time she would hold him for months.

He traced a finger down her side. His hands had roamed her body so often, on and off the ice, that she scarcely noticed.

"How's the rib?"

"What? Oh, it's fine. It was just a pull, I think. Now that I won't be doing throws and twists, it shouldn't be a problem."

"It's hard to believe that you're going back. Are you sure, Maggie? Do you really want to do this?"

She looked at him almost angrily. "Of course I don't *want* to go. I hate the idea of being away from you, and as for going back . . . well, there've been times, the last couple of days, when I felt like being sick when I thought about it. But it's the only way that makes sense."

She lowered her head to his shoulder, savoring the smell of him. "I've tried to think of another way that made as much sense, and I couldn't. This has to be."

She felt tears starting again. "Damn it!" She rolled away and sat up, blotting her eyes with her blouse. "We've so little time left."

"Have you decided how long you'll stay?"

"I can't—not until I see how I come along." She groaned. "If only it weren't so far away."

"You've got to come back as soon as you can, at least for a few days."

"I will." She propped her head on her hands and looked at the embers. "Imagine—coming to Boston as a visitor. It'll be like when we were young." She forced a smile. "Race you around the pond?"

"No way. You'd win."

"You bet I would."

"Besides—the pond's gone, along with the farm."

She nestled back against him. "We had fun then, didn't we?"

"We sure did. But when Dad lost his money, and had to sell the farm, and then my partner quit, I wondered if I'd ever have fun again." He stroked her thigh. "Then your father called and said you were moving back, and I knew everything would be all right."

"Oh, Clay." She rubbed her head against his shoulder.

"I mean it. You became my partner, and life was better than ever."

"For me, too." The fire toasted her back. "As soon as we started skating together, everything ugly was behind me. You took it away."

"I hope it's not there, waiting for you."

"I'm not worried. I know who I am now. What I am. And what I'm doing there. There won't be any surprises. I won't let there be."

He rolled over onto his back and stared at the ceiling. "That's okay, then. Did I ever tell you I used to think about buying the farm back?"

"Really?"

"Um. After we won the Olympics, and the promoters were showering us with money. I imagined us living there, if you wanted."

"Of course I'd want to. Is it for sale?"

"Well, in a fantasy you don't have to worry about details like that, but I guess most things are for sale, at a price."

"Then we'll do it!" She laughed, rolling over and straddling him. "Right after the games." She thrust her arm overhead. "Price is no object! Goose Hill Farm must be ours!"

It brought a grin. His hand worked her flank. "Well, I better find that job, if I don't want to be a kept man."

She leaned over and kissed him. "I'm skating for both of us, remember?"

"You're an angel, Maggie, but I intend to hold up my end. I'll contribute something to the pot, believe me."

"I have every confidence in you, Mr. Bartlett."

"That's my girl." He kissed her. "The next year and a half is going to be hell."

Slowly, reluctantly, she rose. "It will be. But we have to remember it's for a purpose, and then we'll have the rest of our lives together. I promise." She prodded his side with her toe. "On the farm."

Her brother, she noticed, was blinking back tears when he said good-bye before leaving for school. She hugged him, and he mumbled something. She turned to speak to her mother, and when she turned back he was gone.

She hoped he'd be all right; he had none of her self-assurance, and she wasn't sure any of the gawky boys and occasional girls who came by to look at his fish tanks or consult on sick pets had replaced her as confidante. She would have to write often.

Her mother came in as she was finishing packing. "Lofton Weeks called again; don't you think you should talk to him?"

Maggie inspected her skates. The Riedell boots were breaking down, and she'd need new ones soon. The Gold Seal blades, sharpened every month, might last a year, but she was doing well if she got eight months out of the boots. She shook her head at the thought of another thousand dollars. With no more financial assistance from the association, and no prize or appearance money, things were going to be tight.

"I said, aren't you going to get back to Mr. Weeks?"

Maggie noticed how much gray her mother had in her hair. It seemed to have happened suddenly, or perhaps she'd been dyeing it and had stopped.

"All he wants is to nag me to stay here and get a new partner."

"Maybe you should listen to him. He only wants to help."

"Mother, he's an agent and a promoter; he wants to ingratiate himself with me so that I'll sign with him someday." She put the guards on the blades and packed the skates in their bag.

Em sank onto her daughter's bed, next to the suitcase, and picked at the bedspread. "Are you sure, Maggie? Sure this is the right thing?" She sounded tired.

Maggie sat down, putting her arm around her mother's waist. "I'm sure. Did you stay up last night? You said you were going to bed."

"Not too long."

"You shouldn't work so hard." She got to her feet, voicing an old worry. "You're all right, aren't you? I mean, you have enough money? I know I've taken a lot."

Em held up her hand. "I'm fine, that way. Your father left us quite comfortable. You needn't worry."

Maggie, packing, nodded uncertainly. She held out a sweater, studying it doubtfully.

Her mother took it out of her hands. "You'll need it." She folded it and put it in the suitcase. "Don't be afraid to come home if it doesn't work out."

"I won't be. Mother . . ." She hesitated.

"Yes, dear?"

"You'll keep in touch with Clay, won't you?"

"Well, of course. If he's moving in with his parents, I expect I'll see him often."

"You *do* like him, don't you?"

"He's a charming young man. Don't forget warm socks. It can get very cold, you know. And damp."

"Mother, I lived there for almost fourteen years." She let out a sigh. She wasn't going to do any better than "charming young man."

"Yes, dear. Did you pack your raincoat?"

Downstairs, waiting in the front hall, her mother pushed a folder of traveler's checks into her hand. "You'll need these—you won't believe how expensive it's gotten."

"I can't take that. You've given me too much as it is."

"Take it—I'll feel better."

"I appreciate it, really, but I wouldn't feel right about it. Please don't press me." Maggie put the money on the table and folded her arms over her chest.

"All right, dear." Em smiled. "You look so like your father when you stand that way."

Maggie looked in the mirror. "I do, don't I?" She let her hands fall.

"Sometimes, when you come in the room, and I look up, it's as though . . ." Her mother shook her head.

"I know." Maggie took her mother in her arms. "I used to wish I looked like you, though."

"Your brother looks like me. It's amazing, really, how that happens." She touched the auburn coils on her daughter's head. "Your father's hair."

Maggie laughed. "Impossible hair."

Em's finger traced Maggie's face. "His nose, his chin, even his freckles."

"True." She didn't mind anymore.

"And his eyes, at least the color."

"I used to hate my eyes."

"I know."

"Now I don't."

"Good." Em studied Maggie's face. "Remember when I told you that you had emeralds in your eyes?"

"Yes."

"Your father had them, too." She stepped back, canting her head. "I'm glad you look like him."

"I am, too, now. But I got your personality."

Em shook her head. "You're a mixture. My temper, your father's idealism."

"I'm not idealistic."

Em snorted. "Of course you are, and at your age, you should be. But it took your father a long time to learn that we have to make concessions to the way the world is. I hope you'll learn sooner than he did."

"I learned the same time he did, Mother."

"Ah. Well, maybe you did. I hope so; it was a harsh lesson."

"Yes. Promise you won't work too hard?"

"Oh, don't worry about me. Did you remember a hat?"

Her mother was still inventorying her wardrobe when Clay pulled up. Maggie looked back as they drove away, photographing with her eyes.

She loved the big old yellow frame colonial perched on

the rise. It had become her first new friend when they'd moved to Boston. In the small, musty, out-of-the-way places under the eaves, the house had offered a sixteen-year-old girl a solitude she'd never known before. She'd sat in the windowless rooms for hours, sometimes reading, sometimes just trying to know what she was. Gradually she'd come to a kind of understanding. Skating with Clay had had the biggest part in bringing back her sense of self, but she'd always think of the house as her friend.

Her mother was still standing in the doorway as the car rounded the bend and the house disappeared. It was hard for her. She would worry, no matter what Maggie said. She felt the folder of checks in her pocket. Her mother must have slipped it in when Maggie was holding her.

All too soon they'd parked the car and reached the "Ticketed Passengers Only" sign. She stepped into Clay's arms.

"Hold me, just for a second," she whispered.

"I love you, Maggie." His cheek rested on her hair.

"I love you, too."

"Whatever happens, I'll always love you." His voice was husky. "Remember that."

"I will." She was determined not to cry. "I better go."

"Oh, Mag." He squeezed the breath out of her. "I'm not good enough. I don't deserve you."

"We deserve each other." She kissed him lightly. "We're together forever." She turned, not looking back.

Northwest flight 932 took off two hours later. Maggie leaned back, reluctant to start the book tucked in her skate bag. It was a fourteen-hour flight over the Pole to Tokyo, and the book had to last.

Chapter 4

She looked around the *cha-no-ma* while Grandmother and Aunt Mariko busied themselves in the kitchen. Grandfather had insisted she take the seat of honor in front of the *tokonoma*, the raised alcove holding a wall scroll. Everything in the combination living, dining, and sleeping room seemed the same, only smaller. The scroll was the same, the vase of pussy willows underneath it was the same, and the low table in front of her still had the chip in the black lacquer finish from the time she'd dropped a bowl on it.

She wondered briefly about the smell of fresh hay, then realized it came from the new tatami on which they sat. Every few years she'd smelled that smell, in her house, her grandparents' house, in everybody's house. It made her think of the green countryside, and rice paddies, and country people in conical hats, cutting the stalks that would make the mats that would never feel the touch of a shoe.

It pleased her that little had changed. She was even glad that Grandmother had already made a barbed comment at Grandfather's expense, clucked disapprovingly about her mother's business, and implied Maggie was anorexic; it reassured her that some things never changed. She'd thought she'd never sit again in the little room where she'd played and eaten, two Sundays a month, for fourteen years, listening to the drone of adult talk, her grandmother's acid asides, Grandfather's mild replies, the clatter from the kitchen. At times, living in the big yellow house outside Boston, she'd wondered if she'd imagined it. The previous weeks had brought nothing but uncertainty; it soothed her, finding a constant.

She realized her grandfather was speaking to her and brought herself back. "I'm sorry—I didn't hear."

He smiled indulgently. Studying his face, she thought, he seems the same, too. Old, but he's always been old. Unflappable, kind, and gentle. Comfortable with himself and his world.

He was sitting *seiza,* his haunches resting on his heels, just as she remembered. He seemed serene, fully satisfied to have his family around him, food on the way, his granddaughter back.

"It is a long flight, and you must be exhausted. Eat, then sleep. I asked about your mother."

"She's well. She sends her love. So does Kenji."

The gray head nodded. "Good. I worry about her."

"She's all right. She's strong."

"Yes, she is. She always was. After your father died, though, I thought she might come back."

"I don't think so, Grandfather. Kenji has school, and she has her friends, and her translating business. She is very American now. And I think she likes being where Father grew up and . . . is."

"Of course. Well, perhaps she will visit soon." His eyes seemed to seek physical connection with her. "We were so happy when you said you were coming. It is a long trip, at our age. Last year your grandmother complained about the jet lag for weeks after we got back. She said it ruined her appetite." He dropped his voice. "I didn't notice."

Uncle Katsumi nodded dolorously. "We were afraid you would never come back."

Maggie wrenched the subject to something unthreatening. "Please, Uncle—tell me about Cousin Nobuo. How is he?"

"He is well. He is sorry he could not be here tonight, but we are building a new production line, and he must supervise the installation."

"Please tell him I look forward to seeing him. And how are things at Kofuku?"

Both men smiled, Katsumi deferring to his father for an answer. The old man nodded happily. "Very good, thank you. Very good." He leaned over the table. "Your uncle and I believe we have developed a product that will revolutionize the business. We believe we have solved the bandwidth problem."

Katsumi added, "We've managed to compress the signal in a way that's never been tried before."

"That's wonderful." Maggie nodded, having no idea what they were talking about.

Her uncle seemed to swell. "If all goes well, it will be worth a great deal, Megumi-*chan*." He stopped abruptly, looked at her uncertainly. "It is acceptable, to call you that?"

"Of course." She hadn't been called by her Japanese name in years. Three, if she'd heard her father's whisper right, but he'd been unconscious and she hadn't been sure. The last person to use it for certain had been her brother, and that had been the only time she'd ever really hit him. Now it sounded odd to her, like a strange noise.

Her grandfather was waving his hand impatiently, unaware she'd drifted away again. "What is important is what it can mean to the public, not what it may be worth to us. Why . . ."

The arrival of Grandmother and Aunt Mariko bearing trays cut off further explanation. Grandmother deposited her tray heavily, passing out dishes while she scolded. "I hope, Husband, that *this* time you will consider what this thing might be worth to your family. Or perhaps we already have so much we need no more?"

"I only meant that Kofuku provides us with a good living; we can't eat any more than we already do."

Grandfather's right eyebrow twitched, and Maggie had to stifle a giggle; she and her grandfather had always had a private language.

Grandmother sniffed. "Let Fukawa-*san* decide he is tired of financing Kofuku and you will see how well we eat. Now, no more of this talk; we will see what comes, and I will believe it then."

She placed a plate in front of Maggie. "You must be starving. I thought Americans all ate too much, but you're nothing but bones. That's what comes when a mother is too busy to look after her family. Eat, eat."

Maggie looked up. "Western food, Grandmother?"

Her grandmother, nodding, passed over a knife and fork, still in their store wrapping. "We weren't sure you ate Japanese food anymore," Aunt Mariko mumbled.

"Oh." The small steak looked delicious; the fried potatoes gave off a fine smell. Broccoli flowerets glistened with oil. Suddenly she was very hungry. She paused only long enough to say, "Thank you, but I would love anything you fix for me. I am very happy to be here."

The smiles and nods the lie drew felt good. Ravenous, she cut into the meat. Chopsticks dipped into lacquer bowls, the soft cricket clicks so much more soothing than the clatter of steel on china. Lips smacked. Maggie felt her eyelids drooping. Around her swirled scents of *dashi* and *shoyu,* the iodine bite of fresh seaweed, the clean salt fragrance of bream, the flowery smell of rice, stirring her thoughts, making her think back to her childhood and wonder why she had been so certain it would be impossible for her to return to the place where she'd once been so happy.

Chapter 5

May 1981: Tokyo

*N*o one was more surprised to find Emiko Tanaka Campbell—"Em" to her husband and American friends—back in Tokyo, with an American husband and two-year-old daughter, than Emiko Tanaka Campbell. She'd left Japan six years before, at eighteen, and had long given up thought of returning. After graduating from Harvard, marrying a young lawyer named Nicholas Stuart Campbell, settling in Boston, and delivering a child whose birth certificate may have read "Megumi," meaning "Blessing," but who was known to all as Maggie, she felt well on the way to becoming an American.

When her husband had come home one day to announce that his law firm had asked him to manage their Tokyo office, she'd objected. She and her mother couldn't be in the same room without fighting, she wasn't at all sure she liked the idea of raising Maggie as Megumi, she had no intention of assuming the life of a Japanese housewife she'd gone to such lengths to escape, and she thought her tall, lanky, red-haired, green-eyed *gaijin* husband had a wildly idealized view of Japanese life, born of a junior year at Keio University. Had she not adored him, had he not assured her that they could leave any time she wanted, and had he not added that it would be an important career boost, she might well have refused.

Eventually Em and her mother reached an uneasy truce, with Maggie the agent of reconciliation. "How strange looking she is," sister-in-law Mariko exclaimed when the child wobbled into the house in which Em had grown up. "Look at her eyes. *Gaijin* eyes—she isn't normal!"

After six years in America Em no longer spoke in nuanced circumlocutions, and she rounded on the older woman. "It's a pity, Sister-in-Law, you don't have bigger eyes—*and* a smaller mouth!" She swept the little girl into her arms, ready to walk out and never return.

Mariko blanched; no one had ever spoken to her so bluntly before. Lacking the ability to reply, she froze, her mouth working like a fish's. Nick, barely able to follow his wife's outburst, smiled uneasily, while Eriko Tanaka murmured conciliatory pap that Em found intensely, irrationally annoying. Katsumi, unnerved by the presence of conflict, began to giggle. She whirled on him, fixing him with a glare that made him giggle more. Seven-year-old Nobuo played with his blocks, oblivious.

Em's father broke the tension, walking over and wordlessly taking Maggie from his daughter. He held the toddler at arm's length, while each inspected the other. They smiled at the same time.

"She has grown so," Shingo Tanaka marveled. He hugged the child, kissing her curls. "Grown even more beautiful." Cradling her with one arm, he tapped his chest, saying slowly, "Sofu. So . . . fu."

Maggie stared at him wordlessly, eyes wide with wonder, until suddenly she understood. "So . . . fu!" Her hand closed on his stubby nose, squeezing. "Sofu!" Both laughed. Shingo Tanaka walked her around the room, Maggie riding easily in his arms, each member of the family suffering the small indignity.

Sobo, stretched out on cushions with a bad back, tried to maintain her dowager image, but it cracked and Em actually saw her mother smile as the little hand reached down; even Katsumi let his natural pomposity slip enough to clap his hands over his face, pretending great pain, after his introduction. Finally they came to Aunt Mariko. "Mariko-*oba-san,* Megumi," her father said. Mariko tried to turn away, but Shingo Tanaka's look brought her head around and she endured her fate.

Eriko Tanaka, beaming up from the floor, said, "*Oba-san* wants to bring you an ice-cream bar, Megumi. She was just going for it." She reached up, taking the child from her husband and settling her on her ample stomach, while Mariko bowed deeply, whispered hoarse apologies for forgetting, and scurried from the room.

The desire to keep up with the child had Mrs. Tanaka on her feet sooner than expected. Before the recovery period was over she was overheard calling for "Maggie." Though nothing would induce her to call Em anything but "Daughter," by subtle gestures she conveyed a certain softening toward her wayward child.

The Campbells fell into a routine. Twice a month, on Sunday, they took the train from Ueno to Nerima. Arriving in early afternoon, they would sit in the *cha-no-ma* and chat, until the Tanaka women served an early supper.

Mariko would bring in miso soup, rice, and pickles, then

grill shellfish and bits of meat over a small gas burner while Eriko Tanaka pushed morsels into Maggie's mouth, if she could grab her as she darted by. The men made desultory conversation while Em held newly arrived Kenji and hoped her father wouldn't say anything to provoke one of her mother's caustic retorts.

Shortly before the Campbells arrived in Japan, Shingo Tanaka had reached fifty-five, the retirement age at Japan Radio & Television Company. As a reward for his service as the JRT director of research and development, and at the personal direction of Seizo Fukawa, JRT's founder, controlling shareholder, and chairman, JRT created a small company, gave it to Mr. Tanaka, and bade him produce cellular telephone equipment, for sale to JRT and others. Since old age pensions didn't begin paying until sixty-five, the arrangement spared Mr. Tanaka the fate of many older men whose affiliations were less advantageous—a poorly paid job as a shop clerk—and allowed him to continue the work he loved. Reflecting his view of this development, he named the new company Kofuku, or "Good Fortune," Corporation.

It was understood by all that Kofuku was bound to the JRT *kereitsu*, or business group, though JRT owned but a single, symbolic share of Kofuku stock. Kofuku would endeavor to produce products that corresponded to JRT's needs. In return, Kofuku would always have a customer and, should the need arrive, a source of capital. When JRT thrived, Kofuku would thrive; when the economy soured, it would be the Kofukus that accepted instructions from above to lay off workers and cut prices, so that the great companies like JRT could maintain the myth of lifetime employment and invincible growth. It did not require great managerial acumen to function in such an environment.

Day-to-day management of the company was left to Katsumi Tanaka, who was named president and who compensated for a limited imagination with a prodigious appetite for mind-numbing detail. Shingo Tanaka felt like a child given the deed to a toy store. Katsumi was well pleased with the title he'd never have achieved in a larger business, and the prospect of an eventual sinecure for his son, Nubuo. Mariko, satisfied that her son's future was ensured, could envision nothing more. Only Eriko Tanaka felt slighted by life, a feeling she was only too ready to share.

Six months after the Campbells arrived in Tokyo, Nick's questions and a second flask of sake caused Mr. Tanaka to overlook his wife's proximity and allow that Kofuku's profits were down.

The scorn in Eriko Tanaka's interjection was palpable. "Fukawa-*san*'s profits aren't down, you can be sure. He'll squeeze you until you're dry to keep *his* profits up!"

"Shh." Em's father looked around until he was satisfied Maggie was playing out of earshot. "You'll upset the children, Wife." His tone was mild, less reproachful than resigned. He had learned long before that wifely deference was something put on for public appearances; like shoes, it was left outside the *uchi*.

She glared at him. "If you owned your fair share of JRT, you could provide for your grandchildren."

"Why would I want to own JRT, Wife? I'd sooner own an elephant. All I ever wanted to own was a business like Kofuku, where I could do my own work, and now I have it." Mr. Tanaka spoke calmly, as he almost always did, with the assurance of a man who knows what he knows and has all he wants. "JRT provided the money to start Kofuku; surely that shows the chairman's goodwill."

"Money you earned for JRT! And in return he gets you and my son working like dogs for him. You take all the risk and he takes all the profit. He leaves you enough to keep you eating, while he hobnobs with the bigwigs."

"Enough to keep us all eating, I think." Mr. Tanaka cast a glance at his wife, adding under his breath, "Some more than others, maybe." He continued: "With JRT we will always have a customer. It is a comfortable arrangement."

"With JRT you will always have a boss! You should be the boss, and after you, Katsumi. Why should you be with some little business nobody ever heard of?"

Mr. Tanaka sighed the sigh of a man for whom a discussion held nothing new. "I reached the retirement age—you know that."

"The retirement age for salaried employees! There is no retirement age for owners, is there? You don't see Fukawa retiring, do you? You should be an owner. This way Fukawa still gets the benefit of your work, and he doesn't even have to pay your salary. And do you think it means anything to the people I meet when I say my husband owns Kofuku Corporation? They say, 'What is that?' The other day a woman said to me, 'Don't they make toilets?' Toilets! And *her* husband sells underwear!"

Finally Mr. Tanaka smiled helplessly, got up, and took Maggie out to the minuscule plot of ground that passed for a garden—"no bigger than a cat's forehead," he said of it— and the sound of laughter replaced the din of combat. Em, her head pounding, rummaged in her purse for the aspirin she always brought with her to the family gatherings and glanced surreptitiously at her watch, willing the hands to move.

Chapter 6

October 2000: Boston

*H*unter Rill sat at the Seeing Eye bar. The lounge was dark and quiet, and since it was poked away on a side street in the South End, there was very little chance Rill would encounter anyone from the Charles River Skating Club. The bartender knew Rill's desires, attended to them with a minimum of chat, and otherwise left him to his own company, which was how he wished it.

He'd stopped in on his way home to the brownstone he'd restored twenty years before, with the money he'd saved from his earnings with the Ice Capades. Not much money, but enough, back when the South End was an urban frontier. People sent home from the Olympics in disgrace didn't have a lot of marquee value, didn't make the kind of money that put someone on Louisburg Square.

Sometimes, after a few drinks, he'd risk thinking about it, seeing if he could make it come out differently; but it never did. He'd celebrated one night too early, that was all, and there were only two things that could help him forget:

enough vodka and creating the champion he should have been.

Everybody who was anybody in skating knew his name. A lot of them preceded it with a four-letter word or followed it with a snicker about his long-ago debacle, but they knew it.

But when you came *that* close to being the defining skater of your generation and instead became a fading scandal, just being a coach, even one of the handful of really important coaches, wasn't nearly enough. Having the U.S. ladies' champion wasn't enough; having had the best pairs team in America wasn't enough. Other coaches had held those distinctions; other coaches would again. No, if he were to find redemption as a coach—and he had to, or he might as well die—he had to be *the* coach, the man who altered the sport forever, who molded a champion whose accomplishments on ice so dwarfed those of the competition that a generation later people would still speak of his creation the way, fifty years after, people still spoke of Babe Ruth, Bill Tilden, Bobby Jones, or Sonja Henie.

Well, he thought, tapping his glass on the bar for another double gimlet, I can buy enough vodka, and soon I'm going to have that champion: the Olympic gold medalist in ladies' figure skating. The most prestigious award the Olympics had to offer. The most prestigious award in all of sport, and Doe Rawlings was going to win it. No—*he* was going to win it. Doe Rawlings would accept it, but Hunter Rill would win it. And it wouldn't just be a little gold disk ratifying Doe as the best woman skater at a particular Olympiad, either; those were given out every four years. Doe Rawlings's medal—like the medal that should have been his—would be given for a performance that would be remembered decades later. Talked about a generation later, the way Torvill and Dean's performance at Sarajevo would always be the benchmark against which every dance team would be measured.

He'd been ready to give such a performance and had wasted the opportunity; now Doe Rawlings would give it for him, but everyone would know it was Hunter Rill's masterwork.

Less than a year and a half to wait. Not to wait, to work. To work on bringing Doe Rawlings to her full, unlimited potential.

Rill knew exactly what was required. He'd spent years in this very bar, often this very chair, thinking about the long program that would exploit to the hilt Doe Rawlings's extraordinary on-ice persona, and he was just about there. They'd begin work as soon as they returned from Düsseldorf in March, with the World title. Eleven months until the Olympics; plenty of time.

He felt a frisson as he contemplated his masterstroke: they would develop the new long program in secret. No one—not association officials, not a choreographer, not other skaters—would see it until it burst upon the world in the Olympic finals. In the interim, in competitions and in public practices, Doe would continue to skate her current program, exactly as though they were satisfied to rely on it at the Olympics.

The apparent failure to develop a new program would be second-guessed throughout the skating world. The closed practices would be ascribed to injury, mental collapse, heaven knew what. But years afterward, people would look back and say, "It was unprecedented, it was extraordinarily risky, and it was brilliant."

It would alter the strategy of skating forever; once people saw how the dramatic impact of a program increased exponentially when no one except the skater and the coach knew what was coming next, once the Lofton Weeks types were deprived of their ability to declaim, "She has a flying camel coming up that she's struggled with all week," everyone was going to realize that it was idiotic to deprive skating of the element of surprise, of the awe that people feel when they see a great athlete produce the unexpected. And some gray-beard—perhaps Lofton Weeks, since no one was quicker to jump on the new—would dredge up a long-forgotten fact: The last great skater to provide novelty in competition, to toss in a wholly unexpected, previously unknown element, was . . . Hunter Rill. Why, someone would recall, it was only after Rill stunned everyone with an unscripted back flip in the finals at Chamonix, instantly rendering the other skaters cloddish, that the ISU banned the move.

Doe would open to something gentle. Soft, caressing, haunting, a study in dreamy languor.

The bartender brought the rebuilt drink, but Rill let it sit—he didn't like to interrupt this reverie, not even for al-cohol—while he pondered, for the thousandth time, the right music for the slow opening. The more he thought about it, the more certain he became: Wagner.

Start with something from the beginning of *Das Rhein-gold:* fresh, naive, and vulnerable.

Let the tension build, let everyone in the hall feel Doe's skin temperature rising, then cut to Brunhilde's "Ride of the Valkyries" and . . . watch out! Because it was here that she was going to do something no woman, and damn few men, had ever done before: Doe Rawlings was going to hit a quad. *Four* airborne revolutions.

Doe already hit triple Axels with the ease of men, but there were a few other women who'd had the Axel. No woman, and few men, had a quad. When the announcers saw the quad, when Weeks told the world what it had just witnessed, Hunter Rill and Doe Rawlings would be linked together with the greatest moment in skating history—one of the greatest moments in the history of sport, in fact.

He took a sip of the drink to slow his heart rate; the thought of the quad, the knowledge that he, Hunter Rill, had the skater who could do it, was almost enough to make him believe in a merciful God. He took another swallow, relaxing.

Close with something suggesting satiation—the finale to *Die Götterdämmerung,* maybe. Or no—stick with *Die Walküre:* the immolation scene. Let things slow down, unwind. Show the glories of the slow, even lay-back and toe spins.

He felt so good about where he was with the choreography that he decided to have another drink after he finished the one in hand. Yes, no doubt about it—God had shown him the route to redemption.

He knew how to handle the girl; that was the key. Had known, the day her mother brought Doe for her lesson, instead of the handsome, weak-faced father who'd always brought her before. The father who could do no wrong in the little girl's eyes.

"Her father . . . left," was how her mother answered his inquiry. That day he saw a new Doe Rawlings, saw a girl who went through her lessons joylessly, stolidly, until gradually he saw the adoring looks again, only directed at him. At him, instead of at the man who'd "left" by putting a bullet through his head.

Rill had done what needed to be done. He'd been firm, certainly, but always thoughtful, always considerate, always predictable. *His* rules didn't change depending on his blood alcohol level; he didn't alternate between sloppy caresses and furious slaps.

He'd let the girl know, without saying it, that he understood about her mother, that Doe could talk about her, that he'd do what he could to be a safe harbor, a place of comfort, and most of all, a refuge of certainty in a life that otherwise knew nothing but uncertainty. He'd won the love that had had no place to go, once her father "left."

He swirled the pale green liquid and listened to the tinkle of the ice. He was never far from ice. He leaned back, imagining his face on the cover of *International Figure Skating:* HUNTER HILL—FROM OLYMPIC GOAT TO SKATING LEGEND; ONE MAN'S ODYSSEY.

The thought was warming, far more so than the drink, but he knew it wasn't the sort of idyll he could indulge without limit. He'd fueled a vision with alcohol twenty years earlier, and it had cost him the reality; he wouldn't make the same mistake again.

"World's greatest skater." It was the role offered him, and he'd thrown it away: stupidly, insanely, self-destructively thrown it away. One more night and he could have basked in glory the rest of his life. Just a few hours, really.

It was so unfair; that was what still baffled him. He'd skated on two hours' sleep dozens of times; he'd won the Nationals on no sleep and a half bottle of cognac. The rink was spinning like a lazy Susan when he went out to center ice, and he'd skated the performance of his life. *He* was different, he was special, the damn rules didn't apply to him.

Except they did. The idiot United States Olympic Committee official had hardly needed to scream at him that he'd never skate in competition again—he'd known that, known it with awful, numb certainty the moment he'd awakened in that unfamiliar room, with some stranger lying next to him, had looked at his watch, looked again, known his competitive career was over.

He'd lain, staring at the ceiling, not realizing he was crying, until he'd become aware of the man's arms around him, a stranger murmuring something soothing in a language he didn't understand.

He'd had to learn not to cry; he had a plan, a goal, a *dream,* and he didn't need to cry. He was so close now, he could taste it. This time there'd be no denying him. This time, by Christ . . .

The glass exploded in his hand. "Shit!" He pulled out a handkerchief and dabbed at a small cut.

He felt a touch on his shoulder and jumped. From behind him, in the gloom, a mellifluous drawl cautioned: "Careful, old dear—thinking about Bartlett and Campbell, are you? All that nice talent, lost? Believe me, I share your disappointment."

"Jesus, Lofton—did you have to sneak up on me like that?" He looked at his finger. "Must have been something defective in the glass, that's all. The damnedest thing, huh?"

Lofton Weeks settled onto the stool next to Rill, lean and elegant in a double-breasted, charcoal pinstripe and starched blue shirt with a straight white collar. "Isn't it, though?"

Weeks caught the bartender's attention. "Another for Mr. Rill, Michael—perhaps in a stronger glass? My usual."

He turned, leaning one elbow on the bar. "Tell me: Did the silly girl explain why she wanted to take up singles? I mean, with Doe Rawlings in the way, among others? It's absolute folly."

Rill shrugged, tucking away the handkerchief. "She's a romantic. Something about 'only one man for me,' I imagine."

"Oh my." Weeks rolled his eyes theatrically. "Thank God *I* never felt that way." He sniffed, "She wouldn't even return my calls."

"How humbling."

"I contacted skaters all over the country. I had half a dozen men dying to fly in and try out with her. Damn good skaters, too: Sessions, LaTourette, Barnes . . ." He trailed off morosely. "Men ready to dump their partners like a five-dollar trick to team with her. Maybe they wouldn't have been ready for the Olympics, but who knows? In a year or two she would at least have gotten a shot at a World title. *Think* of the offers a World champion American pairs team would draw in today's market—oh, my God."

"Is that all it is to you—the money they represent?" Rill looked at him with genuine curiosity.

Weeks harumphed imperiously. "Now, now—no attitude, Hunter; I appreciated good skating before you were born. But without the money, good skaters won't keep on skating, will they?"

"And you won't keep on getting your cut, and stocking your tour."

"Damn right. Good for me, good for them."

The bartender brought their drinks. Rill raised his. "Cheers. And speaking of stocking your tour—you can buy me drinks all night and I'm still not going to tell Doe to sign that contract you have in your pocket. I assume that's why you came in." Rill's eyebrows rose expectantly.

"Actually, Hunter, I came in to see if there was any new talent here, but pickings are depressingly thin, eh?"

"Give it a rest, Lofton."

"Tsk, tsk. You must be wound tight, if you've stopped looking. Of course, I suppose having the best skater in the world *is* a bit nerve-racking. I mean, if Rawlings does repeat at the Nationals, then goes on to win the Worlds and Olympics, everyone says, 'Of course.' If, perish forbid, she doesn't . . ." He shrugged. "Well, it would simply revive memories of other extraordinary talents who fell short of expectations, what?"

Rill chuckled. "You won't get to me today, Lofton. And by the way—tell your hairstylist to lighten up on the dye; you're starting to look like Bert Parks."

Weeks's eyes darted to the mirror behind the bar. "I think it looks fine," he announced, his hand smoothing the back of his head.

"God, Lofton," Rill said, "I've never known anyone as vain as you."

Weeks pulled his shoulders back. Though close to seventy, he still had the aristocratic bearing that had earned him the sobriquet "Lord Lofton" when he'd dominated men's skating almost half a century earlier. "You've known few with as much to be vain about, dear boy. Now—why won't you let Doe sign a contract with me?"

Rill nodded. "Let's see—your asking means that Doe turned you down again. At your party, is my guess. I saw you whispering in her ear, and somehow I just knew you weren't trying to talk your way into her knickers. Do I have that right?"

"Damn it, Hunter—she's over eighteen. She ought to be able to decide for herself."

"She has; she's decided to follow my advice, since she's been taking it since she was five and it hasn't served her badly. And my advice is, As much as we *adore* Lofton Weeks, and as much as the skating world revolves around him, don't even *think* of signing a contract with him now, because when you're ready to turn professional you're going to be in the driver's seat, and, Doe dearest, it is far, far better to drive Lofton Weeks than to be driven by him." Rill raised his glass. "Cheers."

Weeks shook his head. "You've got her taking a hell of a

risk, Hunter. Right now you and Doe are in a position to negotiate a fantastic deal. If she signs now, I'll guarantee a
multiyear contract with my pro tour, starting right after the
Olympics. A million a year for ten years, and no matter how
she does in the Olympics, she gets the money. But if she
doesn't sign now, and doesn't win . . . well, you'll be awfully unhappy she didn't grab it while she could."

Rill looked bored. "After she wins the Worlds you'll double whatever you're offering now. Don't bother. After she
wins the Olympics, and is ready to turn professional, we'll
accept bids. Until then, Doe isn't going to even listen to an
offer."

"'Bids'?" Weeks studied his drink as though he'd spotted
a worm. "You expect me to bid against a bog Irish upstart
like Patrick Coyle, who wouldn't know the difference between Doe Rawlings and Wayne Gretzky?"

Rill chuckled. "Ah, Lofton—you are a delight. It will be a
treat watching you go against Coyle. I expect to see records
set. Let's see—you paid Rischer a million five to appear in
ten events over a year and a half, and that was before Coyle
set up his tour. After the Olympics I figure the bidding for
Doe will start at three and go from there, um?"

"If I were you, my friend, I wouldn't count on Mr. Coyle
being around skating by the Olympics. I don't think he's
finding it as easy as he expected. I may be the only buyer.
And if she falls on her face in the meantime . . ." Weeks
arched his eyebrows knowingly.

Rill shrugged. "Who knows—Doe may decide to start her
own company, not sign with anybody. That's how you got
started, isn't it?"

"Now you're joking." Weeks's eyes narrowed, the bantering tone gone.

It was one thing to bait Weeks, another to challenge him.

Rill knew that under Weeks's veneer of mannered elegance was a hard man. He was certain Weeks was not above using his position as television commentator for Olympic-eligible competition to deprecate a skater he viewed as a threat to his near monopoly in professional skating. Judges listened to Lofton Weeks; Rill retreated.

"Of course," he agreed. He downed his drink and slid off the stool. He gave Weeks a quick hug. "But a little advice: If you want us to be receptive after the Olympics, stay away from Doe now. I've turned down every commercial, interview, modeling opportunity, and hustler, including Pat Coyle, and I'm not making an exception for you. There's only one thing she needs to be thinking about, and I don't want her distracted."

Weeks looked disgusted. "One of these days the girl's got to start thinking for herself, you know."

"Right—and I'll tell her when. Now, I'm going home to listen to Wagner. Ciao."

Chapter 7

October 2000: Tokyo

*M*aggie, her inner clock confused, woke just before dawn. She sat up and swung her feet to the floor, only they already were on the floor. Then she remembered where she was, and that she'd gone to sleep on a futon in the *cha-no-ma.*

The thin walls were no bar to the snores and rhythmic breathing coming from the other rooms, and she knew that further sleep was unlikely. She'd had a notion as she'd drifted off; now that she had a morning to kill, she decided to indulge it. After dressing quickly, she slipped out of the house. Zipping her jacket against the fall chill, she hurried to the train station.

A *sarariman,* on his way to the office in his dark pin-striped suit and white shirt, sat across the aisle, reading a thick comic book. The cover displayed a naked blond woman tied to a chair. The man glanced up, catching Maggie's eye before she could look away. He grinned, looking her up and down. *"Kirei-na karada-dane,"* he declared hoarsely.

She shrugged apologetically, shaking her head.

"Ahh." He nodded sympathetically. *"Ocha shinai?"* He leered at her.

She looked at him uncomprehendingly, palms upturned. Smiling shyly, she leaned across the aisle. His head came toward hers. When they were almost touching she whispered: *"Tansho hokei, kono hoentai!"* "Your tool is too small, you pervert."

Gasping, the man bolted for the next car. Maggie turned to look out the window. It had been night when she'd landed in Japan; now, the pale morning light brought her her first view of Tokyo in five years.

She hadn't remembered it was so dreary. She recalled thinking the city vast and majestic, thrilling in its promise of infinite variety, endless surprises. Instead, as the train approached downtown, she saw only countless blocks of concrete apartment buildings, the laundry hanging from the balconies almost the only color against the dirty gray sky. Highways and rail lines crisscrossed randomly. Squat gas stations and commercial buildings seemed to have been flung among the apartment blocks like dice among dominoes. An occasional postage-stamp patch of green marked a spot where someone still farmed. Roofs bristled with antennas, telephone and electric poles canted every which way, golf driving ranges cloaked the tops of parking garages, looking like huge aviaries.

The city still seemed vast, but depressing, hardly thrilling. A spasm of loneliness passed over her, and she was glad when the brake squeal signaled arrival in Ueno Station.

It was only a little past seven, but the concourse teemed with commuters. Maggie worked her way through the crowds to the row of stalls outside the station. Picking one, she ordered noodles.

"If I may say so, the young lady speaks excellent Japanese." The counterman looked at the slender young *yanki* with the wild mass of auburn curls and large green eyes. She compressed her lips, and he sensed that in some obscure way he'd amused her. The corners of her mouth twitched.

"Thank you," she said, turning away with the steaming bowl, "I used to be Japanese."

Maggie stood, eating the noodles. She'd approached them warily, as though uncertain they were edible, but after a few minutes her chopsticks were flying and she was slurping as loudly as anybody.

Her thoughts turned to the noodles she'd eaten at Mrs. Araki's noodle parlor; hundreds of bowls, probably. She wondered if they really were better than those she was eating now, or if it was another example of time working on memory. She could find out, of course—the little *ramen ya* was no more than a five-minute walk—but she had no right to walk in and force a welcome that she didn't deserve. And Hiro Araki—what would he be now? It no longer hurt to think of him. Married with children, probably. She shrugged and returned to work on the noodles.

Chapter 8

August 1997: Tokyo

*T*he two hundred men in dark suits chatting in the banquet room of the Lotus Garden Hotel might have been on a break from a symposium. The room could have been a meeting room in any hotel in the world, except for the Shinto shrine at one end and its appurtenances: a flask, two earthenware sake cups, and three dishes, holding respectively fish scales, a pile of rock salt, and rice.

The guests included a cabinet minister, who was exchanging pleasantries with the CEOs of several leading companies. An assistant chief of the Tokyo Police Department joked convivially with a four-hundred-pound sumo wrestler, while a popular singer described his new act to a newspaper reporter.

The soft buzz ceased when a pair of doors opened in the wall near the shrine. Through them stepped an older man with steel gray hair, flanked by two associates. The gray-haired man wore a black kimono, his two associates suits. The guests turned, faced the newcomers, bowed. The older man returned the collective bow and allowed one of his escorts to lead him to the shrine alcove, where he sank to his knees, bowed to the shrine, and sat impassively.

His associate, who had escorted him to the shrine, turned to address the assembly: "We gather today, in this eighth year of Heisei, to welcome a new brother and son through the ceremony of *sakazuki*. The *oyabun* waits. Where is the *kobun?*"

A tall, muscular man, younger than the others, stepped forward. He wore a charcoal kimono, severe and elegant, but it was the bright, amused animation of his eyes that focused the crowd's attention. "I am the *kobun*," he announced.

The man who had spoken before said: "And who guarantees this man?"

An older man, perhaps fifty, not nearly as tall as the younger man, appeared at his side: "I, Tsuto Hata, known to you all, offer myself as *torimochinin*." The two men then advanced to the shrine alcove, where the gray-haired man waited. The one identifying himself as the *kobun* went to his knees, bowing first to the shrine and then to the gray-haired man: "May the *oyabun* have health."

Tsuto Hata squatted on his heels next to his charge: *"Oyabun,"* he said, "it is my honor to present this man for membership in the Yamagouchi-*gumi*. I know him to be brave, strong, and a man of honor. He will practice *giri*, and be true to the family."

The eyes of the *oyabun* roamed the face of the younger man, whose own eyes remained lowered. The *oyabun* nodded almost imperceptibly, and his retainer and Tsuto Hata rose to their feet.

Hata and the retainer each took a sake cup from the front of the shrine. They added fish scales and salt to the cups, then poured in sake. When they finished, one cup held fractionally more than the other, and both men nodded approvingly. They turned to the young man, still seated motionlessly, his eyes closed.

Raising the cups, the men said in unison: "From now on, the *oyabun* is your only parent; follow him through fire and flood."

The fuller cup was handed to the *oyabun*, the other to the young man. Holding the cups between their hands, each man toasted the other, then drank. When the cups were empty the two standing figures took them, wrapped them in rice paper, and handed them back. *Oyabun* and *kobun* each put his cup inside the folds of his kimono, then clasped hands.

A low hiss escaped from the ranks of onlookers, followed by another refrain from the two men attending the seated figures: "Having drunk from the *oyabun*'s cup and he from yours, you now owe loyalty to the family and devotion to your *oyabun*. Even should your wife and children starve, even at the cost of your life, your duty is now to the family and to the *oyabun*."

Placing their hands over those of the seated men, the two retainers intoned: "The *sakazuki* is now over."

The seated men bowed once more and rose, the attendant helping the older man while the younger uncoiled in a single, unbroken motion. Tsuto Hata stepped up to his charge, bowing. "Let me be the first to welcome my new younger brother into the *kumi*."

The young man returned the bow. Swiveling, he lowered his head to the onlookers. As they reciprocated, some noticed that while the young man's face was impassive, his eyes seemed to reflect some inner joke and looked into theirs perhaps more directly than was strictly polite. Hiro

Araki did not appear as awed as most new members of the *yakuza*.

Hiro found the next months intriguing. Many of the newer *yakuza*, he saw, quavered in the company of their seniors, some of Japan's best-known criminals; Hiro found the exaggerated swagger, the elaborate posturing, rather amusing, as though he'd dropped into the middle of one of the samurai costume dramas at the *kabukiza*. He masked his feelings, showed proper deference, and reminded himself that the code of conduct would have been even sillier if he'd taken a job in one of the ministries or with one of the great companies, as most of his classmates had. At least he didn't have to live in a company dorm and sing the company song every morning.

Certainly the average University of Tokyo graduate didn't get a mentor as entertaining as Koji Sano. The older man's bluff manner was a refreshing change from the stiff formality that characterized most relationships outside the *kumi*. Sano was a student of psychology and a homespun philosopher, too. Every time they made rounds together, Hiro learned something new about the infinite variety of human nature. He'd studied anthropology at the university, and in many ways he thought of his job as graduate work.

Now it was Friday, collection day, and Sano had met Hiro at the *kumi*'s district office, to begin their rounds. It was still new enough to Hiro to be exciting, this direct contact with those foolish or unfortunate enough to have become involved with the *yakuza*. Most of the time he did research, looking for new sources of income: hanging around bars frequented by politicians, picking up stray bits of gossip from bar girls, passing information along to more senior people. On collection day, though, he got to sit down and sip tea with truly bad people—thieves, liars, cheats of all types. People who would have scorned him, had he just been himself. The common denominator was that they all preferred to pay money to the *yakuza* rather than acknowledge what they had done, or did.

Hiro and Sano worked their territory, the Toronomon and Ginza districts in central Tokyo, on Hiro's motorcycle. The area included most of the major government offices, many corporate headquarters, the world's most expensive shops, and an almost limitless array of bars and restaurants. It was a fruitful franchise, since any place where government and business met, there were sure to be people who would pay to keep their activities private.

The first stop was a restaurant on the twelfth floor of an office building that housed the headquarters of one of Japan's largest savings and loan banks. The president of the bank was waiting for them at their regular table in the back. He stood, smiling, as they approached.

"Sano-*san*, Araki-*san*."

"Nomo-*san*."

There were bows all around, and then a waitress shuffled up and deposited tea. Half an hour later Hiro and his mentor were back on the street, a brown envelope in Sano's pocket.

"It's good he quit smoking; I was worried about his heart." Sano was something of a hypochondriac, tending to project his own health concerns onto others.

"He looks as though he's good for a long time to come." Mr. Nomo had been a client of Mr. Sano's for many years, since well before Hiro's time. As a young bank officer, he'd loaned money to a company controlled by the *kumi*. A substantial portion of the loan had come back to him, under the table, and from then on he made regular payments to the *kumi*. It was an amicable relationship, since over the years

Mr. Nomo had found the *yakuza* quite useful in helping him collect problem loans, for which Japanese courts were useless. Indeed, it was no longer clear who profited off whom, which Mr. Sano said was as it should be, if a congenial, long-term relationship were to be maintained. Hiro thought this an interesting insight.

He fired up the big Harley and tweaked the throttle. He loved the way the deep *burpeta, burpeta* turned heads. It was such an American noise—loud, self-assertive, unapologetic. It said, "No excuses; I'm here, and if you don't like it, too bad for you. Now, get out of my way."

The next client hadn't had a relationship with the *kumi* as long as the savings and loan president's, and it showed in a certain chill in the atmosphere when they all sat down in a small bar. Mr. Sano was at pains to put the man at ease.

"A beer, Ozawa-*san?*"

The man shook his head nervously and reached for his briefcase. "I have your money."

"Tsh!" Mr. Sano shook his head. "Let us relax a minute first; we've been out in that filthy traffic, and the air is poison. I need to wash it out of my system."

The man, a small, pale-faced fellow in his early thirties, said, "I have to get back to my office; people will wonder where I've gone."

Mr. Sano found this vastly amusing. When he stopped chuckling he said, "Just tell them you ducked out to wash up."

The man was a highly placed trade specialist in MITI who'd been in the habit of stopping off at a *soapland* on his way home after work. There he would have a young lady named Koko give him a pleasant bath, followed by a soothing, if somewhat localized, massage.

Had it stopped there, the MITI official would have had no

problem; no onus attached to men who found prostitutes
more enthusiastic than wives, less bother than mistresses.
But Ozawa made the mistake of becoming hopelessly smit-
ten, and little Koko had expensive tastes. Soon, to provide
the baubles she found so alluring, the official was accepting
bribes for import licenses.

Ozawa had shown extremely bad judgment, both in al-
lowing emotion to intrude into the realm of the senses and in
failing to realize that those who owned the *soapland* would
quickly conclude that their employee's new Rolexes and
furs weren't coming out of a civil servant's salary. Now the
gentleman had sponsors at least as concerned with his future
as any superior at MITI, and nothing at all to fear, as long as
he cooperated, but he was not yet comfortable with the relationship. He did not laugh at Mr. Sano's little joke.

"Relax, friend—enjoy life a little." Mr. Sano ordered beer
all around. "Now," he said after it arrived, "with a new baby
on the way, no doubt you need to save every yen you can.
Well, we will pay a handsome finder's fee to you, if you can
help us obtain new clients. For example . . ."

The next stop was the one Hiro had been waiting for, the
first client he had developed himself: a Mr. Hashimoto, the
chief financial officer of a major hotel. As a mark of favor,
Sano told him he could lead the discussion. Hiro was in high
spirits as they walked toward the *yakitori ya* near the hotel
where they were to meet the new client.

Sano had helped him develop a business plan. "Remember," the older man lectured, "it's no good asking for so
much that the fellow is driven to desperate ends. It's long-
term partnerships we're looking for, not a quick shakedown.
Now—how much do you figure Hashimoto should pay?"

"He can afford to pay well, and he should. I told him to
bring his pay stubs for the last year. I think twenty percent of

his weekly pay would be about right, since my source says he's been doubling what he takes home through his theft."

Mr. Hashimoto was in charge of all of the hotel's financial records and had several bookkeepers working for him. One of them, a pretty young thing named Junko, had been crying in a bar one night when Hiro encountered her. Three nights and several bottles of sake later, Junko had her revenge on the man who'd talked her into an empty hotel room with the promise of marriage, left her in the family way, and gone home to his wife and children. Hiro had the entries with Mr. Hashimoto's seal on them that established that he was a quite ambitious embezzler.

Sano cocked his head to one side, asking offhandedly, "Why his pay stubs, Araki-*san?* Why not a portion of what he has taken from his employer? Surely that would be more."

"Because we know he falsifies records, and we would never know if he was dealing with us honestly. The pay stubs tell us what we can count on. There is no point in starting the relationship with a lie. His pay will go up over time, and our fee can rise with it."

Sano looked at him respectfully. "You have thought well."

Hashimoto was the sick-looking man standing by the counter where the grilled chicken was dispensed. The evening trade was beginning, and the place was filling fast, which was why Hiro had selected it when he'd called Mr. Hashimoto. He handled introductions, leading the party to a table in the back.

"Yakitori, Hashimoto-*san?*" Hiro was at home in the noisy, smoky restaurant, filled with good smells and the banter and friendly insults shouted back and forth between customers and grill men. He felt in control.

The client, sweating profusely, shook his head.

"A mistake—it is good here." Hiro called out an order to the counterman. Turning back to the bookkeeper, he asked pleasantly: "You have the pay stubs, Hashimoto-*san?*"

The man's legs crossed and uncrossed nervously. "I . . . I didn't see any reason for that. I have brought some money, which I will give you." He coughed hesitantly. "In return for the, ah . . . papers you have."

He'd started to reach for his breast pocket when Hiro took the man's elbow between his thumb and forefinger. The man gasped, his face turning white under the pressure on his nerve. His fingers drew into a claw.

Hiro held the elbow, gazing impassively in the man's eyes. When he saw what he wanted to see, he released him. He waited while the man rubbed the elbow, then said sympathetically, "I am sorry—I thought we had an understanding."

The man wiped his forehead. "I . . . only, only thought, that . . ." He winced, flexing his fingers. "I am sorry. I misunderstood. I have the pay stubs here. Please, I—"

"Hashimoto-*san,*" Hiro interrupted, "forgive me, but I feel I must have spoken poorly on the telephone. Any misunderstanding is entirely my fault. I am so sorry. We look forward to a long and harmonious relationship. Now, perhaps there are some ways in which we could be of assistance to you, ways that would bring you credit with your employer—and increased pay?"

The waiter arrived with plates of grilled chicken on skewers. Hiro held one up. "You must change your mind, Hashimoto-*san.* Have some, please." Soon the three men were chewing chicken, drinking beer, and talking about baseball.

Chapter 9

October 2000: Tokyo

*M*aggie put aside the empty bowl, drained the last of the tea. She was tempted to have another cup, but now that she was in Ueno she felt her curiosity growing, and she was due at the rink at one. She strode off, oblivious of the stares of the counterman and the regulars gathered around him, buzzing about the *yanki* with the quick, purposeful stride, who'd said the oddest thing, in a Tokyo accent at that.

In three minutes she was in Ueno Park. She passed Shinobazu Pond, wondering briefly if the ducks had been among the hatchlings she'd fed rice wafers as she'd dashed from her house to the skating rink.

She saw the rink and her pace quickened, just as it had when she was six and was tugging her mother's hand. It wasn't yet open, but she rested her hands on the rail, hearing the cacophony of steel on ice, tinny music, calls, and laughter. It was a small rink, less than half regulation size. The boards were rutted and flaking, the seats just backless benches. Yet all the joy a child could imagine had seemed centered in this small space.

She slumped onto a bench. Her fingers found the patch on her jacket, idly stroking the embroidered "USFSA." She lowered her chin to her stacked fists, staring blankly at the smooth, milk white surface, remembering. . . .

Chapter 10

February 1985: Tokyo

*M*aggie, six, darted around the rink on her new skates. Though the ice was heavily rutted, her blades bit cleanly as she shifted her weight. The cold damp air held laughter, excited cries, the scrunch of skidding steel. A scratchy "Greensleeves" struggled to escape an overstressed loudspeaker.

Maggie cut and accelerated without apparent effort, a minnow in a pond. She threaded improbably narrow spaces, unnerving larger, less agile skaters. She'd hear them as she flew by.

"Look how fast she's going," one woman exclaimed.

"She's awfully good for someone so little," she heard another say.

Then, loudly, from a fat man whose sudden, sideways lurch Maggie just managed to avoid: "She nearly knocked me over!"

Maggie looked back. Satisfied she'd done no harm, she turned her head again, only to have her vision fill with a dark form, appearing from nowhere. Then all she could see was gray, and pinpricks of flashing light, coming from somewhere behind her eyes. A weight seemed to be pressing the breath out of her. From somewhere far away she heard a vague, rushing sound, like a waterfall. She thought she might be dreaming.

The boy with whom Maggie had collided was much older, and stocky. He'd been skating in the wrong direction; she might as well have run headlong into the boards.

She had no memory of the impact. She wasn't sure how long she'd been lying on the ice before she began to understand what had happened.

Her eyes teared as she struggled to sit up, and she thought about crying, but only for a second. By the time she rolled over she'd gotten her breath and given up the idea of tears. When she looked up, her assailant was bending over her, concerned. His hand enveloped hers and pulled her to her feet. She was standing, wobbly but intact, when she saw her mother working her way through the crowd.

Em Campbell was still several feet away when the boy, smiling sheepishly, announced to the onlookers: *"Otchoko-choi na gaijin no ko da na."* "Clumsy little foreigner." He started to skate away.

Cheeks reddening, mittened hands clenching, Maggie called out an indignant snap that stopped the boy cold: *"Baka iwanai deyo!"* "Don't say stupid things—it was *your* fault!" She puffed up like an angry cat, hissing: *"Kono, kono . . . kuso-ttare!"* "You, you . . . asshole!"

He spun around, slack-jawed. The crowd drew back as though part of a single organism. A loud, collective gasp hung over the rink as Em broke through the last rank and ran to her daughter.

The boy gaped at Maggie's rosy cheeks, the fair skin. Her

cap had come off in the collision, and her springy hair stood out from her head as though she'd received an electric shock.

"You speak . . . Japanese?" he gasped.

"Certainly I speak Japanese. I *am* Japanese." Her forehead furrowed.

Again there came an audible inrush from the onlookers. Em heard a woman importune her companion: "What? Did the little *gaijin* say she's . . . ?"

"You *can't* be!" the boy stammered.

"Of course I am!" Maggie protested.

Her jaw starting to quiver, the crowd's exclamations rolling over her: "The little *yanki* says she's Japanese!" "It's impossible—look at her hair!" "Look at her *eyes!*" "Did you hear what she shouted? No Japanese girl would say that!" "That can't be her *mother?*" "The *gaijin* says she's one of us!"

The word echoed like a drumbeat, heads shaking at the wonder of it: "The *gaijin* says she's Japanese . . . the *gaijin* says she's Japanese," until Maggie clapped her hands over her ears. "The foreigner says . . . the foreigner . . . foreigner . . ." Em, shuddering at the atavistic power of the word, swept her daughter off the ice.

"Shush, shush, Megumi. It's all right." Em patted her daughter's back. "It's all right now. They didn't mean any harm."

"But, but . . . why? Why were they all pointing at *me*— what did *I* do? It was that boy's fault."

"It wasn't about the accident. You see, you"—she searched for the words—"frightened them. Yes, that's it— you frightened them, and they forgot themselves and were rude. I'm sure they're sorry now."

Maggie's head pulled back. "*Frightened* them? But how? Was it what I said?"

"What you said?" Remembering, Em stifled a smile. "No, but you mustn't say that, ever again. Wherever did you hear it?"

"Father said it to a truck driver the other day. What does it mean?"

"Never mind—it's just very rude. Sometimes your father forgets we're not in America anymore." She hurried on: "Anyway, I think you frightened those people by speaking Japanese so well. They weren't expecting that, from someone looking like you."

Maggie's lower lip came out. "Because of my eyes."

"Well, yes, among other things. You have beautiful, big eyes—Campbell eyes, only a tiny bit more pointed here." Her finger traced the upturned corners.

"I *hate* my eyes."

"Shh, shh. Your eyes are wonderful—like one of the Egyptian queens in the museum. And their color! When you were a baby, I looked into your eyes and I thought they held emeralds, one of the most precious jewels there is. You got jewels, and all I have are two little lumps of coal." She pointed to her black irises, affecting a kabuki frown. "That's all that most Japanese people get—the *kami-sama* made you special."

Her finger slid down the satin cheek, lingered on the chin. "And usually our skin is wheat colored, not rosy like yours." Her hand stroked her daughter's tight, rust-colored curls. "See how black and straight my hair is. Most Japanese people have hair like mine. You got your father's, and some of his red, too." She clasped the little face in her hands. "It makes you very beautiful, Megumi. The most beautiful

Japanese girl in Tokyo. *And* the most beautiful *American* girl in Tokyo. Nobody else in the whole world can say that!"

Her daughter frowned as a new thought arose. "Why does Kenji have eyes like yours, and black hair?"

"It's just the way it happens. When two people have children, some will look more like one parent, and others will look more like the other parent. Kenji got my features, and you got your father's."

"I wish I looked like you."

Em pulled her back into her arms, letting her nestle against her shoulder. "That's a lovely thing to say, but I wouldn't want you to look any other way. You're perfect, just the way you are." She stood, her knee reminding her that it wanted more rest. "We better go, Megumi—there's just time for a bath before dinner."

They walked off, hand in hand, skates hanging over their shoulders—across Ueno Park, around Shinobazu Pond, past the statue of Saigo and his dog, into the dark warren of streets that led to their house. The faint sun was disappearing, the sky at the divide between sooty gray and black. Though the cherry blossoms would appear in only a few weeks, Tokyo in winter is a dank, dreary place, and as they walked home Maggie and her mother were both envisioning the steamy cheer of the neighborhood bathhouse and the blistering water that would soon enfold them.

The Campbells enjoyed a small measure of the greatest luxury to be found in Japan: privacy. Em and Nick had their own bedroom, sparing them the need to sleep in the *cha-no-ma*, as many of their acquaintances did. Maggie and Kenji slept in the other bedroom. Both rooms were plain and sparsely furnished. Nick and Em each had a dresser, although they shared a wardrobe. The children had a single dresser, a wardrobe, and a pair of desks and chairs.

The two rooms, together with the landing and a small bathroom, formed the upstairs. The downstairs consisted of a yard-square anteroom inside the front door, where shoes were exchanged for slippers before their owners could step onto the inviolate, tatami-matted floor beyond; a kitchen the size of an American walk-in closet; and the *cha-no-ma*, containing a low, square table set over a leg well, a bookshelf, a toy box, an easel, a television, a record player, and in deference to Nick Campbell's long, American frame, a reclining lounger. Color was provided by decorative scrolls, an antique Buddhist shrine covered in gold gilt and red lacquer, fresh flowers, and two Currier & Ives prints Nick had inherited from an aunt.

The house itself was an anomaly, a battered, century-old survivor of earthquake, fire, bombing, and relentless rebuilding. Hand-hewn, unpainted boards clad a skeleton that owed as much to the abutting houses for support as it did to any residual strength of its own. A few times a year Namazu, the great catfish, stirred in the waters of Tokyo Bay, and the resulting tremblor would pop some of the clapboards loose. Nick would go out with a hammer and nails and pound the old house back together, as its occupants had been doing forever. The roof, green terra-cotta, was remarkably watertight, except when the fall typhoons carried tiles away.

Asked where they lived, the Campbells would answer, "Ueno," a part of Tokyo known to all, because it holds the zoo, the largest park, and many museums. If they wanted to tell someone how to find their house, though, the Campbells did as all Tokyoites did: they furnished a map, with the house's location marked in ink. They couldn't provide a street name, because there was none. Mail came addressed to "Campbell, 2-3-12, Yanaka, Taito-ku, Tokyo 110"—the twelfth house on the third street of the second subdivision of the Yanaka district of the Taito ward of Tokyo postal zone 110. This was more than enough for Mr. Yamashita, the postman, since he lived around the corner anyway; anyone else got a map, even taxi drivers, because no living person knows more than a tiny fraction of Tokyo's eight hundred square miles and countless, nameless streets.

If the great earthquake of 1923, the U.S. Air Force, and the Japanese passion for the new could be said to have left anything of the Tokyo of the wood-block prints, it is Ueno, part of what was once called *shitamachi,* or "downtown." Here one still finds blocks of creaky wooden houses, each listing under the weight of the next; low, tiled roofs; noodle shops, cracker vendors, and bean paste candy stands; fishmongers and greengrocers. The candlelit lanterns of the fortune-tellers dot the streets, wooden *geta* clip-clop down cobbled alleys, the sweet-potato man's cry pierces the quiet like a birdcall. At eleven every night the *hinoyojin* man still roams the neighborhood, beating his wooden sticks together to remind people to extinguish the charcoal cooking fires no one has used for fifty years.

It was a quirky, idiosyncratic place for the Campbells to settle. Ueno more typically attracted newcomers from northern farms, drawn by the self-fulfilling prophecy that the teeming Tokyo-Osaka corridor was the only place for the competent and ambitious. Tradesmen and artisans made up much of the rest of Ueno's population, with a dollop of people many Japanese mention with voices unconsciously lowered: "other Asians." Ueno was a place for the *sarariman* and his family to visit on weekends for its museums, the zoo, the great park—one wouldn't *live* there.

Nick Campbell thought Ueno was "the real Japan"; Em

was drawn to it precisely because it was anything but Japan as she had known it, the Japan of faceless apartment blocks, *sarariman* husbands, and two-hour commutes—that was the *real* "real Japan," and Em wanted nothing to do with it. Ueno's mixture of types, the fact that her old schoolmates couldn't imagine living there, the hint of disorder in a society that views order as a sacrament—these let her retain a sense of individuality, a feeling that she was just a little bit *bohemian*. She might be back in Japan, but she certainly wasn't back in the Japan for which she'd been groomed and which she was more certain than ever would have crushed her. That certainty had been powerfully reinforced by the incident at the skating rink.

That night she was angry with her husband, who refused to enroll his daughter in a school for foreigners—who refused, in fact, to acknowledge that his children *were* foreigners. It was the one, persistent issue between them.

Nick Campbell's father had had a mediocre career in the foreign service. Nick's childhood had been spent in one foreign posting after another; in each he was placed in a school with other expatriate children, got to watch his parents drink away their lives in expatriate clubs and compounds, and was zealously guarded from all but unavoidable contact with what his parents and their associates called the IP, or "indigenous population."

Nick had loathed the life, loathed the hierarchies and backbiting, loathed the insularity. He was determined his children would grow up equally at home in the two great cultures they represented.

Most of the time the issue was more theoretical than real, months going by without it surfacing. It was never resolved, though, and with the memory of the afternoon fresh, and no time for delay, Em renewed the argument as soon as the children were in their room, presumably asleep.

Nick heard her through respectfully but remained unmoved. Her account concluded, his only response was: "She knows she doesn't look like most Japanese. Of course some people will be surprised to learn she *is* Japanese—she ought to understand that by now."

It was not Nick Campbell's way to raise his voice, but as he unrolled the futon his implacable lawyer's logic caused her to raise hers. "With eyes like that, and that hair? Of course she knows she doesn't look like most Japanese— she's not an idiot. What she doesn't understand is what that's going to *mean* to her, if she thinks of herself *as* Japanese. Today was just a small down payment."

"Just what *does* it mean, Em—that people will get confused when she speaks Japanese? That she'll hear stupid things? Christ, I hear people whisper about 'the hairy ape' when I go to the bathhouse; you laugh it off."

She thought about throttling him. "You can laugh it off because you don't expect people to think of you as Japanese. We're raising our daughter to have that expectation, and we're setting her up to be hurt."

"Em, the law says she's as Japanese as the emperor. I wouldn't send the children to a Japanese school in America just because there're people who resent Asian Americans, and I'm damned if I see why it should be any different over here."

It infuriated her that he could be so bullheadedly wrong, but she would be the one to lose her temper, so that he'd end the argument soothing her. She took deep breaths before continuing: "This isn't like America; it's not that we don't *like* Japanese who look different, it's that if they look different, they *aren't* Japanese."

"It all comes to the same thing."

"Nick, Nick, don't you see? Every time she opens her mouth and Japanese comes pouring out, people are going to look at her the way you would if you heard a dog speaking English. And no law is going to change that."

"Well, it's damn well time they understood there *are* Japanese who don't look like the official model. The children's papers don't say anything about how they have to look. There's no law that says Maggie had to have black eyes and straight hair to get that passport."

"I'd appreciate it if you didn't mention the law to me again. I know what it says. I also know what it means."

"Well, then you know—"

She whirled around, brandishing her hairbrush. "Don't you understand—I'm not talking about the damn law! That's a meaningless piece of paper."

"Shh, shhh . . ."

"Don't 'shush' me! This isn't some experiment in international living we're talking about; this is our daughter's happiness!"

"Please, Em . . . you'll wake the children."

"All right, I'll whisper: I don't want Megumi being used to prove a point." Em harumphed. " 'Megumi.' A likely name for a girl who looks like that."

"She wants to be called Megumi; she hates it when we forget."

"I know, I know." Her shoulders sagged.

"You were about to tell me what you *do* want?"

"I'll tell you what I want. *Megumi* starts school in two weeks. The first time they send her home because her hair isn't straight and black, the first time they bully her because of her looks, we put her in the American school. The very first time."

"I don't want her hurt, either, you know."

"So you agree."

He shrugged, resigned. "I agree."

"Good." She pulled the overhead light cord and slipped under the comforter next to him. "Japanese indeed," she sniffed. Her fingers found his shoulders. She kissed the back of his neck. Soon they were both asleep.

Maggie looked at her reflection in the mirror. The room was dark, but a shaft of streetlight penetrated the shutters, bathing her face. She liked the burnished hue it gave her skin, thinking it much more attractive than the ghostly shade she shared with her father as soon as daylight arrived.

The rule in the Campbell house was Japanese downstairs, English upstairs, to keep everyone bilingual, so Maggie wasn't surprised that the words coming through the thin partition were English, only that they were so loud—at least her mother's.

A dark shirt pulled taut over her head hid the loathsome curls. In the shadows it almost appeared as though she had hair like her mother's, sleek and black as a raven's wing.

". . . eyes like that . . . that hair . . ."

Her father's voice was quiet, reassuring. She could hear little of what he said, but the soft, low murmur was comforting.

". . . no law is going to change that."

She turned her head, first one way, then the other. Sometimes, when she caught the angle just right, she thought she could detect an echo of her mother's face in hers, but always, when she focused, the cheekbones flattened, her nose grew longer, the chin lost its delicacy, and her father's head emerged above her shoulders.

". . . school . . . no curls allowed . . . make her cut it . . ."

She put her forefingers in the outer corners of her eyes, tugging.

". . . not hurt again . . ."

They flattened into narrow slits that looked almost right, but as soon as she removed her fingers her eyes reverted to the big, tilted teardrops she despised.

". . . damn law! That's a meaningless piece of paper!"

Maggie jumped, startled by her mother's outburst. She looked over at her brother, who was making the little whimpering sounds that meant he was having a bad dream. She hoped he wouldn't wake up screaming; she hated that. She went over to him, picking up the stuffed bear that had slipped out of his arms. She waited, patting him, until he grew still and she left to slide under her own comforter.

She heard her father's low whisper. Her mother said something, but softly. There was whispering, then quiet.

Usually all she heard from her parents' room was a soft murmur, almost like the wind, and she liked that. Sometimes she'd hear her mother laugh, and scuffling sounds, and she'd be sorry she wasn't with her parents. When she heard happy sounds from their room she felt warm, no matter how cold it was, and it got very cold, since the wind whistled through the old windows and the cracks in the wooden walls.

Slithering down until only her head was exposed, she looked over at the lump of bedding that was her brother, lying on his futon. Why hadn't *he* gotten eyes like Komuro-*san*'s cat? It wasn't fair! Maybe if she pulled hers long enough, they'd stay like *oka-san*'s. She was still holding them when sleep arrived.

Chapter 11

October 2000: Tokyo

*M*aggie looked at her watch with a start; she'd been wandering the labyrinthian alleyways of Ueno for almost four hours, her feet dictating the route.

She'd spent several minutes standing in front of the canted little house at 2-3-12, Yanaka, measuring the frontage with her eye; the living room in South Natick was wider than the whole house. She looked at her bedroom window, remembering the shadows dancing on the ceiling when the summer breezes stirred the Sawanoyas' maple. The doorway was ringed with vines, many still in flower; she saw her mother putting out cuttings in the spring. Her father was loping down the street, briefcase swinging, calling out greetings in his funny accent, his open, uninhibited American voice. He was picking her up, throwing her high in the air, tucking her under his arm as he ducked his head to clear the lintel.

She saw people she knew: Mrs. Takoaka, standing in the doorway of her pickle stand, gold teeth flashing as she bowed: "Welcome back, welcome back, Campbell-*san!*"

The sweet-potato man with his cart and charcoal stove, pressing a hot tuber into her hands, refusing payment; young Sawanoya and his wife, wheeling their new baby; Mr. Yamashita, so proud in his postman's uniform; Police Officer Tetsu; old Mrs. Ozawa and her even older dog. All welcomed her.

She'd told herself she'd feel nothing, returning to the country she'd sworn she'd never set foot in again. She'd promised she wouldn't let herself feel anything, worrying that if she gave feeling even the smallest purchase, the bitterness she'd harbored when she'd left might return like a cancer, eating at her, keeping her from doing the one thing that mattered, the business that had brought her.

She'd come to do a job, she'd do it, she'd get out. Yet here she was, back no more than hours, and there was feeling, and though she wasn't sure what it was, it wasn't bitter.

She felt loneliness, certainly, waves of it, sweeping over her like nausea, the only cure focusing on the present, the business that had brought her. But as she probed her consciousness—cautiously, ready to retreat and slam the door—she found nothing ugly, nothing threatening; nothing even painful.

Suddenly she recognized what had displaced the bitterness: detachment. She remembered the girl's pain, but that was someone else. The young woman gawking like a tourist felt mostly curiosity and even, as old friends bowed and smiled, pleasure.

She entered Ueno Park, stopped in front of the statue of Saigo and his dog. As a girl she'd loved the story of the last samurai hero; her mother had brought her to see the statue in the winter, after skating, many times.

"Look, Megumi—that's a statue of the great Saigo," her mother said. "He led the fight to overthrow the shoguns and make Japan a modern country. Then he decided the new government was bad, too, because it no longer followed Bushido—the way of honor. So he led a revolt against the new government."

"Is he dead?"

"Oh, yes. This was over one hundred years ago. He lost the revolt and committed *seppuku*."

"What is *seppuku*?"

"He killed himself."

"Why?"

"Because he was wounded on the battlefield, and knew he had lost. He thought it more honorable to die. It was the way of the samurai. It was Bushido."

"How did he kill himself?"

"Why do you need to know how he did it, Megumi?"

"I want to. How did he kill himself?"

"If you must know, he had a friend cut off his head with his sword."

"Did they kill the dog, too?"

"No, dear, I don't think so."

"That's good," Maggie had said.

She crossed Kototoi Dori, the main street through Ueno, and stood outside the schoolyard of the Ueno Elementary School. It was recess, and the children, each in a blue sailor suit, were playing, their bare limbs red in the crisp air. Some, seeing her watching them, began to giggle and elbow each other.

Two girls approached warily. Reaching the gate, one, wide-eyed, said "Hair-ro."

"Hello," Maggie replied.

The girl pointed at Maggie. "America?"

"Yes."

Both girls nodded, echoing in unison: "America." One

added, forming the letters with elaborate movements of her lips: "U . . . S . . . A."

"Yes, U.S.A." Maggie nodded, switching to Japanese, "Tell me please—is Hayashi *sensei* still teaching?"

The girls stepped back, gaping, as though a snake had shot out of Maggie's mouth. One whispered wonderingly: *"Hai."*

"Good. Please—tell him Campbell said hello. Campbell—Maggie Campbell. Can you remember that?"

The girls stared wordlessly, then turned and ran away. Maggie called after them: "No, not Maggie! Please tell Hayashi *sensei Megumi* Campbell said hello."

She watched the two rejoin their classmates. A teacher came out, and in seconds the children had formed a line and were marching back into the school. The last one filed through the door, popped back to steal another look, then disappeared for good.

Maggie chuckled and started for the station. It would not do to keep Madam Goto waiting. Her pulse raced, and suddenly she felt the way she had thirteen years earlier: terrified and eager.

Chapter 12

May 1987: Tokyo

*W*hen Maggie was eight, Em decided it was time to place her in the hands of a professional. The girl loved to skate, and the easy work was done. She took Maggie to the Ikebukuro Skating Club in northeast Tokyo to try out with Asako Groto, who had been Em's instructor until her knee put an end to it.

It had taken all of Em's perseverance to win Maggie an audition. Madam Goto had protested repeatedly that she was taking no more students, that she was too old, and that children no longer had the discipline she demanded. Finally, bowing to Em's persistence, Madam Goto begrudgingly agreed to let Maggie go through her paces, making it clear that there was little chance she would reconsider.

Em sat nervously in the stands while Maggie performed under the critical eyes of the doyenne of Japanese skating. Though the severe hair was steel gray now, and the woman seemed even tinier than Em remembered, there was nothing to suggest she had mellowed. She still stood ramrod straight, still had a look that could melt ice from twenty feet away.

The hooded eyes watched, unblinking, as Maggie, the tip of her tongue peeking out of her mouth, executed the increasingly complex tasks Madam Goto called out from her perch by the boards. Em found herself clenching her fists through left and right crossovers, choctaw and mohawk turns, a waltz three, a two-foot spin, and a series of full-rotation jumps. She didn't relax until the old woman called, "You may stop now," and turned to face her.

"You have taught her well, Emiko-*chan*. She has excellent edge control for one so young. You didn't forget the importance of true edges, I see."

"*Hai,* Goto *sensei.* Thank you very much. She is not completely clumsy."

"I think not." The old woman turned as the little girl skated up to the two adults and came to a stop. "That was excellent, Megumi-*chan*. You skate well."

Maggie bowed. "Thank you very much, Goto *sensei,* but I am not very good, I think."

"Good enough to have many fine coaches who will want to teach you, child." The old woman turned to Em. "Understand—the girl has the gift. But I simply cannot take on another student. I have three girls now, and two young men, and—"

Em was starting to stand when, to her horror, she saw her daughter tug at Madam Goto's sleeve. "But I can do other jumps. Goto *sensei,* harder jumps."

"Megumi! You must not interrupt Goto *sensei.* She has been very kind to let us appear before her." She bowed, mortified: "Excuse me, *sensei.* Her rudeness is unforgivable."

Madam Goto looked at Maggie, whose hand dropped slowly from the sleeve, even while, unblinking, she met the *sensei*'s eyes: "I'm sorry if I was rude, Goto *sensei,* but I want to show what I can do. Goto *sensei* hasn't asked me to do my best jump."

The leathery face softened. "Oh? What have you taught the girl, Emiko-*chan?*"

Maggie shook her head. "My mother didn't teach me, Goto *sensei*. I learned it watching an older girl at the park."

Em started to step out onto the ice. "Megumi, it's time to go now! Goto *sensei*, thank you very much. I will contact another—"

"Well, let us see." The black eyes appraised the child meditatively. "I remember another girl who wanted to skate. If she hadn't been hurt . . ." She shook her head. "You found other ways to perform, I think. But this one . . . why not let us see?"

She nodded to Maggie. "Jump your jump, child. I will watch."

Maggie's head bobbed. *"Hai! Domo arigato,* Goto *sensei."*

She took two strokes, stopped, and turned back. "Goto *sensei*—is there any music, please? It seems to help."

Em's stomach spasmed. "Megumi! That's enough! Do your jump, and don't—"

Madam Goto seemed amused. "Shh, shh—the girl is an artist." She walked over to a tape recorder. In a second Borodin flooded the hall.

"Will that do, Megumi-*chan?*" Em could have sworn the tiny woman was enjoying herself.

Maggie stood, listened for a few bars, then bowed. "That is beautiful, Goto *sensei*. Thank you." She skated away, bringing her strokes into harmony with the music as she approached the end of the rink.

At the moment when the full orchestra cut in, picking up the theme set by the woodwinds, Maggie turned, her face peering over her right shoulder, the pink tongue still in place. She shifted to her left outside edge, bent her left knee sharply, extended her right free leg behind her, and glided in a clockwise arc.

Suddenly, stabbing her right toe pick in the ice, she flew into the air, spinning twice before landing, arms spread, on her right outside edge, still traveling backward. Her left foot swept in a clean arc behind her, the toe pointing down and out at a pleasing angle.

"A double," Em muttered. "She taught herself a double lutz."

"She did. Good height and a clean landing, too." Madam Goto stared at Maggie, her lips pursed. "She is very, very young for that." She tapped her finger against her nose, nodding. "Very young."

Maggie coasted up to Madam Goto, a questioning look on her face. The two small figures, almost sixty years between them, appraised each other.

"When did you learn that, child?"

"I have been practicing it for many weeks, *sensei*. Last weekend was the first time I was able to do it each time."

"You must have fallen many times before you could land that jump, Megumi-*chan*."

"*Hai, sensei.*"

"Was it painful?"

"Sometimes, *sensei*. When my foot twisted under me on the landing."

"Come over here and sit down, child." Madam Goto gestured at the bench. "Take off your right boot, please."

When the boot was off Madam Goto eased down Maggie's sock. Em, looking over her shoulder, gasped at the sight of the ugly, purple-yellow bruise covering the inside of Maggie's ankle. "Oh, Megumi—why didn't you tell me?"

Maggie hung her head. "I was afraid you'd make me stop."

Madam Goto released the foot. "Tell me, Megumi-*chan*—why did you want to learn that jump?"

Maggie's face reflected her perplexity. Finally she shrugged. "When I saw the other girl do it, I had to try, *sensei*."

Madam Goto studied her, rubbing her chin. "Of course," she murmured. "A foolish question." After a long pause she asked: "I meant to retire, Megumi-*chan*. Have you come here to deny me my retirement?"

Maggie looked up into the wizened face. "I don't understand, *sensei*."

Madam Goto placed her hands on Maggie's shoulders. "Megumi-*chan*: what you have learned is very impressive. What is inside you is even more impressive. But as my student that would be the last double you attempt for some time. Your bones are soft, and I will not let a child risk permanent damage. You will spend a great deal more time skating figures than you will jumping and spinning. Are you prepared for that?" Her eyes explored Maggie's.

Maggie nodded solemnly. *"Hai,* Goto *sensei."*

"You would lose your time for play, and you would have to squeeze your schoolwork into less time. It would be hard for you."

"Hai, sensei."

"Much time will go by before you could hope to gain any reward for your hard work, other than the work itself. When the rewards come, they will be in the skating, not pretty ribbons and trophies. My students skate for skating, not for trinkets—the awards are reminders of special moments, never the end in itself. If you need to win medals soon, need to hear yourself called the champion of this or that, you should find a teacher who believes in putting children into competition before their time; I do not."

"*Hai, sensei.* I will wait until the *sensei* says it is time. I only wish to be as good as I can be. I love to skate. My mother says the *sensei* can show me how to be the best skater I can be."

"I know, perhaps, how to help one like you find what there is to be found in skating, but it won't be easy."

Their eyes locked, one set searching, the other trusting. Finally the holder of the older pair sighed. "I wasn't ready to move in with my sister in Kanazawa anyway. Very well."

She touched the bruised ankle lightly. "There will be many more bruises, Megumi-*chan.* Tell your mother when you hurt—she remembers how to care for these things." She turned to Em. "What time does the girl finish school?"

"Four o'clock, *sensei.*"

"She should be here at five, then. For now, Tuesdays and Thursdays only. We will see if the child has the will to work. If she does, we will move to a full schedule."

Within months Maggie was taking the subway to Ikebukuro every day but Sunday. Three days a week Madam Goto gave her an hour lesson, followed by an hour of practice. Half of each session was devoted to figures: circle eights, serpentines, threes, and double threes. Maggie was assigned to a rectangular patch of ice twenty feet by forty, and there she would trace figures, one on top of the other.

Each figure had to be mastered in multiple manifestations prescribed by the rules of the International Skating Union. Even the most basic figure, the circle eight, had eight forms, varying according to the edge and foot used and whether forward or backward. Each form had to be traced hundreds of times, and until each was executed flawlessly, Maggie could not go on to the next.

On Saturdays Maggie had four hours of practice: two hours of patch and two hours of free skating, during which she practiced the elements she would have to perform to pass the tests administered by the Japan Figure Skating Association. Though Maggie's Saturday skating was unsupervised, Madam Goto had an uncanny ability to watch the girl for a few minutes on Monday, then bark: "No free skating today, Megumi-*chan;* you neglected your figures on Saturday."

At first Maggie had a large wooden scribe, like a compass taller than she was, that she kept at the rink. She would set the point of one leg into the ice, and with the pointed end of the other she would mark off circles, each circle having a diameter three times her height. Two abutting circles gave her a pattern to follow. Then she would start at the point where the circles touched and, following the prescribed order of edges and permitted number of strokes, endeavor to lay down a tracing that conformed to the enscribed circles, keeping her head down, her body straight but not stiff, her arms, hands, and free foot in a graceful, relaxed pose. She would repeat each figure three times, then stop and examine the tracings left by her blade. Although Madam Goto often had three or four pupils on the ice at the same time, little escaped her. No sound was more dreaded than the sharp "rap" of a skate guard on the boards, signaling Maggie that her errant edge or forbidden thrust had been spotted. When that happened, "Start over" was the iron rule.

There was no greater sin than failing to hold a true edge throughout a figure; Maggie would wait, breathless, while the old woman circled her figure, hands behind her back, nodding. Just when Maggie would think it safe to relax, a bony finger would shoot out, followed by denunciation: "Flat!" Maggie would gulp, look, see the foot-long stretch where both edges of a blade had been allowed to touch the surface simultaneously, leaving their telltale parallel tracks.

Madam Goto viewed flats as evidence of moral infirmity, stemming from sloth, indolence, and a failure of will. True edges, carved hard by the knifelike apex of a blade, were a sign that a skater was in control of mind and body. Maggie dreaded the sharp hand clap, the imperious command: "Do it again—no flats." Only a visceral refusal to quit under pressure kept her going on those days when she seemed to hear nothing else. Then she would circle her figure's midpoint, her jaw set, face red, eyes narrowed until only the irises showed, determined to prove the tyrant couldn't break her.

Sometimes, when the tracings seemed to have a will of their own, assuming asymmetrical shapes or grotesque protuberances, Madam Goto would make her bring out the scribe and revert to basics. Maggie's cheeks would burn as she hauled the giant implement out on the ice, imagining that everybody in the arena was observing her humiliation.

After six months, occasions for the scribe became increasingly rare, until one day Madam Goto announced that it was time to pass it on to another pupil. That was one of the proudest moments in Maggie's life. Another came a few weeks later, when Maggie passed the preliminary figure and free skating tests.

A year passed before Madam Goto let Maggie enter her first competition, a Tokyo prefecture figures event for girls twelve and under. Maggie couldn't understand why the judges made such a fuss about her figures, dawdling over them far longer than they had with the other girls. Later, Madam Goto said that one girl's coach had insisted that

Maggie had to be overage, since it was impossible for a girl to strike figures with such precision without years of practice.

Maggie came in second. Madam Goto made much of her that day, but not for her award. "Your forward inside eight was quite good," she said. "Really quite good." Maggie remembered that long after she'd forgotten the ribbon.

The more she skated, the more she wanted to skate. Many a night Maggie lay on her back in the dark, next to her sleeping brother, imagining the night when she would accept the medal designating her the senior ladies' figure skating champion of Japan. Then she'd go to the Worlds and compete against the other national champions from around the globe. Finally she would arrive at the Olympics. There was a victory stand, and the Japanese flag being raised, while the national anthem played and the gold medal was placed around her neck. It was acceptable to cry under the circumstances, almost rude not to, so a few tears would slip down her cheeks, and then she would retire from skating, and then . . . she would fall asleep.

This was not a vision she felt comfortable sharing; decent people didn't strive for individual glory. She avoided guilt by assuring herself that she sought victory, not for Megumi Campbell, but for her family, her schoolmates, Madam Goto, and Japan. The scene at the Olympics, with the flag and the anthem, was particularly encouraging in this regard.

It wasn't modesty alone that kept her from sharing her plans with her parents. She had discovered that it was risky to let them think she was dwelling too much on skating, although privately she didn't see how that was possible. From time to time her parents even implied that her life would be just beginning at the very point where, in her Olympic reverie, it ceased holding enough interest to keep her awake.

They had gone so far as to declare that at the first sign of deterioration in her schoolwork, skating was over.

Maggie envied the girls she read about in *Skating World*, an American magazine her parents got her for a Girl's Day present, girls who at her age were going to school part-time or had given up school altogether in favor of a tutor, so that they could skate five or six hours a day. How, she wondered, could she hope to get really good if her parents kept insisting that she had to lead what they called "a normal life"? She couldn't imagine why anyone would want that.

Chapter 13

October 2000: Tokyo

*M*aggie stood just inside the door, glancing about the familiar space until she spotted the tiny woman at the far end of the rink, sitting with Chiako Mori, the former national champion who had become the *sensei*'s *joshu,* or assistant.

She darted forward, almost running, until, remembering protocol, she drew up six feet away from the imperious figure. Bowing deeply, she whispered: "*Sensei*—I am back. I would be honored if you would instruct me."

Maggie was startled at how the woman looked; she'd thought her ancient beyond further aging, yet aged she had. Before, her face had looked like the inside of an old skate, brown and leathery; now the skin had a gray pallor, and the cheeks had sunk.

Only the eyes seemed unaffected, as though all the life remaining in the frail little body was concentrated just behind the irises. They scrutinized Maggie, darting up and down, black and avian.

"So," she finally said, apparently satisfied with what she saw. "Once again you wish to deny me my retirement."

"I am sorry, *sensei*. I am selfish."

"Bah—I tried retirement after you left. All day I sat in a park in Kanazawa and looked at the Japan Sea. In the evening my sister and I played cards, until I discovered she cheated at cards and bored me with her prattle. Then I saw a boy at a local rink who wasn't completely useless. That was that. He is a good junior now."

Then she was nodding, clucking her tongue, tugging at her chin, and finally smiling. "It is good Megumi-*chan* has returned."

Maggie bowed again. "It is good to be back with Goto *sensei*."

"Your mother is well?"

"Yes, *sensei*. She sends her respect."

Madam Goto bowed. "And what is it you wish from us? What is this about wanting to qualify for the Olympics in singles?"

"It is true, *sensei*."

"You have accomplished much in pairs; why would you abandon that?"

"My partner was injured; he cannot skate anymore."

"Surely in America there would be other partners for you?"

"No, *sensei*." Maggie's jaw tightened. "There is no other partner for me, in America or elsewhere."

"Ah." The old woman rubbed her chin appraisingly, her eyes narrowing. She nodded. "I see."

A scowl formed on the worn face. "Megumi-*chan*—it pains me, but in fairness to you, I must point out that, though you are a young woman, you are not young for a woman singles skater. You are twenty-one. You will be twenty-three by the Olympics. That is unexceptional for a pairs skater, but many of the idiots in your skating association will think you too old to have a future in singles, no matter how well you skate. Many judges will be hypercritical. Close calls will go against you. The same, to my disgust, is true here, true everywhere."

"I know. I must try, though."

Madam Goto began to pace. Each limping step was punctuated with a loud thud as she rapped her cane on the floor. "It is a disgrace. Just when a skater becomes capable of expressing a mature aesthetic, she must become a professional or retire, because Olympic eligible competition is becoming nothing but a jumping contest between prepubescents. I am glad I will not have to endure it much longer."

"*Sensei*, I—"

"But perhaps I have time enough to fight one more fight, eh?" She stopped, eyes burning. Arthritic fingers worked each other as a thin, hard smile formed. "Perhaps we three can say something about what skating should be, *ne?*"

She waggled the cane. "A woman, not a child. *Skating*, not barrel jumping. Beauty, not just strength. Every element part of a seamless whole."

She pulled up abruptly, focusing on Maggie. "Do you remember when you said you dreamed of *being* music, Megumi-*chan?* Of becoming the notes?"

The moment returned, as though it had been yesterday. "I do, *sensei*."

"*That* is skating." The cane came down, shaking the floorboards. "That is anything, done right. Perhaps, Megumi-*chan*, you will find what it is to be music. That would show them, *ne?*"

Maggie bowed. "As the gods will." The ritual phrase emerged before she had time to think about it.

The *sensei* grunted. "The gods favor the well prepared. We will plan a schedule that will, perhaps, help the gods get you there. Very well. Patch—tomorrow morning at eight; let us see if that American coach left you with any edges."

Two days later Maggie moved in with Chiako Mori, whose rent, in stylish Harajuku, had risen faster than her income. For $1,000 a month she got to share a single room, a narrow cooking alcove, and a bathroom.

Moving in was simple enough, since she'd brought only her skate bag and a suitcase. She put her clothes in the closet and pictures on a shelf: one of Clay, one of her family, one of their Airedale. Then she wandered down Harajuku's main avenue, poking her head into the chic little shops.

She stepped into a hairdresser's. The proprietress, bowing, inquired in halting English: "Are we . . . helping you?" In Japanese, for her assistant's benefit she added: "I hope she doesn't want us to do anything with hair like that."

"*Hai!* That's exactly what I want!" Maggie snapped. The words were hardly out before she wished she could retrieve them.

The two women flushed, dropping their heads below their waists, arms rigid at their sides. "*Gomen nasai, gomen nasai,*" they implored, bobbing up and down. "I'm sorry, I'm sorry." The phrase rang in Maggie's ears, drowning her own apology. She backed out of the shop, teeth grinding.

Maggie passed the plastic pail between the spigots until she had the mix right, then poured the hot water over her head. "Ahh." She slumped down on the low stool. A week of wind sprints and six-hour-a-day practices had left her exhausted; she was glad she'd let Chiako talk her into going to the bathhouse. She picked up a brush and started in on her legs again; when she slipped into the bath she wasn't going to hear muttering about "the dirty *yanki*" if she could help it.

"Your Clay is very handsome, Megumi-*chan*." Chiako was sitting next to her, completing her second soaping. All around them naked women from six to eighty were going through their ablutions.

Maggie smiled. "He is. He's also smart, and funny, and thoughtful, and he can do just about anything." She scrubbed her face with the little towel the *sento* provided.

Chiako's eyes widened. "Are there many men like that in America, Megumi-*chan*? I will send for one. He sounds perfect."

"I'm afraid they're rare any place."

"Have you known him long?"

"You know my American name, Maggie?"

"*Hai.*"

"Well, he gave it to me. When I was only a few weeks old, and he was three. My parents were great friends of his parents, and I guess he couldn't say 'Megumi'—it came out 'Maggie.' Since my mother wanted me to have an American name anyway, it stuck."

"What a nice story. So you have known him forever?"

"Forever. And after we moved to Japan we spent a week every year at his house outside Boston, while my father visited his home office."

Chiako clapped her hand over her mouth. "They had room for your whole family?"

Maggie nodded. "It was the biggest house I'd ever seen, an old farmhouse on a huge piece of land. Clay's parents bought him anything he wanted, too, so it was like going to an amusement park. He had a pony, and an electric car, and every game imaginable. We'd skate on their pond, or if it was summer, we'd catch fish and cook them."

"Their own pond? A pony?"

"I know—I couldn't believe it either."

Chiako filled her pail with cold water; the shock as it cascaded over her shoulders vaulted her toward the bath. Maggie rinsed repeatedly, lest a lingering soap bubble provoke a disapproving glance from one of the ladies soaking.

She lowered herself into the water. She'd forgotten how numbingly hot the baths could be. She nodded to the other women, extended her legs, leaned back, and rested her head on the rim, the water lapping just below her chin. It bubbled up from hot springs, bringing with it a faintly sulfurous odor. She found it almost sinfully relaxing. In Boston she would have sworn there was nothing in Japan she'd missed except her family, yet here was something else America could use.

Chiako turned to her, perplexed. "There is a matter I do not understand, Megumi-*chan*, if you do not mind my asking about your friend's accident?"

"Of course not. Ask anything."

"Rawlings-*san* did not even apologize for what she did?"

"She did not."

"That is unforgivable."

"I agree. Clay made excuses: it was too hard for her, she was never taught how to behave, what could she say that would make any difference. He was always making excuses for her."

"He is a forgiving man."

Maggie's voice turned hard. "Too forgiving, but I make up for it."

Chiako splashed water onto her chest. "Permit me, please, to speak of something that is not my place?"

Maggie eyed her uncertainly. "Please speak freely."

"Megumi-*chan*, do you not think it difficult to skate well

when you are skating, not for yourself, but to be better than someone else?"

"We always skate to be better than someone else. That's what competition is."

"Excuse me, but no; that is not the *sensei*'s way, nor mine. The goal is to skate as well as we can; if that is better than anyone else, we win. We do not set out simply to be better than someone else. If you do that, aren't you in effect letting this woman control your performance?"

Maggie slipped lower in the water. "Forgive me, Chiako-*chan*, but this is too subtle. Perhaps I lived in the States too long, but I see things in simple terms: I want to beat her. If I do, I have little doubt I will win the gold, so perhaps it comes to the same thing, *ne*?"

Chiako, sighing, changed the subject. "I always wondered what it would be like to skate pairs; you must become so close."

Maggie welcomed the shift. "After a while, like two bodies with one brain and one heart."

Chiako shut her eyes, smiling. "That is a beautiful image, Megumi-*chan*. I am so sorry I never skated pairs; I would like to know what it is to be bound to someone that way. What woman wouldn't?"

"Mmm." Someone was adding more hot water. Maggie's legs had lost feeling, a delicious deadness. "I can't imagine." She groaned contentedly.

Chapter 14

June 1995: Boston

*D*oe Rawlings studied the girl in the mirror, turning first one hip, then the other, seeing how her new skating dress fit in different poses.

The top part was demure, with a high neckline and a floppy, open collar. Big, puffy, short sleeves added to the impression of youthful innocence, as did the large blue polka dots scattered across the snowy background.

She thought the dress was lovely. The white panties under the short skirt were the problem. No matter how many times she tugged them down, the elastic rode back up, exposing the rounded swell of her bottom. It wouldn't be as obvious when she had tights on, but it made her uncomfortable. The thought of Clay Bartlett seeing her that way was mortifying. Hunter couldn't have meant the panties to be cut so high, she thought; maybe they could be redone.

She got a tingling sensation as she thought about Clay Bartlett and her plan. Spinning away from the mirror on her toes, she spread her arms, declaiming: "And intro . . . duc-

ing the pairs team of Doe Rawlings and Clay . . . ton
Bart . . . lett!"

She stood, looking over her right shoulder, arm extended
as though to take a man's hand. Dropping the pose, she ran
over to her dresser and picked through tapes until she found
the one she wanted.

"There." She resumed her pose, holding it until *Show
Boat* filled the room. She began long, sliding steps around
the floor, crooning softly: "Only make believe, I love you,
only make believe, that you love me . . ."

Her thirteen-year-old body was already more a woman's
than a girl's, breasts rising and falling with the bounce of her
bobbed, blond hair. She felt as though her bare feet were
scarcely making contact with the floor and that she could
dance forever.

She had a light, pleasant voice, which she dropped an oc-
tave as she assumed another role, gliding and turning: "Although Doreen Rawlings has been skating with Clayton
Bartlett for less than two years, they move together as
though they've been a team forever. Already they're heavy
favorites to win the gold."

As the song drew to a close, she stopped, raised her
hands, and, holding them as though cradling a face, formed
a kiss. She curtsied, nodded to the opposite walls of her
room, and blew kisses.

"What a *magnificent* performance," she intoned in her announcer's voice. "Poetry on ice! Bartlett and Rawlings, ladies
and gentlemen—soon to be the world's greatest pairs team!"

Exhaling languorously, she stopped the tape. She picked
up a program from the skating club's most recent ice show,
letting it flop open to her page. After running her hand over
the picture of Clay Bartlett, she took a pair of scissors and
began cutting. When she finished there was a hole in the

page next to Clay's picture. She tore the piece with Janice Siegel's picture on it into scraps, then turned back to the page where her own picture appeared. It was bigger than the one she'd excised, since she'd been the Ice Princess and Clay and his partner had only been members of her court, but when she put it behind the space she'd cut out, it did look as though Clay were holding her.

She was pawing through her desk, looking for tape, and didn't hear her mother until she was directly behind her. "Damn it, Doe, five hundred dollars for a dress, and you're wearing it like a sweatshirt? Now hook me up."

Doe jumped guiltily. "I . . . I was just trying it on."

Her mother eyed her over her shoulder. "Well, take care of it. The association doesn't begin to cover all your expenses, you know."

"I know." Doe caught a whiff of her mother's breath. No more than a drink or two, she calculated, because she was a lot louder when she'd had more. Her mother was in her good mood, probably because she was going out. She was wearing her highest heels and a low-cut black dress Doe hadn't seen before. She reached up and fastened it. "You look great, Mama. Is this a new dress?"

Phyllis Rawlins pirouetted. "Yep. I said to myself, why should my daughter be the only one with pretty clothes?"

Doe, unsure if her mother was about to launch one of her tirades, rushed to humor her. "It's beautiful."

"Thanks, baby." She looked into Doe's mirror, pushing hair into place. "I only hope this doesn't give him a heart attack." She looked down at her cleavage. "The way he was trying to look down the front of my blouse yesterday, I figure he hasn't seen many of these in a while."

"Did you meet this man at work, Mama?" Doe knew that

the best way to avoid subjects that provoked her mother was by feeding her self-regard.

"In a manner of speaking." Phyllis Rawlings shook herself deeper into the dress, chuckling. "He owns our largest distributor. He walked up to the desk, asking for Schmidt. When I saw the way he was staring I said, 'You can go right in now, or I can say Mr. Schmidt's tied up and you can stay out here for a while.' Two minutes later he'd asked me out."

Phyllis Rawlings fluttered her lavender eyelids while Doe clapped her hands appreciatively. "That's wonderful, Mama! I hope you have a terrific time."

"The trick, baby doll, is to make sure *he* has a terrific time. The man's *rolling* in it."

"He'll have a good time, Mama, how could he help it?"

Phyllis Rawlings beamed. "I'll do my part." She chuckled naughtily and winked.

Since her mother was in such a good mood, Doe decided to risk a question: "Mama, do you like the way my dress fits?"

Her mother scowled, and for a second Doe was afraid she'd misread the moment. "I pay a week's wages for it, and you're complaining about the way it fits?"

"No, Mama. I just . . ."

Her mother laughed. "But if any more of your rear end hung out, you might as well not bother wearing the panties."

Doe reddened. "So you think maybe it . . . it's cut too high around my . . . legs?"

"Too high?" Phyllis Rawlings grabbed her daughter's shoulder and turned her around. "Mmm. I don't think so. Rill knows what he's doing. Of course, he ought to, considering what he charges. You're developing a terrific figure, and you might as well use it."

"Oh. I . . . I guess that's right." Doe tugged the skirt down. "If you say so, Mama."

"Sure it is." Mrs. Rawlings looked at her daughter, shaking her head appreciatively. "You are one beautiful girl, baby—in a few years, you're going to have sponsors falling all over you. You'll need a truck to take your loot to the bank." She pinched Doe's cheek. "Just don't you forget your old mother then, huh?"

"Of course not, Mama—you've done everything for me."

"That's my girl." She pulled Doe to her, pressing a wet kiss against her forehead.

Doe cleared her throat nervously. "Um, Mama, uh . . ."

Mrs. Rawlings, who'd turned to leave, stopped impatiently. "What, baby? I'm in kind of a hurry, you know."

"There's . . . there's something else I wanted to ask you."

"Well, what is it?" She glanced at her watch.

Doe's courage evaporated. "Why, uh . . . I only wondered—will you be late, Mama?"

"Don't wait up for me, you know what I mean? Mr. Berg looks like he might be a night owl." She winked and walked out.

Doe waited until she heard the door slam, then slid into her desk chair and resumed her search for tape. She found some but didn't get up right away, looking dreamily at the wall instead.

She'd been right not to ask her mother if she could try pairs. It made more sense to talk to Hunter first. If she'd told her mother that she wanted to be Clay Bartlett's partner, she would have just lost her temper and screamed at her, something like "Are you crazy? You're a few years from the really big money, and you want to risk it all to skate pairs? No . . . damn . . . way, you ungrateful little snit." Then it would have been impossible to change her mind.

Hunter would explain that she could skate singles *and* pairs. Other girls had. And if she couldn't do both, she would just give up singles, no matter what her mother said. Hunter would want her to stay with him, and if he understood that was the only way, he'd let her skate pairs, she knew he would. She sighed happily, letting the words slide through her lips: "Clay Bartlett's partner."

She held up the montage, knowing they looked wonderful together. Hunter would see how good they'd be for each other, how well they'd get along, with none of the fights Janice Siegel caused. She brought the picture to her lips.

She stared at Clay, memories tracing a wistful smile on her full mouth. The way he'd skate by, winking, when Hunter was in one of his moods; his grin, the friendly laugh, the little, teasing questions. The way he noticed when she'd change her hair or wear a new sweater. The way he didn't talk just about skating, but about lots of things, as though her opinions mattered. The way they'd laugh when he told her secrets about his partner. The way he'd pat her arm, give her shoulders a little squeeze.

She knew men's touches. Her mother had brought home lots of men who'd bump into her in the hall or just happen to brush a forearm across her breasts while they reached across to open a car door. Little pats on the bottom, hands dropping onto a knee at the movies—oh, yes, her mother's men knew how to touch.

When Clay touched her, though, it didn't make her skin crawl, didn't make her want to scrub it off. She thought of how he rubbed her neck. The feel of his fingers on her back. How strange her breasts felt, when he'd see Hunter had left the rink and swoop by, taking her in dance position, guiding her around the rink, chests touching.

She thought how his mouth had felt on hers, the first time he'd given her a quick, playful kiss. How it had felt the second, not-quite-as-quick time.

Chapter 15

November 2000: Boston

Clay gave his name to the receptionist, then circled the waiting room, admiring the indicia of success: elegant chairs of beige kid and brushed steel; glass-topped tables bearing handsome, small-circulation magazines; shelves of trophies, sparkling under bullet spots. The gray walls, bearing rows of skaters' pictures, most with adulatory inscriptions. Lofton Weeks's Olympic gold medal, encased in a shadow box, enjoying pride of place at the center of the wall behind the reception desk.

Framed pictures of Weeks: one of him in front of a skating rink, wearing his signature black dinner jacket, talking to a ten-year-old who later became the United States ladies' champion. Others with various members of his stable of professionals, looking not unlike a rich breeder with his entries at Churchill Downs, except the horses couldn't supply autographs.

Clay studied the black-and-white photos of the young Weeks: standing in front of an outdoor skating rink in a Yale letter sweater; afloat in a stag leap, head thrown back, arms flung wide; bending over as an official put the World championship medal around his neck.

Clay's jaw muscles tightened. He took a deep breath, exhaled. It was happening less frequently, but in odd moments reality would hit him in the gut like a well-aimed fist. Then the self-hatred would wash over him until he'd wonder others didn't flee the stink of it.

He wandered over to a floor-to-ceiling window and forced his mind to think of other things. It was just before Thanksgiving, but the weather had held, and even from the fiftieth floor of the Hancock Tower, Copley Square sparkled. He imagined how much sheer, sybaritic pleasure he could find in the square mile below him. He let his fantasies play, taking him away from reminders of successes he would never know.

He couldn't resist gadgets; he'd start at Brookstone, then wander over to Eric Fuchs and admire the model trains. When that palled he'd stop by Brooks Brothers and see if there were any new suspenders, the kind with embroidered scenes. He'd take coffee in one of the elegant little cafés, enjoying the buzz of smart chatter and upscale vowels. Refreshed, he'd get a haircut next. The barbershop at the Ritz offered a barber, not a hairstylist, and he liked that, the old-fashioned luxury of the scalp massage, the straight-razor shave, the feel of the old man's fingers rubbing saddle soap into his shoes.

He was starting to enjoy art, and he'd browse the Newberry Street galleries, perhaps buy a print; he'd passed a fine Barry Moser in one window, and he suspected Moser hadn't exhausted his upside potential. Certainly he'd drop in at Waterstone's, where there was a book on trout fishing he'd been coveting.

Of course, he'd be on the lookout for something to send

Maggie. The jewelry at Firestone & Parson and Shreve's
was a bit matronly; perhaps a scarf or sweater from Est! She
could buy anything she wanted in Tokyo, of course, but she
wanted little. Too little, considering what she deserved.
She'd appreciate the thought more than the thing. He owed
her a letter, anyway. Two, in fact.

"Maggie." It escaped involuntarily, at the image of her.
Startled, he noticed the mark his breath had left on the window and looked around to see if anyone had heard.

Maggie was a part of him, and part of him was missing.
No mere lover could know what it was to have a pairs partner. If there was a human activity offering a more intimate
linkage, he didn't know what it was.

That train of thought was a trap. Angrily he willed himself
to return to his travels around Copley Square: a drink at the
Ritz bar, dinner at Cafe Budapest. Maggie always liked . . .

Clay turned from the window, disgusted. There would be
no shopping, no drink at the Ritz bar, and no Maggie. Not
for a long time. He took a seat, began flipping through a
magazine.

Weeks was pacing his office, talking to a *Globe* sportswriter, an earnest young woman named Moorman. As
Weeks paced he kept his hands thrust into the side pockets
of his jacket, occasionally removing one to make a point
with a crisp chop. He moved with short, precise strides on
small feet. With his economical movements and his dark
blue, double-breasted Rizzo blazer, gray flannel trousers,
and black loafers, he might have been a dancing instructor.
He spoke in the assured, old-money voice that lent such authority to his television commentary.

"A very good question," he was saying. Miss Moorman
beamed. "Yes, much of skating's *huge* audience—mostly

women, as you point out—otherwise has no interest in spectator sport. You are really very astute to pick up on that."

"Thank you." Miss Moorman gazed up worshipfully, journalistic objectivity in tatters. Weeks seduced the media with practiced ease.

"The reason," Weeks continued, "is that skating, at the higher levels, is unique in the world of sport." He cocked an eye at the reporter. "It offers athleticism of the highest order, certainly, but athleticism that must always be yoked to art."

"As though you crossed a ballet dancer with a, a . . ."

"An NBA basketball player. Very good. I like that." Weeks paused, watching as his words were recorded on the reporter's stenopad, then continued: "Exactly right. A world-class skater is a world-class athlete, have no doubt of that, but at the same time world-class skaters have to be world-class artists. When they are performing, they are expressing feelings, emotions. The audience gets the beauty, the flow, the sound, and the color of ballet, and at the same time the thrill of watching a magnificent athlete poised on the knife edge between magnificence and humiliation, victory and defeat. Imagine if ballerinas competed against each other: first one jumps, then the other, each striving for greater and greater distance, until one falls on her dainty little derriere and the other's declared the winner."

Miss Moorman nodded appreciatively. "You'd certainly draw a new audience to ballet."

"It's what I call the 'edge of the cliff' aspect of skating. People don't want to see skaters fall, but they're riveted by the *possibility*. After years of work and staggering expense, the goal is within reach. The skater has performed flawlessly, she's thirty seconds from the National title or Olympic gold, and then this exquisite young creature places an edge wrong, and phht!—it's gone forever. I *still* feel the tension."

"I do, too. My stomach knots. Not in the professional shows so much, but with the amateurs."

Weeks clamped his hands over his ears. "Please, please, dear lady—*never* say 'amateurs' when you're talking about skating, at least not what's called Olympic-eligible skating—the National titles, the World titles, numerous international competitions, and of course the Olympics. It calls forth images of, oh, I don't know . . ." He fluttered his hand. "Hans Brinker, I suppose. Club competitions, that sort of thing. But skaters competing at the international level . . . well, they're hardly 'amateurs.' "

Miss Moorman's breathing accelerated. "You mean . . . they *cheat?* They get paid under the table?" She held her pen poised.

"Good heavens, no. That's not what I'm saying at all." He could imagine the flak if such a charge were attributed to him. "Absolutely not. Olympic-eligible skaters *have* to be able to make money; it takes at least fifty thousand dollars a year, for eight, ten, or twelve years, to train a serious skater. The International Skating Union recognizes that if it insisted on pure amateurism, the only people competing in the Olympic division would be the children of the very rich." He smiled engagingly. "Like me."

Miss Moorman seemed to sag as he continued. "Every spring the Tour of World Figure Skating Champions travels across the country. It's all top Olympic-division skaters, it's sanctioned by the USFSA, and it pays each skater a minimum of two thousand dollars a night as it moves from city to city. Some skaters make as much as one hundred and fifty thousand dollars from that tour alone. That's hardly 'amateur,' wouldn't you say? The only difference between

Olympic-division skaters and professionals is that the professionals have more money-earning opportunities, and there are theoretical limits on how the Olympic-eligible skaters can spend their earnings. Now . . ."

He stopped, seeing Clay standing in the door. He waved him in, arms outstretched.

"Clayton, Clayton—it *is* good to see you." He placed his hands on Clay's shoulders, studying him. "You look *wonderful*. Retirement must agree with you. I thought you were a shade too thin at my party, but now you look *perfect*."

Clay groaned. "Oh, Lord—I've gotten fat."

"Not at all, not at all. Believe me, I'd tell you." He dropped to a stage whisper. "Between us, I told Jennie Niedermyer she could skate as the back end of Dumbo without a costume. I don't believe in coddling skaters." His eyes dropped. "How's the hand?"

Clay turned it back and forth. "Good for swatting flies, not much else."

Weeks clucked his tongue sympathetically. "I so admire your attitude. I've known countless skaters who've suffered career-ending injuries, and few have taken it with as much grace."

He turned to the reporter. "Miss Moorman, let me introduce Clayton Bartlett, a marvelous pairs skater whose career ended in a tragic accident a few months ago. You may have heard?"

The woman's eyes widened. "Oh, yes—I read about that. I'm so sorry, Mr. Bartlett."

"Thank you."

"Miss Moorman's a sportswriter for the *Globe*, doing a piece on the popularity of figure skating."

Weeks turned back to the reporter. "Did you see Clayton

and his partner, Maggie Campbell, at the Summer Skating Festival, in Denver?"

She shook her head. "I'm afraid not."

Weeks frowned. "Well, get the tape, and you'll understand exactly what I mean about the art, the emotion, the *tension,* of great skaters performing at the absolute apex of their art. It was a magnificent performance."

He clamped an arm over Clay's shoulders. "As far as I'm concerned, Clayton, you and Miss Campbell are the American champions, and I think you had a good chance of becoming the best pairs team of all time. It's a great, great loss."

The reporter looked at Clay admiringly. He lowered his eyes modestly, assuming Weeks's flattery had a purpose. It felt good, and he wanted to show he knew how to play his role.

Miss Moorman stood. "Well, thank you so much, Mr. Weeks. You've been a tremendous help. You have such a gift for conveying your passion. May I call you if I think of anything else?"

"By all means." Weeks escorted her to the door. "But one other thing. You spoke of professional 'shows.' I assure you: the events *I* promote aren't 'shows'; they are most definitely competitions. First prize in this June's Champions Cup is a quarter million dollars. I only invite skaters who've medaled at their nationals, and these are highly competitive people. For that kind of money, most of them would murder their mothers."

"Oh." Miss Moorman struggled to hold her coat and scribble notes at the same time.

"I'd appreciate it if you wouldn't quote that last bit, Miss Moorman. It's perhaps a bit indelicate."

There was a flash of disappointment, but she nodded.

"Off the record, though, some of the johnny-come-latelies *do* put on 'competitions' that are about as legitimate as professional wrestling."

"Oh? Who?"

Weeks clucked his tongue. "I'm afraid I've already said too much. But do call if you have any other questions."

When she was ten feet down the hall he called to her: "But you might ask Patrick Coyle why certain people *always* win those farces he puts on." He shut the door, returning to Clay. "Sorry to keep you waiting. Now—"

His intercom buzzed. "Damn it."

A woman said: "Mr. Coyle again."

"Tell him I'm busy, Doris." Weeks sat down across from Clay. "The *nerve* of some people. He thought that just because he'd promoted *automobile races,* for Christ's sake, he could show up one day and be a force in professional skating. Now he's found out the reason Crouvisier was available was that, as anyone who knows anything about skating could have told him, she has a *major* drug problem. So Coyle's got Madison Square Garden booked for three nights, his headliner's in a clinic somewhere, and there isn't a single gold medalist on the marquee. Now he has the unbelievable gall to call and *demand* that I let Suslov skate for him: 'We loan drivers all the time—it's good for the sport.' Fine, I said—call Richard Petty; let's see *his* triple triple! Can you imagine the man's cheek?"

Weeks, not expecting an answer, steepled his fingers under his chin. "Now, you're probably wondering why I asked you to come in, eh?"

"Well, I hoped it was to offer me a contract with the WPT."

Weeks winced. "My dear boy—unfortunately, you stopped being box office the night you stopped being one-half of America's best pairs team. Campbell and Bartlett I'd hire in a thrice, but you alone—I'm afraid not. If you were a good enough singles skater to skate for me, you wouldn't be sitting here—you'd be training for the Olympics, like your former partner."

He looked at Clay benignly. "Of course, you could talk to Coyle."

Clay met Weeks's appraisal coolly. "I wanted to approach you first; you're the top tier."

"What a nice compliment." Weeks pursed his lips. "Of course, I know Coyle already turned you down—he told me so, when I suggested he call you. But I like the way you fed me that absolutely shameless line. You'll go far."

Clay, chuckling, raised his hands in surrender. "You got me, Lofton; I knew you were a long shot, after Coyle said no. But thanks for pitching me to him; I appreciate the thought. So why *did* you ask me in?"

"I have a proposition to make you."

"What sort of proposition?"

"A damned good one. How'd you like to work for me?"

"Work for you? But you just said—"

"Not to skate with WTP—work here, at World Skating Management."

"Good Lord—doing what?"

"Everything. I've got two dozen top pros under contract to the tour, but we serve as agents for a dozen more besides. Much as it rankles me, we have to negotiate on their behalf with competing programs. There's the media to deal with, advertising to buy, arenas to rent, transportation arrangements, product endorsements, personal appearances to arrange. And, of course, skaters retire or jump ship; they've got to be replaced. I'd like you to help me."

"Me, an agent?"

"Why not? You're bright, you know skating and skaters, and you need a job. I've reached an age where I don't care to be on the road all the time, and the younger skaters think I'm a dinosaur. I'll pay you a base salary of forty thousand a year to start, plus expenses. You'll also share commission income. With some skaters the agency takes fifteen percent of everything earned—prize and appearance money, endorsement fees, whatever. You'd get a third of that, for anyone you sign."

He began doodling on a pad, his voice turning ruminative. "Take somebody like Doe Rawlings, for example. . . ."

"Doe? She won't turn pro until after the Olympics. I didn't think you represented Olympic-division skaters."

"I don't; with the association dictating where they can compete, and what they can get, there's no need for an agent, and not enough money to make it worthwhile anyway. But signing her to a contract now, binding her to us *after* she turns professional, that's different."

"I didn't know you did that."

"I haven't, but I'd rather sign her now than later."

"Before the bidding starts, in other words."

Weeks winced. "I don't even like to think about it. Now, let's just run some numbers." His forehead furrowed as he jotted figures. "I'm hopelessly retro, I'm afraid; the staff can't believe I can't use a calculator, but . . . ah."

He looked up. "Let's say you get Miss Rawlings to agree we'll represent her after she turns pro. She'll bring in two, three million a year, *minimum,* from skating alone. Scads more if we do our job right and get the endorsements, movie deals, all the rest. A gorgeous girl like that, it shouldn't be hard. Let's say a total of four million a year. At fifteen percent a year commission, that's six hundred thousand to the agency. One-third to you . . . well, unlike a lot of your peers,

I expect you can do that arithmetic in your head. What do you think?"

"I think two hundred thousand a year is a lot of money."

"It is, but it's quite realistic."

"I suppose. But tell me—why Doe Rawlings in particular?"

"Because she's the defining skater of her generation."

"Don't you think the Olympics are going to have some bearing on that?"

Weeks looked skeptical. "She's as close to a sure thing for the gold as you can get, don't you think?"

"I know at least one woman who'd disagree."

"Ah—Miss Campbell, yes. Well, she's a wonderful girl, and a marvelous skater, but I'm afraid that's a bit quixotic. A year and a half isn't much time when you haven't been competing in singles, and if she *does* get to the Olympics, which I dearly hope, she'll be twenty-three years old, running into the best woman skater alive, probably the best who ever lived, at her absolute physical peak."

Clay set his jaw. "Maggie's as competitive as they come; I wouldn't count her out."

Weeks smiled condescendingly. "Of course, of course. Look, dear boy—I'm not saying the girl isn't a beautiful skater; she is. In fact, she's the only pairs skater I can think of who could reasonably expect to go into singles and almost immediately be credible. All I'm saying is, a Doe Rawlings comes along once in a generation. It's just bad luck for everyone else."

"You may be surprised, Lofton."

Weeks threw up his hands. "All right, all right—your loyalty is commendable. But since I lack the sentimental attachment, I'm prepared to offer Doe Rawlings an incentive to sign with us that I'm afraid I can't offer anyone else, including Miss Campbell."

"Which is?"

"If she signs with us before the Olympics, I'm prepared to guarantee her one million dollars a year, in return for giving WTP a first call on her services for ten years."

Clay looked pensive. "I thought you just said she'd be worth two to three million a year, after the Olympics."

Weeks smiled vaguely. "Yes, yes, I suppose I did."

"So you want to sign her to a contract that'll let her keep about a third of what she earns, and you'll take the rest?"

Weeks shrugged. "I'm willing to guarantee that money to her, regardless how she does in the Olympics."

"But you think she's a lock for the gold."

"That's my bet."

"She'd have to be insane to take that deal."

Weeks smiled thinly. "A bird in the hand, you know. A million a year might look pretty good to an eighteen-year-old. And I'll tell you another incentive I'm ready to offer. You get Doe Rawlings to sign that contract, and on the day she does, you get one hundred thousand dollars. That's over and above your share of the agency's earnings."

Clay whistled silently. "You really want her."

Weeks's hands clenched. "I've got to have her." He thrust himself to his feet, pacing. "For thirty years professional skating was a joke. You could have a trunkload of gold medals, and once you retired from the Olympic division the best you could hope for was a few years with the Ice Capades or the Ice Follies. Meaningless exhibitions, and if you weren't careful, they'd have you skating around in a clown suit while someone pushed a pie in your face. I was the person who realized there was going to be a market for professional competition, that more and more people were going to be willing to pay to see former Olympic-division stars if they were really competing. It took a long time to develop, and for years I underwrote the WPT, but now it's coining money, and all of a sudden every hustler who ever put on a variety night at a Moose lodge thinks he can sign up some skaters and make a bundle. When Doe Rawlings turns pro, God knows what they'll offer her. Rill will have us beating the hell out of each other, and at best we'll wind up with five percent of her gross. Or some egomaniac like Coyle will make an offer Rill can't resist and she'll be gone before I can even respond. And anybody who doesn't have her might as well have the Ice Capades. So I need her, and I want her tied up *now*."

"Why don't you approach her?"

"I have, but she won't talk to me unless Rill says it's all right, and he's told her to hold off until after the Olympics."

"Well, then, why would I have any better luck? She's not going to go against Hunter."

"Not for just anybody, no." He looked at Clay's hand, shook his head sadly. "I thought . . . you and she must be great friends, you see. I thought perhaps you'd have greater . . . influence than I do."

"'Great friends'?" Clay shifted his weight uneasily. "Hardly. She offered to drive me home, that's all."

"Ah." Weeks tapped his forefinger against his nose. "Actually, it's more that when I saw you at my party the two of you seemed to be chatting so . . . amicably."

Clay hesitated, blinking, then smiled. "Really, Lofton—Doe and I shared the same coach and the same ice for nine years; of course I talked to her. She's had a pretty rough life, you know, and I try to drop a friendly word every now and then."

"Very decent of you, then. And the way you had your arm

around that trim little waist as you went out to the parking lot? Just offering a helping hand, were you?"

Clay studied the man. Finally he shook his head. "I don't think you saw that, Lofton. I've made no secret I'd had more to drink than I should have, but I'd certainly remember if I'd been pawing the girl, and I wasn't. And incidentally, I'm planning to marry Maggie Campbell, so I'd appreciate it if you wouldn't repeat that story."

Weeks sighed lackadaisically, as though tiring of the discussion. "I must have been mistaken. Oh, dear . . . I did hope you'd be particularly simpatico with Miss Rawlings."

Clay looked at him levelly. "No more than anyone else she trained with."

The older man managed to make even his shrugs crisp and elegant. "But you'd be willing to talk to her about a contract with us?" Looking at Clay's hand, he added: "I mean, you're in a unique position to point out to her the uncertainties that every skater faces. She might jump at the thought of a guaranteed income, come what may."

After a pause, Clay nodded. "I'll give it a try, but I can't promise anything."

Weeks held up his hand. "What more could I ask? The job's yours."

"I was planning to go back to college next semester."

"Take night classes. By the way—were they able to fix that Porsche of yours?"

"No, it was a total loss."

"Pity, a beautiful thing. What do you drive now?"

Clay flushed. "I borrow my parents' car when I need one."

"Good heavens—I couldn't have a representative of this agency showing up for appointments in a *Volvo,* or whatever."

He rubbed his chin, looking off into the distance. "It's important that we make the right impression, because people know we prosper only if our clients do. Prosperous, but not ostentatious; I leave vulgarity to people like our friend Coyle—it comes so naturally to him. Now, let's see: I drive a Mercedes, but perhaps that's a bit *stodgy* for your generation." He leaned across the desk. "What say we lease you a BMW, one of those little two-seater convertibles; I think that makes a tasteful statement, don't you?"

Clay tried but couldn't keep the grin off his face. "Very tasteful." He cleared his throat. "I could use an advance, though." He looked at his watch as he got to his feet. "I should pick up some clothes. I can swing by Brooks Brothers on the way home—I want to make a tasteful statement when I get out of the car, too."

Weeks bent over the intercom. "Doris, I'm sending Mr. Bartlett out; get him twenty-five hundred dollars from petty cash, would you?" When he looked up, Clay was on his way to the door.

Weeks canted his head. "When the cat's away," he murmured, "when the cat's away." He smiled. "And she really couldn't be much farther away."

Chapter 16

November 2000: Boston

*C*lay rested his hands on the steering wheel, asking himself for the hundredth time if he was making a mistake. Finally, swallowing hard, he got out and mounted the brownstone's steps.

He cleared his throat. When the door opened he smiled. "Hello, Doe."

Her eyes widened as she stepped back. "Clay—what are you doing here?" She fluffed her hair nervously.

Clay had rehearsed his speech, and it flowed smoothly. "I was in the neighborhood, and when I saw your place I just had a sudden impulse to stop and say hello. It's been too long."

"I . . . I'm glad you did."

"I should have called before, but I wasn't sure how you and Hunter might feel about me. You know—after what happened. Is Hunter home? I'd like to say hello."

"No, he's with some juniors in Worcester. He won't be home until later."

Clay knew, having checked at the club. Rill took his guardian duties seriously, and Clay wasn't sure how he'd feel about him calling on his ward. "Ah—I'm sorry to miss him."

"I'll tell him, but I'm glad you stopped. I've . . . missed you."

"Well, I better get going. I'm on my way to the Museum of Fine Arts. Can you believe it? I've become an art buff."

He eyed her appreciatively. She looked fresh, scrubbed, and radiant.

"You're going to a museum?" She was still trying to take in the apparition on her doorstep.

"Yep—I really like it. It relaxes me."

"I've never been to the art museum."

"No? Well, you ought to go sometime."

"Maybe I will."

Clay snapped his fingers. "Well, why not now, with me? If you're not busy, that is." He could feel his pulse racing.

"No," she said, "I'm not busy. I take Sunday off." She stood, rooted, her eyes drawn to his hand.

He caught her look and held it up. "Not too bad, is it? I mean, just seeing it, you wouldn't know anything was wrong, would you?" He turned it like an exhibit.

She stared, fascinated and horrified, shaking her head. "No. It looks . . . fine."

"I've gotten so I can get some use out of it, too."

"Use?" She was still staring.

"Like driving. Now, how about my idea? It's freezing, just standing here."

"Your idea?" She wrenched her eyes up to his face. "Oh, the museum. Sure. I'd like that."

He smiled. "Come on, then." He turned and beckoned. "Grab a coat. We'll get you some culture."

*   *   *

"It's beautiful." Doe ran her hand over the beige leather seat. "It must have been terribly expensive."

Clay drove easily, weaving the BMW through the light Sunday traffic. "It's leased; comes with the job."

"Oh—what are you doing?"

"I'm working for Lofton Weeks. You know, World Skating Management?"

"I didn't know that."

"No reason you should—we don't represent you."

"No." She settled back against the seat as Clay accelerated. "Lofton wanted me to sign something with him, but Hunter says I won't need an agent until I'm ready to turn pro."

"Umm. Well, between us, in most cases he's right." Clay punched the pedal, and the car snaked into an opening. "Although there might be some security in taking Lofton's deal."

Doe fluttered her hand. "I don't know anything about that. I let Hunter take care of that stuff."

"Probably a smart thing—lets you concentrate on skating. By the way, you were terrific in Portland."

Doe turned excitedly. "Oh—you saw me?"

"I sure did. Let me tell you, Doe—they might as well give you the World championship right now and save you the trouble of going to Düsseldorf to pick it up. There's no one out there who even comes close."

Doe looked like a child at Christmas. "You really think so?"

"I know it. The only thing that could derail you is an injury." He looked her up and down. "And you look pretty healthy."

"No, I'm not worried about that. I've never had a serious injury."

"You're lucky. Of course, I'd never had a bad one either."

She looked at him sadly. "I know. I can't tell you how—"

He cut her off. "Things happen, that's all. You just never know when. Here we are." He parked the car and led her into the building.

"Do you like your job?" Doe looked around the lobby, decorated for the holidays; a medieval carol hung in the air. "What do you do?"

"All sorts of things. Come on—let's go into the American gallery first."

He led the way, talking: "I've only been at it a little while, and I'm still learning, of course, but I enjoy it. I went to dinner with Schuyler and Drummond the other night, and they were great. When we were competing I thought they were pretty aloof, but they're quite pleasant when you get to know them."

"I never cared for Kim Schuyler."

"She's fun, actually. She did an imitation of Lofton that had me on the floor. I think that when you're Olympic eligible the pressure's so great that it's hard to be loose with other skaters. But the pros have done all that. They compete for a lot of money, but somehow that doesn't seem to be as stressful as competing for a medal. So they can let down their hair and just enjoy skating."

He stopped her in front of a painting of a man pointing to a rolled-up parchment. "Isn't that terrific?"

Doe studied the painting, then read the label next to it. "Who's Samuel Adams?" she asked, straightening.

"Lord, Doe—he was one of the major revolutionary figures. Try this one." He stepped on, pointing.

"I know who George Washington was."

He laughed. "That's a start." He was feeling more comfortable than he'd expected. The museum had been a good idea.

"I don't know much history, I guess. My tutors never seemed to care, so I didn't, either." She looked around uncomfortably. "I must sound pretty stupid."

"Not at all. You just need to read a few books. Come on— you don't need to know about the subject of the painting to enjoy it."

They strolled through the galleries. Clay had spent a lot of time in them and knew the collection well.

Doe stared uncertainly at a canvas covered with multicolored drips of paint. "It doesn't look like anything. It looks like he threw the paint at it."

Clay chuckled. "He did. That's a Jackson Pollock. He was one of the founders of abstract expressionism. But it does look like something."

She tilted her head dubiously: "What?"

"Itself."

"What do you mean?" She sounded as though she thought he was trying to trick her.

"I mean, don't ask the art to *be* anything other than itself. This is an arrangement of paint on a surface. It may please you to look at it, or it may not, but it doesn't claim to be a picture *of* anything. Except itself."

Doe stepped back, trying to understand. She shook her head. "I don't get it."

Clay beckoned her closer. "Look at the paint." He pointed at the surface. "Closer. See the different thicknesses? It's really three-dimensional, like a sculpture. And there's so much energy *in* the paint. Look at that! And over there! He's letting the paint speak." He rested his hand lightly on her shoulder as she bent over, squinting.

"Oh." Doe, conscious of the weight of his hand, tried to

follow his explanation. She stepped back, taking in the whole canvas again. "It's kind of interesting," she remarked uncertainly, "now that you've explained it. But where did you learn so much about art?"

"I'm taking a night course in art appreciation at BU. See that?" He pointed across the gallery, to a plastic box with a three-dimensional cardboard city inside. "That's a Red Grooms. I bought one of his constructions with my first paycheck. It looks terrific in my new apartment on Long Wharf—lights the whole room up."

She looked at it with delight. "It's wonderful. Like a toy. I didn't know art could be like that."

"Sure it can. You don't have to say, 'What is it?' It is what it is. It's pleasing to the eye, it's fun, and you can spend a lot of time trying to figure out what it means to you."

They strolled on. He led Doe into the gift shop. "Let's get you a catalog. You can look at it at home, and decide what you'd like to see next time."

"Next time?"

"Well, I hope you'll come again. There's always something new to see."

She blushed. "I, uh . . . wouldn't come alone—I wouldn't know what's what."

He handed her the catalog. "Come with me. Next Sunday, say?"

She flipped through the catalog, glad to have an excuse to look away. "I'd like that."

"It's a date."

There was a pause while Doe thought of something else to say. "Those apartments are expensive, aren't they?"

"Oh, I'm paying too much, but I'm getting pretty good money from Lofton, between my salary and my cut of the commissions. Not as much as I could have made skating professionally, if things had worked out, but about as much as I made skating last year. And I hope to make a lot more in the future."

He glanced at his watch. "Now I better get you home, before Hunter has a fit."

"I'm allowed out."

"But he keeps a pretty tight rein on you, doesn't he?" He steered her toward the exit.

"I guess. Too tight, sometimes."

"Well, he cares about you, and I wouldn't want to get on his bad side."

"He acts like I'm still a child—telling me what time to come in, what to eat, what to wear. It's ridiculous."

He helped her on with her coat. "He may think you *want* him to tell you want to do."

They were in the car before she asked: "Why would Hunter think I *want* him to be telling me what to do all the time?"

Clay waited for an opening in the oncoming traffic, then pulled out carefully. "Oh, you know—things like leaving all the financial stuff to him. Someone thinks you don't care enough about something as important as your financial future to take an interest in it, they probably think you need their guidance in everything else."

She looked out the window, frowning. "Do you really think so? I never thought of that."

"Count on it. Boy—this traffic is something."

A heavy snow was falling, and the traffic on Huntington Avenue had slowed to a crawl. Doe wished it would stop altogether, but all too soon they were pulling up in front of her house.

"Here we are." He pulled over to the curb. "I hope you enjoyed yourself."

"You're a good teacher—I learned a lot. And thank you for this." She fanned the pages of the catalog, making no move to open the door. "Maybe I should know more about the business side of skating," she murmured.

"Well, I'm no expert yet, but if you'd ever like to talk about it, I'd be glad to tell you what I know."

"I'd like that." She reached for the door handle but turned back to him abruptly. "I've never told you how sorry I am about . . . what happened."

Clay tensed. His good hand squeezed the steering wheel until the knuckles went white. "It was my own damn fault."

He took a deep breath. "And I never told you how grateful I am for what you did. I probably wouldn't be driving anything, much less this beauty, if you hadn't come through for me."

"That's okay—I was glad to do it." She looked down at her hands, folded in her lap. "You know, Clay, I've always liked you. That night—"

He cut her off hurriedly. "I'd had a lot to drink, Doe. Between the drink, and the accident, I don't remember too much. From the time we left the club until we were waiting for the police, there's kind of a haze."

She studied his face, his nervous eyes. Her lips parted as the corners of her mouth drew into a slow half smile. "That's understandable. But I remember everything."

Clay suddenly found the car stifling. He snapped off the heater and cranked down the window. The blast of winter air revived him. "Doe, you have to understand something. Maggie Campbell and I are . . ." He stopped, swallowing, wishing he had a drink.

She looked at him steadily, her hands balled in her lap.

"Maggie and I . . ." He stopped and looked at the steering wheel as though it held the words.

"Yes?"

His shoulders heaved. "We're . . . friends. Good friends, I mean."

The smile brightened, confident and knowing, much older than eighteen. "Well, of course you are. After all that time together, I'd expect that."

"Yes, but what I mean is—"

"Obviously, after that night I knew you weren't . . . involved."

He turned and looked out the window, letting the sharp cold tear his eyes. The phrase "Oh, God" turned over in his mind.

She went on in a matter-of-fact voice: "Because if you were, I wouldn't dream of interfering. It wouldn't be right, not with her on the other side of the world."

He turned back. "I just want you to understand that, that . . ." He trailed off, staring through the windshield.

"Yes? What is it you want me to understand, Clay?" she asked.

"Just that . . . I can't . . . you see . . ."

"Yes?" She wore the little half smile and nodded encouragingly. "You can't what, Clay?"

What he'd been about to say died deep inside him. He felt nauseated, as though he'd swallowed something putrid. "I only meant . . . I wouldn't want her to know."

"Yes?" Her eyes were clear and guileless. "What wouldn't you want her to know?"

He took a deep breath. "She mustn't know we're . . . seeing each other. She doesn't know, you see, that I . . ." He stopped, swallowed, went on: "That we're just . . . friends, now. I couldn't . . . well, until after the Olympics, I just don't want to say anything, you see? I owe her that much."

Doe's fingers closed briefly on Clay's hand. "That's fine. But it doesn't really matter what she knows, does it?"

"Doesn't matter?" he whispered.

"No. Because if we compete, I'll beat her."

She let herself out of the car and came around to Clay's open window. Leaning in, she said: "I'd like to see how that funny picture looks in your place."

She was halfway up the steps when she turned and walked back to the car. Leaning in his window, she put her face close to his. "I'll beat her . . . on the ice, or off it."

Chapter 17

December 2000: Tokyo

*S*pend the next two weeks practicing your old programs while Mori-*san* and I plan new ones, Megumi-*chan*," had been Madam Goto's directive when Maggie arrived. "We will do the choreography ourselves." Maggie was astounded when the old woman rattled off each element of her old singles programs, with a description of arm positions and, note by note, where the music fit.

She was still marveling when a gnarled hand gestured toward the ice. "Go, go—you must recover the feeling of being on the ice alone."

Yet she never was on the ice alone. She found herself looking around at odd moments, half expecting a pair of arms to be circling her waist, a hand to touch her hip, saying, "Follow me—I'll lead you." She heard his voice, saw his grin, heard his laugh. She remembered the games, the first, sweet kisses in the workout room, his whispered, "Breathe, damn it, breathe," when she'd started turning blue in the middle of a tango camel in their first big competition.

The first time she looked over and remembered he was

nowhere around, she had to leave the ice. She squeezed her head between her hands. "Oh, Clay," she whispered, "how I miss you."

As the days passed, the sense that she was an incomplete pairs team, not a singles skater, became more manageable, and she learned how to invoke his image when she needed it most: late at night, after hours of practice, when her legs felt as though they couldn't stroke another foot; when the task she had set herself seemed hopeless, and she was tempted by despair; when the jump combination that had seemed so effortless to the sixteen-year-old sent her crashing to the ice, and she wondered if she could take any more pain. Then she would see him, beating his hand against the armchair, and she'd gather her resources, stand, and skate on, grimly determined.

The two weeks became three, then a month, with no new programs. Instead, day after day, Madam Goto watched Maggie skate. All but hidden by a shapeless overcoat, supported by her cane, she stood in her familiar spot behind the boards, watching intently. For long periods she said nothing, scarcely moving.

Occasionally she grunted, jotting a cryptic note on scraps of paper she kept in her pockets. Once or twice a day she'd bark an order: "The double triple, Megumi-*chan*," or, "Change foot spin." Hooded eyes followed Maggie everywhere.

Maggie's tenth day back, Chiako heard the *sensei* mutter: "Where is it? Where can it have gone?"

It became an almost daily refrain: "What is *wrong* with the girl?" Brooding, the old head would stare, tracking Maggie's progress around the rink. Chiako, standing next to her, would hear the disgusted grumble: "Work, that's all it is, just work."

The *joshu*'s queries were met with blank stares or a shake of the head. And when Maggie asked how the programs were coming, whether there were not at least elements she could begin working on, she was met with a curt, "You will be advised when they are ready." As Maggie, bowing, retreated to the ice, Chiako heard Madam Goto whisper grimly: "And when you are ready."

Maggie was doing wind sprints, back and forth across the rink. Full speed, arms pumping, head down. Slam to a stop, turn, repeat. Sets of ten, a thirty-second rest, repeat.

Finally Chiako called to her: "Enough, Megumi-*chan!* You will make yourself sick." As though she hadn't heard, Maggie set off again. Ten minutes later she was heaving bile into a wastebasket, but when she felt Chiako's hand on her shoulder she shook it off angrily and stepped back onto the ice.

"Leave her, *joshu*," Madam Goto commanded when Chiako seemed about to pursue her. "She is breaking rocks, not skating; we have nothing to teach her. She must burn it out of herself. I only hope she will do so in time."

Chiako, confused, asked: "What, *sensei?* Do you think Campbell has lost her skill? She appears very strong to me—far stronger than when I competed against her, and she was formidable then."

"No, no—physically she is marvelous; the pair lifts have given her great upper body strength. And look at those leg thrusts—hockey players would envy those. It is not strength that she's lost, or technical skill. But they are useless to her without the other thing."

"What other thing, *sensei?*"

"Joy! She has no joy. Look at her!"

Maggie was practicing a step sequence. Her mouth was set in taut concentration, her eyes were narrowed, her hands locked in front of her. The white boots were making all the right steps, but there was no ease to it; it looked like work, not dance.

"She is tense, *sensei*."

"She is all locked up inside!" Madam Goto shook her head. "When she was fourteen and just becoming a woman, it was all I could do to make her skate within herself. There was so much life, so much passion and romance. They threatened to take her over, so that at times she carried on like a kabuki actor. She learned to control it, so that it was always just beneath the surface. You will remember, I think."

"*Hai,*" Chiako agreed. "She had such expressive movements, yet never overdone."

"Well," Madam Goto said dryly, "you would certainly say her movements aren't overdone now. It is as though all the passion has gone, and only determination is left. She has set herself a goal, and she sees herself as Mother Courage, struggling indomitably against fearful odds. But I tell you, all the determination in the world won't make music. Music can come from joy, it can come from sorrow, but it cannot come from effort alone. She skates like those girls whose smiles are painted on, as though performing a job, a duty. There is no point in working on new programs when she is like this. She will go no place."

By the time she'd been back three weeks, Maggie was fighting panic; every morning she would wonder: Will we start the new programs today? Every night she would tell herself: Another day wasted.

Though she was skating hours every day, there was no form to her practices. Except for Madam Goto's occasional seemingly random instructions, Maggie was free to skate as she wished. Some days she'd fall into a rut and perform spin combinations for hours; other days she'd find herself reprising a program she'd last skated when she was twelve. On yet other days she didn't free skate at all but spent the entire session on figures and wind sprints.

She hinted of her concern, only to draw blank stares or a dismissive gesture. She wondered if Madam Goto was losing her memory and if she'd made a horrible, irrecoverable misjudgment. When she took her worries to Chiako, the *joshu* smiled with a confidence she didn't feel and said, "I do not know what Goto *sensei* is thinking, but that she is thinking I have no doubt. She will propose your programs soon."

"But there is so little time!"

"Too little, I think, to make a mistake in designing them. Have patience."

The more she fretted, the harder Maggie pushed, and the harder she pushed, the stiffer she became. Every day she set her jaw and worked harder, her mind filled with one thought: I must succeed. I am skating for both of us, and I must succeed.

Most of the time Maggie was too busy or too tired to think about anything except skating and Clay. She would crawl home, pick at some sashimi and pickles she'd buy in the subway station, then roll out her futon and fall asleep while Chiako watched television or went out with friends.

Chiako said the best thing about retirement was being able to eat again and burbled that she'd gained five kilos since she quit and was looking forward to the next five. The second best thing, she said, was being able to have a social life: going out, having friends, having time for men.

She asked Maggie to join her when she was going out, but Maggie always declined. She had no time for any of that, and no interest. She had her goal, and it left no time for frivolity.

Then, one night in late November, after a long, frustrating day at the rink, hours of exercises, no programs, no progress, as she walked out into the dark, bone weary and on the edge of tears, she heard a quiet voice: *"Konbanwa."* She stopped warily, still too close to urban America to hear a deep male voice in the night without tensing.

"Who . . ." She took a step toward the dark form in front of her. "Is it—"

"Konbanwa . . . Maggie."

She took another step, and another, then dropped her bag and ran to the man sitting sideways on the giant motorcycle, his gleaming white smile lighting the way. Her arms flew around him.

Hiro Araki was holding her off the ground, and she was laughing. Laughing, and mussing his black hair, pummeling his big shoulders, saying: *"Baka, baka, baka!"* "Stupid, stupid stupid! I was so stupid. So very stupid." She was still laughing when she climbed onto the seat behind him and they sped off into the night, her arms around his waist, her face pressed into the soft leather jacket. Through her fingertips she felt the vital power of him, the security, as she'd felt it the day, half a lifetime before, when he'd first appeared from nowhere, to rescue her from despair. She threw back her head and laughed into the rushing wind.

Chapter 18

September 1990

*M*aggie was in a hurry. On Saturdays school was a half day; in the afternoon she took ballet, to help her movement on the ice, then skated for four hours. But it had been her turn to clean the classroom, and it had taken longer than usual, since at the last minute Hayashi *sensei* had told her to wash the floor, not just sweep it. Now she had scarcely two hours to go home, change, eat lunch, and get to Ikebukuro. Rounding the corner of the school at a near run, she almost collided with the new teacher, Natsume *sensei*.

"Be careful, you!" The man had a high, almost feminine voice. He was barely as tall as Maggie but still made her uneasy. He carried his hands in an odd way, reminding her of a praying mantis. She'd often felt he was watching her, and though he wasn't her teacher, on several occasions he'd stopped her in the hall and accused her of talking in line, or standing wrong, or some other silly thing. He was a praying mantis, and he gave her the feeling that she looked like prey.

She bowed contritely. "Excuse me, Natsume *sensei*—I

am so sorry. That was very clumsy of me." She bowed again.

The little man gave her a quick head nod, and she started to step around him. "Just a minute, Megumi-*chan*," he squeaked, "I haven't excused you. What were you doing in the school building at this hour?"

"*Sensei*, it was my day to clean my classroom. I just finished."

He glared. "You wouldn't by any chance have been in my room, would you?"

She couldn't imagine what he was driving at. "No, *sensei*, just the sixth-grade room."

He went on as though he hadn't heard. "Because, Megumi-*chan*, someone has been taking change from my desk drawer. Do you by any chance know anything about that?"

Maggie's mind refused to process the words; ears ringing, she struggled to reply: "No, Natsume *sensei*—nothing!"

"I suppose if I looked in your pockets, I wouldn't find any change, eh?"

Maggie felt her pulse racing. "*Sensei*, it is forbidden to bring money to school. I don't have any money with me. I—"

The little man's yip cut her off: "Open your book bag—now!"

Maggie's legs went rubbery. She'd unslung the leather case and was reaching for the clasp when her hand froze. Someone else, another voice from a long way away, was saying: "No, *sensei*. Excuse me, but I will not. I am not a thief, and I should not be suspected for no reason."

The hand that lashed out slapped *her*, though, not someone else. "Open that book bag! How dare you defy me! Open it! Open it now!"

With every bark Natsume rose to a higher frenzy. Maggie's cheek was numb; flecks of spittle landed on her face as the little hand flailed at her. Most of the blows were ineffectual, more shocking than painful, but enough landed that after a few seconds she felt disoriented. Yet something wouldn't let her raise her arms, wouldn't let her step back. Between slaps she felt her mouth tightening contemptuously, provoking other, even more agitated flurries from the little man's hand.

Then there *was* another voice, a deeper voice, from somewhere behind her. "*Sensei!* Iwakura *sensei* wants you—he says it's an emergency."

Maggie's eyes, blinking, followed the hand as it slowed its backward, wind-up arc. "Heh? Iwakura *sensei* wants me? Why?"

A boy—young man, really—was suddenly standing alongside Maggie. He'd materialized so suddenly that Maggie had time to catch only a glimpse of him out of the corner of her eye before he bowed to Natsume. He stepped sideways just enough to come between Maggie and the teacher, and then she could see only a broad back and wide shoulders.

"He didn't say, *sensei,* just that if I saw you, I should ask you if you would come quickly."

Reluctantly the little man lowered his hand. "Very well." He looked like a child as he strained to see Maggie, craning his scrawny neck around the young man's shoulder. "Your kind knows no respect; I will deal with you later." He spun on his heel, striding rapidly toward the school building.

The young man looked at Maggie. He hadn't paid attention to her before, had merely acted impulsively when he'd seen the little bully whaling a girl, and now he took his time studying her, running his gaze over her as though he'd spotted her at the zoo. Damn, he thought—what an extraordinary girl. I wonder what she is—she's certainly not Japanese.

She stood before him, arms across her chest, staring back through enormous, glistening eyes. Her body was that of a girl, only the almost unnoticeable bumps on her chest heralding approaching womanhood. The strange eyes held neither the awe to which he was accustomed in young girls nor the coquetry he'd experienced with older ones.

She carried herself like a dancer: feet splayed, knees slightly bent, shoulders squared, back arched, chin high. There was an easy balance in her stance, a grace at rest. The top of her head, crowned with a tangle of reddish brown curls, reached his shoulders. She made him think of the mountain sprites his grandfather spoke of; they too were said to have eyes that could burn flesh.

Her right hand started to stray toward the bright red patch on her cheek. It got within a foot of her face when she jerked it back.

"Hurt much?" He touched her cheek lightly. She started, then held her place.

She shook her head wordlessly, and he thought perhaps she didn't even understand Japanese.

"Why was he hitting you?" he asked slowly, forming the words distinctly, as though talking to someone hard of hearing.

She swallowed. She felt tears welling and knew they'd bring more mortification than she could bear, so she drew on her anger. "He accused me of stealing his money! He wanted me to open my book bag." Her jaw jutted out, indignation flooding back.

Her voice was a girl's, not yet dropped. The young man was startled by her fluid Tokyo-accented Japanese. "*Did* you take his money? I don't care, I'm just curious."

Maggie's eyes flashed. "Of course not! I don't have any money on me."

"Then why not show him?"

She shook her head, lips tightening. "I don't know." She shrugged thin shoulders.

He looked at her approvingly. "You weren't going to let the little bastard make you crawl."

He spoke as though to a contemporary, although his uniform was that of a middle-schooler. "I guess that's right." The grown-up feeling his words gave her chased away thought of tears.

"You didn't cry, either."

She tried to grin, but it hurt too much. "I hate to cry."

"There you go." He chucked her under the chin. "That's Bushido. You've got guts, girl."

He might have been talking to an old friend. The words and grammer he used were for speech between males, too, not for an older boy talking to a younger girl. She found it disconcerting, as though the teacher's slaps had shaken loose the normal social order.

"Thank you. But it is good that Iwakura *sensei* sent you when he did, or I might have had to start crying." Maggie hoisted the book bag onto her shoulders.

"He didn't—I made that up." The stranger grinned, exposing even white teeth. "It was all I could think of at the moment."

Maggie's eyes widened. "You made it up?" She blanched. "But when he doesn't find Iwakura *sensei* . . ."

The young man chuckled. "You afraid?"

"No." She tried to meet his eye but found herself looking back at the school instead. She gulped. "Actually, yes."

"That's fine—it's good to know your feelings, and to be able to admit them. So let's leave."

He started to amble toward the street, as though he hadn't a concern in the world. For a few steps Maggie tried to match his easy pace, until fear took over and she broke for the gate at a run. She heard him laugh, and she thought he wasn't coming, but then he was alongside her.

He had long legs, much longer than hers, but her skating had given her powerful strides, and she set a fast pace. Only when they were across Kototoi Dori and deep in the maze of winding alleys did she pull up.

"You run . . ." The stranger, panting, had his hands resting on his knees while he looked up at Maggie, standing easily, her chest hardly moving. "You run damn fast for a girl."

"For a girl?" He's so tall, she thought. I wonder who he is?

"Okay—you run fast, period." He took another breath, straightening.

She nodded, satisfied. "I ice-skate. It builds your legs."

"Something sure did. Whew!" He leaned against a building, pulling a crumpled pack of Marlboros out of the breast pocket of his jacket. "Want one?" He offered the pack.

She shook her head. His fingers are so long, she thought. He had a large, muscular frame that stretched his blue-and-white uniform.

He lit the cigarette, pulling hard. "Ahh!" The smoke circled his head, six inches above Maggie's. "That's good." He smiled. "Was this the first time a teacher's hit you?"

His eyes, she saw, had a sparkle, as though getting hit by a teacher was the most amusing thing two people could talk about. Black, sparkling eyes, with long lashes, set over high cheekbones. She shook her head. "Once, a few years ago, Honda *sensei* slapped me because I asked a question about something she said."

His hand waved dismissively. "Honda? That old crow

couldn't swat a fly. Now Yonakawa, that man could hit. Knocked my head back against a wall once, and I was out! Nakasone wasn't bad, either."

"You've been hit a lot?"

He grinned sheepishly. "People say no student in the Ueno schools has been hit more than Hiro Araki."

Maggie's jaw dropped. "You're Araki-*san*?" A fabled name in the Ueno Lower School, one whispered breathlessly, down through the grades; Maggie couldn't remember when she'd first heard of him, but it was a name to conjure visions: a *ronin*, it was said—the rogue samurai they couldn't break. She stared, frozen by his presence.

Araki chuckled. "*Hai*—but not *san*, please. Hiro—first names among old friends, eh? And now we're old friends."

Maggie had never heard anything like it. It was unthinkable for a girl to call an older boy by his first name: a slapping offense in its own right. She gulped. "Thank you, Araki-*san*. I mean . . . Hiro. I am Campbell." Maggie bowed. Then, hesitantly, "But please . . . I would be so honored if you would call me . . . Megumi?"

She waited uneasily, concerned that she had presumed too much, but his answer, as his eyes roamed over her, took her by surprise. "You're the *yanki* I've heard about, hum? They say no one messes with you, and now I can see why."

Maggie felt her temperature rising. "Excuse me, but I'm not a *yanki*."

Hiro's eyebrows lifted. "Well, if you're not a *yanki*, what are you?"

"My father's American, but *I'm* Japanese."

He took in her wild coils of auburn hair; the big, elliptical green eyes and pink skin; the strong, outthrust jaw; and the Western nose, sprayed with freckles. He took in, too, the combative pose, the pugnacious tone, so unusual in a girl, particularly a girl confronting an older boy. He decided she was the most fascinating, unclassifiable, singular creature he'd ever seen. He laughed for the joy of their meeting and the improbability of her claim.

Not just a chuckle, either, but genuine, bent-from-the-waist spasms. Peals of them, as he struggled to recover the faculty of speech.

When he regained his composure she was looking at him loftily, as though she'd surprised him in the middle of an unseemly act. "I am, you know; I'm a Japanese citizen."

Her imperious glare checked the laugh that wanted to follow the others. "Think that little pansy slapping you would say you're Japanese?" he asked, arching his eyebrows.

Hauteur dissolved into confusion. "Of course he would. He knows I am."

"'Your kind knows no respect'?" He laughed again, a dry, knowing sound that infuriated her.

Her voice rose as she stepped toward him with her fists clenched. "I tell you I'm as Japanese as you are!" she hissed.

His laugh faded. His face assumed a tight smile, lasting no more than seconds, transmuting into an impassive mask. He started to say something, then checked himself. "Easy— I didn't mean anything. You want to be Japanese, be my guest."

His voice lightened, the edge evaporating into a banter. "But if you're so eager to be Japanese, you can call me Araki-*san*. Okay, Megumi-*chan?* Like good Japanese, eh? 'Mr. Araki' to you, 'Young Megumi' to me."

He invoked the titles mockingly, eyes sparkling. "Remember to use honorific Japanese when addressing me, too, because I'm older, and I'm a male. That's right, isn't it? Isn't that the way you've been taught, as a proper young Japanese girl?"

Gritting her teeth, she forced herself to answer: "Yes, Araki-*san*."

"Very good, Megumi-*chan*." He nodded. "But it's not so easy to be friends that way, is it? In fact, that's the whole point, don't you think—we're not *supposed* to be friends, you and I. You're a younger girl, I'm an older boy, and that's the end of that. Everybody in his or her place, and the language rules remind you what that place is. I think I prefer the American way. What about you?"

Thoughts, muddled, came at her too fast; finally, abruptly, she nodded.

"Good." His forehead furrowed. "Say—I bet you have a *yanki* name, don't you? Something they call you at home?"

Reeling, she tried to decide whether to answer such an impertinent question. Curiosity won. "Sometimes my parents call me . . . Maggie," she mumbled, adding hastily: "But no one else does."

"'Migi'?" He looked at her quizzically.

"No, no—*Maggie*." She made a bleating sound: "Aa, Aa. As in *magajin*."

"'Mag—gie.'" He formed the unfamiliar sound deliberately, drawing it out.

It seemed extraordinary to be hearing her American name on a stranger's lips, much less hearing it pronounced like two, separate nonsense words, and she giggled. Her cheek didn't hurt anymore.

"'Maggie.' Say it fast, like that. You make it sound . . . silly."

He bowed elaborately. "Very well—with your permission, I will call you . . . Maggie." He pronounced it adequately. "Or, if you prefer, Megumi-*chan* to my Araki-*san*. Which will it be—*yanki* way or *Nihon* way? Friends or big boy, little girl?" He folded his arms, smiling.

With the boys in her class she always felt in control; over the years they'd learned not to provoke her, and recently more and more of them seemed either totally unaware of their female classmates or so aware of them that they became hopelessly tongue-tied any time they were alone with a girl. Hiro Araki, though, kept throwing her off balance— one minute talking to her like an adult and the next patronizing her like a three-year-old. One minute intriguing, the next maddening.

It was on her mind to leave without another word when he added: "I've never had a friend named Maggie." He extended his right hand.

She stared at it; her own rose to meet it. Long fingers wrapped over hers. She had never shaken hands with a boy before.

She found her voice. "Please call me Maggie . . . Hiro."

He nodded decisively. "Good." As though expressing satisfaction at business settled, he again ran his eyes over her. "Say—how old are you?"

Maggie felt goose bumps forming on her arms. "Eleven," she said as casually as she could, adding, "but I'll be twelve soon." As soon as it tumbled out she was sorry.

He looked at her pose, laughed, and shook his head. "Too young for me, that way."

Her chest fell. Turning scarlet, she spun on her heel. His hand turned her back. "You're a prickly one, aren't you? I just meant"—he tried to find the right words, then gave up—"nothing. I'd like to be your friend. I'm sorry, okay? Friends?"

They looked at each other for several seconds before she nodded. "Sure. Friends."

"Good. Maybe someday soon you'll come to my mother's noodle parlor for *udon?* The Makino, over by the Daimyo

Clock Museum? Best noddles in Ueno. I bet your English is good, eh?"

He was putting her off pace again. "Not very good."

He cocked his head. "Now, Maggie. Is that the truth, or are you just being the polite little Japanese girl?"

His unblinking, direct way of looking at her, so unaccustomed, made her feel as though his gaze could see inside of her, and she shifted from foot to foot. "I . . . guess my English is pretty good."

"You guess?"

"All right! I speak English well. We speak it at home. Why do you keep asking me questions?" She stamped her foot. "What do you want from me?"

"The truth, Maggie, always the truth, between friends. And with yourself, eh? If you do something well, admit it." Without pausing he added, "Are you a good skater?"

She'd started to deny it when she saw the way he was looking at her. "Yes."

"Good. Now we're getting somewhere. Well, I'll never be a skater, but I'd love to improve my English. Would you be willing to speak it with me? My teacher never has us speak English, just lots of written stuff; I don't think he can speak it himself."

She hesitated, then nodded. "Sure . . . only I don't get a lot of free time." Afraid she sounded unaware of the honor his suggestion conferred, she added, "Because of my skating, I mean."

"Oh." He looked disappointed. "Well, maybe sometime. So long, Maggie."

Before she could stop herself Maggie blurted, "But we live right around the corner—would you . . . would you like to come in and have lunch with me? I have to hurry, but we could speak English, if you want."

The seconds before he answered seemed eternal, and then she heard, "I *would* like that. Thank you."

She stopped at her front door. "Does it show? Where he slapped me, I mean."

His hand, cool and dry, lingered on her cheek. "It's gone. No one will know."

They stood in the doorway after lunch. "Thank you," he said, "that was good. Next time we'll go to my mother's noodle parlor, okay?" He tilted his head, studying the brooding look she'd carried through the meal. "You're worried about Monday, aren't you? About what that little maggot Natsume might do?"

"I can't help thinking about it."

"You could have told your parents. They seem warm—they could talk to the principal."

She shook her head. "It would upset my mother. She's always asking me if everything at school's okay. She asks that a lot."

He tousled her hair. She liked the feeling. "Well, you may be worrying needlessly. Perhaps Natsume will realize he could lose face by behaving so unreasonably."

Maggie nodded forlornly. "Maybe."

"Sure. See if he doesn't have a much better attitude on Monday. Until the next time, then."

"Until the next time." She started to bow when she felt his hand on her upper arm, stopping her.

"*Yanki* style, eh?" He extended his hand, saying in labored English, "Good-bye, Maggie."

"Good-bye, Hiro."

His fingers slipped from hers. He turned and sauntered off in the direction of the school, whistling tunelessly, hands in his pockets.

* * *

The first thing Maggie did upon waking on Monday was take an inventory of every symptom of illness she'd ever heard of. She was crushed she could discern no sign of fever, sore throat, headache, or digestive trouble. Her stomach *was* in knots, but even if such a nonverifiable condition would buy her a day off, she'd only have to face Natsume *sensei* the following day. Reluctantly she forced herself to confront her fate.

Yet when she saw Teacher Natsume walking toward her in the hallway and she broke out in a cold sweat, he kept going, moving past her as though she were invisible. When she turned to look, the little man was drawing away from her at a near trot. She found it perplexing beyond words.

Later, as she was rushing home to exchange her book bag for skating gear, she encountered Hiro Araki. She rushed to tell him her news, but he was unimpressed.

"So, Maggie—how is your day . . . being?" Hiro's expression was placid, his tone relaxed. He raised his eyebrows quizzically. "Is my English correct?"

"Going. How is your day *going*. It's fine, thank you. Wonderful, really."

"Ah. Good. That is pleasing me."

"Pleases me. But the reason is, the most amazing thing happened! Natsume *sensei*—"

Hiro interrupted her. "You will be telling me, no, when I am wrong in English?"

Maggie waved her hand frantically. "Yes, but listen, please. Natsume *sensei* didn't do anything! He seemed not even to see me. What do you suppose that means?"

He shrugged. "As I said, perhaps he realized he could lose face, acting so foolish. That can be painful."

"But it's amazing he would change so fast, don't you think?" Maggie cocked her head, seeking confirmation.

"He is of no importance. Now, what is the English for . . ." He would entertain no more talk of Natsume *sensei*.

Chapter 19

December 2000: Tokyo

*H*e was looking at her the way he had in the schoolyard, and it made her shiver the way it had then. She heard herself chattering, words pouring out, and wondered if she was making any sense at all. "But how did you know I was here?" She swirled the cup of sake, grateful to have something to do with her hands, took a deep swallow, giddy, not caring if it put fifteen pounds on.

"I didn't, until I read in yesterday's *Asabi Shimbun* that you were back, working with Goto *sensei* and Mori-*san*."

Her jaw dropped. "*Asahi Shimbun* reported that I was training here? You must be joking."

"You didn't know?"

"I don't read the papers much."

"Well, my *yanki* is a celebrity. Here." He reached inside his pocket and pulled out a folded clipping.

She looked at it incredulously. There was a picture of her with Clay, the night they took the silver in the Nationals, and a large header: AMERICAN SKATER TRAINING IN JAPAN.

She scanned the clipping quickly. It was clear the newspaper thought it a great tribute to Japan that she was training under Goto and Mori. It wasn't nearly as clear—was almost lost in a maze of allusion and nuance, in fact—that she was a Japanese citizen who had grown up in Japan and left.

She laid the article on the table, shaking her head. "Five years ago I was going to be a disgrace to Japanese skating; now I honor it by coming back. I don't understand."

Hiro smiled. "Sure you do—it's the national inferiority complex. You made it in America, so you have to be good. Notice it says 'American skating star.' You can read the whole article and hardly know you're Japanese, but they'd probably make you head of the Japanese Figure Skating Association if you wanted."

"It's so strange." Everything else in Japan had gotten smaller since she'd left, but he was so much bigger. The low table between them seemed little more than an armrest for him as his eyes drank her in.

She thought how much courage it must have taken for him to have come to her. Looking away, she said, "My first day back I went to Ueno. I thought about coming to your mother's noodle parlor. But I was . . . ashamed. I didn't know how you'd . . . feel about seeing me." She forced herself to look at him. "I'm so sorry about what happened. The things I said."

He waved his hand. "You're back, that's all that matters. You were a young girl. You've grown up." His eyes roamed her face until, blushing, she looked away.

"Yes." Nervously she went on: "How are your mother and grandfather?"

"Grandfather is the same, only older." He shook his head. "Mother is gone—a stroke, four years ago."

"I'm sorry." Her hand closed on his. Guiltily, liking its warmth, she let it go. "She was so kind to me."

"Thank you. Yes, I miss her, but I think at the end, when she knew she was going, it was a relief. She was worn out— she'd worked long hours, and she was afraid all the time, that someone would guess our secret. Fear is exhausting. Now she needn't be afraid."

"She was a wonderful woman."

"She was. She loved you, you know. She missed you." He signaled the waitress, adding, "So did I."

When he'd ordered, he asked: "And your parents?"

"My father's dead—his heart. My mother's coping."

His face fell. "He was a good man. He was good to me."

"As your mother was to me. Like a second mother."

"I'm glad you felt this." He lightened. "I once said you were like a sister to me, remember?"

"I remember." She winced. "I was such a little ninny. I acted like a fool."

"You were young."

Her mouth tightened, then they were both speaking at once: "Tell me about . . ."

"What are you . . ."

They were laughing like children when the waitress put the fresh *tokkuri* of sake in front of them. When she left, he asked, "Why *did* you come back, Maggie?"

"It's a long story."

"I've waited a long time to hear your voice again. I wouldn't mind a long story."

She looked around the room, the second floor of a restaurant in Asakasa. There were three long, low tables and a stage at one end. The middle table was filled with people who didn't dress or act the way Maggie remembered anyone in Japan dressing or acting, though they were Japanese. Some of the men were in Hawaiian shirts and black denims held up with big, silver-buckled belts. Others, their eyes hidden behind sunglasses, had cropped hair and wore dark blue double-breasted suits with white neckties. The women, several bare-midriffed, laughed often, their arms draped around the man next to them. At one end of the table a young man, fat but powerful looking, had a black leather satchel from which he took a portable telephone from time to time. The satchel brimmed with yen notes, which the young man made no effort to conceal.

When Maggie and Hiro had arrived, several of the people at the middle table had called out to Hiro, beckoning him over, but he'd shushed them with a wave of his hand, taking her to a far corner. "Acquaintances of mine," was all he'd said. "Good people, but a little loud."

She looked at Hiro. His eyes were on her, black and gleaming, the little lances of light darting from under his long lashes the way she remembered, the upturned corners of his mouth as familiar as though she'd seen them the day before. Her hand shook as she held out the tiny *ochoku*.

She sipped the warm liquid, felt it slide down, relaxing her. She set down the cup, letting her fingertips play over the picture of Clay. "He's . . ." She stopped. "He *was* my skating partner. I love him." She drew a deep breath and began.

Finishing, she felt his disgust. "Criminal. And your friend was only trying to do the right thing." He made an angry sound, deep in his throat. *"Ano ama."*

"Yes, she's a bitch." Her fingers turned the cup, finding the flaw in the lip. "We had everything figured out. We were going to win the U.S. Nationals, you see, and we probably would have medaled in the Worlds in March. Plotov and Gagarin are retiring, and next year we'd have been favored to win the Olympics. I think we would have. A month after that, the World championship. Then Clay wanted us to skate professionally for a few years, do some endorsements and commercials, so we'd have all the money we needed."

She shrugged. "We worked so hard, and came so close. All over."

"So you go against her instead."

Maggie's eyes narrowed. "If everything works out, I will."

"It's so important to you, this medal?"

"Not just for me; it's also for Clay, and for my father."

"Your father?"

"He didn't know a Salchow from a sit spin, but he never begrudged the expense, and never missed a competition. I know he felt in some way . . . responsible for what happened to me here. Even after he got sick, and should have been in bed, he'd drag himself wherever we were competing. I promised him a medal. I mean to get it for him."

He nodded. "If will can do it, you'll win. I told you once before: My little *yanki* follows Bushido."

She snorted. "Will is necessary, but not sufficient; your little *yanki* wouldn't mind a triple Axel to go along with the Bushido."

"I'm sorry?"

"Just something I've been thinking about. The Axel's a triple jump, the hardest one. Only three or four women in the world have hit it, and Doe Rawlings's one of them. I don't know if I can." She held out her cup. "Now, what about you? I've given you my life story, it's your turn."

A commotion caused them to turn before he could respond. The man who'd been the center of attention at the middle table was mounting the stage. "Shh," Hiro said, "listen to this first. He's good."

Two of the waitresses had followed the big man, one carrying a stringed instrument, the other something like a flute.

When the man was comfortable behind the microphone, he nodded, and they began to play. After a few measures the man sang.

It was a strange, haunting sound. Soon the baritone voice was deep in Maggie's bones.

Hiro leaned over. "It's called 'Kyodai Gingi'—'Vows of Brotherhood.' It's about loyalty between men."

"It's beautiful," she whispered, "very sentimental."

"Yes, it is. We *yakuza* love it. We're very sentimental."

Maggie cheered as lustily as anyone at the end of the performance. Before the noise had subsided, she leaned over again. "What did you say?"

"I said: 'We *yakuza* love it.' That's what I am." He gestured toward the middle table. "That's what they are—the men, anyway. Come on—I'll introduce you."

"I can't believe it." They were sitting in a café near Chiako's apartment, drinking tea.

"That I'm a 'gangster,' as you Americans say?" He laughed. "This isn't the States; we don't go around shooting each other. We have an office with our seal on the door in Asakasa, there's a monthly magazine, and I carry business cards with my name and the *kumi*'s on them. Working on an assembly line's more dangerous, and the businessmen and politicians are more dishonest." He snorted. "I ought to know—we work for enough of them."

"But why did you become a *yakuza?* How?"

"By accident, really. At Tokyo University I studied cultural anthropology. I was interested in the way people live, how their cultural institutions develop. I was particularly interested in the *burakumin*."

"The Hamlet People," she said, remembering.

"Exactly. Remember what I told you, about my being one?"

She nodded. "I'll never forget our day in the country."

"Nor I. Well, after my mother died I stopped concealing it. I joined the BLL—the *Burakumin* Liberation League— became active in the *Burakumin* Students Association."

He shrugged, smiling. "When I graduated and applied for jobs, I quickly discovered that there was at least one class of student for whom Tokyo University diploma didn't open doors. I had classmates who hadn't read a book in four years who were showered with offers, while it became clear to me that I was going to be lucky to get a job as a ticket seller in the subway."

"How horrible."

He pulled a face. "I didn't see myself as a *sarariman* or bureaucrat anyway, so I was really just going through the motions. But I did need a job. While I was working for the BLL, I learned that the *yakuza* are one of the few Japanese institutions that don't care if you're *burakumin*, and I started visiting places they frequent. As you could see at the restaurant, they aren't hard to spot, and I got to know some easily enough. They were flattered, I think, that a Todai boy was interested in them. Really interested, I mean, not just titillated, the way most people are."

"Weren't your afraid?"

"A little at first, since you hear such wild stories. Then, after a few months, one of them, just a kid, really, tried me out."

"Tried you out?"

"You know—provoked me, to see what I was made of. Playground stuff, really."

"What happened?"

"I put up with it for a while, then I broke his nose. After

that, they treated me like a brother. The *oyabun,* the group leader, had an older man ask me if I'd be interested in joining the *kumi*—that's a group—sort of a clan, you might say. I thought, Why not? I figured I could always quit if I didn't like it, and it wasn't as though I was overwhelmed with other opportunities. I haven't been sorry."

"And what do you do? Can you tell me?"

"Nothing very exciting." He swirled his teacup. "I work with information."

"What does that mean?"

"Well, as you know, in Japan the face people present to the public is very important. Many will pay handsomely to make sure that the face they present puts them in the best possible light. I help them manage problems they might have with their public face if certain *lapses* in their private lives were to become known. You might call it public relations."

Maggie cocked her head dubiously. "In English the word would be blackmail, I think."

He repeated the word carefully, nodding appreciatively. "My *yanki* has come back, and she's giving me English lessons again."

He grew serious. "But before thinking too badly of me, you might consider this: You can't blackmail someone who has nothing to hide, who has done nothing wrong. Say a big executive pays off a politician in return for a government contract, and we find out; well, both the executive and the politician are crooks, robbing the public. We simply take some of their stolen money for ourselves. We punish them, in effect."

"You could report them."

"I think you have been in America too long. Here, what would happen? Some scandal, certainly. The businessman might have to pay a small fine, and he'd apologize. The politician would have to resign. That is what they pay to avoid. But nobody would go to jail, and the politician would keep the money he'd squirreled away. In a few years he'd be back in office, and the businessman would still have the profits from all the government contracts he'd bought."

Chuckling, he threw back his tea. "Besides, if we reported them, we would get no money, so we would have no incentive to find out about them in the first place, so there would be nothing to report, would there?" He turned up his palms.

Maggie wondered if she'd have had an answer if she hadn't drunk so much. "But don't people get hurt?" she asked.

"Innocent people? Let me tell you what happened a few months ago."

He poured more tea. "Two men from another *kumi* were sent to talk to a man who was breaking into cars to steal radios. He was hurting business in a whole neighborhood, and the businessmen asked the *yakuza* to stop him. The man fled, and the two *yakuza* foolishly gave chase in their car. Regrettably, they hit a person crossing the street. Well, the next day the leader of the *kumi* accompanied the two men to the police station, where they turned themselves in. The *kumi* settled a large sum on the injured man, and the two *yakuza* paid a fine, after visiting the victim and expressing their sorrow. No, Maggie—it is not like the States."

Hiro watched her struggle with it, leaning across the table with a smile on his face. "You asked me what I do; I hurt no one, I promise you. No honest person fears my visit."

"You make it sound so . . . reasonable."

His eyes shone. "In America, I would be a lawyer, no?"

She laughed. "But is it right for you? Are they people you're comfortable with?"

He shrugged. "There are all kinds. Many, certainly, have pretty rough edges. Some are quite well educated. But no one messes with anyone else in the *kumi,* so it doesn't really matter. And there's one big factor."

"What?"

"I'm judged by what I do, not what I am. I like that, and there aren't many places you can find that in Japan. No one cares that I'm *burakumin.* The *kumi* is one of the few places in Japan where a misfit can fit in. And don't tell me you don't understand the appeal of that, Maggie the *yanki.*"

"Because I'm a misfit."

"Thank the gods you are," he said. "If you weren't, I wouldn't have missed you so much."

She shifted nervously. "I'm too young for you, remember?" She smiled to show it was a joke.

Looking her over appreciatively, he said, "I don't think so. Not anymore."

"I . . ." She cleared her throat. "I love Clay. I'm here for both of us, and I'm here to work."

Now his smile was more like the one that used to infuriate her. "Then I will be doubly grateful for such time as you can spare me."

"Chiako-*chan,* who is that young man?" Madam Goto pointed her cane at the figure sitting halfway up the stands.

"His name is Araki, *sensei.*"

"Campbell seems to know him. I am certain I saw her wave."

"He is an old friend of hers, *sensei.* She asked if he could attend practice, and as you were not here, I took the liberty of telling her he could."

"He is distracting her! Look—just look." She jabbed the cane impatiently at the center of the rink. Chiako turned to see Maggie coming out of a cross-foot spin, a blue blur as her arms rose overhead. She finished with an exaggerated flourish.

Nervously, Chiako nodded. "That is a difficult spin, *sensei*—I could never do it."

"She is grinning like a fool, showing off for the young man!"

Maggie struck off. After half a dozen strokes she was speeding diagonally down the rink. Another skater had put on music from *Carmen,* and Maggie began to strut, matador-style, twitching her hips, waving her arms coquettishly. She ended with butterflies, landing them as lightly as a real butterfly. She came to rest, panting, against the boards beneath Hiro. "Well?" they heard her call. "Think the bull's ready?" She put her hand behind her head, batting her eyes.

Chiako blanched. "You are right, *sensei*—he *is* distracting her."

Madam Goto rapped her cane sharply on the floor. "I won't have him up there!"

"I will ask him to leave, *sensei*." Chiako bowed and started up the steps.

Madam Goto's bark stopped her. "Leave? I don't want him to leave. I want him down here."

"Here, *sensei?*"

"Of course. The joy is back."

Chiako looked at Maggie uncertainly. "She does seem more animated, *sensei*. Yet she said he was just . . . a friend." She wrung her hands. "She has a young man in America, *sensei*."

"And that means she cannot respond to another? Bah— you sound older than I am, Chiako-*chan*. Perhaps she does not even know."

She rapped her cane impatiently. "Come—let them gabble a while. Seeing her skate that way has given me an idea for her long program. If we can capture the simple joy, the simplicity of line she was displaying . . . A child's spontaneity in a woman's body, with her skills, well . . ." She trailed off, mumbling.

Chiako had to hurry to keep up with the suddenly animated old woman. She almost ran her over when the *sensei* stopped abruptly, looking back pensively. "I thought there might have been a young man before—for a time the girl carried on like a sick calf. I wonder . . ." She shook her head, grunted, and hurried off.

Chapter 20

April 1993: Tokyo

*Y*ou are six minutes late, Megumi-*chan*."

Madam Goto was in a foul mood when Maggie got to the rink. She stood ramrod straight, all four feet eleven inches of her, tapping her watch and glaring. "This is the fourth time."

"I'm sorry, Goto *sensei*."

"If you have lost interest, if you are no longer prepared to work, to exhibit perseverance, you will never be a skater. *Gaman*, Megumi-*chan*, always *gaman*. Ceaseless perseverance is the only way!"

Maggie had heard it dozens of times in the last months. "*Hai*, Goto *sensei*. Please forgive me." She laced on her skates as quickly as she could.

"You will never realize your potential. You have started—"

"*Hai*, Goto *sensei*."

"—treating skating as though it were a hobby, like origami. It is a way of life, not a hobby, Megumi-*chan*. If you want a hobby, fold paper cranes."

"*Hai,* Goto *sensei.* Excuse me." She scrambled to her feet. "May I please start my warm-ups, Goto *sensei?*"

"Very well, but I hope you are prepared to work today. We have had some very careless practices recently. Careless practice habits . . ."

Maggie could recite the lecture in her sleep. "Lead to careless competitions."

She began with a series of stretching exercises, using the boards that surrounded the rink as an exercise bar, hooking the heel of first one and then the other skate over the top of the boards and lowering her forehead to her knee.

While she stretched, she brooded. Setsuko had recently seen Ryoko kissing a boy from the high school; it seemed to Maggie that if she was going to get chapped lips, that would be a more interesting way than getting them from the cold dry air of the skating rink.

It would be different if she were training to enter the Nationals, maybe; certainly if she were competing as a senior. She doubted becoming the junior ladies' champion of the Hokkaido Winter Festival, which was the next event Madam Goto had her entering, would give her as much pleasure as Ryoko was having. Her forehead smacked her knee.

Wincing, she unhooked her leg and received permission for warm-up laps. She began a series of crossovers, her body knowing what to do while she put her mind to other things.

She replayed recent conversations with Hiro Araki, concentrating more on the impressions than the words. She did not find them altogether unpromising. True, he was seventeen to her thirteen, but that wasn't necessarily an unbridgeable gap. She knew what it was to have an older boy look at her with as much interest as he might show a rock; that was not, she was certain, the look she was receiving from Hiro. The possibilities excited her. A scratchy rendition of

Tchaikovsky's First Piano Concerto, one of her favorites, was blaring over the loudspeaker, and she tried to give herself up to the music.

"Do not bounce your arms, Megumi-*chan!* They must be relaxed, but steady!" Goto *sensei* didn't raise her voice as Maggie sped by, but somehow Maggie always heard; sometimes she wondered if the woman had really spoken at all, or if after almost six years she could simply read her mind. She adjusted her arms fractionally, switching to back crossovers before slamming to a T-stop a few feet from the impassive *sensei* and removing her warm-up jacket. She'd started to perspire, and the cold felt good on her arms.

"We need more work on the combination, Megumi-*chan.* You have been releasing your left arm too soon. That is why you singled your loop the other night."

Maggie stroked hard, circling the great rink, one, two, three . . . seven hard strokes, arms pistoning, then executing a quick three turn, three back crossovers, then the setup: gliding backward on her right foot, arms slightly away from her sides. Lean over to assume a strong outside edge, reach the left free foot back, *plant* the left toe pick, *push* with the right leg, *pull* your arms in, *hold* them there. Hearing Goto *sensei:* "Don't lift your shoulders, keep your ankles crossed, your body vertical, or you'll fall!"

She had timed it so that the jump occurred just as the orchestra struck the first rising note after the four falling notes that formed the concerto's signature—exactly the way she would have liked Hiro to see it. The effect was dramatic.

She liked to think of it as an explosion launching her toward the roof thirty feet overhead, but actually all that happened was that the energy of her backward travel was transferred through the thrusting right leg, aided by the pole-vaulting effect of the extended left leg, into vertical motion, so that the one hundred pounds that had been traveling horizontally at twenty miles an hour were redirected upward.

It was supposed to be a triple toe loop/double loop combination. The force of her takeoff and the strength of her legs gave her plenty of altitude, but once again she opened her arms a fraction too soon in the first jump, braking the speed of her rotation so that she had to fight to make two complete turns before landing. Still, she did manage a solid double and had enough momentum remaining to spring off the ice again, into the double loop. After two clean revolutions she landed, the toe of her left foot at a forty-five-degree angle above the ice. For a few dizzying beats, she had felt magic.

The sequence had taken no more than seconds. Hands on hips and breathing hard, she glided over to the boards. As soon as she saw the scowling face she knew that what had been beautiful was about to be ruined.

"You set up long enough for the audience to fall asleep. Do you think you're a dying swan? You struggled to make the jump because you haven't been doing your exercises, and your arms might as well be jellyfish. You cheated on your takeoff edge, and the judges will see the ice crystals and know you two-footed your first landing as easily as I did. Do it again."

"Again, Goto *sensei?*"

"*Hai! Kata,* Megumi-*chan, kata.* Endless repetition. Like kabuki. Again! And this time, no music." She reached over and clicked off the tape recorder. Instantly the hall seemed lifeless.

"No music, *sensei?*"

"No music. Let your skating be the music."

"But *sensei*—"

"Enough! Now skate." The taskmistress folded her arms across her chest, waiting.

Maggie felt a drumming in her head, louder and louder. It sounded like the subway station just before the train arrived, the same sense of rising pressure, of power, of potential danger. It burst forth from her mouth, as with a great roar the *chika-tetsu* burst out of the mouth of the subway tunnel. "No, *sensei*. I won't skate without music."

The words were out before Maggie could stop them, and then she was glad. Her arms came up, and she was locked in the same pose as her teacher, staring back at the woman who had held her in thrall for years. Her jaw jutted out. "Without the music, there is no point. I have to *feel* it. It is not just a matter of perfect movements. I have to feel it in . . . here." Her hand felt the pounding heart. "If I can't compete seriously, there must at least be beauty, or there is no point. I am tired of pointless exercises. I have to *skate, sensei!* Or I will . . . quit."

She felt her anger, the dark eyes sucking it out of her, and she rushed on, before it was exhausted. "Goto *sensei* doesn't understand. Goto *sensei* hasn't felt . . ." Her voice trailed off into a whisper. "My *sensei* doesn't know."

Madam Goto's lined face paled, her eyes closed. When she opened them she unfolded her arms, reached a hand into her pocket. "Megumi-*chan*—come here!" When Maggie hesitated, she repeated gently, "Come here; I have something to show you."

Slowly, warily, Maggie approached her. She'd seen coaches beat their charges with a skate guard for infractions far less serious than hers.

"Sit down." Sighing, Madam Goto patted the wood next to her. "Here, please." Infinitely tired, she tapped the worn surface. "It's all right."

Tentatively Maggie sat, her hands holding her weight as though readying herself to flee.

"Let me show you something." Madam Goto's birdlike hand pulled a small black leather case out of her pocket. Arthritic fingers pried open the medal clasp and opened the case. She looked at the contents, then held out the case for Maggie's inspection.

It contained a yellowing photograph of a young man in a white military uniform. He sat stiffly against a studio backdrop, his hands resting on the handle of a sword. He stared straight ahead, expressionless, yet the artless picture had captured the life in his eyes.

Inside the right-hand side of the case, beneath cracked celluloid, was a small lock of black hair. Under the hair was an inscription on a little square of paper.

Maggie looked at her teacher with raised eyebrows. At her nod she picked the case out of Madam Goto's hands.

The minute brushstrokes had faded, but Maggie could follow them. She read, in a soft, wondering voice: "Having a dream, I will go up into the sky."

She looked up slowly, feeling as though a hand were clamped on her throat. "What does it mean, *sensei?*" she whispered.

"Nothing." The gnarled fingers reached out and rested briefly on the picture. "And everything." She paused, her mouth tightening. She snorted. "Forgive me. That's an old woman's nonsense." Her fingers closed over the case and withdrew it from Maggie's hands. She drew it to her, looked once, closed it slowly. "It is a young man I knew."

She nodded. "A young man I was to marry. Only the war came, and he was a naval aviator. Toward the end he volunteered for a Special Attack Squadron—the 'Wind of the Gods,' they were called—kamikaze. It was a great honor to be selected." She paused, looking at the case. "Or so they said."

Her hands rubbed the little memory case. "When he flew for the last time, he left this behind for me. I was twenty-two. What the words mean . . . well, perhaps one thing to one, something else to another."

"*Sensei*, I . . ." Maggie felt her heart was coming to a stop. "I'm so sorry for what I said."

Madam Goto fluttered her hand. "It is no matter. I only wanted you to see that I *do* know. I know what young hearts need. I know what happens to hearts starved of magic."

Tears trickled down Maggie's face. "*Sensei*, I only meant—"

"It is all right, Megumi-*chan;* when we first recognize beauty, we all believe it is something *we* discovered. Each generation *must* believe that, because that is part of the beauty—part of its power."

Maggie wiped the back of her hand across her eyes. "I didn't know."

Madam Goto placed her tiny hand on Maggie's. "I remember a little girl. I wasn't going to accept any more students, but then a mother brought me this little girl and I watched her skate. She was a fine skater for her age, with good balance and good edges. But what made me take this little girl wasn't her skill—it was the fire inside her. I could feel it, and it warmed my bones. I thought: This girl will skate through the boards if I challenge her to. This girl will skate over me if I get in her way. I *want* this girl. I was selfish, you see.

"But fire alone isn't enough." Her hand, surprisingly strong, clamped on the large one under it. "Or perhaps it is too much. The fire has to last a lifetime; I could not live with myself if I let a pupil spend it all on a few years of skating, as too many coaches do. I have tried to show you how to focus the fire, control it, so it lasts and does not burn out.

"You are not yet fourteen. Too young, I've told myself, to be faced with the pressure of senior competition. Your bone plates are still forming; the demands of a senior program can do great damage. So I have held you back." She sighed, her shoulders sagging. "These last months, I sensed perhaps I had gone too far, smothered the fire. Fires need air, and perhaps I did not allow enough. Perhaps my old eyes were too weak to see that the little girl had left me, that it was a young woman I was keeping down. I should have trusted you more."

Maggie struggled to find her voice, but when words finally came, they came in a tumble. "I need to skate, Goto *sensei, really* skate, not just practice and enter . . ."

She stopped, unsure how far she could go, but Madam Goto helped her. "You may say it—unchallenging competitions, *ne?*"

Gratefully Maggie nodded. "*Hai.* I need to go as far as I can as a skater. I need . . ." She shook her head hopelessly. "I *want* something," she gasped. "It seems to be growing inside of me. I have to find it." She clasped her hands, released them hopelessly. "But I don't even know what it is."

Madam Goto looked down at the leather case lying in her lap. When she turned to Maggie she was smiling, a small, faraway smile. She took Maggie's hands in hers, shaking them gently. "Of course you want something. You want to *be* the music. You want to feel as though you are making the music, that it and you are one. That is why you skate." A small, dry, indulgent sound escaped.

"Yes," Maggie whispered, "yes!" She looked up in wonder. "But how do you know?"

"I, too, have known what it is to want that."

"Did you . . ." Maggie bit her lip. "Forgive me."

"Did I ever have it happen? Did I ever become the music?"

"I am sorry. I have no business asking."

"It is a fair question." A gnarled hand patted Maggie's knee. "Yes, it happened to me. I knew it once. Only once. But I'll never forget."

"What were you skating, *sensei?*"

"I was not skating."

"Oh." The thing inside Maggie turned. She bit her lip, so that she would have a pain she understood. "Is it wrong to want this? Am I foolish?"

"'Foolish'? No, no, child—why else should you skate? Why else should you live? If you wanted less, I would not keep you. Fame, money, pretty trophies . . . I would not train a person with your gifts who skated for these. I *know,* you see—that is why I showed you this." She nodded at the little case. "Your time will come. You will dance your dance, make your music."

"But when, *sensei?*" She clutched the thin bones of her teacher's hands. "When?"

"Soon, perhaps. But first you must be ready. You say you want to go as far as you can as a skater, but you must be prepared to go farther than you can skate. When the skating is over, there will still be far to go. The magic, the music, they are in many things. Skating is not the first among them—far from it. And if the *kami* should decide you should not find them in one thing, you must be ready to find them elsewhere."

Maggie whispered wonderingly, "My mother said you taught her that—that it was thanks to you that she found what she wanted in life. That it had nothing to do with skating."

"I am glad. I would have failed her if I had taught her things that ceased having value the day she was hurt."

Madam Goto shook her head, smiling. "She was a marvelous skater, though; so graceful. I can see her as though it were yesterday." She chuckled fondly. "I knew, when your mother came to me as an eleven-year-old, that I was being given the chance to work with the best skater I would ever have."

She stood, taking Maggie's face between dry palms. "I just didn't know she would make me wait almost twenty more years to get that skater." Her hands fell to her sides. "Rest for a few minutes. This has not been easy for you."

She started to walk away, then turned back. Maggie was sitting, slumped over, hearing the words again. "I would not get too comfortable, though—five minutes, and then patch." The old tone had returned.

"Patch, Goto *sensei?*"

"Certainly. You have lost your edge control. You have been skating like a novice. Figures may teach you how to control your edges again." She looked down expressionlessly.

Maggie straightened. "Which patch, *sensei?*"

Something lightened in the old woman's face. "Number ten. Waltz eights. They will remind your body about edge control. And I expect to see only true edges, no?"

"*Hai, sensei.*" Maggie stood.

"Good night, daughter."

"Good night, Goto *sensei.*" Maggie bowed low, wondering if she had heard right. By the time she looked up, the little woman was already walking toward another pupil.

The following Monday Maggie arrived early, eager to work, but Madam Goto's expression suggested that the retribution she had miraculously escaped at the time of her rebellion had merely been deferred. The *sensei* stood with her arms folded across her chest, scowling ominously as Maggie approached.

"I have withdrawn you from the Hokkaido Winter Festival, Megumi-*chan*," she growled.

Maggie kept her face and voice emotionless, though her stomach was twisting. "*Hai*, Goto *sensei*."

"After all, you are too good for that, isn't it so?"

"*Sensei*, I—"

"In any case, you will not be ready."

"*Hai, sensei.*" Maggie hung her head; this would be her last day skating.

A bony finger gestured toward the ice. "Well, get stretched and warm up—there is much to do."

"*Hai, sensei*. What does Goto *sensei* desire that I work on?" Maggie asked listlessly as she bent to put on her skates.

"The serpentine step sequence, of course."

Maggie looked up uncertainly. "Excuse me, *sensei,* but what serpentine step sequence? I don't have a serpentine in my program."

"Exactly. But you must have, if you are to pass your senior test. Which is why you will not skate in Hokkaido. The next time you compete, it will be as a senior. When that is depends on you."

Maggie tried to digest Madam Goto's edict as she warmed up, stroking the figures automatically, lost in wonder, her body and some unconnected part of her brain directing her skates while she repeated, over and over. "I'm going to be a senior!"

* * *

Three mornings a week Hiro met Maggie at a gym tucked behind Ueno Station, as he had ever since Maggie passed her senior test, a month shy of her fourteenth birthday. Double jumps—and the Axel only had to be a single—were enough to qualify as a senior; they weren't enough to win as one. For that she would need a double Axel, four or five triple jumps, triple triple combinations, and the stamina to land those jumps three and a half minutes into a four-minute program.

The workouts grew less oppressive over time. After a while Maggie even found herself looking forward to the five-thirty alarm. Still drowsy, carrying a gym bag with her school clothes in it, she would slip out of the still-sleeping house. Threading the quiet alleyways, startling cats, nodding to homeward-bound night workers, she walked to the gym.

She arrived in sweat clothes, ready to go as soon as she gulped down a cup of scalding tea from the urn by the door. Then they went to work.

Hiro waited until their second week at the gym to show Maggie what working out meant. The first few times they worked out together he'd said nothing as Maggie, after half a dozen repetitions with a lightly loaded bar, used all the strength remaining in her quivering arms to press it into his waiting hands. The following Monday he looked down at her as she lay on her back on the bench. "Ready?" The bar he put into her hands had twice as much weight as before.

Her eyes widened as the unexpected weight dropped the bar to her chest. "That's too much—I can't hold it," she gasped.

He stood at her head, looking bored. "I thought you said you were serious about working out."

She struggled to lift the bar. As the backs of her hands

pressed down into her chest, she could hardly breathe. "I am, but—"

"No 'but'! You've got ten repetitions in you. Now do them."

She felt panic as she imagined her arms giving way, the bar crushing her sternum. "I can't. Take it, please!"

"You can," he insisted.

"No—really. It's too heavy!"

"I won't let it hurt you."

"I can't, I tell you!"

"Oh, all right. Stop blubbering like a baby." She saw disgust on his upside-down face. "I should have known I'd be wasting my time coming here with a girl. Well, it won't happen again. All right—here." He reached for the bar.

He watched her eyes narrow. She inched the bar up, lowered it, inched it up again. Between each lift she grunted its number.

On the ninth repetition he placed the bar on the rack.

"What are you doing?" she panted. "I'm not done."

"You're done. Knowing when to quit is as important as knowing when not to quit. Save something for the next set. Here." He held out a pair of dumbbells, holding them in one hand as though they were weightless. "Take a minute, then let's see three sets of ten with these. Reverse curls—I'll show you how." He placed the dumbbells at her feet, then picked up another, much heavier set.

He sat on a bench, curling first one and then the other of the dumbbells as he talked. "You see, girl, it wasn't your arms that were tired, it was your will. People are used to quitting when something starts to hurt. If you train yourself to keep going *through* the pain, you're going to leave a lot of people behind."

Maggie glowered at him. "That was too much weight."

"I know." He nodded.

"You knew? Then, why—"

"Because you've been babying yourself. Pretending you're working when you're not. Quitting when the going got a little rough. Acting like a girl's expected to act."

"I *am* a girl."

"Sure—but *you* decide what that means, no one else. What it means to be a girl, what it means to be Japanese, what it means to be you. Don't let other people define you."

He looked down at his forearm, veins pulsing above the pumping tricep. "You weren't taking the last two or three lifts, and they're the only ones that really matter. Now you know you can do a lot more than you thought, right?"

"I could have been hurt," she said, pouting.

He shrugged complacently. "That was a risk I was willing to take." Only the sweat beading his forehead showed how hard he was working.

"That *you* were willing to take?"

"Sure." His teeth were clenched. "You get hurt, I lose my chance to coach a champion. I wouldn't want that."

She picked up her dumbbells. "Like this?" She started curling the weights, one after the other, glaring at him over the top of her fists.

"Like that." He nodded, grunting. "Just like that. Like a champion. Just one more than the next girl, and you'll be the champion. You're good, Maggie—you're the best. Say it. Say, 'I'm the best.' In English, if the Japanese in you isn't comfortable with it. Each curl, 'I'm the best.' With me, now. 'I'm the best.'"

"It's embarrassing."

"It's the truth, damn it. If you don't believe it, why should some judge? Now: 'I'm the . . .' "

"Best." Catching Hiro's rhythm, Maggie swung first one

and then the other dumbbell up toward her chin. "I'm the best. I'm the *best*. I'm . . ." Soon her dark sweat stains matched his.

"Thank you," she mumbled, leaving the gym after showering, unwilling to meet his eye. He acknowledged her concession with a quick squeeze of her biceps. She couldn't lift her arms the next day, but she never quit again.

On the two weekday mornings she didn't work out, and on Saturday evenings, Maggie went to a ballet studio in Shinjuku. There she went through a barre for thirty minutes, followed by a half hour of floor exercises. She also got a choreographer, a former member of the Kirov Ballet, who worked with Madam Goto on Maggie's new programs, agonizing endlessly over hand placement and arm movement.

After a few months Maggie felt lighter on her feet, more catlike and supple. She could feel herself growing stronger. The soreness that had made the first few weeks of the new regime agony every time she moved faded into a feeling of taut bounciness, and whether she really was stronger or merely thought she was, her jumps started showing more height, better control. She stopped worrying that she was going to develop grotesque muscles and simply rejoiced in the feeling that she was bending her body to her will. Boring spells in the classroom were met with reveries about skating, music, and the way Hiro Araki's shirt looked when he was doing pull-ups. Her friends wondered why she so often had a silly little smile on her face; she met their inquiries with shrugs and a silly little smile.

One day Madam Goto took her to a tea house in lieu of practice. They crawled through the tiny entrance and entered a room that might have come straight from the sixteenth century. For two hours the tea master, a follower of the

Omote Senke school, conducted the *chanoyu* with movements so spare and economical that when the teacup appeared in Maggie's hands, it was as though by magic. Afterward, whenever Maggie would get carried away and her movements began to seem florid, Madam Goto would call out: "Tea, tea!"

Time passed, faster than Maggie would have thought possible. Soon she felt as though the collegial discussions with Madam Goto and the choreographer, the smell of sweat, the feel of muscles worked to exhaustion, the sound of grunts and clanging metal, had always been part of her life.

That winter she entered the Japanese Senior Ladies' Figure Skating Championship and captured the silver medal. *Japan Skates* covered the story under the headline MOVE OVER, OLD LADIES—HERE COMES TROUBLE! At the head of the column was a picture of a beaming fifteen-year-old girl.

Chapter 21

December 2000: Tokyo

C hiako, clutching a black notebook, sat down next to
Maggie, the *sensei* standing behind her. "Megumi-
chan—we have been giving it much thought, and we have
the outline of your programs to propose. Would you care to
review them?"

It was all Maggie could do not to snatch the notebook out
of the *joshu*'s hands. Several minutes passed without a
sound. Finishing, she looked up, confused. "The short program is interesting, *sensei*."

"The short program is what the rules require, no more.
You will make it interesting. And the long?"

Maggie looked down doubtfully. "It is . . . different, I
think, but . . . ." She stopped, afraid to continue.

"Hai?" Madam Goto nodded. "You may say it."

Maggie's fingers played over the notebook. "The long
program—it is so . . . simple. So . . . easy, I suppose I would
say. I see only one jump combination."

The old woman scowled. "That is all the rules require."

"Yes, but . . ." She looked at Chiako helplessly, but the *joshu* said nothing. "And only four triple jumps."

"That is all there will be time for."

"But the others will have six or seven."

"Yes, and they'll look like a flea circus."

Maggie's fingers moved over the page, as though the program were written in braille. "And all the connecting steps, and turns, and arabesques—shouldn't we drop some of them, and put in more jumps and spins? How much weight can such a program be given? I am capable of much more. Or have my skills deteriorated so much?" Her voice cracked.

The old woman rested her hands on the handle of her cane. "Megumi-*chan,* listen to me." She spoke sympathetically. "The program will evolve, of course, as we see how the pieces fit together in practice. But as I envision it, it will be the most challenging program I have ever devised. Simple, yes. But easy? No. And I do not believe there is another skater in the world who could execute it."

Maggie studied the notes, thinking perhaps she'd missed something. "If you will forgive me, *sensei,* my program when I was sixteen was more challenging."

"No! Your program then was more *complicated,* not more challenging. Five years ago, as good as you were, you could not have done well with this program. You lacked the maturity, the grace. You needed the jump combinations and spins because you moved over the ice like a girl. A very capable girl, to be sure, but you weren't ready to skate *simply.*"

"I don't understand, *sensei.*"

"Think of our art, our food. We say: 'Hide nothing. Take the most perfect material obtainable, and let it be itself. Do to it only what displays its essence, never what obscures or masks.' When I practiced *ikebana,* if I found a perfect iris, that alone would be my arrangement; when I had inferior flowers to work with, I had to make more complicated arrangements."

"But—"

"You can be that perfect flower. You say that program is easy. It is not, I assure you. It will require every ounce of your discipline, and more work than you can imagine. You will learn how to sustain an arabesque longer, and more steadily, than any skater in history; your catch foot will look like statuary. The spins and jumps will be a textbook, each finishing as though to say: 'There.' That program is a celebration of skating as it once was, and should be. It has enough difficulty, but most important, it has *beauty*. It will give you your chance to be music. Now think about what I have said; look again at the outline. And think of the music you wish to become. We will be back later for your answer."

Maggie hadn't moved when Madam Goto and Chiako returned. Madam Goto came right to the point. "Have you reached a decision about the long program?"

"*Hai!* I came to you because there is no one whom I trust as well. I put myself in your hands; please forgive me for doubting."

"It was understandable." The light of combat was in her eyes. "Very well, then; let us start immediately." She rubbed her hands together impatiently.

"Certainly, *sensei*. But with respect, there are two additional considerations I have."

"Oh?"

"First, I wish permission to begin competing as soon as possible. The Nagasaki Prefectural Open, perhaps."

Chiako raised her eyebrows. "So soon? But it is impossible—you won't even have the jumps and spins set, much less the choreography."

"I know. But it has been a long time since I competed in singles. I must get the feel back, and I need the pressure of competition."

Madam Goto looked skeptical. "You will do poorly."

"I will, at first. But I can do my best. And as the *joshu* reminded me recently, that is why we skate. The placement is incidental."

Madam Goto nodded, chuckling. "The student has the best of us there, Joshu. Very well. You said there were two considerations—what is the other one, please?"

"It is with the long program—you have me opening with a triple lutz."

"Yes. By placing your most difficult jump first, we tell the judges the rest of the program is simple because we wish it to be so, and not because you cannot do more."

"With the *sensei*'s permission, I wish to open with the Axel instead."

"But the double Axel is not as difficult as the triple lutz."

"No, *sensei*, but the *triple* Axel is far more difficult than the triple lutz. I wish to open with a triple Axel, not the triple lutz."

"You do not have a triple Axel, thank the gods."

"No, *sensei*, but I wish to."

Chiako stared as Madam Goto's nostrils flared. "What foolishness—the few women who have had the Axel haven't won the Olympic gold; they build their programs around their one trick, and the rest of their skating suffers."

"Excuse me, *sensei*, but Doe Rawlings is no one-trick act. She is a great skater. She is the American champion, and soon, I believe, she will be World Champion. She lands triple Axels, and I must have one, or I cannot hope to win, no matter how well I skate otherwise, for she is strong in all elements."

"This is what your years in America have done! I am surprised you don't want to skate naked; that would get attention, *ne?*" The old woman quivered with indignation.

Chiako, seeing Maggie's mouth start to open, cleared her throat nervously. "*Sensei,* it is no doubt true that the Axel would say, more powerfully than the triple lutz, that what follows reflects Megumi-*chan*'s art, not any technical limitations."

The old woman whirled, glaring at her *joshu.* "The Axel is an abomination in woman's skating! It is a man's jump that a few women with freak bodies can achieve, while beautiful skaters are penalized because nature did not endow them with an unnatural musculature. Little girls are tempted to take drugs just so they can perform tricks the gods never meant them to perform. In a woman's program the triple Axel is the symbol of all that is wrong with the art."

"Exactly, *sensei.*" Chiako bowed repeatedly. "Exactly. And if Megumi-*chan* is able to open with the Axel, in effect the rest of the program becomes a statement: See the contrast, see what woman's skating has become and what it was and could be again. See that we should avoid the extremes, not because we cannot do them, but because beauty lies in nuance, not in raw displays of power."

Maggie added softly, "Please, *sensei;* let me try. I must not fail for want of a jump. I will—"

The two young women jumped as the cane slammed down on the rail. "Absurd! I would sooner train a donkey to dance!" The old woman hobbled out of the arena, her breath leaving dragon plumes in the frosty air.

The next morning Maggie and Chiako found Madam Goto already perched in her seat by the rail when they arrived. She glared at them icily as, nervously, they approached, bowing.

"Absurd!" she announced, ignoring their greeting.

Chiako was abject. "*Sensei,* please forgive me. I had no business speaking as I did. It was—"

A harsh bark interrupted her: "What! You expect me to forget that you questioned my judgment? *Ignore* what you said?"

"*Sensei,* I am sorry." Maggie rushed to intervene. "It is all my fault. Please do not think ill of Mori-*san.* I will—"

"Silence! I will not hear any more!" The old black eyes blazed, the sagging cheeks flushed. Madam Goto's mouth worked soundlessly, her chest rose and fell furiously. Maggie thought she might be having a heart attack.

"Absurd!" She began to speak, almost to herself. "I am an absurd, arrogant old woman. When you are old you forget that children grow up; Megumi-*chan* is not a girl anymore, and I should not have forgotten that she is hardly a creature of whims. Chiako-*chan,* what you said makes sense. I thought about it a great deal, and I would be a fool to assume I held all truth about skating. You were right to speak as you did. If I'm too old to learn, I'm too old to teach."

She nodded magisterially, rising to her feet. "Very well, daughter, we will attempt to give you the Axel. If you can develop one, we will substitute it for the lutz."

She scowled, eyebrows beetling ominously. "Of course, it will do you no good to land the Axel if it takes so much out of you that you destroy the rest of your program."

"I know, Goto *sensei.* I can only try. If it does not happen, *shikata ga nai.* It can't be helped."

Maggie began working on her programs, running through the elements, talking with Madam Goto and Chiako about music and choreography. By the time of the Nagasaki Prefectural Open, though Maggie had to improvise her choreography, the only truly embarrassing part of her performance was the spectacular fall she took opening her long program. Observers weren't sure what she'd been attempting, but whatever it was, the result was quite amusing. Even Maggie smiled as she picked herself up and skated on. The competition had not attracted a top field, and Maggie finished eighth in a field of thirty, and fairly content.

Every afternoon, after her regular practice was over, Maggie stayed on to work on the Axel. Madam Goto, as though it were too painful to watch, took that as her cue to leave.

Chiako was watching intently, occasionally calling out a suggestion. When Hiro Araki arrived she was chewing her thumb nervously. She wore a worried frown, but lightened when he joined her. Like many Japanese, Chiako thought the *yakuza* quite romantic, the modern equivalent of the samurai, and enjoyed teasing Maggie about her "mighty outlaw." She wasn't sure Maggie knew it, but whenever he appeared, she seemed to skate with more élan, so Chiako was glad to see him.

Maggie hit the ice with a sound like a fish being slapped on a slab at Sukiji, picked herself up, circled for another attempt.

"Why is it so hard, *Joshu?*" Hiro asked.

"It's the only jump entered skating forward. Since you land backward, it requires an extra half turn in the air. The other triples are three turns, the triple Axel three and a half. Few women have been able to achieve the necessary height. Regrettably, Campbell-*san* isn't one of them, so far."

Maggie was wearing a T-shirt and leotards. She's so slender, Hiro thought, like the willow tree. Slender and pliant.

When the *taifu* has blown out, the willow stands; the oak has fallen.

Each time she fell he felt a tremor in his spine. How can that slight body take such a beating? he wondered. Each time she picked herself up, slapped ice crystals off her leotards, and slowly gathered speed for another attempt.

Chiako made a low, growling sound in the back of her throat. "I worry she will hurt herself. The pressure on the landing foot is terrible. When you see it on tape, in slow motion, the foot is so bent, almost to a right angle with the leg. If the muscles are not strong enough, the ankle can snap. That would be the end of her dream."

He watched, fascinated and apprehensive, as Maggie's back crossovers built her speed. She turned, stepped forward on her left foot, twisted to her left, and brought her right foot forward as though determined to kick the ceiling. Her arms flew up and in, and into the air she rose, spinning counterclockwise. It happened so fast, he couldn't follow her movements, much less count the turns, but he could almost feel the impact when she landed, her foot skittered over the ice, and she collapsed in a heap.

Chiako shook her head. "Your upper body is getting ahead of your hips, Campbell-*san*," she called out. She stepped onto the ice and twisted her shoulders. "You are swinging your takeoff. You can't start to turn until you're in the air."

Maggie struggled to her feet, muttering to herself. Then she repeated the process—time, after time, after time. Almost always she fell.

On those occasions when she finished upright Chiako invariably murmured, "Doubled," while Maggie skated in a tight circle, looking down at the ice as though it were disappointing her. When she finally gave up she let Hiro ease her out of her skates and onto the motorcycle, grimacing as she settled onto the seat. She fell asleep while he was talking to her over tea. The next morning Chiako had to help her up from her futon. Her left ankle was swollen and stiff, her right hip bore a blue-black bruise the size of a plate. She took two aspirin and limped alongside Chiako as they headed for Ikebukuro.

Rain cascaded down the window of the train. It seemed months since Tokyo had seen the sun. On the subway Chiako scanned the newspaper. "It says here, Megumi-*chan*, that the cherry blossoms may appear early this year, perhaps even in March. It seems impossible to believe spring will ever come. Twelve more weeks." She lowered the paper, sighing dreamily. "We will have to plan an *o hana mi* party. We should invite Araki-*san*, *ne?*"

Maggie looked out the window but didn't see the dirty sky, the dingy buildings hurtling past. She saw clouds of pink cherry blossoms falling on her. She didn't hear the roar of the train as it plunged into a tunnel; rather, her ears were filled with the sound of a million laughing voices. She was swaying not in a train car, but in the back of a battered truck, ascending an unpaved, mountain road. "Yes," she murmured, "we will have to celebrate *o hana mi*. And we definitely should invite Araki-*san*. I've waited too long to view the *sakura* with him." Her mouth puckered; she felt the bite of sour plums. Bittersweetness.

Chapter 22

March 1994: Tokyo

*T*he line of cherry blossoms was advancing on Tokyo.
The approach of the *sakura zensen* was the subject of
breathless comment on the evening weather reports; every
morning the newspapers printed maps of Japan, showing the
northernmost point the blossoms had reached, in their annual rite of spring.

It was not the beauty of the blossoms alone that invested
them with such special meaning to the millions awaiting
their arrival, not even that they would herald relief from the
dank gray days of Tokyo winter and introduce a few weeks
of verdant spring before the onset of the sweltering summer.
No, the poignancy of cherry blossom season lay in its tran-
sience. One day the blossoms would be open, the next day
they were falling. The sky rained pink, the trees faded to
green, and the *sakura* would be gone for another year, with
not even a ripening cherry left behind—for the trees were
barren. The *sakura* was a metaphor for the samurai of old—
a brief, glorious life, then only a poignant memory.

Curiously it was Maggie Campbell, not her mother or

brother, for whom anticipation of the cherry blossoms struck a resonance that was Japanese to its core; in that spring of her fifteenth year she alone of the Campbell family heaved the sighs, read the poems, and indulged the aches that gripped the Japanese soul contemplating the cherry blossom.

Her parents had a secret—this she knew—and she thought it possible that this could account for their relative indifference to the impending spectacle. There were the whispered conversations, broken off hastily when she'd surface unexpectedly; the buzz of anxious voices late into the night, as she lay, bone tired but unwilling to yield to sleep until she'd milked the last drop of sentiment from the haiku she was composing in her few spare moments; the odd phrases, seeping through the wall—her mother's voice, rising, ". . . love Boston"; her father's measured, "What about her, what about her skating?" Every effort to wrest an explanation was met with bland reassurances.

It was all very suspicious, and notwithstanding the demands on her time imposed by schoolwork, skating, physical training, and ballet, Maggie might have put more effort into cracking her parents' secret had not this question paled next to the major issue in her life: how to deal with the fact that Hiro Araki was in love with her.

It wasn't the first time a male had shown interest; classmates had passed notes seeking her company after school, and Yoshi Ando, with whom she'd been skating pairs three hours a week for almost a year, had gone so far as to press a wet, off-center kiss on her lips one day when they were practicing lifts.

Her classmates were callow youths she thought of more as litter males than as objects for romance; she turned aside their advances by invoking the imperatives of skating. Yoshi

Ando, whose bad breath had rankled from the start and whom she had tolerated only because Madam Goto said pairs training would help her in singles, was dispatched with a shove that left him, goggle-eyed and stunned, lying on his back. Madam Goto had made no objection when Maggie completed Ando's rout by suggesting that she'd gotten all she was going to get out of pairs.

Hiro Araki was an altogether more complicated problem. She wasn't sure what she should do about it.

The fact of his infatuation had come to her during one of the long reveries that were increasingly her wont. For some reason Hiro was often the focus of those moments, and one day she found herself wondering why this enigmatic young man, almost five years her senior and a student at the prestigious Tokyo University, seemed so eager for her company.

Why she would catch him looking at her when he thought she wouldn't notice. Why he talked to her as though truly interested in her opinions, unlike the boys in her class with their bantering, suggestive comments. Why he was always giving her advice, whether she asked for it or not. Why he seemed to be taking greater and greater pains with his appearance, so that at twenty he was even better looking than he'd been when she'd met him in the schoolyard. Why his manner had become so enigmatic, his eyes so mysterious, his smile so electric. Why his habit of tousling her hair, an annoying reminder of her youth only months before, had begun to feel like a caress. Why, when they worked out, his shirts accented the breadth of his shoulders, the muscles in his chest, as though he'd begun buying them too small.

The more she thought about it, the only rational answer to these and a million other questions was that, notwithstanding the way he pretended to think her little more than a child, he was in love with her. Once it came to her she thought about it daily. It left her confused.

Certainly she was touched that he was so obviously making an effort not to let on, in any way, that his feelings toward her had changed, that he was no longer simply an older male friend, but a suitor. She could understand that he didn't want to be hurt if his feelings weren't reciprocated, and of course he understood that with barely eight months until the Nationals, she had no time for love-struck young men.

Following much deliberation, she decided that there was no reason for her to *do* anything, as long as Hiro continued to exercise self-control. Over the previous years she had grown quite fond of the bowls of noodles at his mother's noodle parlor, the respectful but easy way he engaged with her parents, his ability to draw out her shy little brother, the chats about every subject under the sun on the way to the subway, his company during workouts, the uninhibited way in which he would wrestle with the American idioms she taught him.

After all, she told herself, he is amusing, at least when he isn't being preachy; he does know a lot of interesting things; and he is tall, well built, and increasingly handsome. For some reason she often felt older, stronger, wiser, and better after she'd been with him, and while it would never do to admit it, there had been times when he'd told her something she didn't want to hear, and later she'd been glad he had— as when he'd chided her into understanding what weight work really involved.

True, there were occasions when she found his unconventional behavior acutely embarrassing. The way he would buy food and eat it as they walked along, for instance, indifferent to the disapproving frowns of passersby. The way he would say, flat out, if he thought she was wrong about something, instead of at least coming at it indirectly, the way decent people did. The way he looked into people's eyes when he talked to them, as though he didn't realize how rude that was, or didn't care. His insistence that there had to be a better reason for something than that that was the way things were done.

She found his practice of questioning things that weren't to be questioned particularly unsettling: whether a teacher was wrong about something; whether American beef really was unsuitable for Japanese digestive tracts, as an official claimed; whether the Ministry of Finance really knew what it was doing. She'd almost died of mortification the day he'd asked her, matter-of-factly and not even whispering, if she thought it made sense to do away with the imperial throne.

At times like that she wondered if there were something wrong with *her,* that she kept company with someone so indifferent to society's rules. Then she would reflect that, after all, it was a woman's role to serve as a civilizing influence on men and that, with time and patience, she could accomplish what all the teachers' slaps had failed to accomplish with Hiro Araki and render him fit for his place in life. If he had developed a passion for her, that would simply make him more amenable to acculturation.

If he *did* show signs of becoming squirrelly; if he suddenly flung himself upon her and proclaimed his uncontrollable passion; if he threw his powerful arms around her and pressed his mouth down on hers—why, there'd be time enough to make it clear that there were limits to her willingness to brook unconventionality. Besides, it might be interesting to experience the kiss of someone immeasurably more attractive than Yoshi Ando. Perhaps, if that was *all* he did, she wouldn't even send him packing; maybe she'd give him a second chance.

After a while Maggie even decided that perhaps, in simple decency, she ought to send *some* indication that Hiro didn't have to be *so* circumspect about his new level of emotional attachment; it really wasn't fair of her to deny him even a hint of acknowledgment, some little sign that she certainly didn't view his suit in the same light as she had that of the striplings whose overtures she had so swiftly disdained.

She was just wondering how best to do this when Hiro relieved her of the need. It was a Friday morning, and the cherry blossoms couldn't have been more than a week away. They had just had a particularly good workout and were leaving the gym when Hiro stopped her at the door.

"Maggie," he said, "what are you doing Sunday?"

It was an odd question. "Sunday's my day for catching up with homework. Why?" Maggie was puzzled by Hiro's demeanor. He seemed hesitant, almost ill at ease, something she'd never seen before. Then it dawned on her. Ah, she thought, he can't keep it inside any longer. He wants a rendezvous. It rather made her tingle as she waited.

"I have to go someplace, and I wondered if you'd go with me?"

She thought he could have stammered, or at least had a catch in his voice, but still—she thought it sweet he wanted an assignation. The Meiji Shrine, most likely, a traditional setting for pledges of undying affection.

She couldn't appear too ready, of course. "Well, I'd like to, but I have homework, and . . ."

That should suffice; the tingling sensation was growing stronger, and there was no point in torturing him. "How long would it take?"

"All day, I'm afraid."

The tingle faded; that was rather more of a rendezvous than she'd been expecting. Still, to see him standing there, so obviously in need, gave him a vulnerability that she found quite appealing—indeed, almost irresistible. But what if he had in mind taking her to a love hotel? She didn't want to crush him, but he'd have to understand that anything like that was simply out of the question—at least until he'd proven himself worthy. Perhaps she'd let him start by demonstrating that his kisses were a quantum improvement over Yoshi Ando's. Which she didn't doubt for a second, and she'd given it a lot of thought. Still, they could hardly spend an entire *day* kissing. It was best this be clarified at once, so that no misunderstandings would arise.

"Where on earth would we be going?"

He *did* look nervous, she was sure of it; should she slap him if he said a love hotel? Perhaps his mother was going away, and he meant to take her to their apartment over the noodle parlor. Maybe . . .

"Where?" She couldn't believe she'd heard right.

"Yamanashi. Well, a bit beyond Yamanashi, actually. We'd have to take a train, and then get a ride. That's why it takes all day."

"Wherever is Yamanashi?"

"To the west of us. It's in the mountains."

Ah, in the mountains. Could there be a *ryokan*, an exquisite, rural, lover's bower? It would be too cruel to let him build up his hopes, spend his money, only to spurn his advances when they arrived. *Now* was the time to make things clear. Her eyes narrowed suspiciously. "But why would we be going?"

He grinned playfully. "It's a surprise. Now, will you come with me? I'd really like you to."

That confirmed it! She thought it a remarkably high-handed way to speak to someone you hoped to seduce. She was about to say just that when she stopped herself; very well, she decided—I gave him every chance. I can use a day off, and when we arrive at his little love nest and I tell him the way things are, I'll remind him that he has no one to blame but himself if he's wasted his time and money.

"I'll come."

"He'll have no one to blame but himself if he's disappointed Sunday," she muttered as she hurried toward the high school, the "if" reverberating in her ear.

Outside Yamanashi Station Hiro stopped at a street stall and bought dumplings. They sat, eating, Hiro deflecting Maggie's questions with maddening complacency.

An old truck pulled up. A middle-aged man with a squint stuck his head out the window. "Climb up, then, Araki-*san*." He had a strong rural accent, quite unlike that of Tokyo.

Maggie looked into the cramped, smoky cab. "Is it all right if I ride in the back?"

"Suit yourself," the driver said. "But it will be bumpy."

Hiro looked at her dubiously. "You're sure you'll be all right?"

"I'll be fine."

"You'll hold on tight? We don't want you bouncing out. It gets quite rough."

Maggie felt a flash of irritation at his paternalism; she leapt into the back of the truck with only a grunt for an answer. She just had time to settle back against a bale of hay before the truck lurched forward.

Back and forth the road switched, climbing steadily through dense pine forest, the truck grinding along in the lowest gear as it strained to negotiate the hairpin turns. Maggie clung to a stanchion sticking out of the truck's side and tried not to look at the precipice inches from the bald tires. It was strange to look around and see nothing but forest—no houses, no fields, no people. Especially no people.

Yamanashi appeared, a thousand feet below. Beyond it she could see a brown cloud on the horizon that she assumed was Tokyo. Her parents and Kenji were somewhere in that muddy soup. She decided she was content to let the day play out as it would. She cleared her mind of questions and began to hum snatches of music from her long program. She was still humming when they rounded another turn and shuddered to a stop in a large clearing. Two children in ragged clothes stood, rooted, staring at Maggie.

Hiro hopped out of the cab, grinning. "Like the ride?"

"Once I decided we might survive." She cast a confused look at her surroundings. Not only was there no *ryokan,* there was apparently nothing at all. Try as she might, she couldn't see anyone coming to this desolate spot to attempt a seduction.

Hiro reached up and gripped her waist. "Alley-oop!" He lifted her over the side of the truck and set her on the ground as easily as if she'd been a doll. "Well, what do you think?"

Her eyes followed the sweep of his arm. At first she saw only patches of snow and the pine forest surrounding them. As her eyes adjusted, though, she began to make out the outline of small houses set back in the woods and, beyond them, more cleared areas. The houses were wood, and unpainted, so that they blended in with the trees. A woman was hanging laundry outside one of them. Somewhere children were playing, their shouts echoing off the bare rock faces rising above them.

"What *is* this place? Where are we?"

Hiro waved to a man walking across the clearing toward them. He carried a long stick that he used as a cane, his steps slow and deliberate. "Oi—over here, *Ojii-san,*" Hiro called before answering. "It has no name. People here call it 'the Place for the People Who Have No Place,' or just . . . 'Someplace.'"

"But . . . on the map—what do they call it?" Maggie made out several more houses nestled in the woods, and some of the cleared areas had been recently cultivated. The place *had* to have a name.

"It isn't on any map."

"But who are they?" She pointed to people hoeing a plot. "Surely they live here."

"Oh, yes," Hiro said as the man approached, "they live here. This is their home. They are Hamlet People, Maggie. These are *burakumin*."

The man stopped in front of them and bowed. He was old, though how old Maggie couldn't tell, since sun and wind had aged his skin beyond anything years alone might have done. His hair was thin and white. His right eye was covered with a patch, the left watery and faded.

"*Ojii-san*—I would like you to meet my friend, Campbell." Hiro bowed low.

"Campbell-*san*. I am Nagata." The old man bowed again. "I am honored to meet Grandson's friend."

"Please have some tea, Campbell-*san*."

They had followed the old man back to a small house on the edge of the clearing. A dog of indeterminate type, rushing out to greet them, licked Maggie's hand.

They removed their shoes and the old man ushered them in, holding aside the cowhide that served as a door. The house was dark, since it was sheltered by the trees and little of the spring sun worked its way through the narrow windows. There was only one room, sparsely furnished, with a packed dirt floor topped with worn tatami. In the center of the room was a stone fireplace, a pit ringed with rocks. An iron bar with a hook on the end hung from a beam overhead, and after the old man had filled the kettle from a barrel by the front door he hung it from the hook and lit the fire underneath.

Soon the fire was snapping busily. The smoke drifted out through a hole in the roof. Maggie had seen similar arrangements in a museum but had no idea anyone still used them.

The old man filled a pot with water and added various things: soy, rice wine, some dried mushrooms, bits of dried kelp, chunks of cabbage, potatoes, an onion. He unfolded a bundle wrapped in newspaper and placed its contents in the pot before Maggie could see what it was. He removed the steaming kettle from the fire, replaced it with the pot, and brewed tea. He sat down, facing his visitors.

"So, Grandson—your mother is well?"

"Very well, Grandfather. She sends her love." He passed over a package he'd brought. "Also some books and magazines."

"Ah, I do enjoy those."

"This, too," Hiro handed over an envelope.

"She should keep her money. You need money in the city; there is little to buy here."

"For your cigarettes, Grandfather."

"Well, thank you, and please thank your mother. I was almost out." He reached into a pocket hidden in the folds of the worn robe he wore and pulled out a battered pack of Winstons. He offered it first to Maggie, then to Hiro, before extracting one for himself. He reached into the fire and pulled out an ember. When the cigarette was lit he exhaled appreciatively. "They say cigarettes are bad for you, that they shorten your life. I say, 'I certainly hope so!'" The old man threw back his head, laughing. "When you are young, you cannot imagine dying. When you are old, you cannot imagine living. I'm ready to go any time the *kami* are ready to have me."

"Don't say that, Grandfather—you're not so old." Through the smoke Maggie could see the warmth in Hiro's eyes.

"Oh, I've probably got a few years left." The dog that had greeted them strutted in, sank to the floor, laid his head on the old man's lap. "One thing they have to admit about us— we're not easy to kill." His gnarled hand fondled the dog's ear. "Heaven knows they're tried hard enough!" He laughed again.

Hiro looked at Maggie. "Do you know what Grandfather means, Maggie, by 'us'?"

She was confused. "Japanese?"

Hiro snorted derisively. "Oh, yes, we're Japanese all right, not that a lot of our fellow citizens wouldn't prefer to deny it. No, Grandfather meant *burakumin*—the Hamlet People. That's what we are. What I am. Do you know about the *burakumin*?"

She had heard the word, whispered, behind the school, but all she remembered was someone using it and someone else wrinkling her nose in disgust. "I don't think so."

"Would you tell her, Grandfather—tell her what you've told me?"

"Oh, it is not so interesting." He picked up a wooden spoon and stirred the pot. A rich, sweet smell wafted Maggie's way.

"Please, Grandfather—it is important to me. I want her to understand. That's why I brought her. She is not like the others. She is . . . different. She is my great friend." He smiled across the fire. "I trust her."

Hesitantly, not sure what he meant, she added: "I would like to know, if you would tell me, Nagata-*san*."

"Very well. The stew has a while to go." He stared at a spot midway between Maggie and Hiro.

"Many years ago—many, *many* years ago, even before the Tokugawa shogunate—there were jobs good Buddhists would not do; their religion forbade them to kill animals or handle their skins, to guard prisoners, or to execute criminals. Anything to do with death was forbidden. But as you may imagine, even in a proper Buddhist state there is death, and somebody has to deal with it." The old man chuckled. "Hence the *burakumin* were invented."

As he spoke, Maggie felt herself drawing away from the smoke-filled room, back to the time of mist-shrouded mountains, crashing waterfalls, graceful courtesans, and warrior-poets. The old man's voice, craggy and distant, evoked those days. "And in that time there were great sages and priests. Artists of genius, princesses, and lords. Humble farmers, courtesans and warriors, servants and served. All had their place in society, as low or high as might be—samurai, artisan, merchant, or peasant. Each had a place, as Confucius had taught—except the *burakumin*. The Hamlet People—for that is what *burakumin* means—had no place in a society that could not admit the need for what the Hamlet People did, even though they did it because society needed it. And Confucius taught that there was no greater crime than having no place in society."

The old man stopped and drew on his cigarette. He stared into the fire, but just when Maggie was wondering if he'd gone on an old person's journey, he resumed his tale. "It is confusing, Campbell-*san*, because the Hamlet People are no different from any other Japanese in appearance or language; we are not a race apart, though we are often treated as such. What I meant was that some Japanese did these things that had to be done. In return, they were paid a pittance and kept apart from other people. They were not allowed to wear shoes, and if they were townspeople, they couldn't have windows that faced the streets, lest their gaze light on decent people. They could not enter the temples or shrines, they could not marry outside their own group, and many were forced to live in remote villages like this one. They couldn't even leave their villages from sunset to sunrise. After a while, being *burakumin* became hereditary. We were called 'filth abundant' and 'nonpersons.' Have you heard those terms?"

"I have not, Nagata-*san*."

"Ah." The old man smiled. "I am glad you haven't. That is progress. Yet that is what the *burakumin* were called, for many centuries. Under the shogunate, it was not even a crime to kill a *burakumin*."

Maggie gasped. "How horrible!"

"Oh, things are much improved. In the last century, after the shoguns were overthrown, we had some enlightened leaders. They ended the legal mistreatment of the Hamlet People; now we can live, work, and marry as we will." The old man chuckled. "That is, if anyone will rent a house to us, hire us, or marry us."

"I do not understand."

A soft, bitter laugh came out of the darkness shrouding Hiro. "Why do you think my mother came to Tokyo, Maggie? It was to escape. I will tell you a secret: When she came to Tokyo she obtained false papers, because anyone would know from her real papers that she was *burakumin*. Many did this. And do you know why she did this, Maggie? Why she gave up her identity?"

Her ignorance appalled her. "I . . . I can only guess."

"It is so I would have a chance in life. If our landlord knew, she might lose her restaurant; if an employer knew, I would never get a job with a respectable company. And certainly no decent family would have me as a son-in-law, no 'nice' girl would marry me. Mother wanted me to be able to live in *ippan* society, to be normal. There are thousands like us—passing, pretending." He flung a twig into the fire. "And every day she is afraid, afraid that someone will guess. Have you ever seen someone hold four fingers up behind someone else's back?"

The sudden shift was disconcerting. "I . . . I don't know. I don't remember."

"It means 'four legs'—like an animal. It means this person *is* an animal, this person is *burakumin*. My mother lives in fear that one day someone will do that to her—or to me."

"But, but . . . how can people know?" The more she heard, the more incredible it seemed—not only that such horror should exist in Japan, but that it went on under her nose and she'd never been taught about it.

"Where you were born, where you live now, your accent—all these things can make people suspect," replied the old man. "Certain jobs, too: butchers, shoemakers, shoeshine boys." He laughed. His voice held none of his grandson's anger. "For some reason, flower peddlers—I never did understand that, but there it is."

Hiro broke in. "This is why many *burakumin* change their names, conceal their origins, try to create new identities. But of course in Japan, where we have records of everything, where everybody must be registered in their neighborhood registry, it is not easy. Though they deny it, many of the great companies keep a register of people suspected of being *burakumin;* they share names among themselves. And even if a person succeeds for a time, he or she lives in constant fear of discovery. Many hidden *burakumin* are blackmailed by those who discover their secret."

Their host stirred the pot again. "Many Hamlet People lived in and around Osaka, where I was born and raised. The American air force did us the honor of treating our homes as though they were as worthy of attention as the homes of the rich, so after the war, having no place to come back to, I went to Nagoya, where there was work. I applied for a job in a steel mill, but they found out that I had been a tanner. I might as well have said I was *burakumin,* you see? That was the end of that. So I came here; I was too old to escape, and life is better here than the way we lived in Osaka."

Everything was a terrible muddle; she felt as though she'd fallen off the earth and landed in a different universe. "Nagata-*san*—your grandson says this place has no name, that it isn't even shown on the map; how can that be?"

The old man reached for the pot of stew without answering. After lifting it carefully off the iron hook, he set it on the ground beside him. The dog lifted its head and sniffed, then pounded its tail on the ground, raising little clouds of dust.

"Come around here, young people, so we can eat this stew before the dog gets it."

Maggie and Hiro came over, and the three of them circled the pot. The old man handed each a pair of chopsticks and a small, wooden spoon. It was only after Maggie and Hiro had pulled the first morsels out of the pot that the old man answered Maggie's question. "It is because now we are to be invisible; we do not exist."

Maggie looked up uncertainly. " 'Do not exist,' Nagata-*san?* How can it be, this place does not exist? It is here." It was too dark to see what she was eating, but it was tasty, if somewhat chewy.

"From your questions, I take it they teach you nothing of us in school?"

"No, Nagata-*san*—nothing."

"Then that is the answer to your question: The Japanese people say we do not exist. We Japanese decided long ago that the easiest way to deal with embarrassing situations is to pretend they don't exist. In the cities men and women are sometimes side by side in a public toilet, *ne?* No one minds because everyone simply pretends no one else is there. In the same way, now that there are no more laws against the *burakumin, ippan* society just pretends there never were any *burakumin.* It is embarrassing, and embarrassing things are not mentioned in polite society. Therefore we can't possibly be discriminated against, since we don't exist and never did. Once we were pariahs, now we are ghosts. Some people say there are as many as two million of us, yet we do not exist."

Maggie, stunned by the huge wound she had discovered in her world, said dully: "I am sorry, Nagata-*san,* and ashamed."

"Why should you be ashamed, Campbell-*san?* You have done nothing wrong."

"No, but I am Japanese, and—"

"Excuse me, Campbell-*san,* but that is exactly the problem. You should not be ashamed of something other people have done; it is not your responsibility. I am old, and I have learned that we all will be kept quite busy merely taking responsibility for the things *we* have done; there is no time to feel guilty for the wrongs of others."

His tone softened. "It is because people believe in group responsibility that the *burakumin* have suffered; so while you mean well, never, never, *never* credit yourself with another's accomplishments, or accept fault for another's bad deeds. If you wish to help the Hamlet People and all others who are victims of blood guilt, you will remember this."

Maggie dipped her head. "*Hai,* Nagata-*san;* I will remember."

"Good. Now have some more stew, because soon you will have to leave."

"Thank you. It is delicious."

The old man's face lit up. "Ah—you like meat, then?"

"*Hai,* Nagata-*san.*"

He wheezed contentedly. "Being *burakumin* isn't all bad—we learned centuries ago to enjoy foods good Buddhists wouldn't touch, like meat. Only now is *ippan* society catching up with us."

Maggie looked curiously at the little bone she'd been chewing. "And what is this meat, Nagata-*san?*"

"Why, that is squirrel, Campbell-*san;* you have not had it before?"

Hiro grinned, winking at her. She shrugged, dipping her chopsticks back into the pot. "No, Nagata-*san.* It has been my loss. My education has lacked much."

"Thank you for coming with me, Maggie. I wanted you to meet my grandfather and to . . . know about me. It gets very lonely, not being able to share that."

It was dark by the time they caught the train. Maggie basked in the intimacy of the shared seat in the dimly lit car. "Thank you for bringing me. I'm glad I know. But it's . . . disgusting. I . . . I had no idea." She felt as though she had just passed through a great *jishin* and, like any quake survivor, would never again assume the earth underfoot was stable.

"You won't say anything to anyone? It would kill my

mother if it got out. And if the wrong person learned . . . I am afraid my mother would pay to keep our secret."

"I won't say a word. I understand her worry."

"Well, I don't!" His vehement protest startled her. "It's pathetic. No one should live like that, letting other people's ignorance and hatred control them. I pray my mother has a long life, but the day she dies, I will declare to the whole of Japan that I am *burakumin*. I will *revel* in it!"

"But . . . you will be shunned, you said so yourself."

"Oh, not everyone is like that—there are good people, sensible people, who will not care. As for the rest, well"—he made a spitting sound—"why would I want anything to do with people who despise me, who have made my family suffer for generations, who would make my children, and my children's children, suffer? Let them call me filth, an animal, a nonperson; just so long as they stay out of my way."

Maggie's throat tightened. "But that's why your mother left, why she's trying to . . . pass. So you and your children won't have to suffer as your grandfather did. Why wouldn't you want to . . . escape, I guess you'd call it?"

"Hah! Some 'escape.' 'Escape' so I can live my life like the rest of the herd? Always worrying about what other people think? Japanese people are always worried about being different, being left out. But when you *are* different, are left out, you realize how, how"—he searched for the right word—"liberating it is. No—when I was little, when I first knew that I was different, that if the truth were known I'd be despised and feared, I hated it. I lay awake at night, crying, cursing the fate that had made me *burakumin*. But now, I wouldn't trade with the people who think that way for the world."

He grabbed her arm, so hard that she winced, but he didn't notice. "It's not just what people would say if they knew about me—that's just part of a mind-set, the way people here are trained from infancy to be uncomfortable with anything that sets anyone apart. So many of them never think for themselves, don't care about ideas unless they're ideas they've been told to care about. You hear them talking about what ministry they'll go to, or what company they'll join. They play tennis all day, or bridge, or if they talk about anything, it's whether it's better to go with MITI or Finance if they're men, or whether it's better to marry someone from MITI or Finance if they're women. They can't even *imagine* doing something different, because all their lives they've been taught: 'Different' is bad, 'different' is wrong."

Maggie reeled under the words breaking over her in the half-light. "I . . . I didn't . . . know it was like that. I always heard that Tokyo University was—"

He cut her off, leaning toward her and whispering passionately, "Can you imagine how hard it is to bite your tongue when someone says something vile about your own people? By extension, about your mother, your grandfather, the people you love? To have to join in the laughter, the snickering, so no one will start to suspect?"

In the dusk his dark eyes bored in on her, as though a physical thing tied her to him. "I, I guess so."

"There's no one else I could tell, but I knew you understood how liberating it is to be able to admit you're different, you'll always be different, and you don't have to waste a second trying not to be different. We're soul mates, you and I; I felt it the day I met you. You understand me, what it means to be what I am."

The stabbing pain in her chest disappeared. "I . . . I *do* understand. I really do." Her hand found his and closed on it. She leaned back and closed her eyes. She drifted off to the thought: He has trusted me, only me. He loves me, and I love him. With all my heart, I love him.

She woke as the train slowed to enter Tokyo Station. He was staring at her, his eyes fixed on her face. She shut her eyes for a minute longer, feeling the weight of his gaze, letting it caress her. She wished they could have ridden forever.

They caught the subway to Ueno. At the top of the steps Hiro took Maggie's hands in his. "I owe you more *on* than I can ever repay. Thank you."

She looked up into his eyes. "No, thank *you* for sharing your life with me." Suddenly, impulsively, she stood on tiptoe and kissed him on the mouth. His lips softened, moved, adjusted to hers, just for a second, before he put his hands on her shoulders and stepped back, awkwardly. His eyes, usually so steady and cool, darted nervously, and the touch of his hand on her cheek was little more than the flick of a moth's wing. His voice rasped. "I'll see you soon. Goodbye." He walked quickly away.

The cherry blossoms reached Tokyo in early April, and Maggie was dispatched to buy pickles for the *o hana mi* picnic the following night. At Mrs. Takaoka's pickle shop she encountered her oldest friend, Sachiko Fujita, and they walked down the street together, surreptitiously popping sour plums into their mouths. "I know"—Sachiko discreetly spat a pit into her hand and dropped it into her pocket— "let's go over to Ueno Park after we've eaten. There will be more than a million people there."

Maggie shook her head. "I don't know if I can; I may be doing something else."

Sachiko pouted. "I see so little of you these days."

"I'm sorry—it's the skating."

"You won't be skating tomorrow night—*do* let's go to the park! Don't you want to see what it looks like?"

"I would, but . . ."

"What else can you have to do?" Sachiko eyed Maggie suspiciously.

Maggie stopped walking. "Promise you won't tell?"

"Of course. Now tell me," Sachiko importuned.

Maggie dropped her voice. "Well, I hope to be meeting someone." She paused dramatically. "A young man."

Her friend's eyes widened. "A young man—who? Who's your boyfriend?"

"You gave me your word you won't tell *anyone*, remember?"

"I said I wouldn't, didn't I? Come on, tell me, tell me. Is it Shino Minami?"

Maggie recoiled. "Are you serious—that child? My boyfriend is a *man*. He's in college." She leaned forward conspiratorially. "It's Hiro Araki."

"Araki-*san*? You're joking!" The girl's mouth dropped open.

"Shh! Keep your voice down!" Maggie looked around anxiously. "No, I'm not joking."

"Has he . . . kissed you?"

"Of course." Not wanting to be pressed for details, Maggie hurried on: "But our relationship isn't about sex. It's far more than that. Deeper. There's a special trust. He's . . . told me things."

"What does that mean, he's told you things? Has he told you he *loves* you?" Sachiko's eyes grew until they were almost as big as Maggie's.

"Well, no—not in so many words, that is." Maggie was starting to wish she hadn't confided in Sachiko. "Oh, look at them." She stopped in front of Mr. Imuri's pet shop.

"Yes, they're cute." Sachiko turned back to Maggie, dashing her hope that the tangle of kittens would distract her friend. "Well what, then? What's he told you?"

"That . . . he recognizes this special tie between us. It's like . . . destiny, I guess. He felt it, and I felt it. There's a . . . chemistry. He said we were 'soul mates.'" Maggie could almost *taste* the sweetness of the words, even over the residual bite of the pickled plums.

"He *said* that?"

"Um-huh."

Sachiko's brow furrowed. "But isn't Araki-*san* a little old for you?"

Maggie started walking again, slowly, while Sachiko leaned against her so she could hear. "No, of course not. He's not even five years older than I am. My father's almost eight years older than my mother. The man is usually older than the woman."

Sachiko sounded skeptical. "Yes, but at our age—"

Maggie cut her off. "It's not a problem, I tell you. He teases me about my age, but that's just his way of masking his feelings. He doesn't mean it."

"How do you know he doesn't?"

"Because it's obvious. A woman can tell. The way he looks at me when he thinks I won't notice, that sort of thing. Besides, he wouldn't want to be with me all the time if he thought I was too young for him. He wouldn't . . . share things with me if he didn't think of me as his girlfriend."

Sachiko frowned. "Perhaps I shouldn't say this, but Araki-*san* has a somewhat . . . *bad* reputation. The teachers still talk about what a delinquent he was."

Maggie looked at her friend scornfully. "He wasn't a 'delinquent.' The teachers feared him because he thinks for himself and says what he thinks. We're always being told:

'The nail that sticks up gets hammered down.' Well, nobody's going to hammer *him* down!"

Sachiko took a step back. "I was just telling you what I'd heard, that's all." A frown settled on her round face. "Campbell-*san*, I'm your oldest friend, right?"

"Of course." Maggie eyed her companion cautiously, wondering where she was going.

"As your oldest friend, I owe it to you to point out that Araki-*san* is said to be a real ladies' man. You must be careful." She stepped forward again, so that her nose was only a few inches from Maggie's. "I heard he only has to snap his fingers for girls to . . . you know."

"That's a lie! Araki-*san* has never been anything but a gentleman with me. In fact, I may have to . . . take the lead, when it comes to . . . that." Maggie raised her chin and set her jaw. "*I* don't want to be an old maid."

Flushing, Sachiko retreated. "Well, better an old maid than damaged goods. See who'll marry you then!"

Maggie's eyes flashed. "You're jealous, Fujita-*san*, but you needn't be; no doubt you'll find a boyfriend soon. Perhaps Shino Minami, hum? You certainly wouldn't have to worry about *him* leaving you as damaged goods."

"I see." A pair of tears formed in the corners of Sachiko's eyes and rolled slowly over the plump cheeks. "I'm glad to know how you feel, Campbell-*san;* may you have great good luck in all you do." She bowed stiffly, turned on her heel, and hurried away.

The following night was unseasonably warm, with a gentle breeze that fanned the cherry blossoms until the trees looked like pink clouds scudding across the heavens as the sun set.

The Campbell party sat around a blanket spread on the

plot reserved for them. On all sides, just inches away, sat
friends and neighbors on *their* long-reserved plots—and so
it went, to the very edge of the neighborhood cemetery.

Overhead hung strings of *chochin,* brightly colored paper
lanterns with small light bulbs inside. They poured their
light onto the array of food and drink covering the blanket.

Everywhere sounds of laughter and the buzz of cheerful
talk rose in the still, warm air, punctuated by the busy clicks
of thousands of chopsticks. Moths, drawn by the lights of
the *chochin,* cast their dancing shadows across dinner and
diner alike, so that an observer might have thought it an
image from a kaleidoscope. And everywhere, the rain of
pink petals served as a reminder to savor the moment, for it
would be as fleeting as the *sakura.*

Maggie alone was unsurfeited, having exercised every
ounce of willpower to confine herself to a few pickles, a bit
of sashimi, rice, and some fruit. She could feel her resolve
slipping, hear a malicious little voice whispering, "Go on—
just a *taste* won't hurt," as her eyes, seemingly operating in-
dependently of her brain, fell on one delicacy after another.

She thought about Hiro Araki, thinking that would help.
The problem was, the more she thought about him, the more
disappointed she was that he hadn't asked her to be with him
that evening, not even when she'd hinted rather pointedly
that she wouldn't mind getting away from her family for a
while. That made her feel sorry for herself, which made her
want to eat even more.

She could feel her resolve collapsing. A particularly mis-
chievous *kami* was making short work of her defenses, over-
coming them one by one with facile rationalizations, and she
was just snaking her hand toward a pile of sweets when, to
her immense relief, Sachiko Fujita appeared. *"Konbanwa."*

"*Konbanwa*, Fujita-*san*," they echoed.

"Sit down beside me, please." Maggie tugged the girl's hand until she sank next to her.

"You're not still angry with me, Campbell-*san?*" Sachiko inquired in a nervous whisper.

"Megumi, please. But it is you who should be angry with me. I behaved terribly—please forgive me. Have you eaten?"

"Oh, yes—too much. I came to see if you wanted to go for a walk." She lowered her voice even more. "That is, if you have time before . . . you know?"

Maggie jumped at the chance to get away from food. "Oh, yes—I have time. Let's go."

"Are you meeting Araki-*san* later, then? Do you have time to go over to Ueno Park first?" Sachiko whispered when they were out of earshot.

Maggie's face fell. "I'm not going to see him tonight. He had to be with some other people." Her smile returned. "But I'll see him soon—we work out together."

"That's nice, Megumi-*chan;* he must really like you. I wish I had a boyfriend."

"You will, Sachiko-*chan*, and soon. You're smart, and pretty. Boys will be falling all over you. And not freaks like Shino Minami, either."

They left the cemetery and threaded their way through the maze of streets hardly wider than a cart track that laced through Ueno.

"Would you look at that!" They had passed under the monorail connecting the two halves of the zoo and were suddenly confronted with the panorama of the park.

"I'm not sure I want to go in there after all." Sachiko's

eyes bulged at the sight of a carpet of humanity, stretching in all directions as far as they could see.

"Don't be silly—there's nothing to be afraid of. Come on." Maggie pulled Sachiko into the crowd before she could argue.

"Where are we going?"

"Let's go see the great Saigo's statue. I bet it's mobbed." She set off.

Sachiko stumbled. "Don't go so fast, Megumi. I can't keep up."

"If we get separated, I'll meet you at the statue," Maggie called back just before a line of young people, each holding the hips of the one in front, or a bottle in one hand and a hip in the other, snake-danced between them.

The throng behind her propelled her forward, and it was useless to resist. She declined a young man's offer of a drink from his sake bottle as he pushed past.

In a few minutes the pressure eased, and she stopped to get her bearings. She had reached a part of the park where the crowd wasn't quite as dense, near the shoguns' graveyard, so Saigo wasn't far. She threaded her way toward it.

By the graveyard a row of bushes had been deemed a sufficient assurance of privacy to make space-starved couples decide that this was as good a place as any to satisfy their desires. Oblivious of the hordes around them, couple after couple were locked in embraces, their legs sticking out from under the bushes, their grunts and squeals punctuating the crowd din.

Maggie gaped at one particularly animated foursome of legs, jerking her eyes away in disgust when she realized their owners both had their pants down. She hurried on, eager to leave the carnality behind her.

She looked around for Sachiko, but there was no hope of

picking her out in the dim light. When she turned, a boister-ous group was approaching. She couldn't see their faces, but she could hear them clearly, singing an off-key chorus of a folk song.

They stopped in the middle of the walk, a few yards in front of Maggie. She saw someone extend an arm, pointing at the full, golden moon. The others nodded, murmuring, and then the man who'd been pointing lowered his face and kissed the woman his arm encircled. Maggie heard her laugh, and then her hands came up and cupped his head.

"Everybody's got somebody but us."

Maggie whirled around, startled, to find Sachiko, looking wistfully at the several couples blocking their way, arms around each other, some locked in embraces.

"Mmm." Maggie felt envious, and part of her wished Sachiko hadn't caught up to her just then. "Let's go on," she whispered.

As they drew abreast the first couple broke off their kiss, parting to let the girls through. "Excuse us," the young man murmured. Hiro Araki, his face glowing in the buttery light, looked at them apologetically.

Sachiko, unprepared for Maggie's abrupt halt, bumped her from behind, propelling her into Hiro's hands.

"Easy, Maggie." Hiro's teeth gleamed white as he smiled. "Not like you to lose your balance. But what a nice sur-prise."

The tension in her throat left her speechless. She nodded dumbly.

"Allow me to introduce my friend, Miyoko Sato." Hiro nodded at the young woman he'd been kissing, who smiled and bowed. "Miyoko-*chan*, this is Campbell-*san*. I have told you of her."

In the dim light Maggie could see that the young woman

was quite pretty, though her lipstick was smeared and her hair messed. She had a high, lilting voice. "I am pleased to meet Campbell-*san*. Araki-*san* has told me so much about you. He speaks of you so warmly."

Reflexes drew a bow. Maggie's face felt as though it were on fire. "And my friend, Fujita-*san*." Her voice quavered and broke. "Sachiko-*chan*, this is . . . Araki-*san*. And his . . . friend.

From a distance she heard Hiro speaking to her. "We were on our way to the garden. Won't you join us?" His arm circled Miyoko's waist. "I told Miyoko-*chan* I knew you, and she has been desperate to meet you." He added in a stage whisper: "I think Miyoko only goes out with me because I know such a celebrity."

The young woman giggled. "Silly man." She slapped Hiro's arm. "But skating is so beautiful; perhaps next winter you would be willing to give us lessons?"

Maggie's head whirled. "Give . . . lessons? Skating lessons? To . . . both of you?"

Hiro laughed. "Miyoko-*chan*, Megumi-*chan* has no time to waste on skating lessons for old folks like us."

"No—I would be glad to give you lessons," Maggie said listlessly. "Both of you."

Miyoko bowed as well as she could with Hiro's arm around her waist. "That will be such a great honor."

A hand passed a bottle over Hiro's shoulder. He took it, started to offer it to the two girls, pulled it back. "Your parents would never forgive me if I sent you home smelling of alcohol." He handed it to Miyoko instead.

Behind him the other members of his party were growing noisy. Young women giggled as their escorts stole kisses between drinks. A man said, "Bottoms up"; a young woman squealed.

"What?" Through the fog swirling around her, Maggie heard someone speaking to her. She blinked and realized it was Miyoko, free of Hiro's arm, leaning toward her.

"I said, I am so pleased to meet *Imoto-san*."

Maggie tried to make sense of it. *"Imoto-san?"*

The woman nodded eagerly. "*Hai*. Araki-*san* says that you are his little sister. That is so sweet, I think."

"Little sister?" Maggie tried the phrase; nothing Mrs. Takaoka sold had ever tasted as sour.

"The little sister I always wanted, but 'little sister' is growing up, I think." Hiro's hand came out, tousling Maggie's hair. "She'll have boyfriends soon, and then no time for her big brother, I fear."

"No!" Her voice sounded to her the way it did in dreams. She felt herself backpedaling, drifting away, as the power of movement and the power to feel returned together. "No," she was saying, "it's not true. It's not true!"

"Maggie, why are you . . ." she heard him call, and then she was running, as fast as she could find openings in the crowd, running without regard to the shouts of people she stepped on or bumped against, without regard to the horrible spasms in her stomach, without regard to the tears that streamed down her face as she staggered through the dark streets.

Three days after *o hana mi* Maggie came around the corner near her house to find Hiro leaning against the wall. She'd been dreading the moment.

Straightening, he looked at her curiously. "I missed you at the gym. Were you sick?"

She started to step around him. "I've found a new gym."

"Wait." He stepped away from the wall and blocked her path. "The other night in the park—you ran away; why?"

"It doesn't matter. Would you excuse me, please?"

She tried to step around him again, and again he blocked her. "It was Miyoko, wasn't it? That I was with her?"

She squinted, trying to see what it was she had thought she loved. She felt her eyes starting to betray her and turned away, swiping at them angrily. "You led me on! You lied to me!"

He took a step backward, shaking his head, looking at her uncertainly. "I don't know what you mean. You're my friend. I like you tremendously. I'd never lie to you."

"And her? That, that . . . Miyoko? Is she your friend, too? Do you like her tremendously?"

"She's a nice girl, Maggie, and yes, I like her. She's a good friend."

"Well, how do you decide which of your friends you paw and which ones you don't?"

His shoulders slumped. "That's what I was afraid of." He nodded resignedly. "Maggie, Miyoko's at the university. She's almost my age. It's natural . . ."

Maggie stepped toward him, her voice hissing, "You said we were 'soul mates,' remember? I was the only person you could talk to. I was the only person who could understand what you had been through."

"It's true."

She stepped toward him again. " 'It's *true*'? But how can you be in love with me and carry on like that with her? What kind of a man are you?"

He stared uncomprehendingly. "Be in love with you?" He smacked his palm against his forehead. "Oh, no—you thought *that's* why I took you to meet Grandfather? Why I told you what I am?"

Maggie wanted to vomit. "It doesn't matter what I thought."

"Maggie." He reached for her, but she jerked back. "I *do* love you. But not like that. Not as a man loves a woman. I'm not *in* love with you."

Maggie jerked as though he'd hit her. "Not as a woman?" she croaked.

"You're not even sixteen. I'm almost twenty-one. You've just started high school. I'll be graduating from the university next year. I *couldn't* get involved with you that way. It wouldn't be right."

"So I get to be your 'little sister'?"

"I'm sorry you sneer at the thought, but yes, you're like a little sister to me. There are three people in the world I love as family, Maggie: my mother, my grandfather . . . and you. Isn't that enough?"

Her expression said as much as her reply: "The other day, when we came back from seeing your grandfather, I kissed you, and you kissed me back, you know you did! Was I 'little sister' then?"

He grimaced. "I was surprised, Maggie . . . you took me by surprise." His jaw muscles knotted. "I shouldn't have— I'm sorry."

Maggie stepped closer, her arms rigid at her sides, her hands balling into fists. "And going to see your grandfather, saying we were 'soul mates,' and everything . . . All that was because I was your little sister'?"

He shook his head in frustration. "We're so alike, Maggie; don't you see?"

She shut her eyes. "No, I don't see."

He tried to grab her arms, but she twisted away, and at her sibilant, "Stay away!" he stepped back. "We're both outsiders. We don't fit in. I thought you felt it, too."

"I don't know what you're talking about." She'd thought

she couldn't hate him any more but found she could. "I fit in fine. I have lots of friends."

"Sure—so do I. And what do you think your friends say about you behind your back? That's one advantage I have over you, you know; I *know* what people say about *buraku-min*, because they can't tell with me. And it's no different from what they say about you, about anyone like us. Anyone the least bit different."

"Stop it!" His insistent, self-assured voice enraged her, his probing made her feel violated. Her voice rasped. "Stop saying such horrible things. You . . ."

He caught her wrists, suddenly, before she could step away. "You want to be a woman, not a child? Then open your big eyes and take a look at the real world. You're a half-breed. Most of the people you know will never view you as anything other than a freak."

"A 'half-breed'?" she choked, gasping with rage. "A 'freak'? Is that what you think of me? Well, *you* may not be Japanese, but I am, and I've got papers to prove it!"

He laughed scornfully. " 'Papers'? Why, you little idiot— don't you think my grandfather had papers when he looked for work at the steel mill? You think my mother doesn't have papers? Papers didn't save him from a lifetime of poverty, and they haven't saved her from a lifetime of fear. And your papers won't mean a damn thing when it matters!"

She struggled against the hands manacling her wrists. He brought his face within inches of her. "I thought you understood, that's why I took you up the mountain. You're a Hamlet Person, Maggie. As long as you're in Japan, you'll be *burakumin.* Only you're lucky—there's no way for you to pass, so you won't be tempted to try. At least, you better not." One hand forced her chin up. "You'll get hurt, if you ever forget. And I'd hate that."

Her foot shot out, catching his shin. "Let me go!"

He ignored the kick. "You'll find out plenty fast if you're ever stupid enough to want to go to work in one of the big companies. Think they'll hire someone who looks like you, just because she has citizenship papers?"

"Stop saying these things!"

"Listen to me! When you start thinking about marriage, you're going to find an awful lot of young men will be unavailable. They'll sleep with you, like they sleep with a Thai whore, but they won't marry you any more than they would her."

"You're disgusting!"

"Oh, they won't tell you to your face it's because you're 'tainted,' that their parents would disown them if they were to marry you, that their careers would be over, that your children would sicken them, but that's the fact. Remember that, before you start falling in love. *Really* in love, I mean, not just some puppy crush." He dropped her wrists as suddenly as he'd grabbed them.

Maggie felt a great pressure building in her head. Her voice was a choked rasp that she hated but couldn't control. *"That's* why you kept looking at me, kept coming around, talking to me, wanting to be with me? Because I have funny eyes and funny hair? Because I'm a . . . a *freak?"*

"I didn't say that, and you know it. I'm drawn to you because you're smart, and interesting, and fun. I respect you because you're a fighter, and you go your own way. You think for yourself, Maggie, and you don't worry about what the group thinks. *That's* what comes of being an outsider. *That's* what we have in common." His voice softened. "And you don't have 'funny' eyes or 'funny' hair. *I* don't think you're a 'freak.' You're . . . unique. You're you."

"How . . . how sweet." She was hyperventilating. "Do

you say that to that Miyoko? Or maybe you don't have to, because everything looks the way it's *supposed* to on her."

"You *want* to misunderstand me."

"Does she know? Does she know what you are?"

Sadly he shook his head. "No. Only you."

"Well, you better not let her find out, because it would make her sick. As sick as it makes me!"

Blinking furiously, Maggie advanced another half step. Peering up at him through narrowed eyes, she whispered venomously, "*You* may not be Japanese, but *I* am. I have a Japanese mother, I'm a Japanese citizen, I've grown up in Japan, I speak Japanese, I have Japanese grandparents. I have a medal that says I'm one of the best *Japanese* figure skaters in the country. Someday I'm going to represent *Japan* in the Olympics, and when I win a gold medal they'll raise the *Japanese* flag!" Little drops of saliva sprayed on his jacket as her voice broke and sputtered. "And now I can understand why *my* people don't want to have anything to do with your kind; you *are* filthy, you *do* behave like an animal, and as far as I'm concerned, I never want to see you again!"

His right hand flew back, but she didn't flinch. Slowly it returned to his side. He swallowed, and whatever he'd been about to say died in his throat. Maggie glared at him a few seconds before turning and striding away.

That evening the weatherman announced that the last blossom had fallen; the *sakura* season was officially over.

Chapter 23

February 2001: Boston

*M*aggie sent Clay a valentine: herself. The whoop he'd let out when she called and told him she was coming home swept away the guilt she felt at using the money her mother had given her to buy the plane ticket. Now, curled on his couch after dinner, she marveled at the changes she saw.

He was so ebullient. It was the animated, cheerful Clayton Bartlett from before the accident, not the dispirited man she'd left.

She was disappointed, initially, that they'd spent far more time talking about his job—whom he'd met, what he did, how much he was making—than they had about her training or her life in Japan. Soon she had to go back, and he'd never even asked her to describe her new programs. Over dinner, while she told her mother and Kenji about Hiro, Chiako, Madam Goto, and her programs, she'd sensed his attention wandering. It didn't return until they'd again been talking about life at the agency.

His focus on the moment had grated at first, but she decided she was being silly; of course he was caught up in the excitement of a new career, whereas her training was, at the end of the day, just skating—something he'd known for years. And it wasn't as though he were indifferent to *her;* from the time he'd picked her up at the airport, it had been all she could do to keep his hands off her until they were alone. Certainly she had nothing to match his stories of expense account dinners at Maison Robert, trips all over the country, marketing coups. She'd savor the opportunity to share his ideas and dreams, because it would be months before she'd be able to again. When they'd returned to his apartment and he unrolled his latest purchase, she looked at it eagerly.

"It's a Lindner, one of his best. I picked it up today. That's why I was late for lunch." He stared at the poster proudly.

"Oh." She hadn't wanted him to think that as soon as she came back he had a keeper, so she hadn't asked why he'd kept her waiting half an hour.

"I think up there, don't you?" He pointed to a spot at the head of the stairs.

Maggie tried to imagine going up to the bedroom every night with the baleful eyes of the grim, vaguely fascist figure glowering at her. "I guess. You're running out of wall space."

"I know. I'm thinking about a bigger place already." He returned the print to its tube. "I love collecting this stuff. And guess what?" He flopped down and put his arm around her.

"What?"

"You know Alanna and Fred Turner, the dance team? Third in the Worlds, four or five years ago?"

"Sort of."

"Well, I'm about to close a deal for them with the Cavalcade of Stars. Sixty thousand to the agency, and I get a third of it."

She rolled onto her knees. "Oh, Clay, that's wonderful."

"Yep—that's the Abrams I've been dying for."

"What?" She had no idea what he was talking about.

"A Vivien Abrams construction. Wonderful stuff—huge, abstract designs. A real connoisseur's artist. They've got one at the Pierson Gallery that I've had my eye on for weeks."

"How much is it?"

"Five thousand."

"Five thousand dollars, for a painting?" She thought she might have misheard.

"A print." He waved his hand airily. "It's a good price, Mag—she's bound to go up."

"Yes, but . . ."

His finger went to her lips. "Now, don't begrudge me my pleasures, girl. I'm working hard for them."

"I know, but . . ."

The phone rang and he held up his hand. "Let's hear who it is; if it's my West Coast call, I've got to take it."

They sat silently through Clay's greeting. The message, when it came, was brief. "Hi, Clay, it's Doe. Give me a call when you can. Bye."

Maggie, sitting up, shook her head, echoes of the young, breathless voice still sounding in her ear. "I don't understand," she said carefully.

"Understand what?" He'd begun straightening magazines on the coffee table.

"Why Doe Rawlings was calling you."

He paused, looking at her curiously. "Oh, didn't I tell you?"

"Tell me what?" Maggie wondered if she'd stumbled into a dream world.

"I'm trying to sign her for Weeks. He wants her a lot."

"You're what?" Maggie blurted. "You're trying to do *business* with her?"

"Maggie, settle down."

"I'm as settled as I'm going to get!"

"All right, all right." He sighed. "Lofton's offered me a hundred-thousand-dollar bonus if I sign her before the Olympics. He figures it will be a lot cheaper to sign her now than . . . afterward."

"Because he expects her to win."

Clay shrugged. "Let's face it, Mag—most people do."

"If she wins, she'll be worth a lot more than if she doesn't?"

"Of course."

"And since you'd get a share of her earnings, you'll make more if she wins. If she beats me, among others."

"Maggie, that's a crazy way to look at it."

"I don't think so. What's he offered you to sign me?"

"Maggie, Lofton doesn't represent Olympic-division skaters; going after Doe is the only time he's tried."

"So while I've been practicing eight hours a day, six days a week, you've gotten all friendly with little Miss Rawlings?"

He smoothed his hair. "Maggie, it's business, just business."

She scrambled to her feet. "Do you take her to dinner at Maison Robert? Invite her to the agency box at the Garden? Give her rides in the BMW? Maybe you let her drive, huh? I mean, it's just business." She stood, trembling, her forefinger stabbing the air. "Never mind she almost killed you, never mind she destroyed our chances to win a gold medal, never mind that she's the reason I'm sleeping on the floor in

Japan in a room the size of your, your . . . *bathroom*." She paused for breath.

"Maggie, you're out of control. This is exactly why I didn't say anything. Now—"

"You *bet* I'm out of control! Forget I'm working my *ass* off so I can beat her for *both* of us. Forget I despise her. For enough money you can forget all that, I guess."

"Maggie, be sensible. You know I want you to beat her. I hope you clobber her. But either way, she's going to make a hell of a lot of money as a pro. Probably two, three million a year, easily. Why shouldn't we benefit from it?"

"Because I don't want to, that's why!" Her body quivered. "I wouldn't take one cent she generated."

"Maggie . . ." Clay stood and walked toward her, hands out. "Can't we—"

"No!" She stepped backward. "Not one cent. I don't want you to have anything to do with her. I can't believe *you'd* want to, for any amount of money."

"Maggie, money's money, for Christ's sake."

"No! Nothing." Maggie, her face red, felt as if she were going to burst. "I want your word."

"Can't we—"

"Please, Clay—don't make me say it again." Her voice quavered. "Your word, Clay—you won't have anything to do with her. Let Weeks give her anything he likes, but you won't go near her."

"Come on, Maggie—be reasonable. We—"

"Clay, can't you understand? I *need* you to promise." Her heart raced as though the flywheel had fallen off.

He took a deep breath. "I think I can persuade her to sign, Maggie. I've almost got her talked into it. And we'll be set no matter what."

It was hard to force words out—her throat seemed to have

shut down. "You mean, if I lose. If I go noplace, and I'm just another second-tier singles skater who never made it and has no earning power."

"No. I mean . . ." He looked around, everywhere but at her, as though the solution might lie in one of his prints. His shoulders slumped. "Ah, hell, Maggie—can't we think of it as insurance?"

She took a deep breath. "Maybe I'm being unreasonable, I don't know, but . . . it's not negotiable."

"Meaning?" He looked at her incredulously.

"Don't, Clay. Don't make me say it. Just promise."

She waited, the longest wait in her life, until she heard him sigh. He stepped forward and took her in his arms. "Of course I promise, if that's what you want."

She sagged. "Thank you." Her arms reached around him. "You don't know how much that means to me."

"All the money in the world wouldn't mean anything if I lost you." He kissed the top of her head.

She was able to breathe again. She felt as though she'd been carrying a trunk in either hand and one on her back and had just set them down. "I know I probably overreacted, but . . ."

"It's all right," he whispered. "I only wanted to produce something for the two of us. You're working so hard, and I wanted to say, 'I can contribute, too.' But not if it's that important to you. There's plenty of other business out there. I'll let Weeks worry about her."

"I'm sorry I feel this way, really I am. I hate the thought of hurting you at work." She wiped her eyes and leaned her head against his shoulder.

"I'll be fine. I already told Weeks I didn't see any reason why I could sign her if he couldn't." He grinned. "But since you're feeling grateful . . ."

She put her arms around his neck, kissing him hard as he carried her up the stairs.

Soon after her return to Tokyo, Maggie was competing regularly. Chiako accompanied her, for it was too difficult for Madam Goto to travel. At first Maggie limited her appearances to Japanese events, and at these she was treated as a celebrity, someone whose mere presence conferred honor on the competition. Part of it was having Madam Goto and Chiako Mori as coaches, but the whispers she heard as she walked down the dank hallways and through the gloomy locker rooms were about her: "There's the American pairs skater. She broke up with her partner just so she could come over here and skate singles."

People often forgot she spoke Japanese, and she overheard remarkable things. Chiako was taping her right ankle in a grim dressing room in Nagoya when a woman no more than five feet away said to her companion, in a loud voice, "The *yanki* attempted suicide when her partner, who was also her lover, left her for another." She looked at Chiako, Chiako at her, and they both ran out of the room, laughing.

They stayed in *minshuku*, bed-and-breakfasts in private houses; to save money they rode the local trains that stopped in every town. They ate in noodle parlors and yakitori bars and let local sponsors eager to bask in the company of the renowned Chiako Mori and the perplexing *yanki* buy them tea and sashimi.

It was dispiriting for a while; a third at Sapporo seemed to have been a fluke, for it was followed in rapid order by a fifth in Kobe, a tenth in Nagoya, a seventh in Matsuyama, and a did not finish when her ankle gave out on her in Nikko. She became known as the girl with the most spectacular falls, the girl with more guts than judgment, because she opened every long program with a triple Axel that she never landed cleanly and that often left her so shaken or out of synch that the rest of her still-evolving program collapsed.

"We should drop the Axel, Campbell-*san*," Chiako kept insisting. "As we feared, it is spoiling everything else."

"Has Goto *sensei* said so?"

"You know she will say nothing; she will wait for you to reach the decision."

"I have hit it in practice, Chiako-*chan*."

"What—twice? Perhaps once in every hundred attempts? It is not a matter of practice; you don't have the body for it."

"Please, Chiako-*chan*—just a little longer." She would go out and try it again.

Then, one day at Ikebukuro, she overheard two skaters talking about her. One said she must be crazy to keep trying a jump she'd obviously never make, and the other said that no, it wasn't Maggie's fault, it clearly reflected on Goto *sensei*'s fading judgment. And the other thought, and nodded, and said, *"So desu,"* and clucked his tongue as they walked away.

So she went to Seoul and opened with a clean triple lutz. The rest of her program went smoothly, the boisterous Korean crowd got into it, and she went home with her first singles title since she'd turned fourteen: Samsung Ladies' Open Champion. "It was exquisite, Megumi," Chiako assured her, "a performance that would have won anywhere." Maggie knew it was a coach's lie but liked hearing it.

The next day she bowed low when she arrived at the rink. "My *sensei* was right. Please forgive me for doubting."

"You had to find your own way. Now, your hand position in the sit spin. I have been thinking, and . . ." There was no more talk of the Axel.

Maggie knew she'd made the right decision when Madam Goto greeted her a few days later. Her eyes burned as though she had a fever. She thrust a magazine at Maggie. "So—a 'simple' program still has some appeal, eh? Look!"

Maggie quickly scanned the lead story in *Japan Skates*. The header proclaimed: PURE STYLE CAPTURES WIN FOR JAPANESE SKATER.

Maggie looked up and smiled. "Thanks to my *sensei*, I am Japanese again." She bowed.

The old woman wore a look of triumph. "Thanks to my daughter, they are noticing what women's skating is supposed to be. And you are just beginning!"

During the week she trained: six, sometimes seven hours a day on the ice, until Madam Goto or Chiako turned off the music and insisted she stop. Occasionally she'd lose her focus, get caught up in the music, until, from afar, the smack of a skate guard on the boards would grab her attention. "*Cha, cha,*" the old woman would admonish. "Remember the tea ceremony, Megumi-*chan*—economy of movement, always economy. Suggest, don't show. Beauty in simplicity!" Guiltily Maggie would start again, compressing her movements until the *sensei* said, "Good, good—now you are a tea master."

She spent hours at the barre, stretching. And she returned to the gym, once again rising at dawn to walk through the misty alleyways of Tokyo, often with Hiro accompanying her. Soon it felt as though she'd never stopped working out with him, and their talks leavened days that seemed to unfold forever. When the *sakura* arrived and they sat with Chiako and her friends under the pink shower, laughing and eating, she felt fifteen again.

* * *

By late spring Maggie was on the major international circuit. Two or three times a month she and Chiako boarded a plane for Helsinki or Vancouver or Milan. Wherever she could subject her programs to the pressure cooker of serious competition, there she would be. As a member of the USFSA and an American silver medalist, she had no difficulty gaining invitations to Olympic-eligible competitions. Her one requirement was that Doe Rawlings not be entered. She wouldn't confront her until she felt ready.

In mid-May she finished third in the German Pro-Am, well ahead of the other Japanese women entered. An article appeared in the American magazine *Skater's World* about the American pairs skater who had taken up singles training in Japan after her partner suffered a career-ending injury. The article opined that Ms. Campbell was obviously an emerging force in singles, on a trajectory that made her a serious Olympic contender, although of course she would have to enter the American Nationals if she hoped to be a member of the U.S. Olympic or World teams. It editorialized that she should return to train in America if she expected the United States Figure Skating Association to take an interest in her, especially given that her career could not realistically be expected to continue beyond the coming games.

Two days after returning from Stuttgart with her bronze medal, Maggie came off the ice at Ikebukuro to find Madam Goto and Chiako standing with a little man in a dark suit.

"Megumi-*chan*," Madam Goto announced, "this is Yoshida-*san*. He is with the Japan Figure Skating Association." Her face was a mask.

The little man bowed low. "It is an honor to meet Campbell-*san;* her presence brings great credit to Japan."

He showed no more recognition than he'd have shown a tree.

Maggie stared at the man, speechless.

"Megumi-*chan*," she heard Madam Goto say, "Yoshida-*san* has come to ask if you would honor the association by joining it." The old woman's voice was carefully neutral.

Still Maggie stared. She felt her hands sweating.

"As a member of the JFSA, Campbell-*san* would be eligible to enter the Japanese Nationals. Should she . . ."

The ringing in Maggie's ears made it hard for her to follow the little man's high, scratchy voice. For five years she had dreamed of the day they'd meet, and now all she could do was stare, speechless, when all she had to do was laugh in his face to achieve the humiliation she'd imagined herself visiting upon him.

". . . do as well as appears possible, an invitation to skate for Japan in the Olympics and the Worlds would of course follow."

The little man bowed, waiting expectantly.

"Perhaps you need time to think about it," she heard Chiako whisper.

"Yes," she murmured, at last inclining her head, not half as far as Yoshida had. "Some time, please. I must think about it."

She feared she'd faint. She'd been so smug, telling herself it was all behind her, and all it took was the sight of this little, prune-faced man for the toxins to flow again. "Please . . . if you will excuse me . . ." She backed away as quickly as she could, turned, and hurried out the door.

Chapter 24

January 1995: Tokyo

*M*aggie stopped at Mr. Kasahara's toy store and bought a six-inch-tall, bright red, papier-mâché *Daruma* doll. She reasoned that if the prime minister could be photographed blackening one eye of a *Daruma* to ensure good luck in the coming elections, there was no reason she shouldn't invoke *Daruma*'s aid in her quest for a medal in the coming Nationals. The figure's rounded bottom was weighted, so that if knocked over, it righted itself. Maggie thought it a fitting attribute for a skater.

When she got the doll home she painted one of the white eyes black and made her wish; when it came true she would paint in the other orb, then burn the doll. Since her parents did not maintain a family shrine, she took the doll to her grandparents' house and placed it on the *kamidana,* the god shelf they maintained over a doorway. She tucked it in among the sprigs of *sakaki* tree her grandmother cut to provide the *kami* with a resting place inside the house. Stepping back from the shrine, she thought her *Daruma* looked fat and jolly amid the name tablets of her ancestors.

Aunt Mariko walked in while Maggie was admiring the *Daruma*. "Megumi-*chan*," she burbled. "How nice to see you acknowledging the *Bodhidarma*. I did not know you observed."

"I am learning, Mariko-*oba-san*." It would have been a shame to spoil the moment by admitting she thought of the *Daruma* as being in the nature of a rabbit's foot.

"Well, the *Daruma* is all very well, but you want to study Shinto. *Daruma* is Zen Buddhist, which we imported from China, but Shinto is the true religion of Japan. All Japanese people should attend to it."

"Of course, Mariko-*oba-san*."

"I don't know if you've noticed, Megumi-*chan,* but I visit the shrine every week. I find the *kami* are quite helpful if you treat them respectfully. They seem fond of me."

"I am not surprised, Mariko-*oba-san*."

"Of course, they listen only to Japanese people—one way to find out if you are Japanese in your soul is to get out to a good shrine and call on your personal *kami;* if it answers, well . . . then you know. Of course, one can't expect just to drop in the first time and have the *kami* pay attention; they require sincerity, loyalty, and respect—just like Japanese people."

"I appreciate what I am hearing, *Oba-San;* it is valuable advice."

"I am always happy to advise you on spiritual matters. It is an aunt's role."

That night, as Maggie was drifting off to sleep, it occurred to her that the other skaters might well have their own *Darumas,* setting up offsetting *un*. Goto *sensei* had always admonished her not to think about the competition, that her competition was with herself. But how could she *not* think about the powerful Kazue Kondo, with her incredible triple

Axel; the cool, deliberate Ryoko Suzuki, so elegant and smooth; or especially Chiako Mori, who had won the women's title the previous two years and was rumored to be skating better than ever? They all had more experience, more years, more jumps. If they *also* had better *un* . . . Perhaps Aunt Mariko's advice was worth taking; after all, what was to be lost? And she *was* Japanese in her soul; she *knew* that the *kami* would listen.

She slipped off to the image of dozens of huge, grinning, whey-faced *Darumas,* bobbing back and forth as she skated past them. Only one had both eyes blackened, but she couldn't tell whose it was.

Maggie held the new white skating dress to her chest and twirled. Light caught the sequins, thousands of them, reminding her of diamonds. She would wear it for her long program. "What do you think?"

"It's okay, I guess." Kenji, cleaning his fish tank, barely looked.

"It's gorgeous." She pressed it to her face, then laid it reverentially in the suitcase. There was only one thing left to do.

She took the Ginza line to Asakusa. In a few minutes she was walking past the massive Kaminarimon gate, with its huge white lantern hanging in the middle, flanked by the gods of thunder and rain. She arrived at *Sensoji,* the great complex of Buddhist temple and Shinto shrine.

She walked purposefully down Nakamise Dori, her favorite place in all Tokyo. Though most of the trinket stalls lining the way were closed for the night, enough were still open to give the walkway a feeling of boundless vivacity. Even the moths flapping around the overhead lights sounded cheerful.

She paused and looked up at the towering, five-story pagoda flanking the temple, the grandeur of its height matched by the power of the temple itself, with its massive hanging lanterns and, inside, the statue of the Buddha himself. The smell of incense filled the air as worshipers stopped at the burner to wave the smoke into their faces to ward off illness.

After slipping off her shoes, Maggie went to a counter inside the temple and put one hundred yen in a slot, then removed a long wooden stick from a nearby box. The stick had the number "37" written on it. She went over to a set of small wooden drawers built into the wall. After opening the one marked "37," she extracted the little slip of paper and unrolled it uneasily. "You will be brave enough," she read.

She scratched her head. While the message wasn't as unambiguous as it might have been, she supposed it was unrealistic to hope for one declaring, "You will win the National Figure Skating Championship." You had to be brave to win; very well, she would be brave enough.

Maggie left the temple satisfied, but the main business that had brought her required her to go into the building to the right of the temple, the Asakusa Jinja Shrine. Buddha was fine for fortunes, but Buddha was universal; Shinto was where you turned when you wished to invoke the aid of the *kami,* the spirits of Japan and Japan alone. She stepped through the red *tori* gate.

She stopped at the cleansing pavilion outside the shrine proper. Using one of the long-handled bamboo dippers that hung from ropes attached to the side of a large fountain, she dipped up cool water and poured it over her hands. She scooped up more and rinsed her mouth.

Walking into the main building, where the *kami* lived, Maggie thought hard, trying to remember the way she had seen people initiate dialogue with them. She stepped up to the screen that separated worshipers from the reliquary and flung fifty yen into a wooden tray. She bowed, straightened, bowed again. Hands raised, she clapped, paused, clapped again. She reached up, caught the rope hanging in front of the screen, and pulled.

The low *gong* that followed sounded more than adequate to wake the *kami,* even if the hand claps hadn't. She closed her eyes, concentrating. Aunt Mariko had told her that Shinto was "caught, not taught"—she willed her mind to catch.

She hadn't come to talk to just any *kami.* She'd done research, concluding that Benten, who was the spirit of water and music and one of the Seven Deities of Good Fortune, was as close as she was going to come to a deity for skating. She addressed him:

Benten-*sama:* I know I have not been as faithful as I might have been, so I would not ask anything for myself. However, my parents have made many sacrifices for me, and I would like to repay them, and Goto *sensei,* and my grandparents, by skating as well as I can. I pray you will support me in my quest, and help me bring honor to the people I love. I will be most grateful for any assistance you would give me in this regard. If it should come to pass that this leads to my being chosen to represent Japan in the World championships, or the Olympics, I promise to do everything in my power to make you glad I was chosen. More than anything, I want to make my people proud of me.

She stopped, eyes closed, wondering if she'd gotten through. After bringing her hands up and clapping twice, she backed away from the screen.

An old woman was standing behind her, waiting her turn at the bell rope. Osteoporosis had bent her to a right angle, so that she had to swivel her head sideways to look up. She wore a simple country kimono, white *tabi.* "I hope you get whatever it is you came for," she murmured, the rural accent almost impenetrable. "But the *kami* can be difficult; they have their own way of working things out. You must be prepared for that."

Maggie bowed. "Thank you, old mother. I will remember."

The old woman nodded and shuffled toward the bell rope. She stopped midway. "You will have a successful journey, child, but only the *kami* know where it ends." She turned to her business.

At the end of the Nakamise Dori Maggie stopped, looking back at the looming bulk of the temple buildings. Somewhere someone was playing a *shamisen;* the plaintive strains brought tears to her eyes. There was no more beautiful place on earth, she thought, and no more beautiful moment to be alive.

She walked rapidly to the subway station, wondering what the old woman had meant. Perhaps Benten was saying he had heard her.

The next day Madam Goto met her in the foyer of Osaka's Okazki Hall. Everywhere Maggie looked she saw skaters arriving. Many she knew from other competitions, and with these she exchanged waves and bows. Some she felt watching her, and she knew what they were thinking: That's Megumi Campbell—she placed second last year; she could win it all this time.

Yes, she thought, you keep that in mind—because I plan to.

Registration complete, Madam Goto took her aside.

"They held the draw this morning. You skate next to last Friday night."

"Ah . . . that is good." The first skaters were at a disadvantage, since the judges tended to keep their scores low so they'd have room to award higher scores if they later saw better performances. Perhaps, Maggie mused, Benten might already be at work on her behalf.

"Yes, I think it is good. Kondo skates right before you. After seeing her, your grace and youth should be well received, assuming the judges do their job right."

"Kazue Kondo, Goto *sensei?*"

"*Soyo*—that one, over there." Madam Goto pointed with her chin.

Maggie's eyes followed Madam Goto's gesture until she saw, lounging on a big Naugahyde settee, a woman of perhaps twenty talking with a young man Maggie recognized as Issei Abe, the men's titlist. Kondo had missed last year's Nationals with an injury, but she'd finished second the year before that, and she was said to be fully recovered. Even from a distance the woman appeared powerful—short, thick limbed, conveying a sense of coiled energy.

Kondo must have sensed she was being studied, for she suddenly looked up, for a few seconds returning Maggie's stare. Then, with a flicker of dismissal, she smiled superciliously and turned back to the young man.

Madam Goto had caught the exchange of looks. "Do not expect a warm reception from that one, Megumi-*chan;* she will do anything to hang on to her silver; she would stop at little to take the gold."

"She is very strong, Goto *sensei.*"

"Hah!" The older woman snorted. "She is an acrobat, not a skater. Between jumps she skates as though she were in geta. If she draws judges who know anything of skating, she will not score well. I tell you frankly, you're twice the skater she is, Megumi-*chan*."

"Thank you, Goto *sensei*." Maggie sneaked another look at the stocky skater, wondering. The few times she'd attempted a triple Axel—on days when her teacher was away, for the old woman would have skinned her alive had she seen it—she had landed in a heap, and Kondo was said to hit the Axel at will.

"Listen to me, Megumi-*chan,* and stop thinking about things you can't control." The rebuke snapped Maggie's head around. "That's better. She has drawn the same practice times as you. Concentrate on your own practice and stay out of her way; she has been known to 'accidentally' hit another skater coming out of a jump. Two years ago she cut a girl's foot open that way."

"*Hai,* Goto *sensei*." Maggie looked again at Kondo. The thick body was laughing at something the young man had said, a bray loud enough to be heard above the din, as though she were telling everyone she didn't care whom she disturbed.

At rinkside, as Maggie prepared for the first practice, Madam Goto whispered to her: "Remember not to leave your skates or your costumes unattended for even a second; some of these coaches will stoop to anything." As Maggie was stepping onto the ice, the old woman touched her shoulder and added, "Also remember that you came to find magic. Be the music, daughter."

Maggie was working on segments of her program when Kondo made her appearance. In her warm-up pants and jacket she looked shapeless and unprepossessing, but after a few minutes circling the ice she shed her outer garments;

leotards and a T-shirt revealed powerful haunches and broad, well-muscled shoulders.

Kondo took up a position in center ice, raised her arms, began her routine. Maggie watched as the stocky legs accelerated her to what seemed an incredible speed within a few strokes. Soon Kondo was hitting triple after triple, although no Axels. Maggie turned her mind back to the work at hand. Within seconds she was once again fully focused on her own program.

At each practice session each skater's music would be played once—the short program selection in the morning, the long program's in the afternoon. While a girl's music was on, the other five were supposed to yield right-of-way to her. When Maggie's turn was announced she took her place at center ice and waited. The world seemed to close in, the people in the stands disappeared, the other skaters were forgotten. At the right note she struck off.

She was just coming out of the triple Salchow in her triple/double combination when she heard a guttural bark: "Look out!" Stepping out before she could launch the double toe loop, she was looking around, disoriented, when she felt the breeze generated by the speeding Kazue Kondo, shouting as she passed: "Keep out of my way!"

Shaken, Maggie stood in place, panting. She had been told a thousand times that if she fell, she had to get up immediately and press on as though nothing had happened. She hadn't fallen, but she wanted to start over. She spotted her *sensei* waving her on.

She resumed skating, trying to get back into her program, falling further and further behind. The music, no longer synchronized with the elements it was supposed to accompany, confused her, as though another girl's tape were playing. She started thinking about each approaching move, becoming increasingly ragged. She finished awkwardly, long after the music stopped and the hall had grown still. Madam Goto's hand clap brought her over to the rail.

"Well, she succeeded, I see."

"I'm sorry, I don't understand, *sensei*—who succeeded?"

"Why, Kondo, of course. She wanted to throw you off your routine, and she did. Come off the ice."

Maggie shook her head. "Goto *sensei,* there is time left. I need the practice."

"Come off the ice, I said. You don't need to practice slop." Her tone didn't permit further argument.

Seething, Maggie slumped down on the bench and began removing her skates. Goto settled beside her. "Listen to me, Megumi-*chan;* learn, don't sulk. Why do you think Kondo went after you?"

" 'Went after me'? She should have stayed out of my way, but—"

"Don't be a child—that was no accident. She deliberately encroached on your space, to break your concentration. But she hasn't gone near the other girls. Why?"

Maggie, rubbing her toes through the thin sock, shrugged apathetically. "I don't know, *sensei.*"

"Because she doesn't fear them—she knows they have no chance. But she watched you. I saw her sitting in the stands, studying your every move. She knows the other top girls. She's competed against them, but she wasn't here last year, so she isn't sure what you can do. No doubt she has been wondering whether your performance last year was a fluke. Now she knows you are a real threat—unless you lose your nerve. You did. She intimidated you."

Maggie flinched. "Goto *sensei,* excuse me, but I do not think I was intimidated. I just—"

"You lost your concentration! You were watching out for

her with half your mind—that is intimidation. You were already intimidated in the lobby, and now she has completed the job."

Nervously, Maggie studied Kondo. She was taking long lead-ups to jumps, then hitting them with an explosion of energy that sent her to heights Maggie could scarcely believe. Each jump was dramatized by the loud scrunch of the woman's blades carving into the ice as she launched herself, followed a second later by another scrunch as she landed. There was an almost palpable sense of vital, animal force washing up on the stands. Yet in between jumps Kondo looked clumsy and graceless, as Goto *sensei* had said.

Madam Goto's voice interrupted her observation. "It takes more than physical skill to be a champion. It takes *will*, it takes the ability to shut everything else out—*everything*. Pains, worries, fears, other people—everything. I can teach you jumps and spins, but I can't give you will; that must come from you. Last year you proved you have the technique to be a champion, but there are dozens of skaters who have that. Kondo's betting you don't have the will." She left Maggie slumped on the bench.

The next morning Maggie was the first skater on the ice as her group's forty-five-minute practice began. She took several warm-up laps, but then, instead of continuing with her program, she took center ice, carving small circles, taking slow, single jumps, concentrating on getting a true edge before takeoff.

She was preparing for a lutz when Kazue Kondo skated up beside her. "You keep out of my way today, *yanki*. Go skate at the far end. This is my ice."

Maggie slowed, casting an elaborate look around the rink.

" 'Your ice'? I'm sorry. I didn't know that. I didn't see the sign."

Incredulity came over Kondo's coarse features. "Listen, you—don't you smart-mouth me, or I'll knock you on your ass. Now get off this ice."

Maggie smiled sweetly at the stands as she talked out of the side of her mouth. "Kondo-*san*—when your music is called, I'll make way for you. Until then, you make sure you stay out of my way." She stroked twice, hard, then turned to set up for the lutz.

Kondo stared at her, then slowly turned away, a single, malevolent look over her shoulder saying: It isn't over.

Maggie continued skating as she had been, moving at a pace, not trying to execute the elements of her program so much as re-create the process by which, over the years, she had acquired those elements. She ran through the double jumps, then moved on to the basic spins and simple step sequences. She concentrated on achieving perfect execution, refusing to move on until she had it.

She settled into something approaching a trance, scarcely aware as she added increments of difficulty. The doubles became triples, the spins combinations, then combinations with a change of foot, the step sequences an increasingly elaborate tap dance that had her feet moving faster and faster until they were a blur of flashing chrome.

Dimly, as though from a great distance, she became aware of a noise from the stands—soft at first, then swelling until it was a roar.

As she continued her sweep around the rink, she was startled to see people standing and applauding. She wondered if Kondo was practicing her Axel and quickly scanned the ice ahead, eager to see one in spite of the woman's menace. Kondo was not to be seen.

She was just accelerating, frustrated, when her eye caught a movement, no more than a blur, approaching from behind. A heavy, dark squall bearing down on her. Her brain, registering the threat, commanded: "Do it!" She did.

A shower of frozen shards flew ahead of her as she rotated ninety degrees, dug her blades into the ice, bent her knees, dropped her right shoulder. A half second later she was lying on the ice, dazed. She lifted her head and peered around, the room swimming.

A few feet away Kazue Kondo lay sprawled on her side in an undignified heap, looking like a pile of old laundry. Her mouth hung open, tongue protruding. The heavy legs were making slow, bicycling motions.

Hesitantly Maggie pushed herself to her hands and knees, the position she was in when Madam Goto reached her.

"Are you all right, Megumi?" Madam Goto kneeled down, putting an arm around her. "Can you get up?"

"I . . . I think so."

"What happened?" Maggie, wobbly but upright, looked over at Kondo. A man was helping her to her feet while others watched.

Madam Goto eyed her curiously. "That one was coming up hard on you when you stopped; didn't you see her?"

Maggie looked pained. "I'm afraid not."

After a long, reflective pause Madam Goto nodded.

"Ah. Most unfortunate. An unavoidable accident, that is all."

"*Hai, sensei.* I stopped because I wanted to see what the applause was for; I thought Kondo-*san* must have been putting on a display. I am most regretful."

Maggie thought she saw something in her *sensei*'s eyes. "The people were applauding you, for your magnificent practice. Kondo-*san was* putting on a display, though. Apparently, it was not as well received."

"I should apologize."

"It would be a nice gesture. She will be most grateful."

Maggie bent over the prostrate figure. "Kondo-*san*—I am so sorry. It was most heedless of me to stop so suddenly. I hope you will forgive me."

The woman stared at her through unfocused eyes, her mouth working wordlessly. It was the man holding her who answered, screeching: "You little animal—you did that on purpose! I'll have you thrown out of the competition! I'll . . ." His prune face was an apoplectic scarlet.

Madam Goto appeared at Maggie's side. "Yoshida *sensei*—may we speak privately?"

Without waiting for an answer, she stepped toward the rail, beckoning the man to follow. With obvious reluctance, he handed his charge off to the others and joined her.

Though they were out of earshot, Maggie saw that something Madam Goto said caused the man to suck air. His lips drew back, he seemed about to speak, and then he bowed, stiffly and quickly, before swiveling to follow the group helping Kondo off the ice.

Madam Goto returned to Maggie's side. "There will be no more talk like that. Yoshida *sensei* understands that an inquiry into the cause of this little mishap would not be in his interests. Too many people saw what Kondo was up to when it happened. Now, perhaps you should rest."

Maggie bowed. "Goto *sensei,* thank you, but with your permission I should like to resume practice; I have already missed too much."

The old woman cocked her head, casting an appraising eye before nodding. "Certainly, Megumi-*chan*—I respect your judgment."

That night Maggie tried not to think about skating. It helped that she could hear her parents, who were in the adjacent room, talking late into the evening. It was a comforting sound, the soft buzz that had accompanied her to sleep so many nights. An occasional word drifted through the thin door: "America," "Boston," "foreigners." She drifted off.

Maggie skated her short program brilliantly. At the end of the evening she was in second place, behind Chiako Mori, the reigning champion. One judge had actually placed her first, and the five who'd put her second had awarded her scores that couldn't have been closer to Mori's. The only anomaly were the placements of the remaining three judges. Two placed her fourth, and one, a moon-faced man from Okinawa, had her an insulting fifth, with a score for presentation that implied she belonged back in the juniors.

Madam Goto had been correct in her prediction that Kazue Kondo would suffer by comparison to Maggie. It was immediately obvious that Kondo's repertoire was embarrassingly unbalanced.

True, her jumps were spectacular, her squat legs propelling her far higher than any of the other women, but the short program, designed to display the skater's mastery of the basic elements of skating, allowed only two jumps and a jump combination—Kondo couldn't lard it with six or seven triples to help disguise her other weaknesses, as she would in the long program.

Even her jumps seemed curiously graceless and awkward, more like those of someone being violently expelled from the earth's surface than one taking flight through her own efforts. Yet it was her connecting steps and step sequences that revealed most clearly the gross asymmetry of Kondo's development as a skater. As one writer for a skating magazine would put it: "When Kondo came down the ice, uncharitable observers were heard questioning whether they were seeing a finalist in the senior ladies' figure skating championships or a bull walrus that's just spotted a female."

Madam Goto looked as though she'd been sucking sour plums when she saw Kondo's scores, which put her in fourth place. She turned to her pupil. "You have done all you can do tonight, and you did it well. Go and get some sleep—tomorrow will be a long day." She turned and stalked off.

Em Campbell ran after her. Catching up, she took the woman aside. "Goto *sensei*—please tell me what this could mean? Three of the judges gave Kondo better scores for presentation than Megumi. It is absurd!"

The old woman nodded. "It is an outrage. I don't know what it means, but I am going to try to find out. Something about the way your daughter presented must have bothered them. To think that that kangaroo Kondo is within reach of a medal—bah!"

She stopped and put out a restraining hand. "Campbell-*san*—it's just probably a quirk of judging. You mustn't say anything to disturb your daughter. I tell you frankly, I knew she was technically prepared, but I had no idea she was ready to skate like that. She skated as though pressure did not exist. She must go into tomorrow's performance focused only on maintaining her poise, not worrying about the judging. Whether she will win or not I cannot say, but she deserves to skate as well as she is able. And if she does, she will deserve to win. She is a great skater, with a warrior's heart."

She stood at center ice, skating last, knowing what she had to do. Nothing existed for her except the ice. She could not hear the audience, was unaware of the announcer, had not thought of anything but the job ahead of her. She felt no fear, merely a great calm.

Her music began. She raised her arms, threw back her head. For eight years she had been preparing for the next four minutes.

Her note sounded, her arms came down, her right foot thrust. She was ready.

When she came off, she knew it was hers: the vision of an eight-year-old, the moment she'd worked for, Benten-*sama*'s promise. She'd earned it, and she'd won. She was the ladies' figure skating champion of Japan.

The hotel room was a morgue. Maggie sat by herself, looking sightlessly out the window. Sometimes her parents saw her swallow, but they didn't see her cry. For over an hour she had sat by the window, not speaking, not crying, just looking.

She hadn't cried once, not even when her scores for presentation were posted, and she knew she wouldn't even medal. Not even when the crowd, jolted out of character by the irrationally low scores, whistled and booed.

Her parents had rushed to her side, fearing the worst, and had found her in shock, unable to speak. Madam Goto, her face a mask, had her arms around her. She passed her over to her father, pulling Em out of the girl's hearing.

"I will file a protest, of course." Fury caused Madam Goto to hiss. "But it won't make any difference."

Em was quivering with rage. "How? How could they have done this? She was perfect. And for the placements to be scattered like that. Something is very wrong."

Maggie's scores had been crazily distributed. The judge who'd placed her first the night before had her first in the long program, too, but three of the five judges who'd had her second in the short program had dropped her to fourth in the long, joined by the two who'd had her fourth the night before. A majority had placed Kondo third in the long program; the combined placements meant Maggie finished fourth overall, behind Mori, another woman, and Kondo.

The old lady grunted. "I told her that tonight I saw a great skater, in the performance of her life. I told her that is enough, that she must find her reward in the act itself. I have taught her this for years. This is why, I think, she will not say what she is feeling about this. What she has every right to feel."

The low growl grew louder. "It is a disgrace, a rank injustice! She has been cheated. She will not say it, and that is as it should be—but *I* will. They have no right to deny her the recognition that she earned. It is unforgivable."

She walked back to Maggie and put a hand on her shoulder. "Megumi-*chan*. You danced with the gods tonight. You know that, I know that, thousands of people know that. That is your reward today. You have many years of skating before you, and I promise you—you can be the best in the world. When I told you the act must be its own reward, I did not mean that other rewards should not follow. They will come, believe me. Little people will not always be able to deny you what is yours."

Maggie turned dull eyes on her. "Thank you, *sensei*."

"We will talk later. Now, I must go."

Two hours passed before there was a knock on the door. Nick opened it to find Madam Goto.

"I have some information. I believe I know what happened."

Nick gestured for her to step in, but she shook her head.

"It is better I talk to you and her mother. You must decide how much to tell her."

She looked past Nick to Maggie. "How is she?"

"She just sits like that."

"It is a terrible thing they did to her. If you will step out into the hall . . ."

"No!" Maggie's cry pierced the gloom. "I have a right to know." She ran over to the door. "Tell me, Goto *sensei*—it's my life." She stood between the two adults. "Please tell me!"

The old woman looked from daughter to father and back again. "It is up to your parents, Megumi-*chan*."

"Tell her. She's right. It's her life. The life we've given her." Em, her face ashen, had come up behind her husband. "I know, you see."

"You know—what do you know?" Nick turned, incomprehension twisting his face. "What's going on?"

"Please come in, Goto *sensei*." Em, standing by her daughter, had never been more aware of the differences between them. Putting her arm around the girl's shoulders, she turned to Goto. "It's her, isn't it? The way she looks."

Nick looked at his wife blankly. " 'The way she looks'? She looked wonderful. Do you mean her costume? It's beautiful. This is crazy." His head swiveled back and forth, eyes lighting on his wife, Madam Goto, his wife again.

Em held up a restraining hand. "Stop, please. Just stop talking for a second, Nick."

His chin set, and Em saw again how alike they were, her husband and her daughter. "I'm not talking about dresses." Deliberately she turned to the old woman. "It was her, Goto *sensei*, wasn't it? What she is?"

Goto didn't answer at first. Finally, though, she bowed slightly and breathed, *"Hai."*

"What about what I am? Will somebody please explain what you're talking about?" Maggie was swaying slightly, but she wouldn't cry. She'd claw her eyes out before she'd cry.

"What have you heard, Goto *sensei?*" Em asked.

Madam Goto's eyes flashed contempt. "Most of the judges wouldn't talk, or just said some drivel about not thinking well of the program. But Saito, the one who scored honestly, he told me what happened. The others, he said, were 'uncomfortable'—the word he used—with a *hakujin* winning a medal. Not only a *hakujin*, but one with a *yanki* name."

She snorted. "He said they claimed she 'could not radiate the indefinable thing that is the Japanese spirit,' and that national team members must have that. An association official I complained to told me he 'did not think she had the manners of a Japanese woman.' Forgive me, but that is what he said. Garbage." Goto made a spitting sound. "Yoshida, Kondo's coach, he started it, even before the competition began. Saito said he was whispering, insinuating, talking to association officials about it for weeks. After Megumi's run-in with Kondo he redoubled his efforts: she lacked discipline, she would disgrace Japan in international competition, lies like that. Unfortunately he has much influence with the association, and it was an unusually weak group of judges."

"I knew it was something like that." Em nodded, running her hand over Maggie's head, down her cheek, cupping the defiant chin while she looked her in the eyes, the round, green eyes. "I am so sorry—so terribly sorry."

Maggie, blankly, whispered: "A *'hakujin'?* I never thought of myself as a *hakujin*. Even when people would talk about 'white people' around me, I never thought they meant *me*. I was Japanese. I thought if you felt Japanese, and were proud of being Japanese, it didn't matter what color your skin was. I didn't know." Then, in a faint, high, far-away voice: "He was right. He was right all the time."

"Who was right?" Em searched her daughter's face.

"It doesn't matter." Maggie shook her head. "Just some-body I know." She corrected herself. "Somebody I knew."

Madam Goto sagged, a tired old woman. "That's just an excuse, Megumi-*chan*—it wasn't used against you last year. That piece of filth Yoshida saw a way to hurt you, and used it. He would have used whatever he could, because he knew they could not beat you fairly."

"If you say so, *sensei*," Maggie responded listlessly.

The steel came back into Madam Goto as quickly as it had left. "I *do* say so! You did what you came to do—you skated magnificently. You cannot control what little people will do."

"Thank you, Goto *sensei*."

"I am honored to instruct you."

Maggie returned the bow. "No, no—it is I who am hon-ored to be instructed by you."

The old woman stepped back and bowed again. "Your time will come." She left.

"I'm not Japanese."

Maggie had settled on the edge of the couch. "I'm not Japanese," she repeated, whispering wonderingly.

"Of course you are." Her father settled beside her. "You're as Japanese as any one of those women. You just ran into a pack of idiots. It didn't happen last year, and it won't happen again."

"You're the idiot." Em's voice—quiet, low, cutting—overrode her husband's.

He snapped his head around. "Jesus, Em—why would you—"

"How can you lie to her like that? Are you *trying* to set her up to be hurt again? Why don't you tell the truth?"

Nick stood, his big American face coloring. "That *is* the truth."

"What—that what happened was *unusual?* That she can relax now, it won't happen again? Don't you understand . . . this was *overdue!* She's been living in a fool's paradise, and we built it for her."

"You heard Madam Goto—one man got them stirred up. It didn't happen last year, did it? Listen, we're going to raise such hell, why—"

"No, and it might not happen next year, either. Or it might. She'll never know, will she? A skating competition, a school, a job, a man; she'll just have to walk in and see what happens, is that your idea?"

Nick pinched his lips together; his hands balled into fists. "I don't think this is the time for this."

"You're damned right this isn't the time for this; the time for this was fifteen years ago, when I told you we shouldn't move here. But you wouldn't listen then, so you can listen now." She shook her head. "You still don't understand, do you?" She looked at him as though he were dull witted. "I think I know why, too. You think sure, the Japanese may despise the Filipinos, loathe Koreans, and pretend their own *burakumin* don't exist, but *my* daughter has round eyes and fair skin—who can object to that?"

He squared his wide shoulders. "I might remind you who *I* married, and it's the best thing I ever did. But you can hardly charge me with being a racist. *I'm* the one who's saying my daughter's Japanese and damn well has the right to be treated like a Japanese."

"She *is* being treated like a Japanese, Nick!" She advanced on him, glad to see him retreat. "That's not your complaint; your complaint is, she isn't being treated like an *American*. You said you wanted her treated like a Japanese, and now she *has been*—don't you get it? She was treated the way we treat Japanese people who aren't . . . what . . . they . . . should . . . be. And I *told* you this would happen."

"Em, you're talking nonsense. I—"

"No, Nick, I'm *not* talking nonsense. You came over here, and you presumed all sorts of wonderful things would follow. You had your sweet little Japanese wife, and your sweet little Japanese children, and you were going to live with all the sweet little Japanese people, and if you showed them you liked their raw fish, and their hot baths, and you learned their language and a few of their customs, they were going to be sweet little members of the world America was offering. Only this is about *being* Japanese. Don't you understand the difference *yet?* I've told you often enough. I told you back in Boston, but you wouldn't believe me. I told you here, but you wouldn't believe me. Now believe me: people live in tribes, and my tribe says our daughter doesn't belong! And I *told* you it would."

Nick looked at Maggie. "Can't we at least wait until—"

"No! She should have heard this years ago. *Chigau,* Nick. What's it mean?"

"Em, for Christ's sake—"

"What's it mean, damn it!"

"Different," he snapped. "Now—"

"What else?" she demanded. "Megumi knows. After tonight, she'll never forget, either. Have you forgotten what else *chigau* means, Nick?"

"Em, *please* . . ."

"What else, Nick?"

"For God's sake, won't you stop?"

"It also means 'wrong,' doesn't it? Maybe now you won't forget again, either."

He stood, frozen, staring at her.

"Doesn't it?"

"Yes," he answered numbly.

"Very good, Nick, *very* good. In other words, in Japan to be *different* is the same as being *wrong*. And our daughter is different, isn't she?"

"Stop it, Em."

"Look at these—" She jabbed her forefingers against the corners of her eyes. "Go on, look at them! *That's* being Japanese! Look at this—" She squeezed a wad of flesh on her forearm until the color disappeared. "*That's* Japanese skin. Look at this—" She grabbed a hank of hair. "That's Japanese hair! *That's* what these people are saying. If you look different, speak different, or act different, you *aren't* Japanese, no matter what some passport or meaningless law says. That's what I tried to tell you, but you weren't going to listen."

She looked at her daughter. "Oh, Maggie—I'm so sorry. So terribly sorry. We should never have done this to you."

The thought brought her back to her husband, who was standing, mouth half-open, as though she'd driven a knife into him. "So like you—so like Americans—to think that all you have to do is go talk to somebody and everything will turn out nice and reasonable. Like you had me talk to her elementary school principal, so they'd leave her alone."

Nick straightened. "Exactly—and they did! Most people are decent, and—"

"They treated her like a *foreigner*, Nick! The principal was so proud." She adopted a mocking tone: " 'Now that Japan is prosperous, we have *many* foreigners living here. The Ministry of Education says we must accommodate them, and we do.' He told me all the ways they made exceptions for foreign students."

Her mouth twisted. "He assured me the rule against curled hair wouldn't apply to Maggie! Wasn't that nice, Nick? Unlike little *Japanese* girls who make the mistake of curling their hair, or, heaven forbid, are born with it, *our* daughter wasn't going to come home with her head shaved! You see, we make allowances for barbarians. Ever since we stopped killing them, we've been polite to our foreign visitors. So I decided to let the school think of our daughter as a little Japanese-speaking foreigner."

Nick started to speak, but the words strangled in his throat. Em, ignoring him, continued. "I hate myself for that decision. I should have *demanded* they treat her as Japanese, just like you wanted. It would have been far better if they'd sent her home in the first grade and told her not to come back until her hair was straight and black. Until her skin was yellow and her eyes were slits."

"Em, for God's—"

"Because then, you see, she'd have known what to expect, as a 'Japanese.' And what should we do now, Nick, since apparently you're determined to stay? Should I talk to the colleges? Go around with her on job interviews, explaining how she's really a good Japanese girl in spite of her hair and eyes and color? Talk to the parents who'll gag at the thought of their little prince marrying a *gaijin?* I *told* you."

Nick swayed. "I never thought—"

"Have you told our daughter what happens when she becomes an adult and goes to register as a Japanese citizen? Have you told her they won't register her unless she changes her last name to Honda or Takaoka or some other good *Japanese* name? Have you told her that to millions of 'her' people she's *deformed?* Grotesque, a monstrosity?"

"Em, stop! Think what you're saying!"

She advanced on him, pounding her hands on his chest, as hard as she could, crying the tears her daughter wouldn't cry, saying over and over: "I told you! I told you!"

He stood expressionless, letting the small fists flail at him until he caught his wife's hands in his and held them against his chest, waiting while her gasps died. He pulled her to him. "Shh. Shh," he whispered into her hair, "that's enough now." He held her until she settled, the tears stopped.

"That's enough now," he whispered again. Looking over her head, he spoke to Maggie. "There's something you should know. I wasn't sure . . . before, but we've been asked to move back to America, to Boston. The firm wants me back there. Maybe we should go?"

He put his hands on Em's shoulders, easing her away. "That's right, isn't it—that's what you want?"

Maggie answered for her mother. "That's what *I* want. I want to leave. I want to be an American." Her jaw stiffened. "I don't ever want to come back!"

A month later they were at Narita, sitting in the business-class section of a Northwest Airlines 747 as the steps were rolled away, the hatches fastened. They had been seen off by the Tanakas. The house was relet, neighbors and classmates and friends bade farewell. They'd been so busy, there was little time to reflect on the change their lives were about to undergo.

Maggie found the parting from Madam Goto far harder than saying good-bye to her grandparents. They would visit America; she would never see her *sensei* again.

A letter arrived for Maggie, two weeks before they left, from Chiako Mori. "My medal is lead. I hope we meet again, on the ice or off. It was an honor to compete with you."

Maggie thought of little else than meeting Japanese skaters again. She had a new vision, well polished now.

She rested her head against the seatback, conjuring it. She was a member of the American Olympic team. A Japanese girl posted the highest scores of the night. Only Maggie Campbell could deny her the gold. And she did, with perfect scores. She stood on the stand, looking down at the sobbing young woman as the American flag went up, "The Star-Spangled Banner" played. She looked over at the Japanese delegation, led by the vile Yoshida, her eyes telling them what she was thinking. She was only sorry she couldn't imagine Yoshida committing seppuku on the spot.

The plane accelerated down the runway. As the last physical contact was broken, Maggie looked down at the retreating surface. Her tongue betrayed her. *"Sayonara,"* she whispered.

Chapter 25

May 2001: Boston

L ofton Weeks gave his guests his most dazzling smile. "Igor, Luda. What *can* I say, except that we're simply thrilled you'll be joining us?"

They'd risen from the table in the private dining room on the third floor of Locke-Ober. Several empty wine bottles testified to the conviviality of dinner.

Weeks put his arms around the shoulders of the handsome couple, bussing cheeks noisily as he steered them toward the door. The woman, balking, brought them to a halt. Swaying slightly, she assumed a dark, appraising look. "You are sure now you can get us commercial opportunity? This is not bullshit?" She inspected him with the eyes of a Soviet border guard.

Her husband scowled. "Luda, Luda—don't be *nekulturny*. Mr. Weeks will take good care of us."

Weeks chuckled. "Don't worry, Igor—I've heard a lot worse." He turned to Luda Lupskaya. "Clay will be sending you some proposals for endorsements, media appearances, perhaps some charitable activity. He'll—"

Her heavy brows met in the middle of her forehead. "Charity? You mean, like, skate for nothing?"

She shouldn't do that, Weeks thought—her makeup looks as though it could slide off any moment. He smiled benignly. "Sometimes that's very good business, my dear. With you and Igor not all that well-known here—"

"Bullshit!"

"Luda!" Her husband had her arm and was trying to tug her out the door.

"We want to get nothing for skating, we could stay in bullshit, stupid Russia!"

She was anchored to the floor, going nowhere until this affront was removed. Weeks sighed. "Clay, forget about charitable appearances in the proposals you send Luda and Igor, all right? Just throw out some solid, high-profile suggestions."

The woman peered around Weeks. "Expensive, okay?"

Clay nodded. "Nothing but the best for the best."

"You are dear boy." She stood on tiptoe and kissed Clay on both cheeks, then on the mouth. "This is fine young man, Lofton. Beautiful. Take good care. Come, Igor."

She swept out of the small room like Anastasia, followed by an eye-rolling, hands-in-the-air husband.

Weeks shut the door and staggered to his seat. "Sweet, suffering Jesus." He took a long pull on his Armagnac. "A European championship four years ago, never medaled in the Worlds or the Olympics, and she talks like they're Rodnina and Zaitsev. Could you believe she put away two hundred dollars' worth of caviar? Washed down with a bottle of Cristal?"

"Apparently she appreciates the good life." Clay poured a glass of the Chassagne-Montrachet he'd had with his lobster Savannah. Raising it, he added, "As do I, Lofton. Thanks for bringing me. As a matter of fact, thank you for hiring me—I'm loving it."

"Ah, yes." Weeks wafted the snifter under his nose. "I wanted to talk with you about that. I was going over your expense reports."

Clay lowered his glass. "Nothing wrong, I hope. I haven't been having *too* good a time, have I?"

Weeks lowered the snifter and twisted it on the tablecloth. "Not at all. Not good enough, as a matter of fact."

"I'm sorry—I'm not following you. You want me to run up higher expenses?"

The neat little hands stilled. "I want to know why, as far as I can tell from those reports, you haven't spent one minute with Doe Rawlings since mid-February. Almost three months. Perhaps you're wooing her with beer and peanuts? The blue-collar approach? Or am I missing something?"

Clay's eyes darted around the room. "No, you're right. I stopped calling her." He swirled his glass, took a drink. "Look, Lofton, I told you I didn't have any special in with her. I tried it out a few times, she didn't want to talk about it, and I didn't want to waste any more of my time or your money."

Weeks's finger traced the rim of his glass. "Coyle's saying he's brought in investors. Telling people he's going to build a whole new tour around her. Fact is, he gets her, that *becomes* the tour."

"Lofton, she isn't going to sign with anybody until after the Olympics. Rill's adamant."

The forefinger dipped into the glass. Weeks dabbed it against his tongue, nodding. "So I can relax? Start arranging lines of credit, in nine months get in a bidding war with some asshole who'll pay ten times what a property's worth just so he gets his picture in the paper? Knowing that if I lose that war, everything I've worked for all my life is gone?"

Clay threw up his hands. "I did what I could." He shrugged.

"Ah." Weeks shot his French cuffs, nodding. "That's good."

"Sure. What can I say, except I'm sorry that it hasn't panned out?"

"Nothing, really."

"Anyway, for Luda and Igor, I think—"

Weeks leaned forward. "Listen to me, you useless piece of shit."

Clay jerked back as though a cattle prod had been shoved against the base of his spine, the wineglass shattering on the wood floor. "What the . . . I don't have to take that."

"No, you don't. You can get up and walk out now. Leave the keys to the BMW as you go by. Or you can tell me what the *fuck* you take me for."

Clay felt dazed, as though watching it happen to someone else. "I, I don't understand. What the hell's this all about?"

"What this is all about, sonny, is you being too thick to understand what you were hired to do."

"But I *told* you I couldn't make any promises about Doe."

"Right—and I was more than happy to let you spin that cock-and-bull story about you two just being friends, if that was the way you wanted to play it. Or did you *really* think I'd pay you good money to run around the country swilling burgundy with a bunch of has-beens and third-raters? I hired you to sign Doe Rawlings!"

Clay leapt to his feet, anger and hurt overwhelming caution. " 'Has-beens and third-raters'? Just last week you were telling me what a great job I was doing, and now I'm a bum because I can't sign Doe Rawlings?"

"Last week I didn't realize you'd given up on the only business that matters."

Clay, chest heaving, rested his knuckles on the table. "I tried, damn it, and she wasn't having it."

"Then you didn't try hard enough, and you better try again, or you're no use to me."

Clay leaned over the table, beyond all caution. "Well, what does that make you? You didn't have any more luck than I did."

Weeks looked at him coldly. "Yes, but you were fucking her—that gives you an advantage."

"That's a damned lie!" Clay raised a fist. "I told you nothing like that was going on."

Weeks chuckled mirthlessly. "Well, let's put it this way— my parents bred curly-coated retrievers. They had a prize bitch, and every year they'd put her in a pen to be serviced. And do you know what? Until she was ready, the male couldn't get near her. But when she was ready, she'd put her haunches in the air and back around the pen, until the male got the idea. I was reminded of that when I saw you and Miss Rawlings sneaking out that night."

"You're disgusting!"

"You didn't seem very eager to get out of the pen, either."

"I've had enough of this." Clay started around the table.

"Leave the keys."

Clay stopped. "Lofton, this is ridiculous." He felt himself panicking. "Can't we—"

"Leave the keys, and clear out your office. Tomorrow."

"Lofton, I've got a lease I can't get out of. I've got debts. I *need* this job." He heard the pleading tone but was powerless to stop. "*Please!*"

"Leave the keys."

"Maybe I gave up too soon. I'll try again, but if I don't get anywhere—"

"I don't want to hear about it." Weeks drained his glass. Setting it down carefully, he stood. "Get her signed, Clay. You wanted to learn this business, did you? Well, now you are. You do what it takes, boy—you follow me? You get her signed to my contract, by January first, or don't come in on January second."

He waited for almost a week before he made the call. She answered.

He looked at the receiver. He could still hang up.

He cleared his throat. "Hello, Doe."

"Clay?" Her voice was low, uncertain. "Where have you been? Why didn't you return my calls?"

"I'm sorry—I should have, but I've . . . been traveling a lot. But things are slowing down now, and I wondered . . . would you like to get together? There's a symphony tonight, and the agency has a box. If you're not busy, why . . ."

He paused, not sure what answer he wanted. His shoulders slumped when she replied.

"Oh." He paused, collecting his thoughts. After a deep breath he said, "Hey—that's terrific. I'll be by at seven. We can get a drink first."

He replaced the receiver, stood looking at the telephone. He hadn't had a call from Maggie in a while, but he knew she had to watch her money. He could call her. It would be . . . He looked at his watch, trying to figure. Five in the morning? Too early. Or maybe it was too late. All he knew was, he couldn't call. He went up to change.

Chapter 26

July 2001: Tokyo

Maggie doubted Tokyo in July was muggier than it had been when she was a child; no doubt the impression that she was in a steambath the likes of which she'd never known before was simply another example of time embroidering the past. She couldn't understand why her grandfather seemed not to notice.

They were in a long, low building still under construction. A dozen men in green coveralls were muscling machine tools into place while a forklift truck deposited heavy crates around the cement floor. Every few seconds the insistent crackle of an arc welder interrupted Shingo Tanaka's explanation.

"The new product requires an entirely new manufacturing process, you see." He had to raise his voice. "Those extruders were custom designed. They cost almost sixty million yen apiece!"

"You must be very confident in the new product." Her words seemed to evaporate as soon as they left her mouth, but her grandfather nodded. "We are. You will see why when we demonstrate it. Now that," he said, turning her, "will be where the circuit boards are wired. All by robot." He led her across the floor.

With every movement she felt as though she'd dressed in a wet sheet. Her hair clung to her forehead in damp tendrils, her white shirt stuck to her skin, and as she blotted the perspiration mustache on her upper lip she thought with longing of the practice she was skipping to visit Kofuku. When her grandfather finally said, "Come—you're not used to this," she was dizzily grateful.

Inside the main building she could hear herself again, and the overhead fans at least moved the heavy air. "Phew!" Maggie tugged the top of her shirt away from her chest. "That was brutal."

Her grandfather chuckled. "After the Malayan jungle nothing will ever seem hot again." Though he was almost seventy-four, he seemed energized by the tour of the new facility. "The laboratory is air-conditioned. Here." He held open a door. "Now you will see why we are willing to invest so heavily."

The laboratory *was* cooler than the new facility, but it wasn't air-conditioning as five years in America had taught her to like it. While she pretended to be following the bewildering display her cousin Nobuo and uncle Katsumi put on for her, Maggie imagined what it would feel like to stretch full-length on the ice at Ikebukuro.

At one end of the room was something Nobuo called a cellular transmitter, next to which stood telephones, a television camera, and a fax machine. At the other was a table on which sat a cellular telephone, a television monitor, and another fax machine. For half an hour Nobuo, in a crisp white lab coat, broadcast telephone calls, television images, and faxes, while his father sustained a highly technical description of something he called "compressed bandwidth." Every time she got comfortable Maggie would be directed to come to a table and listen or look at something. Sometimes the images or sounds were garbled and indecipherable, and Nobuo or his father would say: "You see?" Sometimes they were distinct, and then the two men would beam and nod while Maggie exclaimed appreciatively.

Shingo Tanaka looked on approvingly, occasionally adding a comment. Maggie found most of the talk impenetrable, but she nodded periodically.

Nobuo concluded with a speech. "So you see, Cousin, with our new technology, the major limitation of cellular telephony has been overcome. This will make fax and graphics transmission, to say nothing of voice, available to areas too poor, or too thinly populated, to install hardwire facilities. Tribesmen in Borneo will be connected to the outside world, at very low cost. This may be the most important development in communication technology since the telephone itself."

His father nodded excitedly. "Kofuku may hold the most valuable telephone patents since America's Alexander Bell."

"That's wonderful. You all must be very proud."

The three generations of Tanaka men murmured self-deprecatingly, but none of them could hide the pleasure they felt. Nobuo reverently shut down the equipment, covering it with plastic sheeting.

"When will I be able to buy one of the new telephones, Grandfather?"

He smiled. "You will not have to buy one; it will be my pleasure to give one of the first ones to you. But it won't be for a while, I fear—the new factory is far from ready."

Katsumi nodded. "And that's why Son and I had better

take our leave, Niece—we must meet with our engineers." The younger Tanakas bowed and left. Maggie was always struck by how much they looked like her brother and how little like her.

"I brought something from home." Shingo Tanaka reached into a bag. "Do you remember him?" He extracted a foot-high mechanical monkey, covered in brown synthetic fuzz.

"Moshi-moshi!" Maggie clapped. "Does he still work?"

Her grandfather set the toy on the table and pushed a switch on his back. With a whirring sound the limbs slowly moved back and forth, and the beast lurched clumsily across the surface. Every few seconds a squeaky voice said, "Moshi-moshi, Megumi. Moshi-moshi."

Maggie ran over and snatched it off the table. She hugged it, kissing the top of its head, where the acrylic fur was worn bald from years of caresses. "Hello, Monkey, hello. It's so good to see you again."

She held it out at arm's length, the arms and legs pawing the air, the shrill voice chanting its one message. "Of all the toys you made us, Grandfather, Moshi-moshi was my favorite. I could never understand how you got him to say my name."

"It was not difficult; just a memory chip and a small speaker. One of the office ladies at JRT did the voice."

Maggie shook her head. "You make it sound so simple. The way Nobuo made the new telephone sound simple. Except I wouldn't have thought of it in a million years."

"And I wouldn't have dreamed of jumping up in the air and spinning around. We all have our strengths and weaknesses."

Maggie pushed the switch on the monkey's back, but it kept moving. She surrendered it helplessly to her grandfather, who took it, tried the switch, and when it still didn't work pulled a screwdriver out of a drawer and began removing a panel from the toy's back.

A knock was followed by an office lady, bearing a tray. She shuffled forward, bowing repeatedly.

Shingo Tanaka looked around. "Granddaughter will stay for lunch?"

"Of course."

The office lady unpacked *bento* boxes and poured orange juice, while Mr. Tanaka made silly jokes and the young woman exclaimed over the monkey, giggled, and bowed. She looked pretty in her powder blue suit and pillbox hat. When she giggled she covered her mouth with her hand. To everything Shingo Tanaka said she answered, *"Hai, hai,"* in a light, birdlike chirp.

After she left he said, "Junko is a good O.L. She graduated from Tokyo Women's College. She is engaged to our assistant sales manager, a fine young man. Ah!"

He extracted a battery, and the monkey went dead as he began unscrewing the switch. "When they marry they will live with her parents. Soon she will get pregnant. Then she will quit, they will move into a flat two hours away from here, and she will raise the child. If the child is a girl, they will have another, hoping it is a boy. She will see very little of her husband, until he retires."

He broke off, smiling. "You are wondering if your grandfather's switch is as broken as Moshi-moshi's. But seeing Junko, with you here, made me remember something. Did your mother ever tell you how she came to go to college in America?"

Reading Maggie's hesitation, he nodded placidly. "She did not get on so well with your grandmother, it is true. Your mother was never willing to accept the role expected of her.

Katsumi always did exactly what your grandmother expected of him, but your mother insisted on asking 'why' all the time. She did not seem to care much what other people thought; if there wasn't a good reason for something, she wouldn't do it. And she didn't think 'because that isn't done' was a reason."

He shook his head gravely. "Your grandmother thinks that's the *only* reason you need." He chuckled. "You see, your mother got my personality, and Katsumi got your grandmother's." He pulled out the switch and held it up. "Corroded. I'll install a new one. We want Moshi-moshi working well when *your* child comes along. Of course, I'll have to put in a new name. What will it be?"

Maggie laughed. "Too soon, Grandfather. But what about the O.L.?"

"Oh, yes. I *am* wandering. Well, when your mother was seventeen she came to me, crying. She had told your grandmother she wanted to go to college in America. She had read that Tokyo University was 'the Harvard of Japan,' and being the girl she was, she wasn't content just to apply to Todai, which would have been rare enough for a girl; she thought she should go to the *real* Harvard. Naturally, your grandmother said it was out of the question."

"Because that wasn't done."

"Exactly. It was unthinkable—your mother might as well have announced she wanted to become a prostitute. So she came to me."

He looked over his lunch, extracting a bit of fish. Chewing thoughtfully, he continued, "It was not my role, of course, to interfere in the raising of the children. Do you know the only other time I did?"

"No, Grandfather."

"When your mother was eleven, and asked to take skating

lessons. Your grandmother was dead set against it—she said it would look as though we didn't care if the girl wasted her time. I could tell your mother loved skating, and since I already had one child who always did exactly as expected, I insisted she be allowed to take lessons."

He folded his hands contentedly over his white shirtfront. "I'm glad I did, too, even though your grandmother was, ah, somewhat irked, you might say. Not so much that your mother got her way, as that I interfered in something that wasn't a man's business. But I think the skating helped your mother be content with her own company and her own accomplishments. Maybe that's why she wanted to go to America, do you think?"

Maggie thought a moment. "I think perhaps that's so."

"Well, that's a good thing, then. But when your grandmother said no to Harvard, your mother was so unhappy that it hurt me in here." He patted his chest. "I asked her why she wanted to leave Japan, and she said it was because she couldn't stand the thought of being an O.L."

He smiled serenely. "You see—I got there eventually."

Maggie furrowed her forehead. "I'm not sure I understand what she meant."

"At first I didn't, either. I said of course she didn't have to be an O.L. if she didn't want to be one, but she didn't have to go to America to avoid it. But she explained, and then I understood. She was saying, you see, she would be *expected* to become an O.L. for a few years, it was what nice girls did after they got out of college. Then she would be *expected* to marry the *sarariman* she'd meet through her mentor, and then *expected* to quit work to have a baby. She was saying she would be expected to live her life through her society's expectations, unless she broke away."

"She could have stayed here, and refused to go along."

"It is not so easy, especially when you are only eighteen. It's easier to go someplace where you aren't making a statement all the time, you see? The years in America gave your mother time to find that strength, so that, when your family moved here, your mother was able to decide for herself what to accept and what to reject. It was what I had hoped would happen."

The pink, pickled ginger crunched coolly in Maggie's mouth, releasing a fresh, sharp, faintly soapy flavor. She swallowed, saying, to keep him talking: "So you overruled Grandmother?"

"I did, and I was never sorry. Your mother grew so much. I watched it happen. Every summer she came home with new ideas. Some were foolish, of course, but she found that out in time. She was like a bud, blossoming into a beautiful flower. Then she moved in with your father, and the next time she came home it was to marry him."

Maggie's eyes widened. "They lived together before they were married?"

"I believe so."

"You weren't upset?"

"Here, she would have gone to a love hotel with her young man, *ne?* Ten thousand yen for an hour at the Venus Joy House, or some such?"

He chuckled as Maggie gaped, speechless. "Granddaughter didn't know her old grandfather knew of such things, eh? Well, the only thing more amazing than how much the world has changed is how little it's changed. Young people find a way to do what young people have always wanted to do. And don't forget—your grandmother and I were young once, and we weren't always married."

"You don't mean . . ."

He held up his hand. "Now, I don't ask your secrets, don't

you ask mine. Anyway, I was glad, when your mother brought your father over to meet us, that she had picked well; that was all that mattered."

"Did it bother you that she married an American?"

"Not at all. I could never understand why people worry about such things. We cross chrysanthemums of different colors and shapes to get even more beautiful flowers, but it horrifies us if our child should marry a Pakistani or American. All nonsense. It would have bothered me only if your mother had married a *sarariman*—that wasn't the life for her."

"You're an unusual man, Grandfather."

He shrugged. "More unusual than I should be, perhaps. People shouldn't still be concerning themselves with silly things like race and nationality."

He broke off. Then, sadly, he added: "The only thing that troubled me was that your father let his law firm transfer him here. I thought that was a mistake. I loved having you and your brother nearby when you were little, I loved having your mother back and getting to know your father, but your mother was right and your father was wrong: you should have stayed in America. At the least, you should not have been raised to think of yourself as a Japanese girl."

"It was all right, Grandfather; everyone meant the best." She drank some juice. It tasted wonderful.

He set his jaw. "When those people did that to you, it was as though they'd attacked me. I could have killed them all." He stared at the remains of his lunch. "We didn't teach you what to expect. We didn't protect you."

She put her hand on his arm. "During the war the American government put the *nisei* in concentration camps. American citizens. They took away their property, locked them up, for no reason except their race. They didn't do that to the

German Americans, only the Japanese Americans. Nobody taught the *nisei* to expect that. What happened to me could have happened anyplace. I know that now."

He nodded sadly. "People are capable of incredible stupidity."

"Yes." They looked at each other; Maggie, eager to move on, asked, "Was Grandmother very upset? When you said Mother could go to Harvard, I mean."

He brightened, rolling his eyes in mock horror. "Oh, my. 'Upset'? You might say so. Your grandmother, you know, is a very forceful woman."

Maggie laughed. "She certainly is."

"She is a good woman, though. She only wants the best for her family."

"I know, but . . ." Maggie hesitated, her chopsticks halfway between the *bento* box and her mouth.

Shingo Tanaka smiled. "It is all right—what would you like to ask?"

"It is none of my business, but why does Grandmother get so angry whenever the subject of JRT or Chairman Fukawa comes up?"

Her grandfather looked at her appraisingly. Before answering, he poured them each a cup of tea. He sipped his slowly, blowing on the surface. "In the jungle hot tea actually seemed cooling. You know I started JRT with Fukawa-*san?*"

"Yes." She'd heard the story dozens of times, but she liked hearing him talk and knew he enjoyed telling it, so she added, "But I forget how you met him."

"Ah." Shingo Tanaka nodded. "It was right after the war. I went home to Osaka, only to find that the house I grew up in was no more—just some burnt timbers. The whole neighborhood—gone."

He shrugged. "There was a skinny fellow about my age in an officer's uniform, picking through the rubble, looking for anything of value. I saw him pull out an old radio. It was in bad shape, and he started to throw it away, but I stopped him. I got it to play, and he traded it for food. That night we ate."

"That was Fukawa-*san?*"

"*Hai.* He was from a rich Osaka family, but they were all gone, as was my family. After a few days we went to Tokyo together; Fukawa-*san* thought there would be more opportunity there, and there was."

The old man sighed. "It was a dreadful time, but there were compensations. Fukawa-*san* was a marvel at scrounging things, and I had a gift for making electronic devices out of odd bits, so we were a good team. He'd find parts—I didn't ask him where—and I'd build simple radios. They had terrible sound, but everybody wanted one, so we had enough to eat. Soon we'd hired some unemployed Imperial Army electrical engineers and were making radios on a volume basis. And that was how Fukawa-*san* and I started JRT.

"In 1951, just before the Occupation ended, the Ministry of Posts and Telegraphs solicited bids for the reconstruction of the entire telephone system. Well, the heart of the system is in the central switches, and I had an idea for a new way to build them. So we bid. But it was really almost a joke, JRT bidding, because we were just a tiny, upstart company, bidding against the great prewar giants. It seemed very unlikely."

He lit a cigarette. "We put everything we had or could borrow into new equipment—we had to be able to show, you see, that we could perform if we got the contract. But it was a huge gamble, because if we didn't get it—phht!

"Well, in the meantime Katsumi had been born, and your

grandmother was desperate to get out of our one-room apartment, just a hovel, really, and into a real house. So I asked Fukawa-*san* if he knew any way I could borrow the money for a house. Much to my surprise, he made me a generous offer for my half of JRT—a very generous offer, under the circumstances. I had a wife and child, he said, whereas he was single. He could take the risk that we would not get the telephone contract and all would be lost; I could not. It made sense to me, so I sold him my half. A few weeks later, JRT got the telephone contract, and that became the basis for its tremendous growth. Fukawa was rich, we were comfortable."

He chuckled. "Your grandmother would have preferred rich. She's never forgiven me for not waiting."

"It was a good decision, Grandfather; had Fukawa-*san* not been lucky, Grandmother would think you a hero."

" 'Lucky.' " He laughed, started to say something, then broke off abruptly, shaking his head. "Ah, well—it doesn't matter. The chairman has what he wants, and I have what I want, and I wouldn't trade with him for a second."

Maggie patted her grandfather's hand. "You did the sensible thing."

He shrugged. "I think so. I've had a good life—work I love, a good salary, and now a business of my own, for Katsumi after me, and Nobuo after him. I am content. I was no businessman. To succeed in business, one must be hard. The chairman is, I am not." He looked up at the ceiling. "The chairman is a very hard man."

Emboldened by her grandfather's frankness, Maggie said, "I always thought there was something . . . ugly about him. That time we paid our New Year's call on him, and he was so horrible to you and Uncle, I hated him."

Her grandfather shook his head. "I'd forgotten about that.

It's best to, you know. Best to forget the things you cannot change."

"I'll never forget." She looked at him ruefully. "I'm afraid I'm not good at forgetting. I'm getting better at forgiving, though."

Chapter 27

January 1994: Tokyo

*I*n honor of the New Year, Nick and Katsumi were in their best suits. Kenji wore a blazer and tie over short pants. Nobuo, sick with the flu, had remained home.

Mr. Tanaka had on the black *happi* coat that he saved for special occasions and was carrying a $100 melon from Matsuya Department Store. It was encased in a fine wooden box that in turn was wrapped in a *furoshiki,* a yard-square cloth used to enfold expensive gifts. In all likelihood Fukawa would pass along the melon in the next day or so to someone to whom he owed *on,* such as a politician who'd done JRT a service. Mr. Tanaka hoped so, because that would mean the gift had been appreciated.

Maggie clip-clopped along in a *furisode* kimono, yards of red and yellow silk, with the long, billowing sleeves that single women wear, her waist girdled by a gold obi tied in a Dancing Fan knot. Embroidered sandals, or zori, and the tailored white socks called tabi completed the outfit. She said she felt ridiculous but secretly considered it shamelessly glamorous.

Her mother was in a married women's kimono, a Moriguchi design. She'd placed wads of cotton above her breasts and a towel around her waist, flattening her curves before slipping on the kimono. Maggie, tugging mightily, had cinched a dozen cloth belts around her before tying off the obi with a Drum knot that resembled a fat sparrow. Maggie thought her mother looked like a courtesan from the days of the Floating World.

Mariko and Mrs. Tanaka were in fine, formal kimonos called *homongi*, less colorful than Maggie's but with delicate flowers embroidered into the silk; they carried their best handbags and had spent hours on their hair. The group made a handsome display as they trooped up the hill from the train station to pay their annual call on the chairman and largest shareholder of the Japan Radio & Telephone Company.

Maggie swept her eyes over the grounds. The Fukawa house, in the staggeringly expensive suburb of Denenchofu, reminded Maggie of the American houses built around golf courses she'd seen when they'd visited Disney World. Short of the imperial palace, she knew of no residence in Japan the equal of Seizo Fukawa's.

The new swimming pool was the final stop on a tour of the grounds that had taken in the topiary bushes in front of the high brick wall around the house, the greenhouse filled with orchids and bonsai, and the garage containing Fumio Fukawa's new white Mercedes convertible. At each stop the visitors trumpeted their admiration, while their host, trailed by his plump grandson, had gone through the motions of deprecating his possessions, not terribly convincingly.

Seizo Fukawa waved at the pool offhandedly. "Of course,

the pool is closed now, but I expect Grandson will find it refreshing this summer."

Maggie was horrified when he added: "Perhaps your lovely daughter would like to join Grandson for a swim from time to time?"

Maggie's prayer was answered when her mother replied, "You are too kind. I am grateful on behalf of my daughter, but I am afraid she will have little time for recreation, between schoolwork and skating."

"Ah, yes. Grandson, too, found that schoolwork imposed great demands on his time. However, now that he will be going to university, perhaps he can relax a little. I thought the pool a suitable reward. He will have to work hard once he joins JRT."

Maggie ventured to speak. "And where are you going to university, Fumio-*san?*"

Grandson's face darkened. "I will be attending Kokubun University, here in Denenchofu. I could have gone elsewhere, but I wished to be close to Grandfather."

"Ahh," said Maggie. "Kokubun, of course." She smiled her sweetest smile. "I have heard much about it. It must be very difficult to get in—last year I don't believe any students from my school even bothered to apply. Not even those who got into Todai."

She was rewarded by the sudden reddening of Grandson's pudgy face. He'd wonder if she knew—as indeed she did—that Kokubun was a *suberidome,* a "skid stopper," the last resort for students rejected everywhere else. No one attended a Kokubun by choice. For years the spoiled lout had conveyed, not very subtly, the sense that the Tanakas and Campbells should be honored to be given the opportunity to pay homage to the Fukawas on New Year's Day; Maggie reveled in his discomfort.

Seizo Fukawa's low, slightly menacing voice broke in: "With my son gone, Grandson is my greatest treasure. I am delighted he agreed to remain here and keep an old man company."

He was not unattractive: rather short, but with an erect bearing and a slow, deliberate way of moving that reflected his character, not his age. He was uncommonly thin, as though he had never caught up with wartime deprivation, but hardly frail: Maggie remembered coming to his house as a little girl, gaping as he cracked a coconut with his hands; she had run off, frightened, when he offered her a piece of the meat. She could still hear his laughter following her.

His narrow head, capped with shiny black hair, was combed straight back, only slightly gray at the temples. His face was not one to forget; though Maggie saw the man only once a year, she could conjure his features at will—the angular planes of the cheeks, the oddly pointed ears, the prominent canines revealed whenever the thin lips drew back—and most of all the drooping, impenetrable eyes, unengaged in anything the rest of the face might undertake.

His voice was soft, formed low in the throat; when he spoke it was as though his mouth were the entrance to a cave, from which an unseen creature's growl escaped.

He led them to a Western-style buffet table, laden with an elaborate assortment of New Year's treats calculated to bring good luck: imported caviar, lobster, smoked salmon, fruit of all kinds, the special New Year's sweet rice cakes called *mochi,* pickles, pastries from the patisserie in one of the great department stores, particularly exotic sushi, thinly sliced rounds of the finest Kobe beef, rosettes of raw chicken, cleverly formed bean paste sweets, carafes of spiced sake, beer, wines from France and California, whiskey, and juices. The buffet was presided over by

Fumio's widowed mother, a dour woman who might as well have been a housemaid for all she contributed to the annual event.

Maggie limited herself to a mineral water and, hoping to minimize contact with Fumio, pretended to be absorbed in the pictures in the entrance hall. Her gambit failed when Fukawa, seeing her interest in his gallery, moved over to her, drawing the others in his wake.

"Megumi-*chan* has good taste. That one is a Braque. And that one"—he pointed to a small watercolor—"is by the American Whistler. He was much influenced by Japanese art. And that . . ."

The pictures led them into his study. He had a taste for the public eye atypical of Japanese executives, reflected in a wall covered with photos of himself in the company of various dignitaries, ranging from prime ministers to a world-renowned conductor.

"That's Marilyn Horne there, the opera singer. JRT underwrote her concert at Suntory Hall. And there's Wolfgang Puck, the chef. We had him cater a reception at Spago for a delegation from China. I never saw anybody eat caviar or drink champagne like those Communists. And that's the prime minister. He dined with me just two weeks before he had to resign over that tax scandal."

He pointed to a new picture, of himself flanked by two men. "The foreign minister and the American trade representative. This is Tomio Ota, the baseball player. Perhaps you have seen the commercial he does for us? The one where he . . ."

Fukawa went on in this vein for another few minutes before breaking off. "I have taken advantage of your patience, and kept you away from the refreshments. Please."

He gestured toward the door. "Grandson, if you would escort our guests. Tanaka-*kun*," he said to Shingo Tanaka, "if my other guests will excuse us, perhaps you and your son would remain behind for a minute? There is something I would like to discuss."

Maggie, the art ploy exhausted, was reduced to studying the buffet with meticulous interest, as though preparing to be tested on its contents. Out of the corner of her eye she noted the quantity Fumio Fukawa managed to push into his mouth while keeping up a stream of comments on his grandfather's accomplishments. She had just cast a surreptitious glance at her watch when the sound of muffled voices broke through the walls of the study.

The level rose, the dominant sound Fukawa's voice. Maggie caught her mother's eye, noted the almost imperceptible head shake before her mother turned and began talking to her husband as though they'd heard nothing.

She heard Fukawa's guttural bark—"You will do as I say!"—and then something else that wasn't clear. Though the words were a blur, the tone was harsh, insulting.

Then there was another voice, high and supplicatory. Maggie blanched as she heard her uncle blubbering. Her parents redoubled their efforts to appear oblivious. Mariko glanced up quickly, listened for a second, then pointedly lowered her gaze to her plate. In a second she was grazing as avidly as before.

Maggie stared fixedly at the study door, willing it to open and release the people inside, but the muffled sounds of Fukawa's anger and Katsumi's contrition continued intermittently, until she heard Fukawa snap: "*Damare!*" "Shut up!" After that, no more than a low murmur emerged.

When the study door finally opened, Maggie hurriedly

turned to the buffet. She was apparently absorbed by a piece of pineapple when the two Tanakas and their host filed in.

Fukawa was all charm. "I trust everyone has had something to eat? Shingo-*san*"—he turned to Maggie's grandfather—"please; I have kept you from the table too long. It is poor stuff, but won't you both partake?" He gestured toward the buffet like a particularly unctuous maître d'.

The two Tanaka men were pale, Katsumi's face slick with sweat. He was breathing rapidly, little shallow pants, as though having a stroke.

"No, no," Shingo Tanaka murmured, "we have imposed too long on the chairman's hospitality. With our gratitude, we must take our leave."

From his protests an onlooker would have assumed that Fukawa wished his visitors to move in permanently. Kenji's sudden entrance from outdoors provided the pretext for Em Campbell to intervene. "We hate to leave, Fukawa-*san,* but the children have no holiday from schoolwork." She stepped forward, bowing. In a second everyone was following suit. Katsumi literally backed out of the room, head bobbing.

On the sidewalk Katsumi trailed behind. Maggie could hear him wheezing, whether struggling for breath or actually crying she couldn't tell. Shingo Tanaka walked alongside his wife, his face a stoic mask.

Maggie cast a worried look from her parents, to the Tanaka men, and back to her mother, whose head shake cautioned silence. Mariko kept glancing backward at her husband, but hurriedly, as though afraid he'd look up and spot her spying.

Maggie moved up alongside her grandfather. "Is everything all right, Grandfather?" she whispered.

Her grandmother heard her. "It is not women's business, Granddaughter," she snapped.

"Shh!" Shingo Tanaka responded to his wife with a passion Maggie hadn't heard before. "I'll not limit her like that. She must know the ways of the world."

Eriko Tanaka glared and hurried ahead, as though unable to witness a further breach of protocol. Her husband turned to his granddaughter. "Everything will be fine," he said. "It is just that the chairman told us that we must cut our prices to JRT. That means we will have to lay workers off. Your uncle made the mistake of objecting. It angered the chairman."

"But he had no right to scream at you and Uncle."

Shingo Tanaka smiled ruefully. "Fukawa-*san* is the chairman, Granddaughter. We are in the JRT *kereitsu*. That means we must accept direction from above. Besides, we depend on JRT for financing. We could not exist without JRT. Not yet, anyway."

Maggie slipped her hand into his. He started at the unprecedented contact, then smiled shyly. She squeezed once. "I hate him," she said.

"The chairman is a hard man." He looked off into the distance. "It has not always been easy, but I am glad I have never wasted my energy on hatred, and I hope you won't. Build something good instead. One's children and grandchildren deserve a legacy. Kofuku is my legacy to my family." He pressed her hand. "Perhaps one day we will not need JRT. Until then, we endure what we must, *ne?*"

Chapter 28

August 2001: Boston

*T*he phone call from her mother had brought the unexpected trip to Boston. Her mother's voice, quavering, fearful: Kenji was hurt, near death; come home. Twenty hours later she was at his bedside, sharing the vigil, looking at her brother's bandaged skull, trying to imagine what kind of animals would have done it, all because a yellow boy and a black boy had strayed into the wrong neighborhood. Emiko Tanaka Campbell prayed; Maggie Campbell cursed.

After five days of almost unbroken attendance, the danger passed, and Maggie stole away from the hospital in the early afternoon; Kenji was being discharged, and there was nothing she could do. A few hours' skating would provide a release.

She took a taxi to the Skating Club of Boston. The professional had said she'd be welcome, and she had no desire to go to the Charles River rink and chance an encounter with Doe Rawlings or Hunter Rill.

It felt wonderful to step onto the ice; after a few minutes

her mind was purged of all the ugliness. She began running through her short program.

At one point she looked up and saw a dark-haired man in the stands, tall and erect; for the merest second she thought, What's Hiro doing here? Then her eye corrected her mind's trick and she smiled, the smile fading when it occurred to her that it *could* have been Clay, had she not thought it imprudent to suggest he come by; not after he'd just told her how full his day would be.

Probably it was for the best anyway. He'd see her skate soon enough, and when he did she wanted to be perfect. She wasn't there yet, so she pressed on. Soon her shirt was sodden.

When she came off the ice two hours had passed. She felt physically spent and in better spirits than she'd enjoyed in days. She was looking forward to going home, having a long soak and something to eat, and waiting for Clay's call.

"You're Maggie Campbell, aren't you?"

Maggie looked up from her boot; a pretty young woman, slightly overweight, was standing in front of her, a pair of skates slung over her shoulder. "That's right."

"You're a beautiful skater; I've been watching you for almost an hour. That's a fascinating program. A lot tougher than you make it look, too."

"Oh—thank you." Maggie thought she looked familiar but couldn't remember where she'd seen her before.

"Do you . . ." The young woman hesitated. "Do you keep in touch with Clay Bartlett?"

"Of course." Suddenly Maggie remembered—she'd seen her picture in Clay's scrapbook. "Aren't you Janice Siegel, Clay's old partner?"

"That's right. How is he?"

"He's fine."

"Are you switching over from the Charles River Club? I haven't seen you in here before."

"No, I'm just visiting. I train in Japan now. In singles."

"Oh, yes." The young woman nodded. "I guess I heard that. I was awfully sorry when I heard Clay got hurt. I wanted nothing but the best for him."

Maggie said, more sharply than she intended, "Really? I wouldn't have guessed."

Janice looked wounded. "Sure—I cared a lot about Clay. Too much, I guess."

Maggie felt her temperature rising. "Then why did you quit on him?"

To her surprise, the young woman laughed. "He didn't tell you?"

Her complaisance nettled Maggie. "No, just that you'd split up. He didn't think it was right to talk about whatever had happened between you."

Janice chuckled. "Well, I'm not surprised." She went on good-naturedly: "I heard he was with Doe Rawlings when the accident happened—is that true?"

Maggie returned to her skate. Through clenched teeth she said, "She was driving, yes."

Janice clucked her tongue indulgently. "I might have known."

Maggie looked up quickly. "What do you mean by that?"

Janice took a step back, eyeing Maggie. Her look mutated from curiosity to sympathy as her hand went to her mouth. "Oh, Lord—you, too?" She shook her head sympathetically. "I'm sorry, I wasn't thinking. I didn't mean anything."

Maggie glared at her. "She offered to drive his car. He didn't know she'd been drinking."

"Sure. I'm sure that's right." The young woman nodded

eagerly. "Well, I better be going. It was nice talking to you, and good luck with your skating."

She was walking away when she turned and added, "And with Clay."

"It's a terrible thing to admit, but since Kenji turned the corner I've been feeling guilty about missing practice." Maggie sat at the kitchen table in Clay's apartment, eating yogurt while he showered in the downstairs bathroom. She still found it amazing that he had a kitchen big enough for a table; Chiako's "kitchen" was a hot plate, a sink, and a refrigerator the size of Clay's breadbox. "But it's coming, Clay, it's really coming. I can feel it."

He came to the door, wearing one towel while he dried his hair with another. He stood, still lean and fit, looking at her admiringly. "You're doing so much better than I'd expected, Mag. I'm really starting to believe you can do it. Frankly, I thought it was a pretty long shot, you being out of singles so long, and having so little time to get ready. But all the skating magazines are talking about you. You've got girls looking over their shoulders all right." He popped back into the bathroom.

"I'm almost afraid to say it, but something strange has been starting to happen with my long program. This afternoon? There were moments when I felt more connected to a program than I ever have before. That's been happening more and more."

"Connected, did you say?"

"Um." She had to raise her voice to be heard over the running water. "I can't really describe it. Something happens and it's as though I'm no longer skating, I'm floating. Yet Madam Goto and Chiako say I'm in better control than ever. It's odd."

"Whatever works." He reappeared with a bottle of bay rum. "The Regionals are coming up fast; think you're ready?" He splashed the after-shave on his body; Maggie loved the smell, the acrid, crisp bite in her nostrils. She sniffed appreciatively.

"I wanted to talk to you about that."

"Oh?"

"I'm thinking about skating for the Japanese team instead."

"What?" His hand paused at his chest.

"I haven't made up my mind," she hastened to add, "but they've asked me. I was horrified at first, but I can see some advantages. For one thing, I'd have a better chance of making it to the games, since there are three open places on the Japanese team. There are really only two places open here, since one is already set aside for Doe Rawlings. Also, it would be a way of honoring Madam Goto and Chiako. What do you think?"

"I thought you hated the Japanese Skating Association." He slowly splashed on more bay rum, looking at her quizzically. "Come to that, I thought you hated anything to do with Japan."

She shrugged. "I'd skate for Botswana if it would get me to Salt Lake City, and I'm not sure I feel much of anything about Japan or any other country anymore. People, particular places, sure. But whole countries? I don't know."

He capped the bottle, studying her. "Well, consider this: Your commercial value after the Olympics will be about fifty times greater if you skated as a member of the U.S. team than if you skated for Japan."

"Why? Foreign skaters skate here all the time."

He looked at her as if she were being thick. "Yes, Maggie, people understand that if you're Ukrainian, you naturally skated for Ukraine. Nobody's going to hold it against you if you then come here to skate professionally. But if you're an American citizen and you choose to skate for someone else in the Olympics, I'm not sure people are going to get it. In fact, if you skate for Japan, I'm not sure people wouldn't think of you as some kind of traitor. It could kill your market value."

Maggie felt her blood growing hot. "Well, it happens I'm as much Japanese as American, so I'll be a traitor either way, won't I?"

"I see," he said, his expression showing he didn't. "I guess I didn't realize you still thought of yourself as Japanese. I was under the impression you'd gotten over that, after what they did to you."

"Oh, but I should think of myself as an American, after what Americans did to my brother, just because of what he was?" She threw down the spoon. "I'm thinking of declaring myself a citizen of a skating rink." She rose abruptly. "And I'm sick of thinking about the money in it, anyway. That's not why I'm doing this."

A pained look came into Clay's eyes. "Lord, Maggie—what set this off? All I was doing was asking questions. You said you wanted my opinion. Obviously it's up to you," he added stiffly. "I'm sorry I said anything."

She sighed. "I'm sorry, that was unfair of me. I *do* want your advice. I'm all mixed up."

"Let me get dressed first, then maybe we can talk this through."

He disappeared into the bathroom. She called after him: "Oh . . . I forgot. I heard the funniest thing today." She inspected the yogurt container to see if there was any left, then licked the lid.

"What?"

She raised her voice over the running water. "Well, you'll never guess who I ran into at the rink—Janice Siegel."

"You're kidding."

"I'm not—and she was kind of . . . strange. Obnoxious, really."

He walked back into the room, still in the towel. "What do you mean?"

"Well, she sort of implied she'd . . . had a crush on you."

He cocked his head, then shrugged. "I suppose she did."

"Oh . . . I didn't know."

"Well, I wasn't going to go around bragging about it. . . . Is *that* what you found so funny, the idea that Janice Siegel once had a crush on me? My feelings are hurt." His eyes twinkled.

"No, no—it's the other thing she said."

He looked at her curiously. "And what was that?"

"Why, she sort of implied you'd had a . . . thing . . . for *Doe Rawlings.* I almost got the impression she was saying that's why she stopped skating with you." Maggie studied the yogurt container as though memorizing the label.

Clay laughed. "That's absurd."

"This only has a hundred and forty calories, did you know that?" Maggie went to the refrigerator. "You don't mind if I take another one, do you?" She began searching. "You weren't, well, fooling around with Doe Rawlings, were you?"

"Jesus, Mag—I think the girl was all of *thirteen* when Janice and I split up. I was almost twenty. What do you take me for?"

"Oh, I knew it was ridiculous. Ah!" Maggie withdrew, holding the plastic container triumphantly. "But why on earth would someone say something like that?"

He walked over to her and lifted her chin until he was

looking into her eyes. "Look, Maggie, I didn't tell you the whole story about Janice; I wanted to leave her with her dignity. The fact is, we had a . . . relationship for a while."

"I see—I didn't realize." Maggie swallowed. "Were you . . . lovers?"

Clay tucked his hands under his arms and looked at her appraisingly. He nodded. "Yes, briefly."

Maggie stepped back. "Oh." She put the yogurt on the table. "I better get going. My mother will—"

He grabbed her. "Maggie, Maggie—you're such an innocent. You didn't think I was a virgin when you and I started skating together, did you?"

"I . . . never thought about it, I guess." She paused. "I suppose I didn't want to."

"Well, I wasn't. But I never lied to her, and never pretended feelings I didn't have. I made it clear to Janice that I liked her, and thought she was a lot of fun, but that I wasn't in love with her. She said that was fine, but in fact, she was insanely jealous. If I so much as *spoke* to another girl, she'd be hysterical. If I said hello to Doe, or Nancy Fordice, the next thing I knew Janice would be yelling or sulking or we'd have a terrible practice. You remember Hallie Perkins, don't you—that incredibly ugly girl with the bad skin and braces? Well, one day Janice accused me of having an affair with her because I loaned her five dollars to get lunch."

"Oh." Maggie rested her hand tentatively on his arm. "She does sound strange."

"Sick, really. Well, I soon regretted I'd had anything to do with her off the ice, but by then it was too late—she wouldn't go back to a purely on-ice relationship. I finally couldn't take it anymore. I started skipping practices because being with her was just too oppressive, and then we broke up. The idea that it had anything to do with me and Doe Rawlings . . ." He shook his head.

"I . . . guess I wasn't thinking. I'm sorry. It's just . . ."

"No more jealousy. It's terribly corrosive, you know." His thumbs massaged her temples. "And believe me, you've nothing to be jealous about. You're my girl, Mag."

She smiled ruefully, feeling like an idiot. "No more jealousy."

His arms enfolded her. "Good—because we shouldn't argue, not with so little time before you have to go back."

"I know." She looked around the apartment. "I better be going."

"So soon? It's not even eleven." His face clouded.

"Yes, but I've got to pack, and I'd like to visit with my mother a little."

"Oh. Mag, do you miss me over there?"

She thought he sounded like a little boy lost in a crowd. "Do you have to ask?"

"I can't tell you how much I miss you."

"You could, if you wrote more often." It slipped out before she had a chance to hold it in.

He drew back. "I'm sorry—I know I'm not much of a correspondent."

She reached for him. "I was just teasing. I love whatever you want to write."

He let her pull him to her. "I worry about you over there, you know."

"Worry? What about? It's the safest place on earth."

"No—I mean, I worry about you and . . . other men."

It was her turn to draw back, astonished. "'Other men'? Clay, I *work*—I'm not playing. And I have no interest in any other man."

"I mean, what about this Araki fellow? You seem to spend a lot of time with him."

"Hiro's a *friend*, Clay, an old friend. But there's no . . . romantic interest there. I'm like a . . . little sister to him."

"Good."

"What happened to 'no more jealousy,' um?"

It was his turn to smile self-mockingly. "I know, I know. It's just . . ."

"Shh." She put her finger to his lips. "You don't have a thing to worry about, Clay—you're stuck with me for life. Now—"

"I do worry, though." He clung to her. "You're traveling all over the world, for Christ's sake. You're beautiful, you're a great skater, and I'm just a has-been with a bad wing. A lot of men must be after you. Aren't you ever tempted?"

"Tempted? Clay, you're the only man I'm interested in. I hate being away from you. After the Olympics I never will be again."

He pulled her against him and kissed her, long and hard. "That's my girl. God, I love you," he said dreamily.

"I love you, too. But really, I—"

"It's going to be a long time, Mag." He cupped the mounds of her bottom.

"Not so long, now."

"A couple of months, at least." His hand found her belt buckle.

"Clay, really—there isn't time."

His towel slipped to the floor. "It won't take much time. Come on."

Afterward, climbing back into her clothes, she thought, It really didn't take much time.

Chapter 29

*H*iro saw the furrows on Maggie's forehead. "What's the matter, little *yanki*—you seem worried." They practiced English at the gym.

She was curling dumbbells, grunting with effort. "Oh, I was thinking about my finances. When I arrived I thought I had enough to get me to the games with ten yen to spare. It turns out I miscalculated by about a half million yen."

"Tokyo is expensive. More slower—make it hurt."

"More slowly, or slower. Unbelievably expensive."

" 'Slower.' " He turned the word over, nodding. "Thank you. I thought the Figure Skating Association was helping, now that you're skating for Japan."

"It is, but everything I get from them has to go for skating. Goto *sensei* and Chiako wanted to keep on working without pay, but I made them take the association money, so I'm really no better off. In fact, I'm nearly broke. I'm going to have to start giving lessons if I want to eat."

He frowned. "You're already skating, dancing, or working out twelve hours a day—you'll collapse."

"What else can I do? I won't ask my mother for help unless I absolutely have to."

He started to say something, saw her warning look, and limited himself to: "Ten more."

"So—your brother is being better?" Hiro was holding Maggie's ankles while she did situps.

"Just better, not . . . unh . . . 'being better.' Yes, thank you. He's out of bed and walking." The sweat streamed down her face, plastering her shirt to her body, but after fifty repetitions she was still breathing easily.

"That is good." His face darkened. "What animals, to do such a thing."

"They caught three of them."

"What will happen to them?"

"Not too much. One had been in jail before; the police said he may be sent back. The others will probably be put on probation." She rose and fell metronomically, her hands locked behind her head. "The police implied my brother and his friend brought it on themselves, by going into South Boston."

"South Boston?"

"An Irish neighborhood. Nonwhite people aren't welcome."

"I thought you said they'd gone to a public beach."

"Yes, but people are supposed to know where their color can get them killed. The gang told my brother and his friend they didn't want 'niggers and gooks' on the beach. My brother made the mistake of challenging them."

"An evil thing. At least here we no longer kill someone just for being different."

Maggie snorted. "A good thing for you and me."

"It certainly is. How is your mother?"

"Well enough, now that Kenji's out of danger."

"And your friend Clay, he is well?"

"Oh, yes, he's fine."

"Good—I would like to meet him. He must be a remarkable man, to win such loyalty."

Maggie paused at forty-five degrees. "What do you mean?"

"Why, just that you are making such sacrifices, working so hard, so that you may have a life together. It is quite beautiful. Like an ancient love story." He pushed her backward. "That is only seventy-six; keep going."

"Oh." Maggie thought through the next two situps. Then, coming up, she said, "Clay's making sacrifices, too."

"Of course he is—he is without his sweetheart."

"No . . . I mean, yes, but also, he is—"

"Working hard, you said, so that he may contribute his share, later. After you are married, I suppose?"

"Yes."

"Perhaps, though . . ." He shook his head. "No."

"What?"

"It is not my business."

"Hiro, really—what did you, unh . . . want to say?" Her stomach muscles were beginning to burn.

"Keep going—that's eighty. I was going to say, perhaps you should not have turned him down."

" 'Turned him down'? What are you talking about?"

"His offer to help support you while you're over here, of course. I mean, it would not be like taking money from a friend. From me, for example."

His upraised hand silenced her protest. "That would clearly be impossible, I understand that. But you and Mr. Bartlett are planning to be married, so surely there could be nothing wrong if you accepted his help now. I really think you should reconsider. You would not be having to work even harder."

"You would not *have* to work even harder, not 'be having,'" she mumbled. She rested on her elbows, trying to read his impassive face. "He hasn't offered me money. And I wouldn't take it if he did."

Hiro winced. "You see, that's what comes of putting your . . . face? . . . in someone else's business."

"Nose. You put your nose in someone else's business, not your whole face."

"Ah. Anyway, please forgive me. I just assumed he had, and that you'd refused."

"Why would you—"

Hiro pushed her back. "Come on, girl—six more. Make it ten, for stopping."

"I can't do any more!"

"Twenty, for saying such an unworthy thing. Now, get going!" He glowered until, groaning, she went back to work. "Good. Excellent. You see, I am thinking"—he held up his hand—"I *thought*, because he was buying those beautiful pictures for both of you, and had that wonderful apartment waiting for you after you're married, and since you are doing this for *both* of you, that he would of course prefer to help you now, and buy a picture later. So I *thought*"—he beamed—"you'd turned him down. Anyway, that's what comes of assuming that other people do things the same way you would. Foolish of me, *ne?*" He released her ankles, putting one hand on her chest, just above her breasts. "Push!"

Maggie strained against the pressure, feeling as though the strength in his forearm were flowing into her. Finally she gasped, "Twenty! That's it!" She wrapped her arms around her knees, shoulders heaving.

"Here." Hiro handed her a towel. "Please forgive me. No doubt your way is best."

Maggie looked at him suspiciously from behind the towel. "Are you trying to tell me something?"

He shrugged apologetically. "Please, Maggie—I am forgetting all my English since you are going. It is good that you are coming back to teach me."

Chiako was out. Maggie lay prone on the futon, penning a letter to Clay. She'd told him before how Hiro had been the one who'd introduced her to serious weight training, but she couldn't remember if she'd mentioned he was helping her with her conditioning now.

Halfway down the page she stopped, wondering if Clay would mind that she was working out with Hiro. She shook her head impatiently and resumed writing:

> Though most Japanese realize, intellectually, that American women tend to be more self-reliant than Japanese women, many still find it difficult to see the implications. Even Hiro, as open-minded as a man can be, has a difficult time understanding that I really *like* making my own way. This morning, while we were working out, I mentioned that money was getting a bit tight, and he said . . .

She chewed the end of the pen, scanning the page with mounting horror. "Oh, my God," she gasped, crumpling it into a ball. She pulled the light cord and slid under a thin blanket.

Hiro really didn't understand, that was the problem. Her lips compressed angrily. He still had a gift for annoying her. That night she dreamed about him.

* * *

The subway was jammed, and she was lucky to find a seat. Soon she was wedged in by a wall of legs, so she was startled when a man suddenly forced his way into the nonexistent space next to her, ignoring the protests of the man he displaced.

As the train accelerated she felt his thigh press against hers. She looked at him sharply, and he smirked. He had his coat across his lap, his right hand under it. The coat twitched and she jerked her eyes away. She'd heard women talk about the repulsive subway *chikan*, perverts taking advantage of the crush to fondle and pinch, but she'd never encountered one before.

His leg rubbed hers. She tried to stand, but a large woman in front of her had her pinned. The *chikan* persisted, ignoring her increasing strident warnings, until he suddenly bolted for the door as the train braked for the stop before hers. "Pig," she hissed.

She noticed a bank envelope in the seat he'd abandoned. Guessing it had slipped out of the man's coat, she opened it, hoping to find some identification. She'd love to report the deviate.

It held $5,000 in yen. If she hadn't been so absorbed by it, and had looked out the window as the train pulled away, she might have seen the man nodding to Hiro Araki, half-hidden by a kiosk.

Later, when she asked him what he thought she should do with the money, he frowned uncertainly. "Ordinarily, of course, you'd turn it in to the police, and they'd return it to the owner. But with no identification . . . well, it just goes to the government, I imagine. And a person like that . . . he doesn't deserve to get it back anyway. I'd keep it." He tapped the envelope against the back of his hand, thinking, then nodded decisively. "Yes. I'd definitely keep it. You need it more than the government. Perhaps this is how the *kami* work, eh? But you have to decide—I've learned my lesson about putting my nose in your business."

Maggie was torn. People turned in a single yen they found, and she liked that. Finally, though, she decided Hiro was right: the rules didn't apply to the disgusting little man. She kept it, relieved that she wouldn't have to take on students.

Chapter 30

*T*here's Kyoto!" Hiro pulled the Harley onto the side of the highway and pointed down at the plain below. Spread out before them was the great imperial city, Japan's capital for the thousand years preceding the advent of Tokyo.

From afar Maggie could see the countless shrines and temples dotting the city and the surrounding hills. "Look," she exclaimed, pointing. "There's Kinkaku-ji."

In the distance the delicate pavilion, built as a shogun's retirement villa, seemed to float on the lake surrounding it, its walls sheathed in gold. Maggie thought it the most beautiful building on earth.

"We have to go there!" she shouted.

She was glad she'd let Hiro and Chiako talk her into the trip. The three of them had been having tea when Hiro suddenly asked if she wanted to go to Kyoto. She'd said no, she had to skate, when Chiako interjected: "You must go—you are training too hard, and you need a rest."

Chiako stopped her protest with a Goto-esque command: "I am the *joshu*, and that is my order."

"Well," Maggie said, "then I have no choice."

Hiro beamed. "Excellent. I know a wonderful *ryokan*. I will book rooms."

Now they were looking down on a fairy-tale building, in a fairy-tale city, and she was excited and happy. "We have to see Kinkaku-ji, and Ryoan-ji, and Nanzen-ji, and, and . . ."

He laughed, bringing her back to the present. "We will, Maggie—we'll go everywhere. But first the *ryokan*, eh?" They descended into the valley.

The *ryokan* was in Gion, the old section in the center of the city. As they threaded the narrow gate across the cobbled drive and pulled into the courtyard, hard by the Kamo River, Maggie thought they might have been transported back to the days of the shoguns. Though it was late summer, and the oppressive, muggy heat had settled over all of central Japan, the tree-shaped courtyard behind the high stone wall was cool and blissfully quiet.

The staff rushed out to greet them as they removed their shoes and stepped into the one-story frame building. Inside it was dark, and even cooler, with a gentle, scented breeze drifting through the shuttered windows.

Her room was large and airy, looking out on a courtyard filled with flowering shrubs, a small pond with a fountain, and singing birds. She slid open the courtyard door, welcoming the fresh smells, the quiet chirps.

Everything was spare but refined, from the scroll on the wall to the low writing desk, with its inlaid wood and antique calligraphy tools. A fresh lily shared a vase with a branch of purple buds. A room for a princess, she thought.

She washed her face but decided to wait until later for a bath. Now she wanted to go to Kiyomizu-dera.

They stood on the broad wooden veranda of the 350-year-old main hall of the sprawling temple complex. It jutted out over a canyon, providing a panoramic view of the city before them. From the woods came birdsong and insects buzzing. Everywhere rose the drone of schoolchild chatter.

Students had already approached her, meticulous in sailor suits, to ask if the American lady would speak English with them, or pose for a picture, or sign their notebooks. It amused her to reply in Japanese with questions like "Is he your boyfriend?" or write, "What am I?" in *kanji* in their books, watching astonishment give way to nervous laughter.

Hiro grabbed her by the hand, rescuing her from a throng of giggling girls, each clamoring to be in a picture with her. "Come on," he said. "There's something we have to do."

Up he led her, past the Jishu Shrine, past a nest of vermilion buildings, statues, and memorials. Ignoring the three-story pagoda, built without a single nail. Past Otowa Fall, where a line of people waited to drink the spring water.

"Where are you taking me?" The girls had infected Maggie with their high spirits, leaving her intoxicated.

"To the stones. To see what your love life will bring."

At the top of the rise where the shrine sat, two stones were set flush with the earth, thirty feet apart. Legend had it that if a woman could walk from one to the other with her eyes closed, thinking of her lover, she would have a rich love life.

She tossed her head, laughing and flushed. "I know what my love life will bring."

"Then no harm, eh? Try it, just for fun."

She surrendered, joining the line of young women filing toward the first stone. The closer she got, the more foolish she felt.

Hiro patted her arm. "Have no fear, Maggie. All will turn out well. Just shut your eyes, think of your Clay."

Her time arrived. Registering her target in her mind, she

closed her eyes. The chirping of the girls behind her faded as her mind turned in on itself.

Clay: she invoked the name, and his image popped into focus. Confidently she stepped off, striding purposefully toward the far stone.

She could see him as though he were standing on the rock, waiting for her. Why, all she had to do was walk to him, just a few more yards. I'm coming, she thought, I'm—

The picture blurred, the outline dissolved. Wait, she thought, confused. Don't!

He faded, evanesced, was gone. Where he had been, there was only a void.

She stopped, uncertain but determined not to peek, since that was supposed to risk very bad *un*. She tried to bring the image back, willing it but finding only an amorphous, shifting specter. Beset with the conviction that, having begun, she must not fail, she set out again, in what she hoped was the right direction. Behind her she could hear squealing and laughter.

Then she heard him, softlly calling: "This way, this way. Come to me." His voice, traveling on the breeze from halfway around the world, whispered, "Come to me." He was there again, standing on the stone, holding out his arms, guiding her in.

She stepped easily toward him, her heart racing. Ten more feet, then five. Her arms came up to meet his, they were entwined, she was back in the hands that had held her so often. "Yes," she said, sighing.

She opened her eyes. There, beneath her feet, was the second stone. Hiro was cradling her.

He tousled her curls. "You found the way, Maggie. You will have much love in your life."

She stood looking down, hearing again the wind-blown whisper. Abruptly, conscious of Hiro's warmth under her hands, the solid mass of him, she stepped back. "A silly superstition," she said with a sniff.

"Perhaps. Time will tell."

They walked back, past the pottery shops that lined Teapot Lane. Halfway down the hill, she stopped, looking back. Night was falling, and up and down the street the *chochin* were lit, competing with the fireflies.

They drank cold sake in a bar, then walked back through the dark warrens of Gion, unchanged for hundreds of years. In the shadows the geisha flitted to their rendezvous, unearthly forms from the past, their ghostly faces intent on the cobbled streets, wood-shod feet punctuating the night with soft, clip-clop sounds. *Maiko,* apprentice geishas, whispered softly behind upraised fans as they shuffled in their mistresses' wake. Through wooden doors and latticed windows came low laughter and *shamisen* music. The smell of grilling meat reminded them how hungry they were.

Back in the *ryokan* they went to their respective baths, then returned to her room in their *yukata.* She opened the door onto the garden and let the singing sounds of night take their place around them as they ate.

The old woman cleared away the last dish, moved aside the table, and laid out the futon, all without ever getting off her knees. Murmuring a "Good night," she exited backward, sliding the door shut behind her.

"Well," Hiro said when she'd gone, "I'd best get to my room."

Maggie laid her hand on his arm. "Not yet—let's go out in the garden. It's so beautiful under the moonlight."

She slid back the screen, and they stepped into the little courtyard. Fireflies flitted through the ornamental shrubs, while a frog croaked a greeting from the miniature waterfall.

The warm, moist night air, rich with strange perfumes, felt like velvet on her skin. The stars formed a crystal tent over their heads, the Milky Way's white belt girdling the boundless black.

"Remember when you took me to your grandfather's village?" Maggie murmured, staring up.

" 'Noplace'? I remember well. Why?"

"It had a feeling of peace like this."

"I'm glad you felt the peace. It comes, I think, of knowing who and what you are, and being where you can be that person. Of feeling free."

Unconsciously she let her weight rest against him. She looked up at the dark outline of his face. "You tried to help me understand who and what I am; you told me I had to define myself, and not let others do it for me. If I'd listened, I'd have saved myself a lot of heartache. I'll always be grateful to you for that."

A breeze came, and she shivered. His arm turned her. "Maggie, I don't want your gratitude. I want your love." He kissed her.

She kissed him back. Only the thin cotton of their *yukata* lay between them. She felt the hardness of him and a burning inside. The cricket drone intensified until it was a shriek. She laced her fingers in his hair, pressing her mouth to his.

"Maggie, Maggie," he whispered, his mouth moving to her ear, "I love you so much."

"Oh, God." She ran her palms up his bare chest, feeling the bands of muscle under the taut skin. "Oh, my God."

His mouth roamed her face, her neck. His hands caressed her back and sides. She felt her belt slip, his flesh against hers. She groaned, wanting him. She didn't want to cradle him, lie with him in her arms, be the earth mother; she wanted him to hold her, protect her, please her. She didn't want an afterglow; she wanted a fire now. She wanted to take and be taken. Her teeth closed on his lip.

"Yes," she panted, feeling the unfamiliar body, so much more massive than—

"No!" She jumped back, horrified. "I . . . we . . . I can't! I mustn't!" Her *yukata,* gaping open, revealed her body, gleaming white in the moonlight. She jerked the robe closed.

He stepped toward her. "Maggie . . ."

"No! No, Hiro," she panted. Savagely, she cinched the belt around her waist. "It isn't right."

"It was right a minute ago—tell me it wasn't!" His arms reached for her.

"I . . . forgot myself. I . . . the night . . . the stars . . . I don't know," she cried. "I only know I can't. Please . . . try to understand."

He stepped back. "Do you love him, Maggie? Really love him?"

"I told you I did!"

"That wasn't my question."

"Then yes, I love him! Please believe me—you have to believe me!" Her voice took on a soft, keening quality.

"No, I don't. There's only one person who has to believe that." Then he was gone. She stood in the garden until her knees stopped shaking.

She lay awake for hours, terrified of the thing she'd felt that had brought her so close to betrayal. She loathed the weakness she'd seen in herself: a romantic setting, a few weeks away from her lover, and she'd been ready to couple like a bitch in heat. And the most disgusting thing was that her body still longed to slip into the room across the hall and do just that, all through the night.

She woke with a feeling of dread, but Hiro made the

morning easier than she'd feared. He came to her after the old woman had cleared away the breakfast tray and said without preliminaries, "I have come to beg your forgiveness." He stood gravely, looking down at her.

She blushed. "It was my fault, really. I—"

He interrupted her: "No. You had told me that you love this man; it was shameful of me to put my desires ahead of yours. But you need have no concern that I will again cross that boundary. May we please remain friends?"

Relief flooded her. She extended her hand. "American style, remember? Friends forever."

"Friends forever." His hand closed on hers.

They spent the morning visiting Kinkaku-ji and the rock garden at Ryoan-ji. They gaped like all the other tourists at the water iris and tried fruitlessly to fathom the Zen of the patterned rocks. They rented bicycles and prowled the back streets along the river. By the time they had their picture taken with their heads stuck through geisha and samurai cutouts, awkwardness was gone. Maggie climbed into the saddle behind Hiro with a great sense of well-being. In Clay she had her great love, in Hiro her best friend; she was the luckiest of women.

As soon as she arrived back in Tokyo and saw the note Chiako had left for her in the apartment, her heart sank:

Campbell: Come to Seiburo Hospital as soon as you return; Goto *sensei* is dying.

She flew out of the apartment.

Maggie crept up to the bed and looked down at the tiny figure. Her eyes were closed, and though she had an oxygen mask over her nose and mouth, there was no movement to indicate she was breathing.

Maggie's hand flew to her mouth. "Is she . . . dead?"

Chiako shook her head. "She still breathes, only not so often."

As though to prove it, the old woman's chest rose and fell. First one eye, and then the other, fluttered open. Slowly the old head turned. A clawlike hand tugged down the oxygen mask.

Maggie was aghast at the changes that had taken place in the *sensei*'s face: The cheeks had collapsed inward, the skin had a liverish pallor, and the eyes—two days earlier black and alive—were faded and filmy.

"*Sensei,*" Chiako whispered, "you must keep your mask on."

The hand gestured dismissively. "Bah—what matter?" The voice was a raspy whisper.

"No," Maggie blurted. "You must get better."

A thin smile formed on the leathery face. "I will, and soon," she rasped. "I am glad you came, Daughter. My only regret is that I will not be with you to the finish."

"My *sensei* will be with me always."

Maggie had to bend close to hear the whispered words. "You have brought me great joy. Now you must bring that joy to your skating. To your life. Pursue your dreams with joy. Do that, and you will surely succeed."

"Yes, *sensei.*" Maggie forced herself to keep her voice even.

Madam Goto's hand reached out. "Take this—it is for you."

With what little strength she had left, Madam Goto pressed the small leather case she'd been clutching into Maggie's hand.

Maggie looked at it numbly, nodding. "Thank you, *sensei*."

"You asked me once what the words meant, and I told you they meant everything, and nothing. Do you remember?"

"I remember." Tears streamed down Maggie's face, dropping from her chin.

"When the time comes, you will know what they mean. I—" She broke off and gestured toward the water bottle.

"Chiako-*chan*," Madam Goto murmured after taking a bird sip, "you are a great soul, and a great teacher. Help my daughter, and never give in."

"Of course, *sensei*," Chiako whispered. She wiped the old woman's mouth.

Her last words were "I must sleep now." Maggie and Chiako sat, unspeaking, for two hours, while the giant heart ran down.

Chiako and Maggie performed the duties to the dead, the sister in Kanazawa too infirm to travel. They had the body brought to a mortuary. They bathed it in warm water and dressed it in the *kyokatabira*, the white shroud of death. The body lay in front of a funeral altar, with the head facing north, to facilitate the passage of the spirit. On the altar were white chrysanthemums, the flowers of the dead, sent by Em Campbell.

They made many calls, and the following night the mortuary filled with former pupils, rival coaches, skaters from all over Japan. They brought *koden*, envelopes of money to buy incense for the forty-nine-day mourning period, and sat through the night while a Buddhist priest recited sutras. At dawn, he pronounced Madam Goto's posthumous name: Shidosha, "She Who Leads."

The next day the body was cremated. When the ashes

were returned, the mourners gathered at the altar. Chiako, reaching into the reliquary box with a pair of long chopsticks, extracted fragments of bone. These she passed to Maggie, who, as Madam Goto's honorary daughter, had the task of taking them with her own chopsticks and depositing them in a jar sitting on the altar.

When Chiako and Maggie left at dawn, they were lightheaded from emotion and lack of sleep. They still had to buy *kodengaeshi,* gifts for the mourners. They would return for services every week for seven weeks, then take the jar of bone fragments to the gravesite for burial. For thirty-three years they would do *kuyo,* or requiem observation, to Madam Goto's spirit; on the thirty-third anniversary of her death her *tama* would merge with the common ancestor of her family, and Maggie and Chiako's duties would be fulfilled.

As Maggie crawled onto her futon she remembered something she'd meant to ask Madam Goto. "Chiako-*chan,* a favor when you wake?"

"Of course," a drowsy voice replied.

"With your permission, I would like to be considered as the Japanese entrant at the Trophée de France. Would you be willing to call Yoshida with that request?"

"Of course. But is there a particular reason you wish to go to the Trophée de France?"

"No, no reason, except there will be a strong field. It will be good preparation for the Nationals. Good night again." And, she thought, *Japan Skates* reports that Doe Rawlings is the American entrant. It is time, time for them to start worrying. Ever since they'd met, Doe Rawlings had acted as though Maggie's very existence offended her. Soon, Maggie hoped, Doe Rawlings would have *reason* to regret Maggie Campbell's existence.

Chapter 31

March 1995: Boston

*F*rom his resting spot at the far corner of the arena, Hunter Rill's eyes followed Doe Rawlings. She was taking methodical warm-up laps, accelerating with an economy of movement that Rill still had trouble believing.

Around and around she traveled, speed building so effortlessly that it wasn't until she turned and hit a triple toe loop that most of the people around the rink had any idea how fast she'd been moving. By the time they did, she had slid to a graceful stop at Rill's side and was removing the red Lycra sweat suit.

Under it she was wearing a new skating dress. Doe tossed the sweat suit over the barrier, standing uneasily as Rill ran an appraising eye over the outfit.

"Not bad at all. I like it, in fact. That woman can do decent work when she wants to." He rubbed his chin, then stepped forward and lifted the crisp material of the short skirt, revealing the tight white panties. Sheer leotards covered the rounded swell of Doe's flanks, otherwise exposed almost to her hipbones. With the modest, unrevealing top the overall impression was of a partially undressed school-girl.

Which was exactly the effect Rill had had in mind when he'd talked to the dressmaker. "Yes," he mused, "I think she got it just right." He stood back and admired his design.

Nervously Doe ran her forefingers into the back of the leg openings, tugging the elastic bands lower on her bottom. "I, uh . . . wondered if, maybe . . . the pants are cut too high?" Her light voice tended to drop to a whisper when she was unsure of herself, as she was whenever she thought Rill might think she was questioning his judgment.

Rill snorted. "Your modesty, dear girl, becomes you. As do those panties. You have marvelous legs, and you must use them, in every way possible. We're moving up to the seniors soon, aren't we?"

He looked into her violet eyes until she nodded. "I hope so."

"Of course we are. That means people will expect you to present as a woman; you're not a little girl anymore, Doreen, and we want to take advantage of your physical assets."

She slumped. "That's what my mother said."

"Well, dear, even mothers are right sometimes."

Doe nodded, content to let the matter go. "All right, Hunter."

"Good." Consulting a clipboard, he said, "I want you to work on the step sequences, Doe; you can do more with them, and they really matter with some judges."

She pulled off her headband, and fluffed the fine, spun gold pixie cut with her fingers. The movement of her arms lifted her breasts under their white covering, and Rill thought again how well the dress had turned out.

"I'd rather work on the Axel, Hunter. I know I can get it."

"So do I, dear—it's just a matter of time. You're going to be the youngest woman who ever hit a triple Axel in competition, count on it. But you're also going to be the youngest woman to have a perfect step sequence in competition, and that's what we want to work on today. I want you to get in more edge shifts. Like this."

He pushed away from the boards, slowly talking her through the steps. "I see you starting with a back, outside three to left forward inside edge, like this"—Rill turned, still talking—"then mohawk to a right back inside. Stroke over to the left back outside, and repeat. Got it?" He curved back to the corner and propped his elbows on the rail.

Doe's lips moved as she talked herself through it. She nodded decisively. "I've got it, but it doesn't seem like much."

"Not at that speed. But with the speed and rhythm you'll have, it'll give you a rolling motion that will draw attention to the really wonderful lines of your arms and legs. The part where the music goes 'duh-da-da-*da*-dum,' I think. Try it." He reached over the rail and punched on *Chariots of Fire*.

"Try it with the passage I'm thinking of," he called to her retreating back, "and let your arms and hands express the roll of the turns. You remember the way Sean suggested you hold them?"

She nodded. The choreographer rarely had to tell her anything twice. Her feet started working the turns; by the time the tape was a minute old she was accelerating down the ice, her body swooping and diving from side to side, her arms forming languid, graceful curves in time to the music. The other skaters were quick to get out of her way.

"That's it, that's it," Rill called out, clapping. "A little more extension on the arms, I think."

All eyes were glued on the beautiful girl with the stunning

figure and liquid technique. The off-ice tentativeness evaporated, her feet and hands moving with a deftness approaching instinct. All that remained of the shy girl of a moment before was the impression of vulnerability projected by her sweetly innocent face. Two-tenths of a point on every set, Rill thought, drumming his fingers with the music. He'd felt the aura the first day he'd seen her skate nine years earlier, and she'd never lost it.

The fringe of the skirt flew up and, as Rill had expected, the briefly cut panties capitalized on her exquisitely proportioned legs. She was only five five in stocking feet yet always looked taller because of her elegant legs, an effect he'd accentuated by having had the panties cut half an inch higher every year since she was ten. Now, at almost fourteen, the deep scallops invited attention to her softly rounded woman's flanks; his only regret was that he wasn't going to be able to push it much farther, or what had been working as an almost subliminal grace note would become so obvious that it could start costing points.

After another twenty feet Doe broke off and skated over to the rail, frowning. "That looks silly, Hunter. I feel like a seagull or something." She looked at him uncertainly.

"Doe, trust me. Let's just give it a try for a while. If you're still not comfortable with it, we'll try something else. But you're ready for a whole new look—a big girl look. If you come in with a step sequence that really presents originally, at the same time emphasizing your youth, your lines, the crispness of your movement, you'll *own* the audience. We want that, don't we?"

She nodded. "Well, sure."

"And we're going to have it." She had a small space between her top front teeth; Rill reminded himself again that if she *was* going to get a retainer, the sooner the better, so the gap would be closed by the time she became a serious threat in the Seniors. On the other hand, he still couldn't decide if the space wasn't a godsend; at the Junior Nationals Lofton Weeks had raved about her "enchanting gamine smile" every time the cameras zoomed in on her. No one had to tell Hunter Rill that, over time, that kind of hype could have a very positive impact.

He glanced at his watch. "Now, why don't you work on the step sequence. Remember to keep the arm motions big, but at the same time *slow*. Mrs. Bartlett's coming in with a new girl, someone from Japan. I promised to audition her, but then I'll be back to you and we can work on the Axel."

Doe's face brightened. "Is Clay Bartlett coming in, too?"

Rill peered over the clipboard. "Dear girl, I really don't know; why do you ask?"

She began shifting her weight uneasily from skate to skate. "No reason, really. But I haven't seen him for a while, and I . . . wondered if he's . . . all right." She looked down at the ice as her voice trailed off.

"He's fine, as far as I know. There hasn't been much point in his coming in, since Janice Siegel quit and he doesn't have a partner."

"I suppose not." Doe began turning slowly in place, first right, then left. "Hunter?"

"Yes?" Rill shook his head, wondering; the girl was acting quite odd.

"There've been girls who skated singles and pairs at the same time, haven't there?"

Good Lord, he thought, *there* it is. He glared at her. "Y-esss, a few. Martin, most recently. But even she decided it was too much. She didn't become the Canadian ladies' champion until she dropped pairs." He looked around absently, as though merely going through rhetorical motions. "Why do you ask?"

"Why, I just thought . . ." Her voice was almost inaudible.

"Yes? What did you think, Doreen?"

She cleared her throat, brightening. "I thought, since Clay had lost his partner, and since you *can* do both, I thought perhaps *I'd* skate pairs with him." The upthrust chin hinted challenge.

Rill, unaccustomed to an assertive Doe Rawlings, nodded. "Ah, I see." He raised his brows inquisitively. "An interesting idea. I never thought of that. You're quite sure you want to take that on?"

"I want to try it, Hunter." Words began tumbling out. "I wouldn't give up singles, of course. But I really want to skate with Clay. I think . . . I *know* we'd be great together. I'm a much better skater than Janice Siegel was, and I'd work twice as hard, and, and . . ."

Rill took advantage of Doe's pause for breath. "Of course, of course. Have you said anything to Clay?"

"Why, no—I wanted to see what you thought about it first."

"I appreciate that, Doe, I really do. But it sounds as though what *I* think about it is irrelevant," he added conversationally, "since you've made up your mind."

Confronted with the significance of her oblique ultimatum, Doe hesitated, her resolve beginning to crumble. "I didn't mean . . . I mean, I want to . . . I only want . . ." She trailed off. "Could I try it for a while?"

Rill rubbed his chin, fuming inside. He knew a harsh word could send the girl into a funk that would destroy her concentration and ruin her practice, so he kept his tone light. "It's an *interesting* idea, Doe. Clay would be very lucky to have such an . . . enthusiastic partner. You get on well, do you?"

She beamed, rising on her toe picks. "Oh, yes—we've been friends for years."

"Of course." Rill felt like kicking himself: it had never occurred to him that the interaction he'd seen between the two was anything other than casual civility; he might have known that someone as desperate for affection as Doe Rawlings would be drawn to someone as engaging as Clay Bartlett, who flirted with pretty females from twelve to forty as reflexively as he breathed. "Well, Clay's a fine young man."

"And he's . . . he's . . ."

"He's what, Doreen?"

She smiled shyly, and Rill decided: The gap stays.

"He's . . . fun, I guess." She hastened to add: "But not . . . fresh, you know?" Mistaking Rill's interest in her mouth for engagement in her reasoning, she forged on. "He's always treated me like, like . . ."

"He treats you with respect, is that it?"

She stopped, nodding uncertainly. "I guess so. Sure, that's it. And he's . . . nice. He's a good skater, too." She ended with an especially bright smile, as though to say: Doesn't that make perfect sense?

"I see. Yes, he *is* a gentleman, and a *fine* skater, dear. A fine *pairs* skater, of course—not the same thing as a singles skater at all." His brain worked feverishly as he cursed his luck: Why hadn't he realized the girl's hormones were kicking in? If he wasn't careful, he was going to have either a sullen, resentful singles skater or a moonstruck, novice pairs skater on his hands. Neither was acceptable.

"Well, Doe, I must say I hadn't thought of this possibility."

"Oh, Hunter, do you think—"

"Let me see. It might just work, the more I think about it. I'll talk with him."

Her head bobbed eagerly, the fine flaxen hair flying. "We'd be great together."

"I wouldn't be surprised. You get working on the step sequence, and I'll talk it over with Clay."

Chapter 32

unter Rill turned to Lettie Bartlett. "I thought you said
you were bringing someone who'd skated in the
Japanese Nationals?"

"I have. This is Megumi Campbell, who just moved here
from Japan. She studied under"—she stumbled over the
name—"Asako Goto?"

Maggie nodded. "How do you do, Mr. Rill."

Rill scrutinized the young woman standing next to Mrs.
Bartlett, taking in the green eyes, the cap of coppery hair,
the peaches-and-cream complexion. She glanced quickly
around the rink, and he thought *perhaps* he saw an Oriental
influence, but then she was facing him again and it was
gone; she might have been any pretty Newton teenager.

"She doesn't look . . ." He shook his head. "Well, I guess
I was expecting somebody older." He extended his hand.
"How old *are* you, Megumi?"

Maggie started to bow before she stopped herself. "I'd
rather be called Maggie, actually. I'm sixteen, Mr. Rill."

He thought he heard a slight accent, flat and clipped, but
her English was flawless. "And you finished fourth this
year? After a second last year?"

Maggie's lips compressed, but she answered dispassionately: "Yes, Mr. Rill."

"Hunter, please. Well, you must be a fine skater indeed. That's quite impressive. Mrs. Goto must be proud of you."

Maggie relaxed a little. "You know Madam Goto, Mr. Rill? Hunter, I mean."

"Of course—I've run into her for years. A great, great teacher. A bit . . . set in her ways, perhaps, but one of the giants."

Now, reflexively, Maggie *did* bow. "Thank you. It was a great honor to be taught by her."

Rill laughed, a pleasant, boyish sound. "Listen to that, Clayton, and be instructed—I expect you to say no less of me."

"That's what I tell everyone, Hunter," Clay's eyes twinkled.

"Good lad." Rill pinched Clay's shoulder muscle. "And are you keeping in shape until we find you a partner? You had a bit of a struggle with that last girl you tried, I recall. Of course, she *did* have a rather low center of gravity."

Without waiting for an answer, he turned to Maggie. "Well, are you ready to try a little skating?"

"*Hai!*" Maggie waggled her head as laughter broke around her. "Excuse me. I mean, yes."

"Then why don't you warm up while I chat with Clay and Mrs. Bartlett."

Maggie left the others by the stands while she stretched, then ventured out onto ice for the first time since the night in Osaka, weeks past. Slowly at first, then with increasing comfort, she circled the rink.

Her legs liked the slight bite at the point of contact between blade and ice. It sent its resistance up her body, bringing tiny tremors to the base of her spine. It was good, hard ice, the kind she favored. Some skaters liked it softer, thinking it easier to carve, more forgiving, but she preferred ice that rewarded edges and punished flats.

After a few laps around the rink she executed bracket, mohawk, choctaw, and rocker turns, linking them with step sequences to regain the feel of her edges. When she arrived back at her starting point, she felt the glow that told her her body was awake and ready for her brain's commands. It felt good, and she knew she'd left it too long.

She stripped off her warm-up clothes, feeling the hairs on her arms and neck bristle as the cold air caressed her skin. She was hopping on her skates, shaking her arms at her sides, when Rill broke off from the others and skated over to her with easy, relaxed strides.

"All ready to go, I see. Is there particular music you'd like?"

"Something classical, please."

"Ah, a romantic; my kind of skater." Rill stroked back to the tape recorder and flipped through a stack of tapes. "Here we go—perfect. Excerpts from the *1812 Overture*—will that do?"

"That's fine . . . Hunter."

"Then you just skate whatever you feel like to this, dear." He smiled and returned to the Bartletts.

Maggie coasted to center ice and stopped, eager to begin, curious how skating would feel after her layoff, the most time she'd gone without skating in over ten years. She waited for a downbeat for her strike-off.

The slow, opening passages were perfect; she tried to coordinate her hand and arm positions with the tempo of the music as she contented herself with an easy arabesque down mid-ice: forward, then backward, alternating easily.

She executed step sequences, a single toe jump, and finally a slow camel that she lowered into a sit spin. Her thigh muscles had tightened during the layoff, and for a second she thought she was going to suffer the indignity of completing the spin on her rear, but control returned and she straightened into a decent scratch spin. When she finished, her arms overhead, she felt her confidence inching back.

The Tchaikovsky changed pace, and she with it, stroking hard toward Rill, Clay, and Mrs. Bartlett. Turning, she assayed a double toe loop, a double flip, and finally a double Axel.

The music slowed again, and Maggie took long connecting steps, catching her breath. Thinking it as good a time as any, she built speed, turned, and threw herself into her triple/double combination.

She had to fight for it, but she landed the second jump cleanly. Her exultant shout burst over the bombast of the music as she stroked down the ice. Clay turned to watch as she sped past, eyes to the roof, fist pumping.

She lost consciousness of time and place. Relieved of the constraints of a formal program, she went as the music moved her. She leapt, she spun, she slowed to a near stop and drifted almost motionless, then burst into full speed before hurtling into a Russian split, her legs splayed wide, traveling sideways through the air, suspended over the ice as though held by wires, reaching out and touching her toes before returning to the hard, familiar surface.

Twisting into a spread-eagle that lapped one end of the rink, her still body drifted by the boards like a leaf in a stream. From the spread-eagle she broke into back crossovers until she had enough speed to launch four butterflies, one after the other, her body parallel to the ice and three feet above it: touching, kicking, springing, reaching, and soaring again until, exhausted, she allowed the last one to turn into a spin that slowed so gradually her audience would not have been able to say exactly when she finished.

She had trouble getting her bearings when she finally came to rest. She looked at the wall clock and realized with a start that she'd been skating flat out for almost six minutes. Beneath the clock she saw a pretty blond girl she hadn't noticed before, executing a sweeping step sequence in the far corner of the rink, her movements precise and spare. Her face was impassive, locked in concentration, and even when her turns brought her line of sight across Maggie's, the blond girl appeared far away, in her own world.

Clay Bartlett was the first to greet Maggie as she returned. "That was incredible." His hand massaged the springy mop of damp hair. "I had no idea you were so good. Damn, that was beautiful."

Lettie Bartlett rushed up and snatched her away. "Oh, my dear. Simply fabulous." Mrs. Bartlett held Maggie at arm's length, beaming. "Wasn't she, Hunter?"

Rill looked the sweat-soaked girl up and down. "And you finished fourth? All I can say is, I'd hate to run into the girls who finished ahead of you."

"Thank you." Her panting covered the stomach spasm he'd evoked. "Thank you. Yes, there are some very good skaters in Japan."

"Well, Hunter, aren't you glad to be getting this girl?" Lettie Bartlett clapped her heavy arm over Maggie's heaving shoulders.

"Mmm." Rill stroked his aquiline nose, pacing. She really is gifted, he mused. That intangible quality that the great ones have—the bearing, the impression that every gesture is inevitable, that easy elegance that makes other girls look like hockey players . . . My God, those edges—every takeoff, every landing on a true edge. And the stroking—it was almost eerie how quiet her blades were. How she moved to the music, the way she expressed its character—completely impromptu, yet she could have been skating that program for years. He glanced over his shoulder, thinking: I'm damned if there are three better skaters in Japan, unless she choked, and I'd bet money this girl's no choker. Most likely they were punishing her, or Goto, for something.

A little voice whispered, *Do it, do it—hedge your bets.*

Spying Doe Rawlings at the far end of the rink, seemingly immersed in her practice and oblivious of the display that had just occurred, Rill shook his head impatiently. God knew how it would affect Doe if he divided his loyalties. It might inspire her, or it might drive a wedge between them, even cause her to leave him.

Any month now Doe would have the Axel, too, the first girl in the world who'd have the Axel without looking like a man. The Campbell girl didn't have the body for it. And while she was elegantly configured and striking looking— really quite unforgettable, in an exotic way—no woman on earth could bring the achingly vulnerable sensuality and breathtaking beauty of Doe Rawlings to the ice. No, he thought with a sigh, his chips were on Doe Rawlings, and there they'd stay.

On the other hand, did he really want to send Campbell to someone like Tobin or that bitch Salvano? That could come back to haunt him. And her parents could pay, Mrs. Bartlett had said—no small consideration, especially now that the Siegel girl was gone and the Bartletts were on their uppers.

"No," he said, looking glum, "I'm sorry." He paused, seemingly deep in thought, then shook his head almost angrily. "It wouldn't work. It just wouldn't be right."

"What on earth do you mean, Hunter? She's a terrific

skater. You could see that." Lettie Bartlett's big bosom heaved indignantly.

Rill nodded, sighed heavily. "Dear, I'm sorry—you're a *marvelous* skater. I would love to train you. You have a great future in front of you, and it breaks my heart that I can't be part of it."

"Oh." Maggie was crestfallen. "I'd hoped I could train with Clay."

"I'm so sorry."

"Hunter, will you talk sense? Whatever do you mean?" Lettie Bartlett looked at him as though he'd started speaking in tongues. "Why did you have her come in, then?"

Rill shrugged. "I should have inquired, before saying she could. But I was expecting someone much older, and frankly, not as good. I assumed, when you said she'd taken a second, then slipped to fourth . . . Well, I assumed this was a skater who'd been around, gone as far as she was going to go, and was on the backside of her competitive career, just wanting to stay in the game a while longer."

Warming to his theme, he turned to Maggie, elaborating. "It even occurred to me, imagining you a grizzled old veteran, you might be able to lend a hand with some of the younger students. Now I see"—he smiled disarmingly— "you are hardly at the end of your career. But I can't take on another top woman singles skater; I'd have a conflict of interest between you and Doe Rawlings, over there."

Maggie's eyes followed the indication of Rill's chin until she picked out the blond girl at the far end of the rink, still skating step sequences.

"You see," he continued, "I have a commitment to her, and I don't see how I could work with two girls who, for all I can see, could well wind up competing head-to-head at the next Nationals."

He spread his hands helplessly. "I mean, which one would I favor? If I thought of something special, that little touch that just might be all it takes, who would I give it to?" He looked as though he had a toothache. "No, it's impossible. I've turned down several good female singles skaters"—he weighted "singles" ever so slightly—"and I just can't make an exception." He drew a deep breath, exhaling painfully. "I know coaches who would do it, but I won't."

He turned to Maggie. "I'm sorry. There are some excellent coaches around Boston, and I'd be happy to speak to—"

"Hunter, you can't be serious!" Clay, hands on hips, glared at Rill. "You've had *lots* of students who compete against each other. Last year you had the Bergers, and they competed against Janice and me. We didn't have any problem with that, and I assume they didn't."

Rill looked at him benevolently. "Dear boy, I knew the Bergers weren't ever going to challenge you—not the same thing at all. And if you quote me, I'll deny I said that."

Clay shook off Rill's smile. "No, Hunter—if you're not willing to coach Maggie, then I'm not going to skate—"

"Clay, stop!" Maggie tugged at his arm. "I appreciate it, but it doesn't matter. There are other coaches. Mr. Rill is right."

She clung to Clay's arm; Rill thought her eyes were misting. "I hoped we'd be able to train together, but . . ."

Rill looked off into space. His sudden finger snap startled them all. Inspecting Maggie, he nodded pensively. "Yes. Ms. Campbell"—he smiled at her—"Maggie, would you mind giving me a minute or two alone with Clay and Mrs. Bartlett? There's something I'd like to bounce off them. Maybe there's a way to handle this."

Maggie looked at him uncertainly. "I don't want to cause any trouble."

Rill waved away her concern. "Just give me a minute with these two, and perhaps something will work out."

"Really, I—"

"Go, go—let us see some more of that *fabulous* technique." He waggled the back of his hand at her until, reluctantly, she turned and skated away.

"We won't be a minute, Mrs. Bartlett. I just need to have a word with Clay."

Rill draped an arm over Clay's shoulders and led him out of his mother's earshot. "Now, Clay—you shouldn't be so quick to talk about leaving; we go back a way, and I'd miss you."

Clay set his jaw. "I'm sorry, Hunter—if you won't take Maggie, I'm gone."

"Now, now." Rill was amused. "A noble gesture, and I could see the young lady was thrilled by your gallantry. Of course, you know and I know that in your, ah, new financial situation, and without a partner in sight, your departure would be more in the way of confirming the status quo than any great personal sacrifice."

Clay tried to look pained, but Rill could see the corners of his mouth twitch. "That's what I've always liked about you, Clay," he continued. "You're such a calculating bastard. If brass alone would do it, you'd already be World champion."

Clay gave up trying to sound indignant. "Last I heard, no matter how much brass you have that still requires *two* skaters, a man and a woman. And as you so kindly noted . . ."

Rill nodded. "Maybe we can work something out; I *love* watching you skate, and I'd love watching you get a gold medal hung around your neck. Which could happen, if you buckled down and exploited your God-given talent. Besides,

I'm fond of you, even if you are the most undependable, spoiled, lazy, irresponsible, and deceitful skater I've ever had. And don't argue—you know it's true, every word of it."

Clay's protest died in a grin. "You've always had a way with compliments, Hunter." He looked the older man in the eye, sobering. "But I've learned a lot the last few months; going broke concentrates the mind. I'm sorry I haven't approached skating more seriously; all of a sudden the idea of skating for a living looks a lot more attractive than the alternatives I see. I've cheated myself, among others."

"Very good, Clay. Fellows like us learn only when we figure out we're cheating ourselves—we don't care about anyone else enough." A shadow flitted across his face. "What's important is that you're gifted, and I gather you're ready to really bear down now. Am I right? You see, I've found a young woman, but I don't think she'd be interested in anything less than a clear shot at the top."

Clay's chin snapped up. "You've got someone? Who?"

Rill squeezed Clay's biceps. "I've found her, but you're going to have to sell her; from the way she looks at you, I think you've got a shot." He turned Clay ninety degrees. They watched Maggie in silence for a minute, until Rill gave him a push. "Go work that charm of yours."

Maggie circled the ice easily, charting a course that brought her close to Doe Rawlings. As she closed on her she saw Doe was even prettier than she'd thought from a distance—beautiful, in fact. The perfect model of an American girl, as Maggie and her friends imagined them. Delicate features, bright, violet eyes, blond hair, and a figure that made Maggie wonder once again why she couldn't have breasts worthy of the name.

Doe's carriage was lovely, a regal ease riveting the eye.

She moved with the languid authority of a young lioness, supple power springing from muscles so harmonized that movement seemed more thought than deed.

Studying the younger girl's steps, Maggie began emulating them. Back and forth, like a shadow, she followed the unfamiliar sequence. There—just like that. It wasn't so . . .

Her feet, unaccustomed to the stylized moves, rebelled. Just before she went down, a strong arm caught her, held her over the ice until her feet steadied. "Careful."

They were stroking together, away from the oblivious Doe Rawlings, Clay's right arm around her waist, his left hand holding hers in front of him. "I see you remember the Kilian position."

She nodded. "You taught me, remember? I thought it was incredibly romantic." Scowling, she added, "Until I skated pairs in Japan. I guess it depends who you're with."

"And now?"

She looked up at him. She'd always thought him attractive, but suddenly she realized he was the most handsome man she'd ever seen. "It's all right."

"Just 'all right'? Better than that, for me. Waltz position." He twirled her, brought her face-to-face. They circled the room, Maggie imagining herself in a ballgown, dancing with a dashing officer on the eve of Waterloo. "When I heard you were moving here, I imagined us doing this, during breaks." He looked around the rink. "I thought that would be fun. You know, the way we used to skate together, when you'd come over in the spring?"

She was surprised he'd nursed the same thought she'd been harboring, and touched. "We'll still skate together. I'll come by here, and you can drop in wherever I am. It would have been fun to train together, but . . ."

"I won't be training here, Mag."

"Clay, that's silly. I mean, thank you for speaking up, but you can't leave Mr. Rill."

He smiled wanly. "It turns out that was a pretty empty gesture."

"What do you mean?"

"I mean the reason Hunter took me aside was to tell me that he was dropping me."

"Dropping you? But why?"

"No partner. He says he can't keep holding open six hours a week in the hope that eventually I find someone. I can't blame him."

She turned, almost fell, liked the feel of his arms as he put her back on track. "Well, I blame him. It wasn't your fault that girl quit." She brightened. "Anyway, then maybe we *can* train together. We'll find someone who takes singles and pairs, someone good, and . . ."

Clay shook his head disconsolately. "Thanks, Mag, but it's no good. Hunter's right—I'm never going to find a partner, at least not anyone any good. It's just too late, and I've gotten a reputation for being 'difficult.' He's offered to let me give lessons here; I can pick up a few bucks that way."

"But you can't give up skating competitively, not when you're so close! You were one of the top juniors in the country, and you would have been a senior soon, and then . . ."

He patted her shoulder. "Shh, shh. Our chickens come home to roost, as Hunter reminded me just now. Let's just enjoy skating together while we can."

"But . . ."

"Please, Maggie? This is kind of a tough moment for me, seeing the handwriting on the wall. Let's just skate together, since I really don't know when the next time will be. Come on."

They resumed stroking, not talking, circling the rink,

Maggie lost in thought. After a long, silent lap, she gave expression to one that seemed to come out of nowhere. "I never skated pairs competitively."

"No? Well, it's a lot different in competition, of course." He pulled her to him so their flanks were pressed together, pumping in tandem. He was only three inches taller than she was, and slender, but the hands that guided her were so sure of themselves that they seemed almost to be speaking. First came the pressure on her far hip, gentle but firm, that said, "Lean right"; then, shortly after, the same hand checked her, saying, "That's enough now." Then came the counterpressure, the wordless instruction, "Follow my left hand, come with me," and finally the reward of silent praise, felt on her hip, as she responded.

She stopped thinking, content to let herself be operated, as though she were an airplane and he the pilot. It was a relaxed, dreamy feeling, a sense of surrender and duality, nothing like Yoshi Ando's clumsy steer wrestling.

She heard him instruct: "Now we're going to try something different. Turn again."

They were both facing in the same direction, only this time Maggie was in front, Clay's hands resting on her hips.

"Are you ready?" She felt his breath in her left ear.

She only had time to say, "Ready for what?"

"This!" His hands gripped her waist. In a single fluid motion, he lifted her over his head, bearing her, his elbows locked, like a trophy.

"Put me down!" she gasped. "Put me down! You'll drop me!" Her hands slapped at his forearms.

"Not if you stop kicking me," he said, chuckling. "You don't weigh anything. I can hold you up all day."

It felt wonderful; when Yoshi Ando'd lifted her she'd always wondered if she was going to come down on her head.

Now she felt as steady as if she were on her own legs. She glanced around the rink. She saw Lettie Bartlett pointing, Hunter Rill's eyes following them. As Clay turned, she saw the blond girl watching impassively.

"Okay," he said, "relax and go limp."

Before she had a chance to think, she was plunging downward. Just when she thought she was returning to the world she controlled, she was accelerating toward the ceiling. He gave her waist a hard twist and let go, so that for a second she was in free flight, watching the rink revolve around her. When she came to rest she was again dangling in the air, facing him, her head a foot above his.

"Put . . . me . . . down." She drubbed her fists on his shoulders, giggling. "Put . . . me . . . down." Her flailing subsided, her hands were cradling the sides of his head. Helplessly, weak with pleasure, she gasped, "I'll lift you by your ears."

He lowered her until her blades made contact with the ice. She slid slowly down his front. His face was inches from hers, her chest pressed against his. Her arms closed around him.

He grinned, looking into her eyes. "All right?"

Coasting backward, she took a deep breath, her heart racing. "I . . . think so."

"Good." He kissed her.

It was over before she realized what had happened. Her first thought was, His breath smelled of toothpaste; I hope mine did. She slumped against him, content to let him steer as she wrestled with the question that had burst upon her.

It had to come out. "Clay," she whispered, her head resting on his chest, "would you . . . would you ever think of . . . taking *me* as a partner?"

He braked to a stop. "You're joking, right?"

"I mean, maybe, just until you found someone good enough. . . . That way, at least you'd stay in practice, and Mr. Rill wouldn't drop you."

"Oh, Maggie." He pulled her to him. "Maggie, Maggie, Maggie. You're the best person on earth. But you're a singles skater; you want to go back and show those judges what you can do in singles, don't you?"

"No, it doesn't have to be singles." Seconds before, she'd wondered, now she didn't. It seemed a meaningless distinction. "Pairs would be just as good."

Rill was immeasurably relieved as he watched Lettie Bartlett, her son, and Maggie Campbell, all in high spirits, heading out the door. Clay Bartlett's career would be set back a bit while the girl worked her way through the tests, but if all went well, she would qualify as a junior soon enough, and they could start competing. She was a far better skater than anyone Rill could have hoped to find, and they'd move on to the seniors soon after that. The girl would know how to work, no doubt about that; with luck she'd get Clay to settle down and stop relying on raw talent. There'd be some income again. On the whole, a most satisfactory disposition.

He'd begun to think about their training schedule when Doe Rawlings suddenly appeared at his side. This, he thought, remembering, would require some finesse.

"Who was that, Hunter, with the Bartletts?" Doe was staring at the doorway, as though they were waiting on the other side.

"The Japanese girl I mentioned. She's quite good, isn't she? Not in your league, of course, but good fundamentals, don't you think?"

"I don't know; I didn't watch her skate. She doesn't look Japanese."

"She doesn't, does she? Striking, though. Rather exotic looking, wouldn't you say? Especially her eyes."

"I didn't notice. Hunter, did you talk to Clay Bartlett about skating pairs with me?"

Rill dropped his voice. "I'm afraid it's a nonstarter. Too late."

Doe froze. Her voice, when she found it, quavered. "What does that mean, 'too late'?"

Rill looked sympathetic. "Clay and the girl were . . . already paired up. That's what he came in to tell me."

Doe's chin quivered. "He and that . . . Japanese girl?"

Rill nodded. "She wanted to quit singles and skate pairs. She begged Clay to take her on, and he agreed. He thinks the chemistry will be right. That's so important, you know?"

"He *said* that? That the 'chemistry' is right?"

"Doe, you can't blame him. I mean, forming a pairs team is like marrying; you've got to be absolutely certain."

"Like getting married," she echoed dully.

"It is, you know. Anyway, her family's known the Bartletts forever, and apparently Clay and the girl practically grew up together. It's a natural."

Doe stared at the floor. "So she's rich."

"Mmm, I suppose. Well off, anyway."

"You won't have to worry about whether she can meet her expenses."

"She made that point, yes." He leaned down, dropping his voice. "Her family even offered to pay his expenses, if he'd take her."

Doe blanched. "She must be used to getting what she wants."

Rill was tiring of the discussion. "Doe, I'm sorry. I was

ready to explore your idea, but it just didn't work out. Frankly, it's probably for the best. Now, as soon as I get back from the office we can get on with the really important business, which is getting you ready for SkateCanada next month."

"Yes, Hunter."

Except when he came back to the rink five minutes later, Doe Rawlings had removed her skates and was running toward the exit. He started to call after her, then gave up; she wasn't going to have a good practice anyway.

Chapter 33

*D*o you suppose, *Ms*. Campbell, that it would make a more satisfying impression if you would *consider* taking the same number of turns in your sit spin as your partner?" Rill's sarcastic drawl became the music to which Maggie and Clay skated.

For weeks they were more like two skaters who happened to be on the ice at the same time than a pairs team. The results were often amusing, sometimes painful, rarely pretty. Missed connections, embarrassing collisions, badly wrenched shoulders, and bruised limbs, all punctuated by Rill's incessant badgering: "Nice height, honey. Maybe next you'll try jumping at the same time as Clay."

One day, though, something happened, some happy confluence of forces, and Maggie found herself in a parallel spin, revolving slowly in place, her free leg extended behind her, far above the ice, Clay in the same position, only facing the opposite direction, their arms circling each other's waists, their torsos pressed together, their heads resting on the other's flanks. As they turned, her hands absorbed the power and tension in his waist, her taut stomach muscles radiated force into his receptive fingertips. She felt herself swelling, her body engorging, chills running through her. When they stopped she was quivering; Clay, as though he knew, skated off to get a drink of water.

After a few months the blushes ceased, hands roaming each other's bodies as impersonally as a masseur's. Some touches tickled, some hurt, some felt good: the gently resistant pressure of young, supple muscles and firm flesh, warm and familiar.

Gradually, glacially, they began to achieve unison. Unison, Rill never tired of reminding them, was the ne plus ultra of pairs.

Rill and Clay showed her how to use the angle of her free leg to match the speed of her spins to his, so that their legs swept their respective circles as though controlled by a single engine. She learned to anticipate, to watch, to whisper instructions. Their shadow skating became more and more congruent, the mirror skating an ever more exact reflection of the partner's movement. They began to develop eye contact, body language, the ability to cover for one another's mistakes.

In the afternoon they practiced lifts in a room off the ice. She'd put her hands in his, lock her elbows, and spring while he took her weight and raised her, slowly, until his hands were at the level of his chin and she towered over him. She would spread her legs, and they would hold the position while he circled the room. Then they would do it again, and again, and again. Every lift, every throw, every twist, had to be mastered on the exercise room mats before it could be hazarded on the unyielding ice.

Clay had a gymnast's physique. Though he weighed less than forty pounds more, his arms and legs were indefatigable; there seemed to be no limit to their ability to sustain her weight.

Accidents happened—many a night Maggie went home to soak deep purple bruises and aching joints, and one day they were practicing side-by-side Salchows, Maggie got too close, and half an hour later she was in an emergency room, having the two-inch gash in her shin stitched. The next day she was back at work.

Hunter Rill was delighted with his new student. Not only was she the best skater he'd ever seen in a pairs team, she was an extraordinarily quick study, with exemplary work habits. She also seemed almost imperturbable, taking his most acerbic gibes with little more than a nod and a faint smile. He was so accustomed to students quaking at his slightest rebuke that at first her composure nettled him; but in his more candid moments he found her indifference to his approbation perversely satisfying. After a few months he tended to accord her far more deference than was his wont.

In one respect he found her immensely useful. He quickly saw that in the new girl he had a powerful device for motivating Doe Rawlings, a utility he discovered purely by accident.

Doe had a weakness for sweets. Rill suspected she found refuge in food, because whenever her termagant mother was being particularly oppressive, the girl's weight increased. Not a lot, never more than a few pounds, but enough to create a problem if left unchecked. Most of the girls could be cowed into weight loss, but bullying didn't work with Doe—it just made her sullen, withdrawn, and uncoachable. It also tended to make her sneak off and eat. So Rill regularly found himself seeking subtle, psychological levers to manage Doe's mood and weight swings.

One day, though, he happened to be standing with Doe as

Maggie and Clay skated by. "What a marvelously trim figure she has," he observed. "They look wonderful together."

That day Doe skipped lunch, and Rill had his epiphany. The next time Doe plumped up two pounds, he said, "You know, Maggie mentioned that a Japanese diet might help you keep the weight off. Raw fish and rice, seaweed, that sort of thing. Said she'd be glad to give you some recipes, if you like." The extra pounds were off in a week.

Maggie Campbell became a key figure in Doe Rawlings's training, a name invoked sparingly but always to powerful effect: "Maggie was saying that figures are the reason she can hold an edge so much longer than you can." He'd find Doe skating patch, which she loathed. "Maggie might be right—you really *don't* get her leg extension." The next day Doe would be at the barre, stretching her thigh muscles. "Maggie offered to work with you at the gym, see if you can't firm up those upper arms." He'd turn around, and Doe would be at the weight machine. It was pure fabrication, but when threats or bribes wouldn't work, Maggie Campbell usually did. Hunter Rill believed in using whatever worked.

Maggie taught Clay what training meant. The first time he quit early she quit with him and spent the rest of the day thinking about how hard her father worked to earn the money, how much it had hurt her mother to lose skating, and especially about Madam Goto. The next time he quit early she kept skating. Not saying a word, just working as though she'd never given up singles. He had one skate off before he realized what she was doing. "Come on, Mag, I'll buy you a Coke," he called. She ignored him. He watched her for a few minutes, put the boot back on, and joined her. They practiced an extra fifteen minutes that day, to make up for the time he'd been off the ice. After a few months Maggie was the one who said when to quit.

So the time passed. Good time for Maggie, the intensity of practice, the warmth and high spirits of Clay Bartlett sustaining her through the interminable last weeks of a Boston winter, the anxiety of a new school, the startling brevity of a New England spring, her seventeenth birthday.

Every month Maggie wrote Madam Goto, reporting on her progress. She'd been uncomfortable confessing that she'd turned to pairs; she wasn't sure her *sensei* would approve and had the feeling that Madam Goto's disapproval wasn't something to be risked, even if she was halfway around the world from her. She was delighted to receive assurance that Madam Goto wished only that Maggie continue to draw joy from skating. Of course, she added, that did not mean Maggie could neglect her figures. Thereafter Maggie gave herself a patch session at least three times a week. On the infrequent occasions she missed one, she was certain there was a steely old woman in Tokyo scowling until she made it up.

Maggie woke at five-thirty, arrived at the skating rink at six-thirty, skated with Clay for an hour and a half, spent twenty minutes doing off-ice exercises and lifts, got a ride to Thatcher Academy, attended classes until three, returned to the rink for an hour lesson, practiced two more hours, rushed home for dinner, did her homework, and went to bed. On Saturday she took ballet in Wellesley, then went to the rink and skated four hours. Sunday was a day off from the rink: homework and an occasional movie.

She found Thatcher Academy, even though it was one of the best schools in Boston, almost laughably easy after the rigors of the Japanese school system; she had little time to make friends, but she also had little time to miss friends.

The only cloud was the worry that Clay would tire of waiting for her, would turn to her one day and say, "I'm really sorry, but this was a mistake. There's this girl who just lost her partner, and . . ."

Yet when she hinted at her concern, hating herself for seeking reassurance, he would laugh and offer it in abundance. "If I got some girl who's been skating pairs for a long time, in effect I get her former partner, too. Better a virgin any day. Besides, where would I find a girl half as pretty?"

Chapter 34

October 2001: Boston

*Y*ou can do it, Doe. You have to will yourself to believe, that's all." Rill stood with his hands on her shoulders, staring intently into her eyes, "I *know* you can do it."

"I don't know, Hunter; only three or four *men* have hit quads in competition. I just don't seem to be able to get enough height to get around before I land, no matter how tight I jump. And it's killing my ankle."

"Doe, you're trying to make history. And you *will*. But we're going to have to work as we never have before. Less than five months, and you can relax."

"Maybe the quad isn't necessary. The Axel is pretty . . ."

"Listen, you aren't going to be the only girl with the Axel at the games, the way you've been before. I hear Campbell has the Axel."

Doe snorted. "Don't make me laugh. I would have read about it."

"She's saving it, dear, just like you're going to save the quad until the Olympics. But I've talked to people who saw her hit them in practice."

"She's been skating places like"—she searched for the country—"Austria."

"Australia, Doe."

"Whatever. Noplace."

"Frankfurt wasn't 'noplace,' Doe, and she finished third in the German Pro-Am." He was delighted she'd been following Campbell's career; that tool was still available.

"Third," she scoffed. "I'd retire if I finished third someplace."

"Well, I don't think Ms. Campbell is retiring quite yet, Doe, since I understand she'd just been named Japan's entrant in the Trophée de France. I have a feeling that ever since your unfortunate accident with Mr. Bartlett, our Japanese friend has had the knife out for you. I suspect she was very much in love with him. Still is, I imagine."

"Well, maybe she should know—" She broke off.

"Know what, dear?"

"Never mind."

"That you weren't driving Clay Bartlett home the night of the accident?"

Her head snapped up. "Why do you say that?"

"Because you weren't driving him anyplace. You weren't driving—he was."

"That's not true." She couldn't meet his eyes.

"Do you think I'm a moron, Doe? I know you can't drive a standard shift. Why'd you take the blame?"

She sat silently for a half minute, then shrugged. "He asked me to. He said he couldn't take a drunk driving charge, he'd lose his license."

Rill, shaking his head, grinned in spite of himself. "Our Clay certainly has a way of getting young women to take care of him."

She shrugged again. "It didn't mean much to me; I don't

need a driver's license anyway. Why didn't you say anything?"

"Believe me, I would have if the police hadn't dropped it. I wasn't about to see you throw away your career for Clay Bartlett. But tell me, were you really just out for a little joyride?"

Her flush told him what her pinched lips wouldn't. "Ah, I see. And speaking of Clay Bartlett, did I by any chance see him pulling away from the house the other day?"

"I really couldn't say."

"Doreen?"

She looked up angrily. "I don't know who you saw, Hunter. It could have been him."

"You've renewed your acquaintance, have you?"

"We see each other sometimes, if that's what you mean."

"Ah; that explains your recent trips to 'the library.'"

"I *do* go to the library. I'm learning about art."

"My dear, I doubt if you know what's inside a library, and I love you for it."

"That's not fair! I—"

He flapped his hand. "Would it make any difference if I told you to stay away from him?"

She glared at him, hugging her knees. "No!"

"I didn't think so, so I won't bother. I suppose he's trying to get you to sign a contract with Weeks?"

"No; he's never even mentioned it."

"Hmm. Well, if he does, you give him a firm 'no,' Doreen. When it comes time to deal with Weeks, I mean to be there."

"I'm not a child, Hunter, and I'm tired of being treated like one."

"I *know* you're not a child, but you'll be acting like one if you get into something you know nothing about."

"You don't have to worry," she said sullenly.

"Let's hope not. And for heaven's sake—as long as you're going to see him anyway, tell him he doesn't have to skulk around like a child molester. I'm not going to put up a fuss."

She looked up, brightening. "Really?"

"Really. I know when to face reality. But let me give *you* a little bit of reality to face. If you want Clay Bartlett to remain interested, you better not neglect your training. Because the Clay Bartletts of this world follow winners."

The smile slid from her mouth. "I don't know why you hate him so much."

"Hate him?" He was taken aback. "I don't hate him; in fact, I'm quite fond of him. It's just that I *know* him. He and I are very much alike, you see."

Doe snickered. "Hunter, Clay likes *women*—believe me, you're nothing alike."

It was Rill's turn to chuckle. "Doe, Doe, you *are* a prize. I have *no* doubt Clay likes women. What I meant has nothing to do with *how* we satisfy our desires and everything to do with the fact that people like us, Clayton and I, feel we're *entitled* to satisfy them, whatever they are. Our loyalties can be rather . . . transient." He studied her. "I care about you; I don't want you hurt."

"He wouldn't do anything to hurt me."

"No, not intentionally. Clay's self-absorbed, not cruel. But if you want to hold his interest, I suggest you keep something back."

He rolled his eyes at the defiant tilt of her chin. "No, dear, not that. I told you, I'm a realist. I *meant* your signature on Week's damn contract. And you better keep on being number one."

"Don't worry, I plan to."

"That's the girl. And, as I say, the Axel isn't necessarily

going to be enough to keep you number one anymore. Hence the quad. I mean, imagine *losing* to Campbell."

"That won't happen." Offhandedly, as though asking for confirmation of the weather report, she added, "Did you really hear she's got the Axel, Hunter?"

Rill contained his smile. "Count on it. Now, you've got almost five months to get the quad down before the Olympics, and you're *this* close." He held his thumb and forefinger a quarter inch apart. "The rest of the program's coming together beautifully. Let's get the quad, okay?"

"If the program's coming together so well, how come you won't let me skate in the Nationals with it?"

Rill hated it when she got in one of these moods. "*Because,* Doe, then everyone in the world would know your program, and the Olympics would be an anticlimax instead of the breakthrough it's going to be."

"But I'd be the National champion."

"You're already the National champion. What good's winning the same title again?"

She shook her head. "How can you be sure I'll make the Olympic team if I don't skate in the Nationals?"

"Doe, I've explained this a dozen times. Dr. Walcott will say that you've got an injury that keeps you out of the Nationals. Believe me, the Olympic Committee will waive you in. There's plenty of precedent. Okay?"

Doe, pouting, shuffled her skates. Rill put his finger under her chin and lifted it until she was staring into his eyes. "Doreen . . . Doe. Have I *ever* let you down?"

She tried to move her chin, but he held his fingers on it until she murmured, "No."

He kept on. "Didn't I get you the titles I said I'd get you, *when* I said I'd get them?"

"I guess so."

"You *know* so. I made you the best woman skater America has produced in a generation. Now I'm telling you how you can become the best skater the world has ever known, man or woman. A skater people will talk about when you're a grandmother. But you've got to trust me."

"I do, Hunter, but—"

"No buts, Doe. You've got to trust me. You've got the American and World titles; now the Olympic gold, and then you retire—the greatest skater of all time. But in the meantime, trust me."

"I trust you, Hunter."

He sighed. "Of course you do." Adopting a businesslike tone, he patted her hair into place. "Ready to try the quad again?"

"Okay."

"Do you want to use the jump harness for a while, get the feeling that way?"

"No. It doesn't feel real."

"That's my girl. Okay, let's take it from the beginning of the *Valkyrie* music. And really *go* for it."

She came into the jump on a back outside edge, at tremendous speed. She planted her right toe pick and went vertical. He held his breath as she rocketed toward the roof. "Yes," he whispered. "Yes!" She seemed to keep going, higher and higher. He counted, although she was revolving almost too fast for even his eyes to follow.

Now down. He flinched as she landed, the impact bending her ankle to nearly ninety degrees. She struggled, fought for it, came within inches of touching her hand down, and then she was standing, shakily, her mouth open, and he was running toward her, across the ice, shouting.

"Oh, yes. Oh, yes! Sweetheart, that was beautiful. You *did* it! The first woman in history to land a quad! You're the most beautiful skater I've ever seen! The most beautiful skater who's ever lived."

He kissed her forehead, walking her off the ice with his arm around her. When they got to the benches he bent down to untie her boots. "Let's go home, Doe. You've earned a break."

He'd fix breakfast while she showered. He'd read the paper, and they'd return to the rink. Spend the day there, like a family business.

Later, when they got home for the evening, she was going to carve a pumpkin for Halloween. He'd warn her about cutting herself, and she'd scoff. She was going to bake cookies, too, for the trick-or-treaters. That meant the kitchen would be an unholy mess for days.

Sometimes he'd hear her upstairs, humming, her radio playing vile music. He'd smell something she was cooking, feel her footsteps as they trod the staircase. He'd grate his teeth because she'd have left all the lights on again or the dishes in the sink.

She'd surprise him with dinner, the table set with candles and flowers. Something burned black on the outside and raw near the bone, or drowned in canned mushroom soup. She'd wait, little white teeth working the full lip, as he brought the fork to his mouth. The dazzling smile his approval brought.

He thought about the sudden impulsive hugs lasting barely seconds but bringing so much more joy than hours in a stranger's arms. The ghastly kitsch she brought him from shopping forays in foreign cities, proudly displayed.

He'd see a brassiere hooked over a doorknob, panty hose lying on the floor of the upstairs hall, a half-eaten apple browning on the television, CDs scattered everywhere, and he'd think, This is what it's like to be normal.

Once, "normal" had been a sneer; now he knew: This is what a normal family, in a normal home, sounds like. This is what it feels like to be the father of a daughter. This is what it feels like to love someone. He wondered how he'd survived before she came, and how he'd survive after she left.

Chapter 35

January 1998: Boston

*D*oe wasn't sure why she'd woken. She cocked a sleepy eye at her alarm clock: one in the morning. She had to be up at five-thirty for practice and was about to drop her head to the pillow again when she heard her mother's off-key singing. Then there was a loud, splintering sound, followed by her mother's rasp: "Goddamn it."

Doe snapped on the living room light. Her mother, on her knees, was flailing at the wreckage of the coffee table. She rose unsteadily, looking foggily at her feet. Her right hand clutched a tumbler of red wine, miraculously preserved.

"Are you all right, Mama?"

A cascade of red splashed on the rug as her mother whirled around. "Damn—you scared me." Mrs. Rawlings coughed. "Made me spill it." More wine slopped onto the floor as she swayed.

"I . . . I'm sorry, Mama. I just wanted to make sure you were okay. I'll get a towel."

Doe was alarmed; her mother's mood could darken faster than the New England sky in winter when she'd been drinking. Spilled wine was more than sufficient provocation, and Doe knew better than to place much faith in the loopy grin her mother was giving her.

"Never mind that now, baby. Come over here and let me show you something."

Warily, Doe approached her mother's outstretched arm. Thinking she meant to enfold her in one of her displays of maudlin affection, Doe stepped in close, ready for the sloppy kiss, only to have her mother draw back.

"No, no, dummy—look!" Mrs. Rawlings thrust out her arm and waggled the fingers on her left hand, flashing a large diamond.

Doe looked from it to her mother's flushed face, then back to the ring. "Why, it's beautiful," she exclaimed. "But, but . . . where did you get it?"

"Now, that's not a polite question, sweetie!" she whooped in her husky voice. "Let's just say he *gave* it to me at dinner." Her raucous chuckles turned into hiccups, and she sank onto the sofa, pushing the last of the coffee table's shards aside with her foot. "Ahh!" She took a long drink.

"But, but . . . I don't understand. Is it . . . an engagement ring?"

Mrs. Rawlings rolled her head back on the sofa. "*No,* you goon—it's my birthstone!" Her hand came around, squeezing Doe's knee. "Of *course* it's an engagement ring."

She raised the ring to her lips. "Had this rock in his pocket, all ready to go." She snorted. "Not the only rock in his pocket, either. Said I was the first woman in a long time, made him feel like Billy Goat Gruff."

Mrs. Rawlings cackled contentedly while thoughts whirled through Doe's mind. Finally she asked hesitantly, "So you said yes, Mama?"

Her mother looked up incredulously. "Did I say yes?

Honey, Art Perkins owns one of the largest plumbing supply companies on the West Coast. He owns a vineyard some-place called Sonoma, for Christ's sake! He's sixty-eight years old, a widower, no children, and the girl asks if I'm going to accept his proposal? What planet are you on, sweetie?"

Doe shook her head, smiling uncertainly. "That's wonder-ful, Mama, I'm happy for you. Now you won't have to work so hard." She settled uneasily onto the arm of the couch.

"Baby, my working days are over. I'm about to become a lady of leisure. Get this!" She grabbed Doe's forearm, drag-ging her down onto the sofa. "Art drives a Mercedes, and he's going to get me one!"

Doe pressed her hands against the cushions, trying to get the room to stay still. "Oh, Mama, he sounds wonderful." The question returned. "One thing, Mama—did you say Mr., uh, Perkins was from the *West* Coast?"

"He sure is, baby. He's got a great big house in Oakland Hills, across the bay from San Francisco. It's got a pool, *and* a three-car garage. I've already told him I want my Mer-cedes to be white. And baby"—her mother smacked Doe's knee—"*your* bedroom opens onto the pool! Just think of that. Why, every morning . . ."

Cold, steely fingers kneaded Doe's insides. She pulled herself upright, staring at her mother. She saw a big, silly-looking, fading woman who'd dyed her hair a color that didn't happen in nature and pulled out all her eyebrows so she could replace them with black, crayon arcs.

She felt light-headed, almost dizzy, as though *she'd* been drinking. "*My* bedroom? You mean . . . you want me to move to California? To, to . . . leave Hunter?"

"I know you're fond of him, sugar, but there are other coaches." She squinted. "I told Art how important that is to us." Her hand rocked Doe's shoulder. "Fact of the matter is, I know Art sees that as a big plus. Why, I showed him your picture, and your clippings, and I could see right away he loved the idea of having a *star* move in."

The playful note returned. "Anyway, Art—that's Mr. Perkins, sweetie—says that some of the very best skating coaches are right there in the Bay Area! Of course, we can ask Rill if he has any suggestions, and I'm sure . . ."

Doe thought that if she could only scratch away her forehead, she might be able to understand. "You took my father away, and now you want to take Hunter away, too?" she blurted, wrestling with a feeling of panic.

Her mother's eyes narrowed. "Your father killed himself—you can hardly blame *me* for that. He was a weak, useless—"

"You made him do it, Mother. I remember. You yelled at him, and yelled at him"—her voice became a singsong—"and yelled at him, night after night. You think I was too little to remember, but I do. You called him terrible things. Night, after night, after night. I remember."

Her mother struggled to sit up. "You shut your mouth. You don't know what you're talking about! Your father was a weakling, a sissy; why, he couldn't even get it up half the time. He—"

"I'd come home and he'd be crying. You made my father cry. You made him leave me."

"I'm warning you . . ." Phyllis Rawlings raised her hand threateningly.

Without breaking the rhythm of her words, Doe rose and stood, facing her mother. She looked down at the woman in front of her, the garish eyes drawn into the points that had always terrified her. "Don't, Mama—don't do this. I've . . . I've had enough!"

Air didn't want to go either way she wanted it. Holding her hands in front of her, she reached for her mother, trying to swallow the space around her. "I can't, don't you see? I can't do it again. Don't take Hunter away, too."

"He's a skating coach, for Christ's sake. They're a dime a dozen."

"He's not just my coach, he's all I've got!"

Mrs. Rawlings lunged forward heavily. Her clumsy swing caught Doe on the hip. "You've got me, you selfish little bitch, and don't you forget it!"

The sound of Doe's heavy panting filled the small room as her hands curled into fists. Her lips came back over her teeth, her eyes narrowing until only the blue centers showed. Her voice grew deeper and rougher. "You're not doing it to me again. I'm sick of your yelling, and your dirty mouth, and your drinking. I'm sick of the men you bring around, with their looks and their touching. I'm sick of losing anybody who's ever meant anything to me. You're . . . not . . . doing . . . it . . . to . . . me . . . again."

Phyllis Rawlings gaped at the apparition before her. Then she, too, was standing.

Her hand caught her daughter just below the ear, staggering her. "You ungrateful little snit." Her chest filled, and she looked twice her daughter's size. "I've worked for years to support your skating. Every penny I could earn or borrow went into it. Now I finally get a chance for something for myself and you say you're not going? Well, the . . . hell . . . you're . . . not. This is my big break, and you're coming!"

Doe straightened. "I'm staying here, Mother."

As her mother drew back her arm again, Doe's hand closed over a piece of the coffee table, canted at her feet. "That's it, Mother—that's the last time. Don't hit me," she hissed. "Don't ever hit me again. Next time I'll hit back, I swear I will. If I have to, I'll wait till you've passed out, and then I'll hit back." She raised the club.

Phyllis Rawlings tensed. Doe looked at her mother's up-raised hand, in her mother's eyes. "Do it"—she nodded—"do it." She tossed her hair back and waited, club poised.

Her mother's hand tensed, wavered, then brushed away the threat. "I wouldn't waste the energy. But don't think you can get away with this. I can make you go, and I will." She kneaded the flesh on her neck, turned wheedling: "Why do you want to be like this, baby? You're barely sixteen—a girl should be with her mother. Haven't I always wanted what's best for you?" She sniffled, old and hollow.

"You want to take care of me, Mother—is that it?"

Her mother sank heavily onto the sofa. "'Course. Can't be running around by herself, pretty girl like you. Men're gonna be swarming round you, baby, especially when you get those medals. Take advantage of you, I'm not there to look out for you."

She lurched to one side as she reached for the wine bottle on the end table. Doe knew it was time to leave.

Grabbing a coat and boots, she walked out of the apartment.

White rage coursed through Hunter Rill. The cow; the bloody, selfish cow, he thought. He rested his forehead against the cool windowpane, staring out at the dirty gray morning. The *Globe* said that it was called suicide weather; he could understand that.

He listened; that might have been a sound from the spare bedroom. He'd have to get her up soon anyway; if her mother sent the police looking for her, it could be sticky. Al-though what was he going to do, turn her away when she shows up at his door at three in the morning?

He turned back to the windowpane. Phyllis Rawlings was going to take her to San Francisco, just like that. Turn her over to someone like Powell-Jones or McLaughlin, and soon he could watch her on television, hugging one of those frauds while someone hung a medal around her neck.

The greedy bitch could think of only one thing: her rich old sugar daddy. The big house, the pool, a *white* Mercedes, for Christ's sake, and a bunch of goddamn *grapevines*. And if it cost Hunter Rill his only remaining chance in life, well then, tough, fucking luck for him.

He could hear the horny old bastard as he patted Phyllis Rawlings's ass. "Why, there's *lots* of good skating coaches in San Francisco, darlin'." And there were, worse luck.

She'd told the girl she could make her go, and he supposed that legally she was right. He'd lose her, lose his one chance in life, unless something changed that sodden excuse for a mind.

Rill resumed staring sightlessly out the window. The girl who'd showed up at his door in the middle of the night before was a different girl from the one he knew. It was as though the steel-nerved artist of the ice had stepped off it and taken over from the off-ice, shy little doll terrified of offending. She said she'd been ready to club the bitch senseless, and he believed her. She said why her mother really wanted her to go, and he believed that, too.

After a few minutes an idea started to form. He rolled his forehead around on the chilled glass—God, it felt wonderful. It helped him think, too. Maybe there was something else to club Phyllis Rawlings with. He walked back to the bedroom to talk to Doe.

"I'll make tea. The two of you need some time together." Rill turned back at the kitchen door: "Doe, listen to your mother. She only wants what's best for you." He looked soberly at Phyllis Rawlings, nodding.

"Yes, Hunter." The girl sounded comfortable, as though she knew exactly what she had to do—which, after her talk with Rill, he prayed she did.

He left the room, stopping to listen as soon as he was past the door. He could see through the crack, hear everything they said.

Phyllis Rawlings looked older than her years. "I, uh, I'm glad you called, Doc. I think maybe I . . . broke things to you a little too abruptly. When you've had a few days to think things over, I know you'll—"

"Mother, it's all right. Hunter told me I have to go, if that's what you want." The girl's voice was flat, decisive, with none of its former tremulousness.

Phyllis Rawlings brightened. "Well, of course that's what I want. I'm your mother, after all."

"You only want what's best for me—that's what Hunter says."

"I heard him. I'm glad he appreciates that." Her confidence seemed to be returning.

"Well, after talking to Hunter, I realized this was really a golden opportunity."

Her mother nodded eagerly. "That's what I was trying to tell you last night, baby. Tell the truth, I think I'd celebrated a little too much, maybe it didn't come out so clear."

"That's all right, Mother. You had a lot to celebrate, didn't you?"

"But you do, too, baby—that's my point." Her mother's head bobbed. "You won't have to worry whether there'll be enough money for your training, and—"

"No, I won't have to worry about that."

"That's right, baby, because Art'll take care of it." Her mother nodded eagerly.

Doe smiled. "No. Because I won't be training."

Mrs. Rawlings's reddened features scrunched into a question mark. "What do you mean, you won't be training?"

"Just that. I'm going to finish high school and go to college. Hunter says California has some wonderful colleges. That's what I mean, this is my golden opportunity. I'm done with skating."

Her mother looked at her uncomprehendingly. "You don't mean it."

"Try me."

Mrs. Rawlings's hand began worrying the flesh on her neck. "You've got to keep skating. You *can't* quit now."

Doe laughed. "Why, Mother—so you can cash in? I thought that was what this old man was for."

The old Phyllis Rawlings revived momentarily. "If you think you can just forget all I've done for you, you got another thing coming! Art's got a lot of money, but . . ."

She sputtered and burned out, but not soon enough. "But not as much as you'll have if I win an Olympic gold? Is that what you were going to say?"

"No, baby—that's unfair. I just . . ."

Doe snickered. "I'm your security, is that it? Afraid Art will catch on to you, the way my father did, the way all the other men you've jumped into bed with have?"

Phyllis Rawlings tensed angrily, but she opened her hands, affecting a wounded smile. "I just meant, why would you want to throw everything away, when you're so close?"

"Well, Mother, I guess I just don't feel like changing coaches. And as far as I know, you may be able to make me come to California, but I don't think you can find a court that will order me to skate."

The young woman who leaned toward her mother, smiling malignantly, was someone neither her mother nor the man watching behind the door knew. "You might say, Mother, that all I want is what's best for you. Why don't you think about what that might be?"

Rill, poised behind the door, took this as his cue. "Well, ladies," he said, setting the tray of tea things down in front of them, "now that you've had a chance to chat, perhaps we can work something out to everyone's satisfaction."

It was arranged in a few days. The lawyer said it wasn't even particularly unusual, a coach getting legal custody of a skater. He'd done one, he said, where the divorcing parents, unable to agree on custody, let the coach *adopt* their child. "He got *all* her earnings, too, Mrs. Rawlings. If your girl does as well as we expect, your share should make you quite comfortable. Quite comfortable indeed." He stood up, the adults shook hands, and Doe Rawlings went home to Hunter Rill's South End brownstone.

Chapter 36

November 2001: Bordeaux

*I*t is a good sign the JFSA selected you to appear for
Japan in the Trophée de France. I was concerned they
would choose Otsuka, just because she's been around so
long."

"It is a tribute to their regard for you, Chiako-*chan*; I am
grateful," Maggie replied. She put her seat back and shut her
eyes.

"No, no—it means that they expect you to win the Nationals. They recognize that you are the best woman skater
in Japan."

Maggie lifted her eyeshade. "The best *gaijin* woman skating in Japan. It is a very small category."

"That is over; Yoshida has told people that nothing could
do more for their program than to have the distinguished
yanki win an Olympic medal for Japan. He said it would val-
idate the Japanese way of training."

"Of course," Maggie chuckled. "If I medal, no doubt it
will be because I eat raw fish and seaweed. It is a heavy responsibility I carry."

"I hope skating for Japan is best for you."

"What is best for me is that I beat Rawlings. I would like to do it as Chiako-*chan's* pupil."

"What is best for you is that you skate in a way worthy of you. Let the order of finish take care of itself."

Maggie's answer was interrupted by the instruction to prepare for landing. "Of course; as my new *sensei* says," she murmured.

Chiako saw Hunter Rill and Doe Rawlings before Maggie did. "Maybe we should come back later?"

Maggie spotted the two of them at the registration desk. "No, there's no point in that."

She strode ahead and was soon abreast of them. "Hello, Hunter. Doe." She didn't offer her hand.

Rill greeted her expansively. "Maggie, what a pleasure. I was thrilled to hear you were entered. So was Doe, I know. Miss Mori." He made a slightly exaggerated bow. Doe and Maggie stood looking at each other, Maggie impassive and unreadable, Doe supercilious.

"Yes," said Doe. "With such a strong field, it's nice to know there're some people you don't have to worry about."

"Now, now, dear"—Rill put his arm around Doe's shoulders, turning her until she was no longer locking eyes with Maggie—"your fangs are showing. I will be very surprised if Ms. Campbell fails to mount a formidable challenge."

"I'll do my best."

"I'm sure you will, dear. Now Doe and I must be off. May the best woman win, and all that." A firm tug got Doe heading toward the exit, with only a glance over her shoulder.

Maggie, seething, stared at their backs. Chiako touched her arm. "You mustn't concentrate on her. Think about the competition instead."

"She's my competition."

"Excuse me, please, but I think not—as Madam Goto would have said, *you* are your competition."

It wasn't clear whether Maggie, still staring, heard her.

Chiako hugged Maggie, saying over and over, "That was so good, that was so good."

The thunderous crowd made it hard to hear, but Maggie knew what she was saying, just as she'd known, as soon as she'd come out of her finishing, flying jump spin and thrown her arms wide to the dying notes of the excerpt from *Rhapsody in Blue*, that her short program was a triumph. When her scores were posted, she set her jaw. "Let's see her top that," she said, staring at the scoreboard.

Chiako shook her head. "She will not," she replied. "But we still have the long program."

The short program was never Doe's strength. She had a touch down on her triple lutz, and while her scores reflected the indulgence given the World champion, they were well below Maggie's. Going into the long program, Maggie was in first place, Doe third.

Then Doe Rawlings demonstrated why she was the reigning World champion, bringing the crowd to its feet when, thirty seconds into her program, she hit a triple lutz, followed by a clean triple Axel, a triple flip, a triple loop, a triple toe/triple toe combination, and a triple Salchow, the jumps punctuated by perfect footwork, an Ina Bauer, a flying camel into a back sit spin, a death-drop spin, and at the end a combination into a perfectly centered scratch spin that turned her into a blue blur at center ice, as the audience exploded. As she came off, a small army of junior skaters was busy picking up the bouquets flung on the ice.

Waiting in the locker room, Maggie, hearing the clamor, turned to the television monitor. "Damn," she whispered as Doe's scores were posted. "Damn it."

"Megumi, listen to me." Chiako stopped rubbing Maggie's shoulders to stride over to the monitor and snap it off. She returned to sit on the bench next to Maggie.

"Stop thinking about that one, do you hear? All you have to do is skate a clean program and you will win. Even if you finish second in the long, you win overall. Just go out and skate for yourself, and forget everyone else."

"*Hai,*" Maggie murmured, still staring at the now blank television screen. "But did you see that Axel?"

"Campbell-*san*, we must talk."

Maggie, mechanically stuffing clothes into her duffel bag, didn't seem to have heard. Chiako walked over to her and closed the bag. "I said, we must talk."

"There's nothing to talk about. I was terrible, and I lost. I'm sorry if I embarrassed you." She opened the bag, threw in a sweater, and zipped it shut. "We better go—we'll miss the plane."

"Just a minute, please." Chiako sat on the bed. "We have to decide if you want me as a coach."

"I told you—I'm sorry I performed so badly. If you want to drop me, I won't blame you. I'm sure I didn't help your reputation any."

Chiako jumped to her feet, her hands closing hard on Maggie's upper arms. "How dare you insult me like that!" She shook her, then dropped her hands in disgust. "You know I'm not thinking about my reputation. If you had skated your program and done badly, I would say nothing; I didn't always skate my best, either. No one does."

Maggie set her mouth in a thin line, nostrils flaring. "I skated my program."

"No! Your program opens with a triple lutz, *not* a triple Axel. We agreed on that long ago. Your program certainly doesn't open with an absurd fall, and that's why the rest of your program doesn't look as though it's being skated by a *drunk!*"

Maggie held the woman's look as long as she could, then crumpled. "Oh, Mori-*san*—I'm so ashamed."

She fell into Chiako's arms. "I wanted to beat her so much. After she skated so well, I *had* to try the Axel. And then, after the fall, I was trying so hard to catch up. It . . . it just all fell apart."

"Shh, shh." Chiako patted her back. "Don't you see? That's what comes of trying to skate *against* someone. You must skate with yourself, for yourself, and let the rest take care of itself."

"That's what Gogo *sensei* said, too. But you told me you understood."

"I do understand. And now I wish to help you by telling you what I think Goto *sensei* would have told you: Though I understand your desire to defeat this woman for the harm she caused you and your beloved, you may do so only if you cease wanting it."

Maggie's hands circled her temples. "That sounds so like her."

"Yes, and it is true. It means you must be able to hear the music with your heart, and you can't if it is filled with thoughts of this woman. You must oppose her, but not with hate or anger. You must oppose her with joy. Your best chance of winning is to skate for the beauty in it, not to win."

"I've tried, but I can't forget my feelings."

"Not forget, no. But feelings are no different from anything else; you must shape them, train them, until once again they serve you, instead of betraying you."

"How can I? I think of her constantly. How do I get her out of me?"

"Remember how you learned to do a spread-eagle? Your feet didn't want to point in opposite directions, did they?"

Maggie stared at the carpet. "No."

Chiako put her arm around her. "Nor did mine. Nor do most people's. So every day we forced them into position. Gradually it became easier. And then, one day, we didn't even have to think about it."

"I know, but—"

The soft voice overrode Maggie's: "You must force yourself to skate with joy, with love in your heart. Whenever you feel bitterness creeping back in, you must deny it space. At once think of other things, good things. The music, the feel of movement, your friends and your family. Bartlett-*san*. Madam Goto. The *kami*, if you are a believer. Araki-*san*, who loves you, I think. There is much for you to think about—too much to leave room for this thing that will only hurt you, if you let it."

Maggie didn't answer, just sat and thought of Chiako's words. If she hadn't been sitting next to her, she would have sworn she was back at the rink in Ikebukuro, listening to Madam Goto explain to her about the little leather case and her airman. If anyone had reason to fill her heart with bitterness, it was Madam Goto, yet she had not, so there had been room in it for a foolish young girl.

She looked up as Chiako whispered. "Now . . . am I your *sensei*, or am I not?"

Maggie wiped her eyes. "I don't deserve Mori-*san* as a

sensei; I am ashamed. But I would be very grateful if you would continue to coach me."

"You will try what I tell you? This woman will not set your program any longer?"

"I will try, Mori-*san.* You will set my program."

"And the *kami,* Campbell-*san,* always the *kami.* They set all our programs." Chiako took her hands. "Then we must go. There's a plane to catch, and much practice before the Olympics."

They were checking out when Maggie saw Doe Rawlings across the lobby and recoiled. She'd started to turn away when she felt a hand between her shoulder blades. "Go," Chiako whispered. "It starts now."

"I . . . I can't. Please."

Chiako crooned softly in her ear, "It is only a new movement. You are anxious, but you will try it."

"No, please. Not yet. I—"

"Think how many years you have been trying new movements. Falling, picking yourself up, trying again. Only *we* know what it is when, on the fourth try, or the tenth, or the hundredth, we make it. People who never try never fall, but they never fly, either. Is this not what our *sensei* would say?"

Maggie swallowed. "Yes."

The pressure of Chiako's hand increased. "Then you must practice, Campbell-*san,*" the lyrical voice whispered, "if you wish to fly."

"Just a minute, please, Mori *sensei,*" Maggie heard herself saying. "I will be right back."

She walked over to Doe, extending her hand. "Congratulations. I didn't belong on the same ice with you."

Doe looked at her incredulously. "You're kidding."

"No. You skated magnificently, and deserved to win."

"What happened to all the things you told Hunter? I thought you could outskate me any day."

Maggie's startled protest died in her throat. She turned up her hands, shrugging. "If I said that, I certainly look foolish now."

Hunter Rill appeared, a broad smile on his face. "Well, I'm happy to see you two chatting so amiably."

Maggie nodded, face set. "I was just congratulating Doe. You, too."

"Why, thank you. That's very gracious. You know, without that fall, it might have been much closer. Still, fifth isn't bad, considering how recently you returned to singles."

"Perhaps. In any case, it's where I finished; there's no point in worrying about it now."

"Very wise. Well, I expect we'll see you in Utah."

"If so, I hope I can provide better competition. I better go now. Congratulations again."

She was walking away when Doe called to her: "You know, I'm grateful to you."

Maggie turned back, puzzled. "Oh? Why?"

"I told Hunter you'd never land the Axel. Now he's going to have to find a new way to motivate me."

Maggie made a stopover in Boston, certain that Clay would lift her spirits. He seemed distracted though, preoccupied with her showing in Bordeaux. Now, less than three hours before she had to leave for Tokyo, they sat in the Ritz Bar while she tried to cheer him.

"It's not going to work, is it, Mag? She's just too good."

"It's coming, I can feel it. I tried to improvise, and that's crazy. It won't happen again. The program's *good*, Clay— really good. I can *feel* Madam Goto in it. It's as though everything she ever believed about skating is crystallized in those four minutes, and it seems so *right* for me. I just didn't give it a chance in France. If I'm on, and I will be, I'll be competitive."

His mouth puckered skeptically. "Without the Axel, Maggie, how can you hope to challenge her? She hits Axels in her sleep. There's a rumor she's putting in a quad, for Christ's sake."

"Really?" Maggie's forefinger traced lazy waltz eights in the mist on the tabletop. "What kind?"

He fiddled with a book of matches. "I don't know. What difference does it make?" The matchbook made a tapping sound on the glass. "Any quad by a woman would make history."

"True." She covered his nervous hand with hers. "But there's more to skating than jumps. Anyway, what's important is that I skate my best, not beating her."

Clay's face registered surprise. "Well—you have changed your attitude."

She nodded. "I'm thinking more clearly now."

"Or more realistically."

Her eyes narrowed as she withdrew her hand. "I've never given up in my life. I just decided I'd start skating for me, and not for her. I think it will work out."

"Bordeaux didn't work out, did it?"

She shrugged. *"Shikata ga nai."*

"What's that mean?"

"It can't be helped." She took a sip of Perrier. "The Japanese say it a lot. They're . . . *we're* fatalistic."

"Now you're not just skating for them, you've become one of them."

She looked at him stonily. "I became one of *them* twenty-two years ago."

He tossed his head. "I suppose; I just never thought of you that way."

"Do you have to think of me as something?" Tiring of the discussion, she pushed her glass away. "All I meant was, we do what we have to do, as well as we can, and we don't worry about what we can't do. Bordeaux's over."

He leaned back, looking at her quizzically. "I suppose that's the Oriental philosophy, eh? Well, I live in the West, and over here performance is what counts."

Maggie flushed. "I'll do my best. I think it'll be enough."

"Maybe if you spent less time hanging around with that Japanese fellow, you'd have the Axel by now."

Maggie recoiled. "Hiro? What's *he* got to do with anything?"

"How do you think I like hearing about all the time you spend with him?"

"Clay, he's an old friend. We grew up together. He's been tremendously supportive." She thought of the hours Hiro had waited at the rink, the rides home, the bracing words when she'd think she couldn't keep going. She felt an image forming of the other memory, from Kyoto, and shut it out. She crossed her arms defiantly. "I don't know if I could have stood it without him. Anyway, I thought you were the one who didn't have any use for jealousy. And I've given you no cause for any."

He passed his hand over his eyes. "Ah, hell, Maggie, I'm sorry. It's just that I've been going half-crazy, missing you so badly. I don't want it to have been for nothing."

She examined him curiously. "I'm doing my best; it won't have been for nothing, no matter how it turns out."

Clay, standing abruptly, put money on the table. He looked at her for a minute, then turned away. "You're right—we do what we have to do. Come on, we better get to the airport."

Chapter 37

December 2001: Tokyo

*Y*ou've been doing an excellent job, Araki-*san*. The *oyabun* is most pleased."

Hiro bowed, taking the opportunity to steal a glance at his watch. He was meeting Maggie later, and as always, the thought quickened his pulse.

Koji Sano missed little. "Ahh—don't tell me: a young lady waits." He chuckled. Sano had had several more beers after their client left and was in a fine mood.

"No, no, Sano-*san*. I am in no hurry."

"What, you think my *kintama* have forgotten what it is to be bursting for a woman?" Sano laughed. "Well, they may have, but I haven't. You've done well today. One more thing, then go to her. I'll get myself home."

"Thank you very much, Sano-*san*." By now the *yakitori ya* was jammed; Hiro and Sano had to raise their voices to talk.

"Because you have done so well, the *oyabun* has instructed me to expand your responsibilities."

Sano reached into his pocket and pulled out an envelope.

"Inside is a list of names and addresses. Study them, then destroy the list."

Hiro took the envelope, looking at it curiously. "*Hai,* Sano-*san.* But what should I do with this information?"

Sano looked at him appraisingly. "You are *burakumin,* no?"

"I make it no secret. Is it a problem?"

Sano, as though he could smell a challenge, held up a placatory hand. "No, no. In the *kumi* are only brothers, and many are Hamlet People—you know that. I mention it only because you ask what to do with the names on the paper I gave you. You will take over these clients. The amount they are paying is set out on the list. From time to time you will increase those amounts, as circumstances warrant. Should your clients be helpful, and give you additional names, then you may adjust their payments accordingly. It is a big responsibility, Araki-*san;* much money is involved. I personally recommended you for this."

"Thank you, Sano-*san,* I am honored. But if I may be permitted to ask, what does this have to do with the Hamlet People?"

Sano smacked his forehead. "I have had too much beer. The point is, all of the people on that list are *burakumin.* They are passing, and they pay to keep their secret."

Hiro, turning the envelope slowly, wanted to understand. "That is all they have done, Sano-*san,* tried to escape their birth role?"

"You will be surprised at some of the names on there— some very prominent people. They pay well."

"But, Sano-*san,* they have done nothing wrong. The people we have been with today, they deserve to pay; they created their problem, they are bad people. But these people"—Hiro tapped the envelope on the table—"all they are doing is trying to get by, *ne?*"

Sano's throat made a guttural sound. "Araki-*san,* these are valuable assets. Some of them have been paying us for years. There are executives, wealthy property owners—it is not for us to question. In the *kumi,* I think we do not question, *ne?*"

Hiro was too focused to heed the threat the neutral words did little to mask. "My mother could have been on such a list; she was passing."

Sano smiled sympathetically, revealing a gold front tooth. His hand flicked away the concern. "Your good mother is beyond all such worries."

"I meant that, like my mother, these people have done nothing."

"Enough, Araki-*san.*" Though Sano's face remained impassive, his voice quiet, his eyes were suddenly little black daggers.

"But—"

"Enough, I said." It was suddenly very quiet in the small space occupied by the two men, as though the silence were being encapsulated by the surrounding din.

Sano rested his palms on the table. "You see the little finger on my right hand, *ne?*"

Hiro knew what the missing tip meant. *"Hai."*

"Once, when I was much younger, I failed to carry out an assignment, to my great shame. The only thing we have, the only thing we value, is absolute loyalty within the *kumi.*"

Hiro spoke deliberately, knowing he was already past the point of safety. "Sano-*san,* I did not become a *yasan* to prey on innocent people. Especially these people—they have enough trouble."

Sano's jaw muscles worked beneath his cheeks. When he

spoke, it was in the growl of a large canine. "You talk like a woman. You did not join our brotherhood to *do* anything, understand? You were permitted to join, so you could *be* something. These people"—he flicked the envelope with the back of his hand—"are nothing; cockroaches, scurrying from the light. It is right they pay to avoid the light. You will collect the money. That is not a request. Am I understood?"

Hiro looked at the man's hooded eyes. His blood was boiling, and he longed to reach across, grab the man behind the head, smash his face into the table. *"Hai,"* he acknowledged. "I understand."

Sano nodded and bowed his head. "Go, then, to your young lady. We will forget this discussion occurred."

Hiro stood and bowed. He'd turned to leave when Sano said, "The young ladies, they like you to have all your fingers when you caress them."

Chapter 38

January 2002: Boston

*P*ull your jacket up." Rill tugged the parka's hood around Doe's head, tucking in stray wisps of silky hair. He spread her muffler across her face until only her eyes showed, and then they disappeared under the sunglasses he rested on her nose.

"I feel ridiculous."

"You should, but not because of the way you're dressed. Come on."

He bundled her into the car waiting behind the brownstone and told the driver where to go. Soon they were heading south.

Rill put up the glass partition and sat in stony silence, his arms crossed. After several wordless minutes Doe said, "I don't see why you're so upset. It's my life."

He glared at her. "Oh, no, dear, not anymore—you just turned your life over to Lofton Weeks. For about one-third of what it's going to be worth."

Doe watched the passing scene through the window.

"Hunter, the contract guarantees me a million dollars a year for ten years." She sounded bored.

"Yes, and Weeks is going to make about three million dollars a year off you in his tour, to say nothing of the money he'll rake in when you skate for other promoters—for which you'll get *nothing*. Did that little shit Bartlett explain that part to you?"

The rage that had been coming in waves every day since she'd come home and announced she'd signed a contract with Lofton Weeks broke over him again. He pulled a copy of the contract out of his coat pocket and flipped it open. "Read it, Doe." He stabbed at the outthrust document. "Read it! Paragraph seventeen. It *screws* you, Doe—it absolutely screws you. Weeks will rent you out like day labor, and there's not a goddamned thing you can do about it."

Her eyes barely glanced at the papers he thrust under her nose. "Clay wouldn't have let me sign anything that wasn't fair."

Rill groaned. "Doe, he *works* for Weeks. That's his fucking signature on this thing! The better he takes advantage of you, the more he gets, for Christ's sake! Are you out of your mind?"

She turned on him. "No! And I'm tired of you treating me like an idiot. For your information, it was in Clay's interest to get me the best possible terms, and he did."

Rill massaged his temples. "Doe, why in God's name would you think that? Because that's what he *told* you?"

Her eyes blazed triumphantly. "No, because we're getting married this spring, that's why!"

For half a minute Rill was speechless. Finally he managed to say, "Oh, I see." He looked at her. "Yes, that does change things."

Doe enjoyed the effect of her announcement. "So if he

really cared all that much about money, the more I make, the more we have together," she declared.

Information was breaking over Rill faster than he could process it. He forced himself to take a deep breath before speaking as calmly as he could. "And when did this . . . exciting development take place?"

"New Year's Eve. He waited till midnight, and then, just as they were playing that song, he asked me." She sighed.

"How romantic. Why didn't you tell me sooner?"

"Clay didn't want me to tell anyone. He's afraid it will get out, and he thinks it would be unfair to . . . her, to find out before the Olympics. As though it would matter," she said with a sniff.

"He always was a gentleman." Rill shut his eyes, trying to think. The only thought that would form was, I can't burst her bubble—not now. Not before the Olympics.

"I'd love to see your engagement ring."

"He hasn't bought it yet."

"Oh." Rill kept his voice carefully neutral.

"But I've been thinking about where to have the wedding. What do you think about the Old North Church?"

Rill's head swam. "The Old North Church?"

Doe's head bobbed. "You know—Paul Revere, the Minute Men? A painting at the museum gave me the idea." Her forehead furrowed. "Do you think they'll let us have it there?"

"I wouldn't be surprised." All he could think was: Oh, dear God, let her go on believing in this until after the Olympics. Don't let the bastard rob her of that.

"Well, I have to find out. We'll want to get the invitations out as soon as we're back from Utah. I've been looking at silver and china settings, too. When we get home, would you like to see the ones I'm thinking about?"

"Of course, of course."

Another thought came to him, like a blow: Maybe he really means to go through with it. Maybe he sees her as the best meal ticket around. Or maybe, just maybe, he really loves her?

As soon as it formed, he dismissed the possibility. "No," he muttered.

"What?"

Doe's voice brought him back. "I'm sorry?"

"What *are* you talking about? 'No' what?"

Rill grunted. "Never mind, dear—just thinking about how happy I am for you." He studied her face for a minute, then reached over and brushed his thumb across her cheek. "You want so little. It makes it so easy."

"I don't understand."

"I know; that's what I mean." Rill studied Doe's profile in the golden light. "Oh, Doreen—what a piece of work you are. Such a lovely, lovely creature. Sometimes, seeing you, I wish . . ." His voice faded away.

"What?"

"Never mind." He made an immense effort to focus on the task at hand. "Let's just keep our minds on the goal. We're so close now. You do your part, and I'll do mine."

"So you're not angry anymore?"

"No, dear, I'm not angry, now that I know about you and Clay. But let me help with the planning, all right? You've got to stay focused. After all, you've got a skating partner now, don't you?"

She glowed. "Yes."

"Well, then, I'll line up the church and take care of invitations and the like."

"I saw some with the prettiest little flowers around the

edge, but they were awfully expensive." She looked at him hopefully.

"I think we can probably swing it, dear. Little flowers it is."

"Thank you, Hunter." She kissed him on the cheek. "I really appreciate your support."

"That's what I'm here for." He snapped his fingers. "Say, what about having the reception at the club? They do a nice job. Perhaps you and Clay could take a turn around the ice together. In your wedding clothes?"

He watched the thought take hold. "What a wonderful idea," she said, nodding eagerly. "We'll waltz!"

"Absolutely. I'll look into it." He put his head back and closed his eyes. After a few minutes he might have been asleep.

In an hour they pulled up before a low building near the New Bedford waterfront. Doe wrinkled her nose as she climbed out. "What a dump."

Rill nodded complacently. "It's not Beacon Hill, I'll grant you that, but I don't think anyone's going to recognize you here. And ice is ice, eh?"

The rink was empty, except for an old Portuguese man who took Rill's money and turned on the lights. Rill said, "Nobody comes in, ¿comprende?" and the old man nodded and walked away. Soon the rink filled with Wagner, and Doe Rawlings was skating her new long program.

Three hours later she limped off the ice, and they headed back to Boston. In the car Rill had her rest her left leg on his lap while he removed her tennis shoe and sock and looked dubiously at her foot. "How's your ankle?" He probed the joint gently.

"Ouch. It hurts."

"It's the quad, isn't it?"

"You bet it's the quad. It feels like my foot's coming off when I land it."

"No one would know from watching you. You've got it down like few men ever have."

"Well, it isn't easy."

"I'll have the doctor look at it when we get back." The rest of the ride he stared thoughtfully out the window.

The doctor had Doe's left heel cupped in his hands, his thumbs prodding her ankle. He looked up at Rill. "I don't like this ankle. It's taken a hell of a pounding."

"I know what the ankle's taken. She's okay to skate, right?"

The doctor frowned. "Well, *I* wouldn't."

Rill snorted. "You wouldn't. Of course you wouldn't— you're not a skater, you're . . . Never mind."

"She should rest it. Stay off it for a few days, and then keep her workouts light. Watch the jumps especially."

Rill sighed. "Damn." He looked at Doe and stroked his chin before nodding reluctantly. "Right. Sorry I snapped, Doctor. I guess I'm feeling the strain."

"No problem—I don't blame you. Try giving the ankle a rest. Pack it in ice now, and after every practice." He stopped at the door. "But the decision to skate is yours. I'd pull her if the ankle's like this, come the Olympics." He let himself out.

" 'Pull her,' " Rill muttered, glaring at the door. "Right— and toss my life down the drain." He shook his head, taking her foot in his hands. "Tell you what, Doe. We're going to take the next couple of days off, and when you resume practice, we'll lay off the quad for a while."

"Do you think we should? I don't want to lose it."

"You won't. I've arranged for a rink an hour away from the Olympic village. You'll have it down pat when the time comes. Anyway, no one you're going to be up against even has the Axel."

She snickered. "Not even Maggie Campbell?"

Rill smiled indulgently. "All right, all right—you've cracked my secret. No, I don't think Ms. Campbell has the Axel. We saw that in Bordeaux. No Axel, and no Clay Bartlett." He got a faraway look for a few seconds and then was all business again, pulling over a bucket of ice and lowering her foot into it. "Okay—from now on, we'll take it a little easier."

Chapter 39

February 2002: Tokyo

"Kampai." Seizo Fukawa hoisted his glass; the other men
echoed the toast: *"Kampai!"* They all drank. The waitress scurried across the tatami mat in a low crouch, passing
the men steaming hand towels.

Seizo Fukawa had been talkative and congenial from the
moment he, Fumio, and Mr. Suzuki, the JRT *bucho,* or bu-
reau chief, had met Shingo and Katsumi Tanaka in the lobby
of the JRT Club, a secluded three-story building buried in
the heart of Rippongi.

It was a great honor to have been invited to dine with the
chairman and his grandson. Katsumi had been guessing for
days about the reasons for the meeting, concluding finally
that it was to give the chairman a chance to express his appreciation for Kofuku's cellular telephone breakthrough,
which was the talk of the trade press. Shingo Tanaka refused
to speculate, offering only that the food would be excellent.

Fukawa had ushered them into one of the private dining
rooms, then caused the liquor to flow freely. The conversation had soon turned to Fumio Fukawa's recently announced

engagement to the daughter of a man whose family owned one of Japan's largest department store chains.

"I understand her great-great-grandfather was a *daimyo*," Katsumi remarked. "Of course, the Fukawas are also a venerable family, if I may be permitted to say so. Fumio-*san*, may you have a long and happy marriage." He raised his glass.

"Thank you, Katsumi-*san*." The younger Fukawa's pudgy features radiated self-satisfaction. "I am grateful to Grandfather for arranging such an attractive union."

Seizo Fukawa smiled complacently. "What does a man live for, but to secure his progeny's future?"

The intimate space was quite attractive, a plain tatami room with a long black lacquered *zataku* table, eighteen inches off the floor, around which the five men sat on wide, flat *zabuton*. The Tanakas sat on one side, Seizo Fukawa, flanked by Fumio and Mr. Suzuki, on the other. As protocol dictated, Shingo Tanaka sat opposite the chairman, Katsumi across from Fumio.

Fukawa was in the best of spirits; Shingo Tanaka could not remember seeing him so animated and attributed it to his grandson's impending marriage. Over cognac Fukawa regaled the group with an account of the latest government corruption scandal.

"Did you hear what Minister Yuasa said when the prosecutor asked him how he happened to have a bank box containing two hundred and fifty million yen's worth of gold?" Fukawa looked around the table expectantly.

His guests shook their heads.

"He said his wife had always been very frugal!" Fukawa, roaring, slapped the table as the others joined in appreciatively.

Fukawa lit a cigarette, exhaling gratefully. "Tanaka-*kun*," he said, "you and your son are to be congratulated. You have completed your new production facility ahead of schedule and under budget."

Shingo Tanaka bowed. "We have been fortunate. No serious problems arose."

"You will be in production soon, *ne?*"

"Yes, Chairman."

"Mmm, that is excellent." Fukawa made a low, contemplative growling sound in the back of his throat. "But did I hear that it is your intention to license this technology liberally?"

"Yes, Chairman. Competition between licensees will drive the price of the telephones down, ensuring that they will be widely affordable."

"Mmm." Fukawa drew on his cigarette, watching the smoke thoughtfully as he exhaled. "But those telephones will be competition for JRT's telephones."

Shingo Tanaka was taken aback. "Of course. But JRT will have access to the new telephones as well."

Fukawa's eyes narrowed. "That is very gracious, Tanaka-*kun*. But perhaps it would be even more gracious to agree that Kofuku will supply the new telephones and the new technology only to JRT, *ne?*"

Katsumi's jaw dropped. "*Only* JRT, Chairman? But JRT could never absorb our total output. It was always understood that we would supply others."

"That was before I appreciated the competitive significance of this technology. And I would remind Katsumi-*san* that Kofuku would have *no* production capacity had JRT not provided the money. Kofuku is part of the JRT *kereitsu*. Kofuku *exists* to serve JRT, and it is not my wish to have JRT's position in cellular telephones challenged by competitors all over the world. As the only supplier, JRT will be able to charge twice as much as would be the case under your preposterous proposal."

Katsumi, sweating, dropped his head. "*Hai, kaicho.*"

Fukawa accepted Katsumi's capitulation with a condescending nod. "We will, of course, compensate Kofuku for the unused capacity. You will not—"

"No."

The word hung over the table like an uninvited guest. It took several seconds before heads swiveled to confront its source.

"No," Shingo Tanaka repeated softly. Slowly he brought his hand up. It came down so hard his glass flew into the air, shattering as it hit the table. He leaned toward Fukawa with his lips drawn back, his eyes narrowed. "My son, my grandson, and I developed this technology, and *we* will decide who gets it, and under what terms, Fukawa-*kun*." Shingo Tanaka emphasized the title, never used by an underling addressing a superior.

Katsumi, stunned, gasped, "Father, Father . . . What—"

Shingo Tanaka didn't look at his son, just held up his hand. "Quiet."

He continued addressing Fukawa in direct, informal words: "We'll sell the new product as *we* decide. It has the potential to enrich the lives of millions around the world, and I will not have it choked off for your narrow purposes. JRT will be treated fairly, but no better than anyone else, and the market will govern. We will forget this conversation occurred, just as I have chosen to forget the circumstances under which you acquired my half of JRT."

Fukawa rested his knuckles on the table and rocked forward. With his neck extended and eyes closed, he looked like a viper, an impression furthered by his seething, venomous hiss: "You were *happy* to sell your share to me. I will assume that your mind has been twisted by envy, and will overlook your rudeness this once. You will do as I instruct, or—"

"No!" Shingo Tanaka looked at his host contemptuously. "My family and I will not again be cheated of that which is ours. This technology is my bequest to the future of my family. And as you said, 'What does a man live for, but to secure his progeny's future.'"

"Careful," Fukawa whispered, "you go too far. I'll—"

Shingo Tanaka interrupted him dismissively: "I saw the letter from the ministry."

For the first time Fukawa wavered. "What letter? What are you talking about?" His tongue darted out, wetting his lips.

"The letter from an official in the ministry, saying the decision had been made to award the contract to JRT. A letter to you, dated a few weeks before you bought my share. When the award was announced, a month later, only days after you'd bought me out, it was a mere formality. You never told me. When you bought my share, you knew we had the contract. You cheated me."

"Absurd. How *dare* you accuse me of such a thing!"

"A year after the contract was signed we received a packet from the ministry. I opened it, thinking it was some technical specifications I had requested, but it was a copy of the contract file, for our records. The letter was in it."

Fukawa's right eye twitched. "Ridiculous. Produce this so-called letter."

"I burned it," Mr. Tanaka said as calmly as if he'd been discussing dinner. "What was done, was done. I had a family to feed. I could not live and support my family while I struggled for years to obtain what was mine, what you stole. I accepted what had to be accepted. Now it is your turn—

you will accept what has to be accepted. You will purchase our products on our terms, or not at all."

For several seconds the only sound was Fukawa's heavy breathing, his chest rising and falling metronomically. He finally whispered, "You can prove none of this ridiculous story."

Mr. Tanaka nodded. "I have no need to. It only matters that I know. If you choose not to accept our terms, you are free to be the one cellular company in the world we will *not* license. Now, I believe we have taken enough of your valuable time." He stood, gesturing to Katsumi to follow.

Fukawa's jaw muscles tightened, fingertips drumming lightly on the tabletop. He nodded almost imperceptibly to Mr. Suzuki, the *bucho,* who cleared his throat.

He had a smooth, unctuous voice. "Tanaka-*san,* before you and your son leave, there is one other matter."

"Yes?" The Tanakas stopped, halfway to the door.

"There is the matter of repayment of the money JRT loaned Kofuku. Almost one billion yen."

Shingo Tanaka looked at the man coolly. "It will be repaid once the new facility goes into production, as agreed at the time of the loan. I am sure it will take very little time."

"Tanaka-*san,* I have reviewed the note your son signed on behalf of Kofuku. It says repayment is due on demand. It says nothing about waiting for production."

"That has always been the understanding within the *kereitsu.*"

Mr. Suzuki turned up his palms, smiling. "Alas, apparently Kofuku is not part of the JRT *kereitsu.*"

Fukawa interjected, speaking slowly. "You pledged Kofuku as security for the loan. Since you are unable to repay upon demand, you will tender the shares. Needless to say, the services of the Tanaka family will no longer be required."

Shingo Tanaka's lips pressed into a thin line. "Absurd. The note gives us thirty days from the demand. We will repay the money. Then there will be no more dealing between us. We will see how JRT does without our technology."

"You're tight. Every muscle is tense. This isn't good, Maggie." Hiro circled his thumbs over the back of Maggie's neck. Chiako had gone away for the weekend, and Maggie was luxuriating in the moments of relative tranquillity that would be her last for some time, with the games only two weeks away.

"I know, but I'm worried sick about my grandfather. All these years he kept his peace, letting a man he knew to be a cheat abuse and bully him. Listening to my grandmother measure him against Fukawa and find him wanting. Never saying anything, all so he could provide for his family."

"He is a courageous man."

"Yes. And now it will all be for nothing. Grandfather and Katsumi have gone everywhere for a loan, but nobody will deal with them; Fukawa has put out the word, and JRT is too powerful. In two weeks everything my grandfather has sacrificed for will be lost. If I could, I'd kill Fukawa tonight."

"He is an evil man. It makes me ashamed I mentioned my problem to you. Please forgive me."

Maggie sat on her futon while Hiro kneaded her shoulders. He thought how fine her bones were and yet how strong she was. Strong, and the bravest person he had ever known, man or woman. To be able to control your body, make it do your will, when your every instinct is to hide, to escape from terrible pressure, from fear . . . Well, he knew what courage that took, was taking, from him, even as he kneeled, rubbing her shoulders.

She smiled. "I'm glad you shared that, that you would confide in me. But this Mr. Sano—he really *threatened* you?"

"This is no time for you to be thinking of such things. Don't worry about Mr. Sano." Hiro regretted he'd mentioned his unexpected meeting with the man, but it was the reason he'd been late to the last evening they'd have together for some time—for a *long* time, if the *kumi* caught up with him.

She was still naive in some ways, very innocent. When he'd told her Sano had stopped him in an alley and said he'd better start making collections from the people whose names he'd been given or the *kumi* would not be pleased, she'd believed it was just that easy to say, "No, thank you," just as she'd believed him when he'd said he'd quit before he'd do what they wanted. Which he would, only it wasn't as easy as she imagined, not nearly that easy.

She didn't know what had really happened. The little time before she left for the States and the moment for which she'd shaped her entire life was no time for her to know that. So he just kept rubbing her shoulders, concentrating on the way they felt, and the way she looked, with her beautiful athlete's body and the wonderful, deep eyes looking back at him.

"What will you do if you quit?"

"I'm not sure." He chuckled. "Maybe become a masseur, eh? *Shiatsushi*, that's the business for me." Sano would have reported what happened by now. He couldn't go home, that was certain. Hiro looked at the hand working the back of the graceful neck; hard to believe that only a short while before, it had broken Mr. Sano's fingers after they'd closed on his upper arm.

"What?" He was lost in the memory of the grunt that had been the only sign the man felt pain; his self-control had been frightening.

"I asked if you had your ticket to Salt Lake City."

"Of course; I've had it for weeks." Even with his fingers broken, Sano hadn't raised his voice; he'd said, "Araki-*san* will regret that," as though commenting on the temperature. It was the same tone he'd used when he'd explained to Hiro that one could not expect to leave the *kumi* without paying a price, and that the price could be quite painful.

If he came back now, expressed sincere remorse, his insubordination would be forgiven. He'd soon be drinking beer with Sano again, the two of them laughing about Sano's broken fingers—and Hiro's missing one. The more he thought about it, the more his stomach knotted, and he knew it was time.

"I better go now, Maggie."

"Do you have to?"

"Mmm." He got to his feet. She started to rise, until his hand checked her. "It will be a while. Stay well."

She looked up sharply. "Where are you going?"

"To spend a little time with Grandfather. You'll be gone before I get back."

"Oh. Please give him my regards." Concern clouded her face. "But you'll make it to Salt Lake City on time, won't you?"

"I'll be with you in Utah, Maggie; count on it." He patted her head and was gone.

"It is always good to see Grandson, but this is an unexpected pleasure."

Hiro sat across from the old man, sipping tea. It was early February, and at six thousand feet the night was cold. Hiro moved closer to the fire. "It seemed a good time to get out of Tokyo; I needed a vacation. If it is agreeable, I will stay a while."

His grandfather smiled. "As long as you like."

Hiro bowed. "Thank you. I think I need a long stay; the mountain air is good for the health, they say. I'm not so sure about my health in Tokyo."

"I'm grateful for the magazines."

"I'm sorry it's such an odd assortment. I was in a hurry at the station, and just grabbed the first ones I saw."

"No, no—I will enjoy these. I don't read many business magazines, but one is never too old to learn something new."

He chopped wood every morning. Within a half hour he'd have his shirt off, enjoying the feel of the pale sun on his bare skin, even though it was below freezing. It was hard, mindless work that gave him time to think. After a week, though, he still couldn't think of a way out, other than to stay in the mountains, hiding like an animal.

He let his thoughts turn to Maggie; in a few days she'd be in America. He could follow her on the radio, he supposed. She'd be in Utah with her American. He had a bad feeling about him, but that could just be his own green eyes. After the Olympics she'd stay, and that would be that; the sweetness of the last sixteen months reduced to an occasional visit, the odd letter. Well, he prayed the gods would give her wings. And if the American treated her badly, he would hunt him down if he had to go through a thousand Sanos to do it.

His thoughts sent wood chips flying. By lunchtime he was famished.

He entered his grandfather's hut to find the old man in

animated conversation with two other men and a woman called Old Auntie. They looked up excitedly at Hiro's approach.

"*Oi*, Grandson," his grandfather said. "Come look at this magazine you brought me. It contains happy news."

Hiro took the magazine, *Nippon Business Week*, studying the picture Old Auntie tapped with a gnarled finger. He read the caption. "I am sorry, I do not understand; why is it such good news that this man is the new head of the Keidanren?"

Old Auntie cackled asthmatically. "One of us, president of the Chamber of Commerce? Those bigwigs would die if they knew."

His grandfather added, "Imagine, a Hamlet Person, becoming so successful. Perhaps, when he retires, he will admit it. Then people would say, 'See? *burakumin* are as good as anyone.' "

Old Auntie hooted. "More likely they'd kill him!"

Hiro looked at the picture again. One of the old men said, "This one will take his secret to his grave; he'd never reveal anything to anyone."

Hiro's head jerked up. "You know him?"

All four nodded proudly. "That's Todeo Tachibana," Old Auntie said. "He disappeared from the *burakumin* district at the beginning of the war. We assumed he'd enlisted. We never saw him again."

"Instead he was passing," one of the men said.

"He always was a smart bastard," Old Auntie added. Her gold teeth gleamed in the soft light.

Hiro was still confused. "But his picture must have appeared in the press many times; how could he have escaped detection all these years?"

His grandfather shrugged. "With good papers, and a good cover story, it is possible. There are only a few who would be able to make the connection, and none, I think, would betray him. We may pray for the day when one of us can achieve such success without hiding our background, but until that day we keep each other's secrets."

"Can you be sure this is the man you knew?" Hiro was trying to gather his wits and make connections, but the excitement of the older people was infectious, and he was having trouble.

"You wouldn't forget that face, Grandson."

"We called him '*Okami-san*,' remember?" Old Auntie chortled.

"Behind his back," someone added. "He wasn't one to trifle with."

Hiro peered at the picture, suddenly getting it. "*Okami-san*," he murmured, nodding. "*Okami-san*. Yes, he *does* look like Mr. Wolf."

The next day he got a ride to Tokoyama, where he caught the train for Tokyo.

Chapter 40

*I*n daylight Tokyo is a monotone: drab, gray, utilitarian. Night transforms it. As the sun drops, it becomes the most colorful of the world's great capitals—vibrant, electric, a pulsating, Day-Glo pastiche. Everywhere neon bursts into life; a refracted spectrum bathes flesh and concrete in surreal, postindustrial pastels.

It thrilled Hiro, the nightly transformation of his city. As he slipped through the Ginza, he could imagine he'd fallen into a holographic world, no more substantial than a vision.

He also liked the night because it offered anonymity. Sometimes he imagined he'd passed back two centuries and that he was one of the ninja—stealthy, silent. Invisible and deadly. He had better be at least invisible, he mused, until he had his business done; it would not do to encounter a member of the *kumi*.

He wasn't invisible to the night receptionist in the lobby of the building he entered, though. She looked up from her magazine, and he announced himself: "I am Todeo Tachibana. I have an appointment."

If the man had decided on extreme measures, he would soon find out. It would be ironic indeed if he'd brought in the *yakuza* to deal with this unexpected threat. Hiro was counting on the man's disinclination to widen his exposure, but one never knew what a trapped animal would do. He was relieved when the pretty young woman stood, smiled, and bowed. "Tachibana-*san* is expected on the twelfth floor."

When he stepped off the elevators the little functionary waiting for him showed no more than appropriate interest, either, and Hiro silently let his breath escape as he followed the man. He stepped into the room to which he'd been led and waited until he heard the man's footsteps retreating down the corridor.

His eyes adjusted to the dim light, and he saw the man he'd come to see, sitting behind a desk. Black, watchful eyes, peering out from under drooping lids; uncommonly long, yellow canine teeth; black hair, edged in silver. He earned his name, Hiro thought.

"You want money, I presume," the man said. He spoke as though to a minion. "How much?"

Hiro shook his head wonderingly, stepping forward into the cone of light cast by the ceiling fixture, looking at the man curiously. "You know, if you only had guts, you wouldn't have to pay a thing. I'm *burakumin*, and I wouldn't pay a yen to keep it secret."

The man growled, a low and ugly sound from the back of his throat. The sound of a carnivore, crouched deep in its lair. "It's easy to be brave when you've nothing to lose. How much?" He held out an envelope. "There's eight million yen here. You'll receive the same amount every month, as long as nothing comes out."

"That won't do."

"Well, how much, then? I warn you, there is a point at which other options become more attractive." The man used provocative, impolite speech, which pleased Hiro; he enjoyed disliking the man.

"Of course. But it is not money I want."

For the first time he saw uncertainty on the hatchet face. "What do you mean? What is it you want?"

"A receipt."

The hooded eyes widened. The overhead light caught their centers, and for a second Hiro felt as though a beam were passing from the man's eyes to his. Then the eyelids dropped again. "A receipt? For what?"

"For nine hundred and sixty million yen. Discharging in full Kofuku Corporation's debt to the Japan Radio and Telephone Company. And you'll give it to me, or tomorrow every newspaper in Tokyo will be writing about the *burakumin* who took over the identity of a dead Imperial Army officer and spent the rest of his life pretending to be someone he wasn't. How a boy known as 'Wolf' crawled out of the Osaka slums to become a great industrialist. How he got his start by cheating his partner. Oh, yes, and about the scandal in the Keidanren, and your grandson's broken engagement. It will be a great story, Tachibana-*san*—or do you prefer your stolen name, Seizo Fukawa?"

Chapter 41

February 2002: Salt Lake City

*T*he three announcers sat in a booth high above the ice. They wore dark blue blazers and the open, earnest faces of their trade. Periodically they talked by wire to Lofton Weeks, resplendent in a black dinner jacket, who was positioned next to the rink, just behind the boards.

They were warming up the American television audience as they waited for the ladies' short program to begin. Tim Dysart and Bob LeFavre were talking with Cathy Perkins, a gold medal winner twenty years before, about "things to look for" in the competition.

"Well, Tim," Cathy answered, "there's no question the American Doe Rawlings is the skater to watch as the competition begins. She's the reigning World champion, and perhaps the most electrifying skater in decades. If she skates a solid short program, this event could be over before anyone realizes it."

"Right, Cathy. But the big story so far is, What is Doe Rawlings doing? While she's been using her practice time to skate a new short program, she's been practicing the same long program she skated last year. Is it possible she doesn't *have* a new long program this year?"

Cathy shook her head. "It's hard to imagine, Tim—the judges could penalize her severely for that. It just isn't done. But I agree, it's a mystery; where's her long program?"

Tim Dysart leaned forward. "Don't forget—Doe Rawlings failed to defend her U.S. title in January, claiming an ankle injury. Do you suppose she's hurt, and that's why we haven't seen a new program?"

Bob LeFavre got a signal from the sound booth and nodded. "Well, in a few hours we'll have these and many other answers, as the countdown to what has become the Olympic games' premier event, and one of the premier events in all of sport, continues. And now, at rinkside, Lofton Weeks."

The camera cut to the graceful figure standing by the rail with Hunter Rill. His right hand was pressed to his ear, his left held a microphone.

"Good evening Tim, Bob, and Cathy. With me I have Hunter Rill, coach of a number of skating champions over the years, including Doe Rawlings. Hunter, what *is* the story? Why are we seeing Doe Rawlings practicing the long program she skated last year?"

Rill's eyes twinkled. "Lofton, the program she skated last year was good enough to make her the United States and World champion. She beat the best in the world with it at the Trophée de France, only three months ago. It has six triples, including a triple Axel. Don't you think maybe that program's got some life left?"

Weeks looked skeptical. "You have to admit, Hunter, it's unusual, to say the least, to hold over a program from year to year."

Rill smiled. "Well, often it's the unusual that wins. They loved it in Bordeaux."

Weeks tossed up his hands. "All right, Coach—I guess you're saying we'll just have to wait. How about Doe Rawlings's ankle? Is she physically one hundred percent?"

"Doe's in the best shape of her life. Nobody should expect an opening on that account."

Weeks stuck the microphone close to Rill's mouth, making one more run at the question of the hour. "Hunter, are you flat out saying Doe Rawlings won't be skating a new long program in these Olympic games? Are you saying you think she can win with her old program?"

Rill seemed to find this vastly amusing. "Sure she can win with her old program—she won everything there was to win with it, didn't she?"

Weeks smiled, but frustration showed. "You answered only part of my question, Coach."

"That's right." Rill looked over his shoulder, then gestured toward the ice. "Now there's someone you ought to cover: Maggie Campbell. Look at that form."

Weeks turned to look, and the camera followed. On the ice Maggie, in a gray warm-up suit, was moving in slow circles. As the men watched she gradually elaborated the circles into single jumps.

Weeks turned back to Rill. "You're right, Coach, there's an interesting story. You coached Maggie Campbell; tell us about her."

Rill nodded. "One of the best I ever had, a terrific pairs skater. A wonderful person, too, I should add. All heart, and great discipline. She could be a factor."

"So her decision to leave you and take up singles didn't reflect any falling-out between you?"

"Good heavens, no. Unfortunately, Maggie's partner, Clay Bartlett, suffered a career-ending injury, and Maggie wanted to return to Japan, where she grew up. She was a promising singles skater before she came to the United States, and she returned to singles when she went back to Japan. That's the whole story. I have great regard for her, and wish her all the luck in the world."

"Well, on that note, good luck to you, too, Hunter, and to Doe Rawlings. Back to you, Bob."

Weeks pulled the earphone out of his ear. "Cut the bullshit, Hunter. You've got something up your sleeve; now what is it?"

"Off the record?"

"Sure."

"Watch Doe's long program very, very carefully, and think about what you're going to say, because you're going to be describing a historic event."

"Can you be more specific?"

"Nope." Rill put his hand on Weeks's shoulder. "Just be there, and you'll find out."

Weeks frowned, then changed tack. Nodding toward the ice, he asked, "What about the Campbell girl—any chance?"

"You going to quote me?"

"No."

"Okay. No chance."

Weeks watched Maggie hit a triple lutz. "She's got great lines. Great technique, too, Hunter: light, high, and easy on those jumps, tight rotation, and terrific speed coming out."

"True. But she just doesn't have the power. Not enough triples, only a double Axel; the program's more like something you would've seen thirty years ago. Time's passed her by. She should have stayed with pairs."

"Hmm. How about we get together for a drink one of these nights?"

Rill patted the older man's shoulder. "You buy a bottle of vintage Dom Pérignon; we'll drink it after the finals."

"That confident, are you?"

"Buy it now." He turned and walked away, whistling. He knew he could count on Weeks to stroke the rumor mills; the largest television audience in history would tune in to see what Doe Rawlings was going to do.

Chapter 42

February 2002: Tokyo

*T*hey made him wait, day after day. It was intended to
unnerve him, reduce him to a state of near catatonia, as
they imagined him huddled in his apartment, wondering if
he'd get his audience or if, at any moment, men would burst
through the door and slice him to ribbons. It just made him
angry.

Maggie was in Salt Lake City, and he wasn't, and if they
didn't agree to see him soon, he was going to march into the
kumi office and grab the *oyabun* by his scrawny throat if it
was the last thing he did—which it undoubtedly would be.

He watched the opening ceremonies on television. When
he saw her march in with her teammates his heart soared,
and he knew he'd made the right decision; he couldn't live
like an animal, hiding in dark spaces, unable to see her. Bad
enough she loved another, but if he couldn't see her at all, he
wasn't sure life would be worth living.

They came for him on the seventh day. Hiro felt calm, almost serene. Either he would be dead in twenty-four hours,
or he'd be in America, watching Maggie skate. It was all he

could do to avoid grinning when the five men fixed their glares on him, pushing him into the huge Cadillac.

The *oyabun* sat silently, never indicating by word or gesture that he was even listening. When Hiro finished he, too, sat still, knowing that it would soon be over, either way.

Finally the older man spoke. "You are offering to trade information for a release from your vows?"

Hiro nodded. *"So desu."*

The *oyabun* looked at Hiro speculatively. "We could make you give us this information."

Hiro shrugged. "Perhaps. Perhaps not. If you wish to try, I am ready."

As the *oyabun* considered this, Hiro added, "Please be so gracious as to remember, though, that if you fail, you will not have the information, and you will have to kill me—or I will kill you."

A collective gasp escaped from the men standing in the background. One of them, pulling a gun from under his jacket, stepped forward. "How dare you speak so!"

The *oyabun* held up his hand. *"So desu,"* he growled. "It is not lack of courage that causes his disloyalty."

He turned back to Hiro. "And if I agree, what is to prevent us from dealing with you after you give us this information?"

"The *oyabun* is known to be a man of honor. Were the *oyabun* to go back on his word, merely to make an example of me, he would lose great face."

"It is so," the *oyabun* acknowledged. He seemed amused.

"Of course." Hiro inclined his head. "And, out of a desire to spare the *oyabun* the pain of loss of face, I have taken steps to insure that this information will become public knowledge, should anything untoward befall me. It would then lose all value to the *oyabun*."

The *oyabun*'s nostrils flared, his jaw tightened. Hiro sat, absorbing the man's stare, knowing that a raised eyebrow or an almost imperceptible nod might be the last thing he'd ever see.

The man made a sound, and Hiro tensed, not relaxing until he realized the *oyabun* was chuckling. "Very well, I accept. Give us what you promise, and you may leave in peace. If all is as you say, you will hear no more from us. If it is not . . ." He smiled, shrugging.

Chapter 43

February 2002: Salt Lake City

*W*hat's the matter? Don't I get a kiss, Mag?"

"I'm sorry—I was thinking about something else."

Maggie stepped into Clay's arms. The dormitory lobby was crowded with young people, not a few of them locked in embraces, and no one paid Maggie and Clay much attention.

"Umm . . . maybe we could slip away to my hotel room for a little while?" He massaged the small of her back. "It's been a long time," he whispered.

She broke away. "Clay—I've got my short program tomorrow."

He winked. "I'll do all the work."

"No!"

His smile evaporated. "Jesus Christ, what's the matter with you? I haven't seen you in weeks, I've been traveling all day, and you act like I'm a leper."

"Clay, I'm sorry. I'm just very worried, that's all."

"Ah." He nodded, understanding. "Well, don't be;

however you do, it'll be okay. Just your being here is enough."

She looked at him oddly. "Well, that's a change. What's come over you?"

He smiled enigmatically. "Let's just say I don't think we're going to starve, no matter how you do."

"Oh." She turned away to hide her distaste. "I guess I wasn't thinking about that."

"Well, one of us better, don't you think?"

"I suppose." She suddenly felt very tired. "Things are going well with Weeks, then?"

His smile returned. "You might say so." He took her arms. "Look, I was an idiot to make such a big thing of Bordeaux." His hand dropped to her bottom. "Just go out there and do your best. There's nothing to be concerned about, not anymore."

"Doing my best is all I was ever concerned about, Clay, not what a medal could earn me. Us," she added absently. She pushed his hand away, shaking her head. "But it's not the skating I'm worried about; it's Hiro Araki—I don't know where he is. He should have been here by now."

He looked at her incredulously. "I don't believe it. I just got here, and you're thinking about another man . . . a *Japanese* man at that?"

Maggie stared at him stonily. "What's his being Japanese have to do with anything?"

He started to answer, stopped abruptly, and canted his head, studying her. "I think I have a right to know: Has something been going on between you two?"

She ran her eyes over him, as though trying to remember who he was. "You have to ask that, as long as you've known me? He's a friend, that's all."

He looked into her eyes until, satisfied, he nodded.

"Right." He turned for the door. "I'm exhausted. When you're ready, I'll be at the hotel."

She fell asleep in one of the Naugahyde-covered armchairs dotting the reception area. She dreamed a man was chasing her across the ice. She couldn't see his face, but she sensed she knew him and knew he wanted something she didn't want to lose, though she didn't know what that was, either. The harder she stroked, the more her blades stuck to the ice. He was gaining on her, reaching out to grab her, and then she felt his hands closing on her. She screamed.

"Shh, shh." A hand rocked her shoulder. "You were having a nightmare."

She bolted upright, blinking. "Who?" A face was looking at her. "Hiro!" Her eyes flew open.

She threw her arms around him. "Thank God you've come—I've been so worried. I . . ." Her mouth found his.

His lips yielded momentarily, then he pulled away, shaking his head. "No, Maggie. I'm no holy man. Don't get me started."

Her mouth moved toward his, as though it had a will of its own, until she saw his eyes. "You're right—that was foolish of me."

He tipped up her chin. "But nice. Now"—he helped her to her feet—"is your Clay here? I've been looking forward to meeting him."

"He went back to his hotel. He's tired from the flight."

He looked at her curiously, then nodded. "Ah—too bad. Well, tomorrow, then. Oddly enough, though, I've never felt more alive. Do you feel like getting something to eat?"

She sprang to her feet, fully awake. "I could eat a cow. Let's go!"

He put his hand on her arm. "But perhaps, with your fiancé here, it would be inappropriate?"

"Nonsense. Come on." She grabbed his arm, tugging him toward the door.

Chapter 44

*W*ell Cathy, Tim—it's the moment we and two billion other people have been waiting for. The largest television audience in history, in fact."

"Right, Bob. In a few minutes, the finals of the ladies' figure skating begin—the biggest sporting event in the world. A few hours from now, the world will welcome a new holder of the most prestigious prize in all of sport. And who will it be? Cathy? Your thoughts, please."

"Tim, right now the gold is Doe Rawlings's to lose. She skated a brilliant short program—not usually her strong suit—and she sits in first place, ahead of Anna Landov of Belarus. And the long program *is* Doe Rawlings's strong suit. Frankly, if she's sharp tonight—and I'm betting she will be, because she's one of the most intense skaters I've ever seen—I don't think anyone can stop her from taking the gold. Certainly neither Landov, the former World champion who lost her title to Doe Rawlings, nor Maggie Campbell, the Japanese national champion who's in third place, has the jumps Doe Rawlings has. And like it or not, nowadays the judges *love* the jumpers."

Bob, distracted, pressed his hand to his ear, nodding.

"I've just gotten word that Loften Weeks is waiting at rink-side to bring our viewers a sense of what it's like down there. Lofton?"

The picture cut to Weeks. Behind him, a slightly out-of-focus Zamboni was working its ponderous way around the rink, consuming the surface like some great, ice-eating beetle. The stands were packed, and the eager buzz of the crowd provided an expectant backdrop as Weeks responded.

"Thank you, Bob, and good evening. Well, it won't be long now. The final group, the ladies with a realistic chance to medal, are taking the ice now for their six-minute warm-up."

The gate opened and five young women burst out onto the ice. Within seconds they had scattered, darting around the rink in their resplendent plumage like tropical birds. "Let's see . . ." Weeks craned his neck. "Yes, there's Violetta Entremont, from France, who's in fourth; Anna Landov, in second; Ilse Rischer of Germany, in sixth; and the young American phenomenon Tina Forbush, only fourteen and a surprising fifth."

The crowd noise swelled, and Weeks had to raise his voice. "And there's Maggie Campbell, standing third, whose touching story has attracted a huge international following. Just listen to the hand she's getting!"

The camera panned to the stands, where row after row stood, applauding the small figure in the scarlet dress. The costume had long sleeves to which were sewn an expanse of fabric running from shoulder to wrist, so that when she raised her arms to wave, she appeared to have wings.

Maggie circled slowly, hands on hips, until she spotted her family at rinkside and skated over. She kissed everybody. When she came to Hiro he rubbed her head. "Good luck, brave little *yanki*."

She hugged him, then turned to her mother. "Where's Clay?"

"I saw him a little while ago, talking to Lofton Weeks. He'll be here."

"Sure." She slipped the tangle of enfolding arms, skated backward a few yards, stopped, and bowed.

She went over to a small patch of ice and began skating figures. As she skated she thought about Madam Goto, and keeping her edges true. The crowd noise swelled to a roar, and she looked up. Doe Rawlings, who'd waited while the others took the ice, had begun taking laps. Instantly all eyes were on her. Maggie noticed she was still wearing her warm-ups, which was odd, but then she went back to her business and thought no more of anything. The crowd, the other skaters, her own body, even time—everything disappeared. There was only a slow drift through white space.

Lofton Weeks hoisted the microphone. It was cold enough at rinkside for his breath to make little puffs punctuate his speech. "Well, you saw Maggie Campbell greeting her family, and now she's engaged in what I understand is a regular ritual, skating school figures in the six-minute warm-up. We don't see figures much anymore, and the other ladies are all doing their jumps and spins, but Ms. Campbell apparently thinks the discipline of the figures helps concentrate her mind. She certainly looks composed."

He looked away from the ice and into the camera. "The big story, though, is Doe Rawlings, and what she's going to do. As many people know, the long program she's been skating in practice is her old program, and a lot of people are saying that because of the ankle injury that kept her from defending her U.S. title, she hasn't been able to develop a new program—which could hurt her with the judges. But I'm going to go out on a limb and predict that Doe Rawlings is going to skate not only a new program, but a truly dramatic program. So stay tuned to your sets, people—you're in for an evening of drama, excitement, and for some, heartbreak. Back to you, Bob."

The three commentators swiveled to face the cameras. "Well," said Cathy Perkins, "if Lofton's right, it *would* be dramatic, because I can't remember anyone presenting a program they haven't shown in practice."

Tim Dysart, who was supposed to bring a certain gravity to the broadcast, looked serious. "Cathy, how would the judges react to that—to a wholly unexpected program, that is?"

Cathy deliberated, then turned up her palms. "I just don't know. They might love it, or they might hate it, and score accordingly."

"Well, we'll know soon. And when we come back, a close-up look at Doe Rawlings, America's hope for a gold medal." Bob stared into the camera until the monitor showed a car climbing a mountain, and they all removed their microphones.

The girl who'd answered the knock on the dressing room door brought an envelope back to Maggie. "An usher delivered this."

Maggie looked at her name on the envelope: it was Hunter Rill's handwriting. She tore it open and extracted the contents, looking first at the thick, legal-size document before putting it aside and turning to a small linen envelope. She opened it and the color drained from her face.

"Not bad news, I hope?"

Maggie looked up, startled because she'd forgotten where she was. The Romanian was looking at her sympathetically.

Maggie looked back down at the envelope, then up at the Romanian. "No, it's not bad news, thank you." Her fingers lingered on the envelope as she shook her head slowly. "No, not bad news." A grin broke across her face. "In fact, it's wonderful news!"

"Megumi—it is time."

Maggie had been stretching in the exercise room when the locket in which she'd placed the airman's inscription slipped out of the front of her dress. Distracted, she'd opened it and didn't know how long she'd been looking when she felt Chiako's hand on her shoulder.

"Oh, yes—good." She closed the locket. Rising, she dropped it between her breasts.

When they got to the waiting area, she stood, shifting slowly from foot to foot, while Chiako rubbed her shoulders. "There is only one skater tonight, Megumi-*chan*. Only one. She skates only for herself."

Nodding, Maggie glanced over her shoulder. "I know, *sensei*, I know. I am ready. Thanks to you and Madam Goto, I am ready." She heard her name announced, adding, "And thanks to Hunter Rill," before stroking for center ice.

"She's skating to Stravinsky's *Firebird*. An unusual choice, not as lyrical as a lot of the ladies prefer, but in that bright red dress with those flowing wings, she certainly *looks* the part."

Cathy Perkins nodded. "It's a smart choice for this skater. Maggie Campbell has beautiful arm movements, and the expressive music and those eye-catching wings really let her show them off."

"Mmm. It's a shame, though, that she only has a double Axel. When Doe Rawlings hits the Axel . . . well, it just rivets the crowd. And let's face it—that has to influence the judges."

"No doubt of it. Maggie Campbell *is* skating flawlessly, though—certainly the best performance we've seen so far tonight. If she can keep this up for another two minutes, Anna Landov, at least, is going to feel some pressure."

The slow portion of Maggie's program opened with a triple toe loop. She adjusted to the change in tempo, landing it effortlessly.

"Look at the flow of that jump." Cathy Perkins leaned forward to get a better view of the monitor. "Many skaters have great jumps, yet they seem almost like an interruption in the program. But every move, every element in this program, is part of a seamless whole."

"An elegant, classical skater, no question about it," Tim Dysart observed. "What strikes me, though, is how *simple* her program is. You have to wonder if it's challenging enough."

Cathy Perkins looked at him impatiently. "Skaters would tell you it's not simple at all, because her technique is flawless, and that's extremely difficult." Bob LeFavre nodded as she continued: "Like her opening triple lutz. A lot of the skaters sneak over to an inside edge just before they launch, because it's easier. But that's really a flip, not a true lutz, even though most of the judges let them get away with it. Maggie stayed on that outside edge the whole way. No, the best make things look easy, and Maggie Campbell is making some of the purest, cleanest skating I've seen in years look very, very easy."

Her attention shifted back to the ice. "*What* a spread-eagle!" she exclaimed. "Very few skaters can achieve that turnout from the hips. And the arm position!"

Maggie was slowly traversing the far end of the arena, her toes pointed in opposite directions, blades tracking a single line as she leaned back, arms extended, following the curve of the rink, no more than inches between her and the boards. The material hanging from her arms made a wild, snapping sound in the still air.

She went into a step sequence that brought her down the center of the ice, toward the broadcast booth, the crowd clapping rhythmically as her feet danced, lances of light flashing off the chrome blades. She wore a bright, natural smile, turning it on first one side of the arena, then the other, her straight back making her appear taller than she was. Her hands, tipped with red, moved with the music as though coaxing it from the air itself.

She slowed and began linking semicircles, coasting the length of the rink, first forward, then backward, inside edge, then outside, her free leg pointing almost straight up, her back a deep crescent, her arms moving sinuously, in perfect time to the music.

"Magnificent, just magnificent," Cathy Perkins exclaimed. "*Look* at that focus. And the leg lift . . . notice the alignment of her free leg as she shifts edges. A lot of skaters lose it there."

Maggie lowered her leg. Three strokes accelerated her to full speed.

"She's got a flying camel coming up, she's setting up . . . *now!*" Cathy's hand chopped the air.

Maggie launched the spin off her forward outside edge, leaping into it after her torso assumed a forty-five-degree angle in the air. She held the camel, perfectly centered, head up, arms back in a V, her right leg straight, the left high in the air behind her, through seven revolutions.

Cathy Perkins clutched her microphone. "Lovely, the lines of her back in that camel. And so much security in her spins, the way they stayed centered. You youngsters out there, pay attention—that's how it's done."

Maggie straightened, still turning, then segued into a fast back scratch spin that turned her into a red blur, a flame bursting from the white surface.

"Oh, my." Cathy Perkins put a palm to her cheek, clucking her tongue. "That really was outstanding—as close to perfect as it gets. Now she'll set up for her double Axel/triple toe, then finish with a death drop."

Bob nodded. "Assuming she finishes as cleanly as she's skated so far, I'd say she's got the bronze locked up."

Cathy Perkins shook her head decisively. "This young lady's looking at the silver, Bob. She's even putting pressure on Doe Rawlings . . . assuming she finishes cleanly."

Maggie came out of the spin with the little locket bouncing against her chest. She headed diagonally down the ice, building speed with back crossovers. When she had the speed she wanted, she coasted toward the takeoff for her combination jump. All she had to do was land it cleanly, and she could do the death drop in her sleep. She turned, facing forward, kicked her right foot skyward, thrust her left edge into the ice as hard as she could.

Madam Goto said that when the time came she'd understand the airman's words. The time had come. All the way down the ice she'd heard them; as she launched, she heard them again: "Having a dream, I will go up into the sky." She rose, rose, rose.

* * *

Loften Weeks was watching the monitor in the warm-up room while Hunter Rill bent over Doe's ankle. The worry that had been nagging him all day was mounting, and he was masking it in mechanical activity.

"It's a *fine* performance, Hunter. The girl's good, *really* good. Look how smoothly she works the transitions in her combo spin. Like satin. And this time she's turning counter-clockwise; Christ, I don't think there's another skater here who has spins in both directions."

Rill didn't look up. Doe gave no sign of hearing, but he knew she had. Most coaches wouldn't have dreamed of letting their skater hear their competitor's performance described, but Hunter Rill hadn't gotten this far by being most coaches.

"*Very* nice spiral sequence; really *very* nice. Amazing leg extension. This is skating of the old school."

Though he was paying little attention to Weeks, enough of the man's commentary was getting through to perplex Rill. He'd half expected an announcement Campbell had scratched, and here the girl was apparently skating quite well. He shrugged, turning his attention back to Doe's ankle; as long as Doe was sound, Campbell could skate her heart out and it wouldn't make any difference. His thumb probed the puffy flesh around the anklebone.

Doe flinched, then asked peevishly, "Does he have to keep talking about her, Hunter?"

"Oh, pay him no attention. He wants to showcase you on a special next week, so let's keep the old queen happy." There seemed to be more swelling than there had been in the morning.

"It's annoying me."

"Don't think about it. Doe"—he dropped his voice—"how's the ankle feel? Really?"

She tossed her head dismissively. "It'll be fine once it's taped."

Rill bit his lip. "We should have laid off the quad longer."

"I needed the practice, Hunter."

"You were limping when we came in."

"I stopped when we saw people, didn't I? Well, I can stop for four more minutes, and that's all I need."

"That's a *great* flying camel." Weeks, in front of the monitor, talked to himself.

"I suppose." He shook his head and began applying tape. Doe grimaced as his fingers touched the swollen joint. He stopped.

"Doe, is it—"

"Jesus Christ!"

Both heads snapped up at Weeks's shout. He was standing, mouth agape, riveted on the television. "Jesus Christ, did I see what I thought I saw?"

An avalanche of sound burst over them, rattling the metal door.

"What is it? What the hell are you talking about?" Rill leapt to his feet. "What is it, damn it?"

High overhead, an incredulous Cathy Perkins, murmuring, "She tripled it, she tripled it," had also sprung out of her chair and was standing, hands pressed against the glass observation window, as Maggie entered her death drop.

Tim Dysart peered at the monitor. "Have you ever seen that before?"

"The thing with her arm?" Bob LeFavre shook his head. "Dexter did it, I think, but not with the Axel; I've never seen a woman do it with any jump, though. Absolutely breathtaking."

"Unbelievable—just unbelievable!" Cathy Perkins was

shaking her head. "She *tripled* her Axel—in a combination, at that. And that death drop . . . Oh! Oh, my!" Clasping her hands to her chest, she exhaled as though she'd held her breath for the entire program. "That was the most . . . the most . . . *perfect* performance I've ever seen."

A cataclysm broke over the small, sweat-drenched figure curtsying at center ice. Twenty thousand people were standing, cheering frantically. A throbbing chorus of "Banzai! Banzai!" broke from the Japanese in the audience, while bouquets cascaded onto the ice. Gliding toward the rail, Maggie bent, retrieved a rose, blew the crowd a kiss. She stepped into the waiting arms of Chiako Mori and held her.

Cathy Perkins struggled to find words. "It was . . . that was, just . . . just . . . unbelievably good. They'll be talking about Maggie Campbell's performance twenty years from now. I'm . . . we're . . . awfully lucky to have been here tonight."

Tim Dysart, who had survived in the business as long as he had by never venturing an opinion until he knew it was safe, asked, "But was it enough to move into second?"

Cathy Perkins looked at him in amazement. "Second? Unless I'm very wrong, Doe Rawlings better skate the performance of her life if she wants the gold."

Weeks was springing up and down, shaking his fists. "She tripled it! She tripled her Axel! In the *combination*, for Christ's sake. No woman's ever done that! Magnificent, absolutely magnificent!" He blew kisses at the screen. "Bravo, Maggie Campbell—bravo, bravo!"

Rill looked at the monitor stupidly. "No! You counted wrong. She doesn't have the Axel."

"Bull . . . shit, Hunter! She's got the prettiest triple Axel *I've* ever seen. And *look* at that death drop!"

The implications of what he had just seen sank in, and Weeks's mouth hardened. "Rill, your girl's in a horse race." His forefinger jabbed Rill's chest. "And she damn well better get across the finish line first. I've got a lot of money riding on her."

He looked back at the screen. "By God, though—that was something." He shook his head in wonder. "Tripling the Axel in a combination . . . Jesus!" Weeks was still exclaiming as he went out the door; when he opened it bedlam poured into the little room.

"Shut up! Shut up, you idiot!" Rill shouted after him. "I'm telling you, she doesn't have the Axel."

He looked up at the monitor. "Come on," he muttered through clenched teeth, "come on, come on, come on!"

His mouth sagged. "Son of a bitch," he whispered, aghast, as Maggie's scores for technical merit spread across the bottom of the screen: five-nine, six, five-nine, six, six . . .

"No, no!" he blurted, staggering back as the scores for presentation followed: nine sixes. In the voice-over Cathy Perkins was exclaiming, breathlessly, "Not since Torville and Dean at Sarajevo has a skater drawn nine perfect scores in the Olympics. What a historic . . ."

"What is it?" Doe was standing by his side, panting. Her face was white, forehead glistening under the makeup.

He forced himself to take a deep breath. After a pause he said, "It's . . . well, it's not what I expected, Doe."

He could not believe the incredible height Maggie had reached. As she jumped, she'd extended her right arm high over her head, so that it looked as though she were pulling herself to the rafters. That spontaneous flourish should have braked her rotation, making the triple toe she'd launched off the Axel all the more amazing.

With the brilliant red soaring wing rising toward the roof,

she looked less like a skater than a blazing, mythological creature. She had *become* the Firebird—a thrusting, electric burst of primal energy. The skater, the moment, and the music had fused.

The twenty thousand people cramming the hall had felt it, the billions watching on television had felt it, the judges had felt it, and though it sickened Rill to admit it, he felt it. He shut his eyes, trying to think.

"I'll beat her." Doe stepped away, but as soon as she put weight on her left foot she stumbled. Gasping, she hopped to the bench. "Finish taping me, Hunter. I've got to get ready."

Rill took a last look at the monitor, trying to expunge the image that lingered even as the picture dissolved into the Olympic logo. He turned, and Doe swam into focus. "You can hardly walk," he whispered.

"I'll walk, damn it. I'll skate, too, and I'm going to beat that sandbagging little bitch. Come on—this is the moment we've been waiting for."

Her eyes held a wild luminosity as she extended her leg. "Just tape me, Hunter—please!"

"Doe, I—" He walked toward her, numb.

"Hunter, I've got to skate! I've got to win! He's waiting, Hunter; he's out there!"

He bent over her leg. Mechanically he pulled off strips of tape and applied them; she paled as the tape compressed the puffy flesh.

Rill squeezed his eyes shut. "You could do permanent damage, Doe."

"Hunter, this is my chance. I've waited for it all my life; it's my one chance!"

"You're twenty years old—you'll have other chances."

"You're forty-five; how many chances did you get?"

He froze momentarily, then pulled off another strip of

tape and brought it down her ankle, under her heel, back up the ankle, teeth clenched. "As many as I deserved."

"Tina Forbush is fourteen; four years from now, do you think I'll stand a chance against her? Against the next one, or the one after that? I'll be too *old* by the next Olympics. Tape me!"

"There's the Worlds. . . ."

"The Worlds! I've already got a World championship, and you're the one who said one Olympic gold is worth *four* World titles. Christ!" she gasped, shutting her eyes as pain shot up her leg like an electric current.

"It's sprained, Doe." He moved automatically, his mind refusing to function clearly. "The muscles are torn."

"I've got to skate!"

"Why, Doe?" he whispered insistently. "Why is it so important to you?"

"Why? You of all people ask me that? It's all you've talked about for years. 'Our big moment.' Well, it's come!"

He reached for her face. "I didn't know. I didn't know before."

She leaned back, avoiding his hand. "Keep taping! Know what?"

"That it wasn't just about *me*."

"You're damn right it isn't. *I* have needs, too. Put more under the arch."

He lowered her foot to the floor, setting it down as though it were an eggshell. He shook his head. "It's no good, Doe. It isn't worth risking the rest of your life for this. I've enough baggage already." He looked into her eyes, feeling his brim. "I'm going to pull you, Doe."

"No—you can't!" She looked around frantically.

"I have to." He straightened up. "There'll be other days."

"Hunter, no!" She staggered to her feet, fingers clutching at him. "If I scratch, she'll win. Landov can't beat her."

"So she'll win. It isn't worth it, Doe."

She grabbed his lapels. "You're the one who said the Clay Bartletts of the world go with winners. She was always saying she was better than me, and now he'll believe it."

"Doe, she never said that!" He pressed his fists to his forehead. "I made that up. I—"

"You're lying, and she'll take him back if I scratch. He'll think it's because I was afraid of her. He'll despise me!" Her voice cracked. "She'll take my medal, and take him, too. I can't lose someone else, don't you see?"

He wrapped his arms around her. "Oh, Doe—what have I done? You're a winner." He swallowed, his vision blurring. "You're a great champion. If he doesn't see that, he doesn't deserve you. Now sit down while I find someone from the committee."

She buried her face in her hands. He was near the door when she whispered lifelessly, "Would you get my bag before you go? It's in there." She gestured over her shoulder.

"Of course." He turned back and went into the dark locker room. "Where's the light, damn it? Ah—"

Doe slammed the door. She dropped to her knees and wedged the rubber doorstop under it. She rested her forehead against the cool metal. "I have to skate, Hunter. I can't lose someone else."

She pulled on her skates, oblivious of the pain, ignoring the muffled pounding behind her. Five minutes later, by the time he'd broken down the door, she was standing at center ice.

[faded text from previous page shows through at top]

Chapter 45

I was right, she thought. I don't feel any pain. I can last four minutes. She let her mind go blank, listening for the first note. In the diaphanous white gown she looked like every man's fantasy of the virginal bride on her wedding night. A chord sounded, and she struck off.

She was only seconds into her program when Tim Dysart exclaimed, "*What* is she skating? This certainly isn't her old program."

Cathy Perkins added wondrously, "No, it sure isn't. Lofton Weeks was exactly right—Doe Rawlings and her coach have sprung a surprise on us. We'll have to wait and see how the judges react." She shook her head. "But it is *spectacular.*"

Seconds went by before Bob LeFavre said almost to himself, "She's *incredibly* graceful."

Cathy Perkins looked at him wryly. "What you mean, Bob, is that this is the sexiest woman in skating, and that is the sexiest program you've ever seen."

The *Wintersturme* began and with it the symbolic disrobing of the bride. Doe's hands played over her body, and suddenly the billowing folds of the wispy train that had been attached to the back of her gown fluttered loose, hanging briefly in the air before descending to the surface like a spring cloud. The young woman was left wearing a short, gauzy white shift, suggesting a peignoir. The collective "Ohhh" said it had had its intended effect.

At rinkside Hunter Rill watched, mesmerized. The crowd had ceased to be twenty thousand people, becoming a single organism with forty thousand hands, clapping rhythmically.

Doubt disappeared. "Oh, sweetness," he whispered. "You're doing it. You're really doing it."

Doe entered a series of butterflies, fluttering down center ice, hurtling through the air, the white dress lifting to reveal her wonderful thighs, capped by lacy white panties that provided tantalizing flashes of satin flesh before the fabric settled back into place.

She moved into the last third of her program, the pace leaping forward. When the "Ride of the Valkyries" sounded, even Rill jumped at the sudden, thunderous percussion.

"Okay, Doe—this is it. Take it down the ice and *do it!*" Rill wasn't aware he was screaming, but even if he had been, he needn't have worried that anyone would notice, because between the sound of the music and the rhythmic clapping, the decibel level was deafening.

Doe turned, looked back over her shoulder. She had more speed going into the jump than he'd ever seen her have— more than most men could manage. Yet she looked rock solid, certain, even serene, as she sped toward the moment that would immortalize her.

"Yes!" Rill blurted. "*Now.* Stretch it, Doe, stretch it," he prayed. "*Feel* it in those shoulders."

Down went her toe pick, *boom!* went the cymbals and the tympani, as though her blade striking the ice brought forth lightning. Twenty thousand people gasped.

She soared, higher and higher, revolving in what seemed to

Rill to be slow motion. Sweet Jesus, he thought. Sweet, sweet Jesus. Yes! *"Yes!"* he screamed. Willing her down: "Okay— *make* the ice, sweetheart, *make* it! Come on down, babe, that's it, that's it, you're down, you're *down!* You've . . ."

And then he was howling—a primitive, instinctive bay, the cry of the mortally wounded, and the crowd, falling silent after a sudden, shuddering groan, heard his dirge clearly, even over the blaring, suddenly grotesque bombast of the music. "Oh, Jesus . . . Oh, Jesus—*no!* No, no, no!"

People were grasping each other or putting their hands over their ears to try to block out the ghastly shrieks coming from the young woman writhing on the ice, her ankle at an impossible angle, as Hunter Rill slipped and scrambled toward her, adding his screams to hers.

Maggie sat in the warm-up room, saying nothing, trying to expunge the awful image. She had gone to the empty room to get away from the hideous chatter, the feverish speculation, and especially the barely concealed delight.

She'd heard the whispers that the ankle was hopelessly shattered, that it would have to be fused. She'd heard the breathless whispers of the coaches and officials, the thinly masked glee with which they contemplated the destruction of Hunter Rill's career, if the rumors that he'd sent the girl onto the ice knowing the ankle to be unsound proved true.

It sickened her, their indignation, their tongue-clucking. She knew how many of them would have done the same in an instant. She knew how many of them were already figuring what the disappearance of Doe Rawlings from international skating would mean for them.

She distracted herself by thinking how satisfying it would be to slip away before the awards ceremony—just disappear. What a fuss it would cause. "You see," some JFSA officials would be only too happy to proclaim, "I told you she would disgrace Japan."

She wouldn't do it, of course: it wouldn't be fair to Chiako, or her family, or the people who'd earned the right to share in the moment. But she suspected Madam Goto might well approve.

A soft tapping brought her back. She assumed it was Chiako, getting her for the awards ceremony, and called, "Come in."

"Maggie!" Clay Bartlett was framed in the open door.

She studied him wordlessly, until he hurried in and threw his arms around her. "My God, you were magnificent!" His voice was husky.

He pressed her face against his waist, stroking her hair. She pulled away, looking up resignedly. "Did you have to come?"

His forehead furrowed. "Of course I came. Why wouldn't I?"

"Because you should be with Doe Rawlings," she said softly.

His head snapped back. "With Doe—why?"

"She needs you."

"I don't understand." He settled onto the bench beside her. "Maggie, what are you saying? Has there been some misunderstanding?"

She looked at him disdainfully. "I hoped you wouldn't come. The other thing I could understand; it's a relief, in fact. But this . . ." She shook her head.

"You're not making sense." Suddenly he blanched. "Did that son of a bitch Rill tell you . . ." He licked his lips nervously. "Look, I was going to tell you, I just wanted to wait until you'd finished. I didn't want to upset you, see? The other day, when I said we wouldn't have to worry about our finances anymore, that's what I meant. I—"

"He *was* kind enough to send this to me, right before I skated." She reached into her bag.

He glanced at the copy of Doe Rawlings's contract with Weeks, nodding. "I thought so—that bastard." His words tumbled out in a rush: "I can explain, Maggie. I know I said I wouldn't, but I had no choice. Weeks was going to fire me if I didn't sign her. After Bordeaux I thought you weren't going to make it. I never dreamed . . ."

He grasped her hands. "I wanted us to have a good life, Maggie. To have enough money. Maybe it was wrong of me to break my promise, but I did it for us. I wanted to do my part. I love you, Maggie. All my life, I've loved you."

She pulled her hands away. "I know how you got her to sign this."

"How I got her to sign it?" He looked at her blankly.

Maggie pulled the rectangle of cream-colored card stock out of the small linen envelope. "Putting these two together, it isn't hard to see, is it?" She handed it to him.

He gasped, going white as he read:

Mr. Hunter C. Rill
Requests the pleasure of your company
at the marriage of
Miss Doreen Anne Rawlings

to

Mr. Clayton Hemmings Bartlett
On Saturday, May 12, 2002
At 4:30 o'clock
The Old North Church
193 Salem Street, Boston, Massachusetts

RSVP

Colorful, hand-appliquéd flowers ringed the border.

Looking up, dazed, he stammered, "What . . . Maggie . . . I've never seen that before in my life. I don't know . . ." He stared at her, horror-stricken. "Maggie, I swear I never—" He broke off to stare at the invitation. His forefinger traced the appliqué border, as though amid the entwined stems and bright blossoms he might find the meaning of it.

"Don't, Clay. When I saw this, I prayed it was the truth. You were back in the States with her, I was in Japan, she's lovely, you were lonely . . . I could accept that. In fact, I was incredibly relieved." She shrugged. "Believe me, I know how it can happen."

He looked up as though she'd hit him. "You don't mean you and that fellow . . ." His face flashed indignation, then fear. "You haven't . . ."

The slight curl of her lips was the only sign she'd heard him. "But to tell me that you coldly, deliberately deceived her, that you *lied* to her, makes me sicken at the sight of you."

"No, no!" He waved his hands frantically. "It wasn't, it's not like that." He was panting, his eyes darting around the room as he tried to think. "I mean, she might have misunderstood, but that's not—"

She went on, ignoring him. "When you tell me you didn't mean it, that you did it for us, or that she misunderstood you, it makes you so tawdry, so squalid. I think your appearing here is the most contemptible thing I've ever seen."

He shut his eyes as if in prayer. "Never anyone but you, Maggie." His voice had a high, keening quality. "There never will be. I wouldn't hurt you for the world. I never imagined this would happen. Don't let this . . . Please don't let this—"

"I knew I was making a terrible mistake; it got clearer and

clearer. I just didn't know how to get out of it. I gave my word, you see. That's always mattered to me."

He swayed. "Maggie, I—"

"Rill made it easy. I'm really quite grateful to him."

"I . . . *need* you, Maggie," he whispered, grasping her wrist. "Oh, Jesus—I need you."

"I know you do." She stood, shaking him off. "But I don't need you."

There was a knock. Chiako's voice, muffled, said, "It is time, Megumi-*chan*."

"Coming." She started for the door. "Go to her, Clay; you've found someone needier than you. Make that invitation be the truth. Do that much for yourself." She walked out.

Maggie looked at the flag, slowly rising, hearing the plaintive strains of "Kimigayo," her lips mouthing the words she'd memorized as a schoolchild. Once she would have been unable to imagine a greater honor than causing this flag to fly, this paean to His Majesty's reign fill the hall. Now it seemed foolish, the suggestion that she had skated for a country.

She looked down at the medal hanging from her neck. She wondered if she'd feel differently about it if Doe Rawlings hadn't gone down; if she'd beaten her on scores. She'd never know.

She did know that Madam Goto had been right: the medal was a reminder, not the goal. Madam Goto had promised her that one day she would dance with the gods, and she had. She would look at the medal and remember the four minutes of magic, when she had become music, as the little leather case had helped Madam Goto to remember her moment of magic.

Before stepping off the stand, she bowed. The spirit of an old woman was watching, and she wanted it to know that finally she understood what she had been taught, those long hours on the ice. Understood the airman's message.

Epilogue

June 2002: Tokyo

*K*oji Sano, chewing ruminatively, vented a low, appre-
ciative moan. "Indians are filthy people, of course, but
I can't resist their food."

He glanced with sudden concern at his companion.
"You're not eating. It's not too spicy, is it?"

The man shook his head. "No, it is fine. I don't have much
appetite."

"A great pity—this is really a very good restaurant."

"I am certain."

"Perhaps, if you're sure you don't want it, I might finish
that eggplant? Ah, thank you so much—you are too generous."

Sano chuckled as he scraped the bowl. "Too generous. Indeed. With your permission, I thought perhaps we could
consider a way to reduce your payments. I understand your
business is not doing so well; you have my sympathy.

"Mmm." Sano wiped *puri* around the dish, then popped it
in his mouth. "Really excellent. It occurs to me that, with

your connections, you no doubt learn much that we might put to mutually advantageous use."

He paused as a waiter entered their room. Sano gestured at the dish he left. " 'Rogan josh,' I think they call it. Absolutely delicious, though no doubt I'll pay for it tomorrow. Ah, well." He reached for the lamb. "I think we could agree to a substantial reduction in your monthly payment, provided we knew certain things. For example—"

He broke off. "Fukawa-*san*, you look ill. Is everything all right? With respect, I'm not sure you're taking good enough care of yourself. Let me recommend a doctor—I'd be honored. Now, at least some curried shrimp? Really—I insist."

Boston

*H*unter Rill had just fixed Doe a cup of tea when the doorbell rang. "I'll get that," he said.

Clay Bartlett stood on the stoop. "Hello, Hunter." He smiled nervously. He was holding a thin, cylindrical package wrapped in white tissue.

"I'll be damned—you really do have balls of brass."

"I'd like to see Doe, if I could."

The smile cracked under Rill's cold stare.

"Five months, two operations, screaming pain every time she takes a step, and all of a sudden you drop in and want to see her, just like that?"

"I had to work some things out." Clay's head dropped. "I'm not proud of myself, but I want to make amends. May I come in?"

"Hell, no. What's really going on? Decide Doe still has some value? Heard about the commercial she's doing?"

"Please, Hunter, it's nothing like that. I just want to tell her how sorry I am. About everything. I want to ask her to, to . . . forgive me. I brought her a sketch I did."

"Well, you can go to—"

"You lied to me."

Doe came up behind Rill. Each step was punctuated with a hoarse gasp. "You said you loved me, that you wanted to marry me."

She reached the door and clung to it, panting. "You left me. I needed you, and you weren't there."

Clay blanched. "I *wasn't* lying, Doe. I meant those things. All of it. I went away because . . ."

"Because you didn't want to be tied to a cripple, someone who'd never skate again. Someone who couldn't make you money."

"No—that's not true!" He held up his hand, smiling shyly, the blue eyes twinkling. "I'm a cripple myself."

She nodded. "Yes, but not because of that."

He swallowed. "I deserve that. I just wanted to say, though, that I'm sorry. About your injury, and about . . . the way I've been. I'd like to . . . see you again, if I could?"

She worked her way around Rill. Her right foot was in a heavy walking cast, giving her an awkward, lurching gait. "No one's ever going to leave me again."

Rill put his arm around her. "I won't leave you, Doe."

Her fingers touched his cheek. "I know you won't."

Clay looked at them uncertainly. "You're kidding, right? I mean, what can *he* give you? He's—"

She swung the door shut, violently. Clay jumped backward just in time.

He stood, stuporously, confronted by the solid, silent door. The fingers of his right hand curled into a soft fist, which he rapped against the hard wood. Slowly at first, and then faster. As his hand flailed ineffectively he groaned. "I never meant to hurt you, Doe! Please—you've got to believe me. Please, Doe . . ."

The thuds faded as Rill coaxed Doe down the hallway toward the kitchen. "This way, Doe—come to me." He walked backward, beckoning to her.

Her knuckles were white where they clutched the walker. "It hurts!" she gasped. "It hurts so much."

He kept walking. "I know, but you've got to do it. Soon you'll be getting around fine. Come on, just a little farther." He backed into the kitchen, staying just out of her reach.

"That's a girl. I need you at the rink, Doe, I really do. Wait till you see the Wallace kid—we're going to make something special out of him. He's dying to work with you. That's the real reason he came to me, you know. Only ten, and he's madly in love with you. A real little imp, but you'll have him eating out of your hand. I'm not sure I could control him alone. Come on, just a few more."

Rill backed around the kitchen table, beckoning to her. "Make it to the chair, Doe, and I'll warm up that tea."

He nodded encouragingly. "That's it—that's my girl. This kid's going to be a great one, Doe. We'll have him in the juniors in no time. That's it, just ease yourself down."

Rill turned his head away at Doe's groan. She settled heavily into the chair and sat, shaking, while he busied himself around the stove.

"We're going to *do* something with this kid, Doe. When you're a grandmother, people will still be talking about what you did with Jeremy Wallace. Now drink the tea, sweetheart. And maybe a cookie?" He pushed the flaxen hair off her damp forehead, murmuring, "A little rest, and then we'll walk some more, okay?" He kissed the top of her head. "I'm telling you, Doe—this could be the defining skater of his generation." He looked away, absentmindedly stroking her hair. His smile took off twenty years. "And he's all ours."

Yamanashi

*T*hough it was mid-August, high in the mountains the night air was cool. Rising mists swirled around her as Maggie rose from the hot spring and stepped onto a rock outcropping, luxuriating as the soft breeze dried her, cloaking her in the scent of pine. Her feet, softened by the baths and the months away from skating, felt the bite of the granite.

It was the last night of the *Bon* festival. For two days the villagers had welcomed the visitors from the spirit realm. They had lit fires to guide them back to the corporeal world, put out straw horses to transport them, danced the *Bon* dances in their kimonos and straw hats, recited sutras in front of the spirit altars. Tonight they had lit the fire on the path leading to the graveyard, but that was only the beginning of the journey back to the spirit world. To help their ancestors the rest of the way, they would set afloat *toro nagashi,* paper boats bearing candles.

Maggie bent to light her candles. Pushing the frail craft into the eddy that ran by her feet, she watched the bobbing lights drop from view, on their way to join the stream that joined the river that joined the sea, thousands of feet below.

Across Japan floating lanterns were working their way toward the sea, guiding their spirits to reunite with the others returning to the spirit world. Her father, Madam Goto, Mrs. Araki, millions of others, returning to a world where tribe no longer mattered.

The wind gusted. She shivered, crossing her arms over her chest, reluctant to seek shelter quite yet. From behind, strong arms circled hers. She felt the warmth of his wet body and wasn't cold anymore.

She rested her head against his chest. Maggie and Hiro stood in the place that had no name, looking up at the heavens.

Acknowledgments

$\mathcal{F}$rederick Hill, my friend and agent, suggested I draw on my business experience in Japan as the background for a novel. One could not ask for a more loyal advocate or more discerning critic. He is second among the many to whom this book owes its existence, behind only my wife, to whom it is dedicated.

The United States Figure Skating Association is generous in its service to those interested in skating, and possesses a wealth of instructional material that proved invaluable to my research. I appreciate the patience with which USFSA employees answered my many questions.

The USFSA retains a quaint usage, dividing the skating universe between "Men" and . . . "*Ladies*," as in Rule 2.2: ". . . the *lady* circles around the man . . ." Until a gracious young woman named Tonia Kwiatkowski agreed to guide me through the complex rules and often baffling ways of skating, I thought it merely an anachronism.

Tonia provided fascinating detail and anecdotes; she failed me only insofar as scoring still remains a mystery, though I'm comforted by the knowledge that no one else understands it either, including the judges.

Yet Tonia unwittingly gave me far more than facts, as I followed the last years of her extraordinarily long tenure as one of the world's leading Olympic-eligible skaters: Tonia gave me the model. Revered by all who follow figure skating, Tonia epitomizes tenacity, courage, and classical beauty on the ice, good cheer, scholarship, and lovely manners off it. As long as there are true ladies like Tonia Kwiatkowski involved in skating, the USFSA's usage will remain apt.

Another fine skater, Marcy Reis, was also a great help, vetting the manuscript and sparing me the embarrassment that would have been occasioned by the several errors she caught.

Megumi Kanda, a young woman raised in Tokyo and now living in America, reviewed the manuscript for Japanese usages and practices, and provided valuable corrections and insights. I also took the liberty of appropriating her first name, and not a few of her engaging characteristics.

In the interests of fiction I have taken certain liberties with both skating and Japanese practice. Departures from reality are entirely my doing, and in no way reflect on the contribution of these three experts.

Once again my friend Deborah Kelbach sacrificed her free time to help prepare the manuscript. I am in her debt.

Gould Electronics, Inc., gave me my entree to Japan. I am particularly grateful to David Ferguson, Gould's president, and Michael Veysey, the general counsel, for their generous professional and personal support.

Through them I was able to work with officers and employees of the Japan Energy Company, Gould's owner, thanks to whom I developed an enduring affection for them, their country, and their culture. Mr. Y. Kasahara, N. Abe, Y. Yamashita, and F. Ito, and others too numerous to mention individually, accorded me, an American lawyer, the privilege of representing them through an arduous experience that was, to them, entirely alien. They were marvelous clients: meticulous, endlessly supportive, resolute. Later, as friends, they and their families extended every courtesy as my wife and I returned to Japan to research this book.

If my Japanese friends read this book, I hope they will find it a fractional repayment of the *on* I owe them. And I hope they will agree that a great people doesn't need to be idealized by its friends, any more than it deserves to be demonized by its adversaries. The Japan I depict has flaws, but those flaws are but a small part of a great, complex society that has much to teach the world. We can have no better friends.

By the year 2000, 2 out of 3 Americans could be illiterate.

It's true.

Today, 75 million adults... about one American in three, can't read adequately. And by the year 2000, U.S. News & World Report envisions an America with a literacy rate of only 30%.

Before that America comes to be, you can stop it... by joining the fight against illiteracy today.

Call the Coalition for Literacy at toll-free **1-800-228-8813** and volunteer.

Volunteer Against Illiteracy. The only degree you need is a degree of caring.

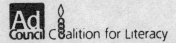

Ad Council Coalition for Literacy